The King's Gold

Book I of
The King's Gold Saga

Martin Jenner

Copyright © 2015 Martin Jenner
All rights reserved.

This book is dedicated to the memory of Wendy Wilson.

Solomon's Map of Bodisha

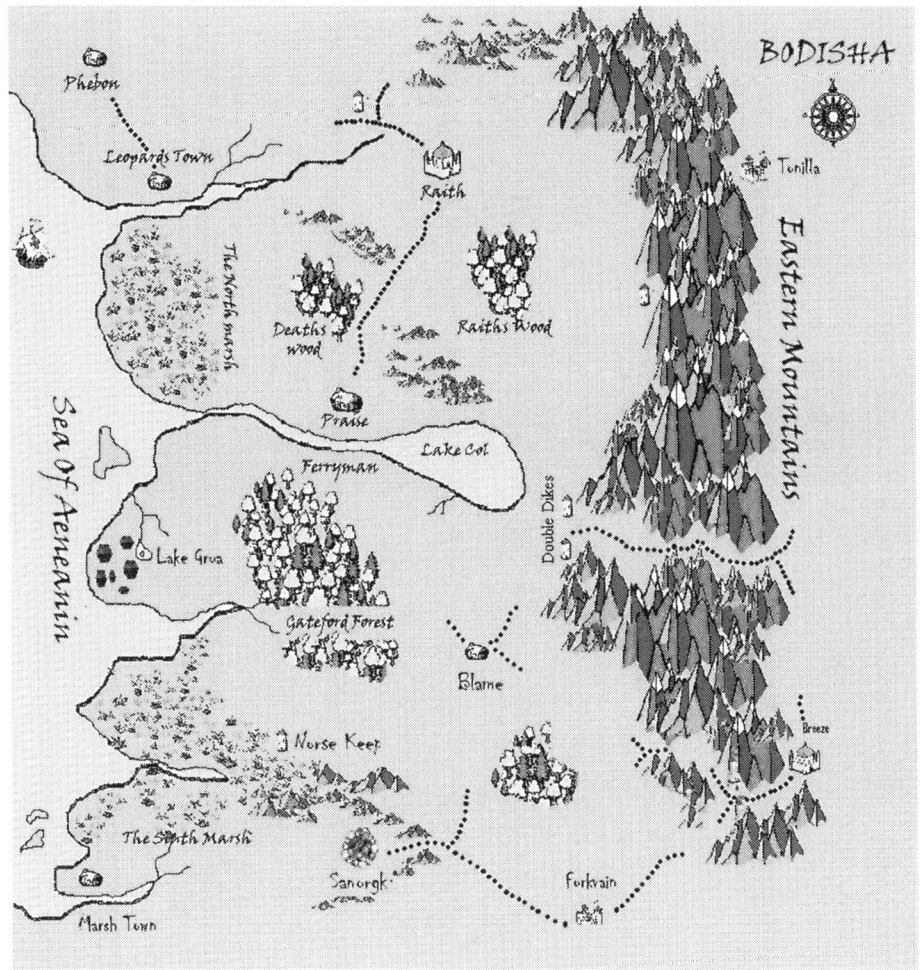

Kern swung his sword in a wild arc in front of him, "Come out and fight me, you little whore!" He spun around, his sword again circling and slicing through the air. "Show yourself, you bastard," he cried as he swung his sword wildly, turning round and round like a blind man. A small cloaked figure holding two daggers stepped out from behind a tree and crouched in front of him, ready to attack.

...

Dreams dance on the fading shadows of the night, taking the wisdom of their secrets deep within... The brief memories left in your waking mind... run fleeing from the morning sun... leaving scars to remind you of something unknown... The unconscious mind is a fearsome thing, filled with power... delve into your worst nightmares and return to us... return to us... return to us...

Chapter One
The Apple Thief

It was early afternoon when Ty and Kern arrived in Raith, and they made their way directly to the marketplace. The city was busy and the market was filled with people trading for goods, weapons, livestock, armour, potions and poisons – just about everything an adventurer or trader might want. Humans, elves, dwarves, halflings and half-orcs mingled together, hustling, bustling, and bartering. The smell of cooked foods, fresh bread, and fruit filled the air.

The biggest city in Bodisha, Raith was often called 'The Heart of Bodisha;' every trader or adventurer, at least once in his or her life, came through here. They used Raith for every type of business; just about everything you could think of was sold here. Some said, if you couldn't get whatever it was you were seeking, it didn't exist. Ty and Kern were keeping an eye out for a good many things as they roamed the marketplace, but primarily they were looking for a way to refill their empty pockets.

Ty, a halfling, roved from stall to stall, oblivious to the glares of several merchants. Ty never really looked clean; his clothes were more suited to an urchin than a thief, his hands and face always discoloured with muck. His cloak, at least, was clean; it was one of Ty's few permanent possessions and he cared for it well. The black wool of its hood mingled with various shades of grey at the shoulders, and dark greens were blended in around chest level. It was very nearly perfect night-time camouflage for both city and wilderness. At the bottom fourth of the cloak the colours all merged to mottled browns, which had the added benefit of helping to cover up any mud that might splatter on the hem. Today, however, it was freshly washed, and hung down to just below Ty's knees, revealing leather boots tied up with leather twine. Whatever else may have lurked underneath the halfling's cloak was anyone's guess. The cloak's hood shadowed Ty's face, giving only a glimpse of his slender features and dark brown eyes. The stall-minders didn't need a soothsayer to tell them to keep an eye on their wares when Ty came near.

Kern, a human who stood two feet taller than Ty, strode easily through the streets. His longer legs gave him the advantage, and Ty complained constantly as he scrambled to catch up with his companion every few paces. Kern's cloak was the typical mottled forest green of a ranger; resembling the colour of the trees and other plants that grew in the woodlands, it gave rangers an almost perfect camouflage. His green light-leather armour, dyed with the same technique, matched perfectly. The dye used to colour the cloak and armour was made by boiling the root of foxgloves, which were found only in the Gateford Forest. It was not a welcoming place, which made the dye all the more sought after, as only the foolhardy would travel into the forest to retrieve it.

Across Kern's back rode a longsword, the hilt peering over his left shoulder; hanging over his right shoulder was a birchwood longbow and a quiver of arrows, and a rapier hung by his side. He walked tall with his hands clasped behind his back, and his hood was down, revealing his handsome features. His dark green eyes and square chin were framed by long golden hair, tied back into a ponytail which hung just below his shoulders. Any of the merchants would gladly have contracted with the likes of Kern – to protect their goods from the likes of Ty.

"Remember, Ty, just keep your hands in your pockets this time. I don't want a repeat of Leopard's Town," Kern said.

"I was stealing to feed us, if you remember!" Ty replied angrily.

"Yes, you just weren't doing it very well, wouldn't you agree?" Kern sniggered.

"If you hadn't lost all our gold in that stupid dice game, I wouldn't have had to try."

"Whatever the reason," Kern said, in a hasty attempt to regain the moral high ground, "just don't steal anything, argue with people, or get drunk. That should be simple."

"All right then, I won't. When we're skint, don't ask me to steal anything, and I won't offer to share if I do." An uncomfortable silence lingered for several moments before Ty continued, "How much have we actually got between the two of us, anyway?"

Kern was about to deflect Ty's question when a young boy came running through the marketplace. He was dressed like a beggar and wore nothing on his dirt-blackened feet, his face nearly as filthy as his toes. The boy's long hair looked like it had gone a moon or two since its last cleaning. Of more immediate interest to Ty, the boy was being chased by two town guards. Their swords were still sheathed, but Ty could tell by the anger on their faces that they meant business.

The crowd milling around the market place seemed to split open for the oncoming guards; many stopped and watched expectantly, willing the guards to catch the boy just to see the punishment that would be dished out. A few cries rang out in protest – "He's just a boy" and "Bullies" – but most of the shouts were lost in the everyday burbling noises of the marketplace.

"Stop, thief! In the name of King Moriak!" shouted one of the chasing guards. Kern noticed the boy was carrying an apple in each hand.

The boy flew past, jumping up and then springing off a barrow full of fine silks collected from the northern silk mines of Bodisha. The trader struggled to keep the barrow upright, cursing at the running boy.

Just as the boy's pursuers reached Ty and Kern, Ty stepped out in front of the first guard and placed his foot firmly down in the dirt, bracing for the collision. The guard ran straight into Ty, and went tumbling over the halfling to land on a vegetable cart, spraying carrots and potatoes everywhere. Ty's hood slipped off in the melee, revealing a topknot dyed red and three identical scars running from his left ear to the corner of his mouth. It looked almost as if a wildcat had clawed him.

The second guard, fatter and slower than the first, stopped and drew his sword. "I saw that!" he shouted, trying to regain his breath.

"You saw what? He ran right into me," Ty began to argue. Kern rolled his eyes.

The first guard had picked himself up; after brushing himself down and straightening his bright red hair, he collected his helmet from the vegetable vendor and jammed it back onto his head. "By the power vested in me by King Moriak, I'm arresting you," he said, still brushing street dirt from his chainmail vest.

"Arresting me!" sputtered Ty. "For what? First you barrel into me, then –"

"For helping that no-good common apple thief escape!" The guard's face was rapidly turning as red as his hair.

Kern stepped forward, thinking to himself, *Here we go again.* "I saw everything that happened – you ran into him. Sir," he added hastily.

"We'll just see what the jailer has to say on the matter, shall we? Now drop your weapons," the larger guard said firmly, glaring at Kern. With a dismissive glance at Ty, he added, "You too, you scar-faced little imp; drop everything before I scratch up your other cheek."

Ty paused, remembering how he'd gotten the scars on his face. Icily he said, "I am not dropping anything. I did nothing wrong." Drawing a bone-handled dagger from each sleeve, he planted his feet firmly in the dirt.

Kern stepped close and placed a hand on Ty's shoulder "Hold on, Ty. Listen, friends, my companion here isn't – well, you know... isn't completely *with us* today. Can't we just forget this whole horrid event ever happened?"

Both guards grinned and slowly shook their heads. Ty turned to his companion. "'Not with us today,' eh?" Kern shrugged his shoulders and reached for the hilt of his sword, knowing deep down this was going to end badly.

By now a crowd had gathered to watch the proceedings, and the usually noisy marketplace was hushed. The two guards stood their ground, as if they were waiting for the tension to break. Suddenly, two crossbow bolts thudded into the dirt inches from the ranger's leather boots. Kern looked up swiftly and saw four more guards standing on a flat-topped roof above them, each one aiming a crossbow at the scene below.

Two of the guards reloaded, but all four gazes remained locked on the human and halfling in the marketplace. The guards shifted positions slightly, revealing a tall man dressed in a black robe with a long black cloak. In one hand he carried a massive wooden staff.

The dark-robed man stepped forward and slammed the staff down onto the wooden beams upon which he stood. "The guards instructed you to drop your weapons, thieves." His voice hissed through the stillness like a snake through dry grass.

Kern looked at Ty and nodded once, curtly. They each dropped their weapons in the dirt, raising small puffs of dust.

The heavier guard chuckled. "You were right, Devon. You said this'd be easy, that two petty thieves wouldn't dare put up a fight."

The red-headed guard nodded and smiled at the compliment. "You stick with me, Don, and you'll wear gold."

"Don't you mean 'wear *shit*'?" Ty smirked and pointed at Devon's leg. As the guard had fallen, he'd rolled in horse manure and the remains were sticking to his leggings. He swore and started scraping it off with his sword.

Two guards stayed on the rooftop, crossbows aimed at the pair in the square below. The others made their way down and around to the captives. Within moments of the guards' arrival, Ty and Kern found their hands behind their backs. The tall man in black walked past the captured duo. "All this for these two clowns," he mumbled, shaking his head as he passed. "Well done, Devon – Don, good work. But Devon, clean yourself up; you look like shit."

"It *is* shit," Ty laughed.

"Shut it, midget," Devon said, nodding to the guard behind the thief, who obligingly smacked Ty on the back of the head.

Soon they were soon being led roughly through the streets, three guards in front and three behind. Leading the procession through the streets was the tall man dressed in black, his long legs setting a quick pace. The townspeople made way without word, evaporating like morning mist, most avoiding the steely glare of the man in black.

As they shuffled through the town, Kern risked a glance at Ty. "This is it. We're finished," he muttered angrily.

"Oh, and I guess it's *my* fault again, is it?" Ty growled back.

"Who else's would it be? *You're* the one barging into town guards."

"Look, they'll throw us into a cell for a few days, then let us go," Ty said, trying to smooth things over. "We only bumped into a guard, not stole the king's crown jewels. And we might get a decent meal for a change."

"I very much doubt it. Look at the crap we ate in Leopard's Town jail; it'll be the same here," Kern replied. "And *we* didn't bump into anyone, *you*—"

The guard struck Kern's shoulder using the flat face of his bastard sword. It was a slightly shorter sword than Kern's, but the force behind it made him wince all the same. "Shut the hell up, you."

Without saying a word, Kern stopped, turned slowly, and stared at the guard. The guard reflexively backed off a step, even though his prisoner was tied up. Without waiting for further reaction, Kern set his expression into a carefully neutral mask and resumed walking.

The pair was led through one cobbled street after another for what seemed like ages, until at last they reached the far side of Raith. Here the streets were visibly cleaner, and the stench of rotten lizard meat from the marketplace could no longer be detected. *This is definitely the richer side of town,* Ty thought.

They came to a halt in front of an imposing building; in a spacious, open-doored barn sitting opposite the main structure, great stallions were being cared for by young stablehands. Ty looked around for clues as to the compound's purpose. He didn't think it was a jail; at least, certainly not the type they were accustomed to. And, he thought ruefully, he and Kern were certainly well-acquainted with small-town jails.

It looked more like the house of a lord – someone powerful and wealthy, for sure. Ty immediately remembered a similar house in Phebon he'd entered one evening, along with two other apprentices from the Dark

Shadow Thieves' Guild. They had ended up with quite a nice haul, and Ty had always resented the fact he'd had to hand his take over to the guild just because he was only an apprentice, not a full-fledged member. Maybe this place would be similarly stuffed with pocketable, portable loot? Then he remembered his hand restraints and cursed under his breath.

Still fearful of the guard's eagerness to use their bastard swords, Kern and Ty simply exchanged a confused and wordless look – but they both had the same thought: A wealthy looking house with big stables; six guards being led by a wizened man leaning on a staff? Definitely not your everyday town-guard capture.

The massive doors of the house opened, and they were prodded and shoved into the cool interior. When their eyes finally adjusted to the glare of sunlight through a glass-topped atrium, twenty feet above them, they registered the splendour of the building's interior. Massive statues of human warriors, twice life-size, dressed in plate mail and carrying two-handed swords, lined the corridors. Suspended from near the ceilings far above, huge tapestries skimmed the floors, most depicting scenes from legendary battles between humans and orcs. The floor tiles were of polished marble, and a grand staircase led to the upper floors. Elaborate vases and priceless ornaments sat atop marble plinths.

Kern could detect the fragrance of sweet-smelling perfumes mingled with the delicious aroma of meats roasting; the sound of boots on the marble floor echoed through the house and blended with the sounds of the brutish guards, shouting orders at the staff.

The man in black turned to the guards. "Put these worms in the cells; I will deal with them later." He turned to walk up the massive staircase, leaning on his staff as he went. He struggled with the stairs, gripping the banister for reassurance – a striking contrast to his bold and energetic march through the town.

Kern and Ty were led through a long corridor past the massive statues. Guards and servants mingled about, but seemed to take no notice of the prisoners. As the friends neared the end of the corridor, they could see a set of double doors barring their way. One of the guards fumbled in his pocket and pulled out a set of keys on an iron ring,

After trying four keys without success, he finally unlocked the doors and, dragging his captives behind him, proceeded down another set of stairs which opened onto a gloomy corridor. On each side of this hallway were three cells, framed and separated by iron bars. Three rusty lanterns hung down from the ceiling, giving just enough light to see halfway into the cells. A guard opened one of the cell doors while another cut the rope binding the prisoners' hands.

Kern didn't recognise either of these two guards; did the full-face helmets they wore override any distinguishing features, or did this black-robed man actually have so many guards at his disposal? For that matter, he wondered, why would a city house of such splendour have six cells in its basements, and this many guards to tend them? Then, with an unpleasant shock, Kern saw a face he *did* remember, as the door clanged shut behind them.

"Sleep tight," Devon said spitting on the cell floor before leaving.

The cell was a windowless square, with no furnishings aside from a bucket and a crude wooden bed, covered with a blanket that looked as though it had been there for a decade. Kern slid down to sit on the floor with his back against the wall and glared at Ty. "I don't believe you. Every *time,* you do it!"

"What's wrong now? You're always moaning about something," Ty replied.

"What's *wrong*? Take a look around! In case you haven't noticed, *we* are locked in a cell because *you* helped a stupid thief steal a couple of apples!"

"It's just in me to help a fellow tradesman," Ty grinned.

"You mean a fellow thief. And here we are, locked up – *again* – because you just had to help a strange urchin swipe a couple of apples!"

Ty shook his head, but didn't reply. Instead, squatting down next to the door, he began to study the lock.

"I suppose you're going to pick the lock, fight your way out, and be in the Orc's Armpit by nightfall, triumphantly drinking a pint of mead?" Kern said, folding his arms. "Is that your plan?"

"At least I'm doing something, not just sitting around complaining," Ty replied.

Moving to the bed, Ty sat to remove his right boot. He poked his hand inside and pulled out a pouch of bound leather about half the size of his fist. After replacing his boot, he unrolled the leather pouch, revealing a bone set of thieves' tools. "I'll get us out of here in no time, trust me," he said smugly. Kern rolled his eyes and made no reply.

"No point bothering, you know," said a voice from the opposite cell.

"Oh? And why is that?" Ty replied, hoping he had masked his surprise. He squinted his eyes, trying to make out a face or form in the darkness of the opposite cell.

"Only one way in and one way out – and that's the way you came in, back up those stairs. And on the other side of the door are two armed guards. I know who *my* money's on. Or would be on, if I had any," the disembodied voice chuckled.

"He's got a point, Ty. They have weapons and armour; we haven't even got a weapon between us. They took everything," Kern said with a hint of despondency. He stood and peered into the darkness of the opposite cell.

"I suppose you're right," agreed Ty, rolling up his tool-pouch. Facing the direction of the voice, he asked, "What's your name, then, and why are you here?"

"I am Galandrik Sabrehargen. I got into a bar fight and ended up injuring a town guard who was trying to break it up. That's what they told me, anyway," he added sheepishly. "I can't really remember much; I was pretty drunk. Again."

Galandrik moved forward from the shadows of his darkened cell, a sturdy dwarf with a long ginger beard. Two braided ponytails hung halfway down his back, his face battle-scarred from years of combat and his red leather armour looking old and worn.

"Pleased to meet you, Galandrik Sabrehargen. I am Ty 'Quickpick,' but most people call me 'The Rat.' This fellow is my old friend, Kern Ocarn, the ranger," Ty said proudly.

"Friend?" Kern said with a small snort, raising an eyebrow. "Friends usually don't get *friends* locked up." Ignoring Ty's look, Kern turned back to the dwarf. "So how long have you been here?"

"About a week," he laughed. "I didn't sober up for two days."

"But clearly this isn't the town's jail. What is this place, and why did they bring us here?" Kern asked, settling on the wooden bed.

"You saw the tall guy dressed in black? That's Conn, King Moriak's personal wizard. I think we're in his house," the dwarf explained.

"But why the hell did they stick us in his house?" Ty asked.

"I don't know; maybe he wants to try out some new spells on us, or practice turning people into toads," the dwarf replied, smiling.

"You're… you're… joking, right?" Ty spluttered.

"Oh, sit down, Rat. No one's going to turn us into toads, you fool," Kern snapped.

Galandrik looked at Kern and began to laugh.

"Who are you laughing at, ginger-beard? Don't make me open this door and come over there," Ty said, squeezing his head as far through the bars as possible.

"Anytime you want it, Rat-boy, I'm right here," replied Galandrik. "I've pushed bigger people than you out of the way to get to a fight, lad!"

"We shall see," Ty said, retreating and sitting down on the bed.

Undaunted by the sullen silence from Ty, Kern moved closer to the bars. "What brought you to Raith, Galandrik?"

As the night grew slowly deeper, the three prisoners swapped their tales of bravery and lawbreaking until, one by one, their voices faded into soft snores. Long after the other two had fallen asleep, Ty continued mumbling improbably heroic stories of his past, but no one was listening.

Chapter Two

The Offering

The next morning, the three prisoners were awakened by what sounded like an army of blacksmiths each battering his anvil. When the cacophony erupted, Ty leapt upright and instinctively reached for his wrist blades. After fumbling sleepily for a few seconds, he vaguely remembered dropping them in the dirt the day before. He looked bleary-eyed down the hallway. The sight of six guards, each one running the blade of his sword along the cell bars, explained the din and prompted Ty's memory of the previous day's events.

The red-haired guard, Devon, stopped outside Kern and Ty's cell. Ty sat down at the foot of the bed as Kern began to get up, slowly stretching his aching limbs. The pair rubbed their eyes, the torchlight ravaging their eyes after so many hours of darkness.

"Right then, thieves, Conn will see you now. We want no trouble," the guard said with a twisted smile, "so give us any shit and you'll be tied hands and feet and carried up like prize pigs. Got it?"

"Yeah, yeah – whatever. You'll get no trouble from us," Kern replied, giving Ty a stern look. "Will they, Ty?"

"No, I'm too hungry to try anything. It's been three moons since I last ate," Ty said, rubbing his aching stomach and yawning.

"Open the cells and bring them up. The dwarf too," Devon ordered before he stalked off down the hallway, leaving the other guards to handle the three prisoners.

All three were led up the stairs and back through the corridor, past the giant statues and up the massive staircase. Servants went about their daily business, scurrying around like worker ants in a nest. At the top of the stairs the prisoners were led down another great corridor, where exquisite paintings of seas, mountains, and forests – landscapes from all over Bodisha – adorned the walls. At the end of the corridor, two large oak double doors barred their way; standing in front of the doors was yet another guard.

Devon snapped to attention and announced, "The prisoners you requested, Captain Svorn." Svorn ignored him, but rapped three times on the door, sending an echo down the great corridor.

"It's toad time," said Galandrik, throwing Ty a smile, only to get a whack in the ribs from the guard and a snarled, "Shut it, dwarf."

The oaken double doors slowly creaked open to reveal a large square room lined with bookshelves and tables littered with parchments, bubbling potions, and stuffed animals. Strange birds and creatures that had once roamed the mountains and forests of Bodisha were mounted on wooden panels, glass eyes staring sightlessly at the clutter below. To one side of the room was a huge oak table furnished with lavish chairs.

At the far end of the room was a massive desk, showing just as much disarray as the rest of the room. Seated behind it was Conn, in his black robe. His cloak and hat hung next to him on a tall stand carved to look like an old oak tree; his long gnarled staff leaned up against a marble fireplace behind him.

"Bring them forward," said Conn, in a commanding voice that echoed around the room. As the three approached the desk, they could see that the staff was topped by a crow's skull. The crow's eye sockets glowed red and seemed to follow them, as if alive. Closer inspection, however, showed that it appeared to be woven into the wood, perhaps by some magical arts, or engraved by a highly skilled woodcarver.

Five paces from the desk, the guards stopped and stood, with one hand on the hilts of their swords, on either side of the prisoners.

"That will be all, Svorn. You may wait outside," Conn said to the larger guard.

"But... surely you Lordship wouldn't want to be left alone with these common cutthroats? It wouldn't be safe," the guard ventured.

Conn rose from his seat and seemed to grow in every direction. The three prisoners looked in awe at him. His thin face seemed sunken, as if it had seen too many battles and yearned to rest; his eyes, as black as his cloak, looked as dead as the night. His clenched fists rested on the desk, and the oak creaked audibly under the stain.

"If I need the Captain of the Guard to help me with three pathetic cutthroats, I will shout!" Conn thundered, barely restraining his anger.

Ty's mouth opened, ready to reply to the "pathetic cutthroat" remark, but he was hushed by a swift elbow to the ribs from Kern, who could foresee the probable outcome of such an outburst. Ty pressed his lips together and glared down at the floor.

"Take your men and go wait outside, Svorn," Conn said calmly.

"Yes, my Lord."

Conn sat back down in his chair, shaking his head and mumbling something that sounded like, "We go through this every week!" The great double doors shut behind the departing guard, their creaking even more pronounced than when they had opened.

Conn sized up the three prisoners. Taking his time, he looked each of them up and down. They all kept quiet, their heads bowed like naughty schoolboys awaiting punishment from a head teacher. Kern wanted to speak up, but his tongue was frozen in fear. He glanced at Ty for reassurance, but Ty just raised one shoulder, and seemed as lost for words as Kern. Galandrik was affected the same – head bowed and silent – when suddenly Conn spoke.

"Kern Ocarn. Human ranger from the north, expelled from your hometown four years ago after you refused to fight for your father's army against the orcs. You've been traveling ever since, living day-to-day and hand-to-mouth, like a common vagrant," he said, staring directly at Kern. Kern struggled to make a reply but his mouth just wouldn't open.

With a cold chuckle, Conn turned to the thief. "Ty 'The Rat' Quickpick; halfling. You never knew your parents. You were raised by thieves in the town of Phebon, and were apprehended while trying to steal a jewelled dagger from another thief – a grave betrayal of the thieves' code of honour. Banished by your own kind, you have been hated by them ever since."

At this speech, Kern looked at Ty with his eyebrows lifted in surprise; Kern had been told quite a different story. Ty merely shrugged his shoulders in return and returned his gaze to the floor. He stood meekly, as if he had just been caught red-handed stealing from the local shopkeeper.

Finally Conn turned his attention to the dwarf. "And Galandrik Sabrehargen. Dwarf warrior from under the great mountain of Grimnoss, you fought on numerous campaigns against the orc armies of the east. You led a platoon of dwarves into an orc ambush and over one hundred dwarves were subsequently slaughtered. Only you and a few others survived. You were stripped of all your honours, and sentenced to work in the mines under Grimnoss. You fled, of course, and have been an outcast ever since."

Kern and Ty could see the truth of each word in the pain etched upon Galandrik's face. Conn stared at all three for a few moments, then steepled his hands to his chin, elbows resting on the table. His brow furrowed, and his face bore the expression of a man wondering if he was making the right decision.

"Now let me tell you a little about *me*," Conn said, rising and walking around the table, grabbing his staff as he went. Kern could see that even though his size projected a younger man, his gait was far from young; he shuffled more than he walked, and leaned heavily on his staff whilst doing so.

"I am Conn, advisor to King Moriak, and I have a problem. Two weeks ago today, a shipment of the King's gold was stolen by orcs just to the south." At the word "orc," Galandrik's head swivelled, like a dog alerting to a knock at the door.

"What I need… is a group of thieves to retrieve it," Conn said, now standing behind the group.

"What if we don't want to help?" Kern said, still facing the desk where the wizard had been.

"That's perfectly fine. Should that be the case, I will simply hand the halfling and dwarf over to their respective towns, and you can rot in jail for a few years," Conn said placidly.

"But that's certain death for Ty, and a life of slavery or worse for Galandrik," Kern said, raising his voice slightly.

"What do we get for doing it, and how do we know you won't just hand us in afterwards?" Ty questioned.

"You have my word that you will walk free after the task is completed. I will speak to the dwarf warlord, Grumlo, and to the grandmaster thief, Cronos of Phebon. You will both receive pardons, in addition to one thousand gold coins each." Upon hearing the words "one thousand gold," Ty swiftly raised his head.

"When do we leave?" he asked, turning to Kern and grinning.

"What's to stop us just taking the King's gold after we find it, or just giving you our promise, then leaving here and walking off into the sunset?" Kern asked.

Conn's staff came down on Kern's shoulder with a thud. The flesh was still aching from the guard's blow the day before, and Conn had struck the exact same spot – as if he knew exactly what would cause Kern the most discomfort. Kern gritted his teeth, inhaling a deep breath to distract himself from the pain.

"That would be very foolish, my friend. It is very unwise to steal from the King. You are already running out of places to hide; where would you run to, exactly?" Conn sneered.

Conn walked back and sat in his chair. "In addition to the pardons and the gold, I will kit you out with weapons, armour, provisions, horses, and even a guide," he said, leaning back in his chair and watching the three prisoners.

Kern, Ty, and Galandrik all looked at each other; it was clear they had no other choice but to do the wizard's bidding.

"All right, we accept the assignment. What is it exactly that we are looking for?" Kern asked.

"All in good time, my friend, all in good time," Conn said. "First we must get you cleaned up and fed. Svorn!"

Within seconds, Svorn entered the room, followed by Devon. "Yes, my lord," Svorn said, bowing slightly.

"Take these men to the bath house and give them the clothes from the cupboard we prepared yesterday. Remember: They are no longer prisoners; they are my *guests*," Conn said. "I know how some guards can be a bit overeager to lash out with the flats of their swords at prisoners." Kern's eyes narrowed at this, but if the wizard noticed the suspicious expression, he did not acknowledge it.

The trio was led back through the enormous house to a large bathing room. Inside were four wooden baths in a row. Filled with hot water and bubbles, each tub boasted a thin cloud of steam; chambermaids flittered about, some scooping buckets of cooling water out of the tubs, while others poured jugs of near-boiling water in. The smell from this room was like a field of roses, Kern thought, as he stripped and slipped into the first bath. He quickly relaxed into the warm water, closing his eyes and rubbing his aching shoulder. Ty and Galandrik followed suit; Ty immediately dunked his head under the surface of the water to wash his face, which felt like it was covered in a lifetime's worth of dirt.

"Kicked out for stealing from one of your own, then, was it?" Kern said after several minutes of silence. "What happened to the escape from prison, picking the locks on your hand- and leg-irons with a sliver of wood you found on the cell floor, and killing five guards on your way out? Not to mention the reason you were there in the first place: Pick-pocketing five mithril pieces from the Prince, who happened to be visiting the week before? And to think I believed you!" Kern shouted at Ty, throwing a bar of rose-petal soap in his direction.

"That Conn is a fool; he doesn't know the real story! They made up that scandalous lie because they were embarrassed by my escape," Ty retorted, raising an arm to throw the soap back.

Just then the red-headed guard appeared, carrying three piles of clothes. As he placed them on the table opposite, Ty thought back to the scene on the street the day before. Devon had just reached the door when Ty threw the bar of soap in the guard's direction. The soap whizzed past the red hair, missing Devon's head by inches – only to hit the door and rebound directly into his forehead.

"Oi! More hot water and more towels, you. And don't be slow about it," Ty commanded. The young serving girls giggled behind their hands, and Devon gave Ty a sinister look. He knew he had to resist the urge to put the annoying little halfling in his place; after all, these were Conn's guests now. Devon had just gotten his irritation under control when Ty added, "And make sure you wash off all the horse shit you've been rolling around in!"

The serving girls' giggles broke into outright laughter, and the guard's face turned as red as his hair. Staring at Ty with a cold smile, Devon slowly backed out of the door, alert for any other missiles that might come his way. When the door closed behind him, all three companions erupted in laughter.

"One day you'll get us into serious trouble, Ty the Rat," Kern joked.

"And one day you'll stop moaning!" Ty answered.

"Here we go again. Don't you two ever stop?" Galandrik laughed as he rubbed the dirt out of his ginger beard.

After an hour in the bathhouse, the three got dressed in the clothes the guard had left on the table. None of them could believe the fit; the garments seemed made to measure, as if their sizes had been known even before they'd arrived. The beautiful green and brown silks had been stitched with a perfect hand; these were good quality clothes, Ty mused. Even the trousers were of fine cloth and fit him to absolute perfection, as did the shoes. He wondered why three thieves should be lavished with silks, but said nothing.

A guard led them back up to Conn's study, where the first meeting had taken place. In the centre of the room was the massive oak table that had previously sat off to one side. Eight lavish chairs surrounded it, three down either side and one at each end. The table held the most luxurious spread of food Ty had ever seen. Kern and Galandrik had seen feasts like this, but only on very special occasions. A suckling pig, complete with the traditional apple in its mouth, lay in the middle of the table, surrounded by every sort of vegetable and bread imaginable, fish such as the red-bellied river cobblers, and large pots laced with baked shrimp and filled with seafood dressings. Fine wine and jugs of ale were placed around the edge of the table, completing the sumptuous array.

"Please, join me; sit down and feast," Conn said from his place at the far end of the table. First to sit was Ty; without another word, a large morsel of pork was in one hand and a chunk of wheat bread in the other. Kern and Galandrik followed suit, and soon all were eating – and eating well.

"This is the best meal I've had since I won that archery competition back in Phebon," Ty commented, grease dripping down his chin. Kern glanced at Galandrik and rolled his eyes. Galandrik shook his head, then returned his attention to his plate. For a long while they feasted without talking, enjoying every mouthful of the splendid buffet.

"I don't think I could manage another bean," Galandrik said, letting out an overly-exaggerated burp and dropping a half-eaten king prawn onto his plate.

"Nor I, sir," Kern offered.

After draining a full jug of mead, Ty finally joined the conversation. "Yes," he said, "that *was* good. Many thanks to your fine cooks," he added as he rubbed his swollen belly.

"I should imagine you have a few questions that need answering, so if you are all satisfied, we will have the table cleared and prepare our strategy. I will be happy to answer any questions you may have and offer any knowledge that might be helpful," Conn said. He clapped his hands twice, and four servants appeared in the room instantly; Ty stared, gaping, and wondered if the wizard had used magic to create such perfectly trained house-servants.

Before long, the table was bare, apart from a couple of jugs of ale and two bottles of Raith red wine, accompanied by four clean cups.

"Fire away," Conn said, leaning forward onto the table.

After a brief silence the dwarf turned to Conn. "I have only one question for you. Why don't you just send an army down there to retrieve your gold? Why send us?"

After a pause, Conn answered patiently. "Simple. An army would be spotted from miles away; the orcs would be well warned before the army was close enough to even pepper their walls with arrows. We believe they have taken the gold for hiding, into some caves in the southeast. If they saw an army coming, they would disappear or blend in to become well nigh invisible." His voice trailed off. "No, we would never find them…"

There was an uncomfortable silence, then Conn resumed his speech. "But you three can get down there undetected and steal the gold from under their noses. Furthermore, King Moriak has armies fighting the orcs in the east and the dark elves in the North." Conn paused and glanced over to Kern, waiting for a reaction, but nothing came. "He doesn't have enough men to spare any for retrieving the gold," Conn finished.

"How much did they steal?" Ty asked, now puffing on a long bone pipe.

"The precise amount is insignificant. There are two chests, though we doubt very much that they have been opened, as most of the orc shamans are being used in the great wars to the east. You needn't worry about the contents of the chests – they are well-secured by powerful spells. Just worry about getting them back here," Conn said, leaning over the table and staring at Ty.

Conn rose from his chair and walked over to one of his untidy bookshelves. After searching through the books, scrolls, parchments, and papers, he eventually selected a long tubular container, hollowed out of what looked like a thigh bone, with a small chain attached towards one end. Whatever beast this came from must have been quite some size, Kern thought.

Returning to the table, Conn twisted the end of bone near the chain until it popped free. Kern realized that the length of bone must be a case of some sort, with a bone cap or lid at one end. Letting the lid hang free on the chain that connected it to the case, Conn pulled a tightly-rolled sheet of parchment from the hollowed-out bone, and smoothed it out upon the table. It was a map of Bodisha.

"The ambush on our troops was two days' ride south of here, just across the River Narv from the town of Praise, slightly north of Gateford Forest. You can pick the orcs' trail up there. We think they either went through Gateford Forest or southeast, around it, towards the Eastern Mountains. Either way their trail is about as hidden as a trail can be, and doesn't want to be found," Conn said, studying the map, finger pointing to the ambush spot.

"Can we cross the river at Praise?" Galandrik asked.

"Yes, there is a ferry crossing," Conn explained.

"You said we would have a guide also; does he know the route through Gateford Forest if need be?" Ty asked, blowing a small smoke ring through a larger one.

Conn lifted his head from the map and looked at Ty. "*No one* knows a route through Gateford Forest. Some even say the forest moves the paths the traders make, to confuse and trap those who venture in."

"The forest moves the paths?" asked Ty sceptically.

"They say the forest is… alive."

Ty slowly pulled the long bone pipe from his mouth and looked at Kern. "Have you been in there?" he questioned shakily.

"No, but I have heard the stories about giant bats and forest ogres eating traders," Kern replied, turning away from Ty and winking cheekily at Galandrik.

"Aye, lad, many a dwarf has been sent through there and never returned. We call it '*Dume Kaziad*,' the Dark Forest," Galandrik added, carefully keeping a straight face.

Ty slumped back into his chair, deep in thought. "I hate ogres, I hate forests, I hate bats, and I hate this quest!" he muttered under his breath.

Picking up on Kern and Galandrik's teasing, Conn smiled to himself as he moved to another table which had been covered up with a white cotton cloth since their arrival. Conn grabbed one corner and turned to Ty. "Maybe this will help you defeat those evil ogres." With a faint grin, he whipped off the cloth with a snap of his wrist.

The cloth fell to the floor alongside the table, revealing a massive display of weapons. Everything on the table looked new and unused, brightly resplendent in the flickering torch light. Ty slowly raised himself from the chair, gazing wide-eyed at the table. Kern and Galandrik also stood and moved toward the table as if in a trance, their eyes widened by the beauty in front of them.

Kern, with his longer legs, reached the table first; his gaze rested on an elven longbow and he gazed at it for several seconds before reaching down and gently lifting the bow into the air. It felt lighter than any bow he had ever held. Made of white yew wood with a maple wood backing, the weapon seemed to shimmer like white smoke when he turned it, and runes swirled along its length from tip to toe. Kern knew at first glance that this bow was special – even aside from the ethereal beauty of the thing, its quality brown buckskin grip and the widened limbs for longevity and decreased bow noise spoke of incomparable craftsmanship. He could smell the tiger balm that had been rubbed into the stave for extra hardness. Twirling it in his hands, he studied its beauty and grace.

Galandrik stepped up next to Kern and selected a two-handed great-axe from the table. "By the great gods of Grimnoss, this is the finest piece of weapon-smithing I have seen since the great battle of Agromarrn." He studied the axe with great interest; its shaft was made of hardwood, the handle covered in buckskin, and the double-bladed head shone like no other axe he had seen before. The engravings on the blade faces were intricate and precise; swirls and circles covered every inch. Only the high dwarf lords carried weapons of such beauty; this would cut through an orc like a hot knife through butter, Galandrik thought to himself.

Ty reached the table at last. Still gaping like a child with mouth wide open, he picked up a bone-handled dagger carved into the shape of a dragon's head. Next to it sat a leather wrist holster, the kind he had only ever seen the elder thieves in Phebon wearing. After examining the dagger's splendour – and cutting his thumb slightly on its sharpness – he lay it gently down onto the table once more. Ty quickly strapped on the wrist holster, complete with leather hand wrap. Raising his hand in front of his face, he slowly turned his wrist round and round while balling his fist open and shut. The leather wrap was a perfect fit. Snatching up the dagger from the table, he locked it in place, then pulled his shirt sleeve over the new toy. Strolling away from the table, Ty fought to conceal a grin. It felt as though there actually *was* nothing on his wrist. Suddenly, with a snap of his arm and a spin, his new dagger flew handle first from his hidden holster; he caught it perfectly, with the tip pointing straight at Conn.

"Very nice," Conn commented drily.

Soon Ty had both holsters on and was practicing releasing the duelling daggers together, trying to perfect the double release motion. Kern had picked up a large brown goatskin quiver filled with fine arrows, while Galandrik stared at his axe – complete with a back holster – still captivated by its beauty. All three of them were like overgrown children, full of enthusiasm and joy.

Conn resumed his seat at the head of the table, waiting for his three guests to follow. Before long the demands of hospitality pulled them back to their own seats, though each of the three still gazed at their new weapons.

Conn cleared his throat with intention. "Tonight you will sleep in town, at the Orc's Armpit. I believe you are all familiar with this place?" Conn looked around the table.

"Yes, Ty and I have been there a few times," Kern answered

Conn looked at Galandrik with a knowing glance; it was the tavern Galandrik had been arrested in. Galandrik looked faintly chastened, then nodded. "Good," Conn continued. "Go to the stable behind the tavern at dawn. There will be three horses and armour – padded leather for the ranger, chainmail for the dwarf, and light leather for the thief," Conn said. Ty was intent on rolling his wrists round and admiring his new holsters – far too busy to notice the wizard's sly insult. Kern didn't miss it, however.

"You will also be provided backpacks with bedding, torches, flint and tinder, rations, oil, ropes, a few random potions, and some poisons to aid you in your journey," Conn finished.

"That's all well and good, but how are we going to find the ambush point? I thought you said we would have a guide," Galandrik said.

"You do; his name is Solomon. He will be ready tomorrow at dawn, complete with maps for the route," Conn said reassuringly. "Leave your weapons here; they will be delivered with the armour and horses tomorrow. That *does* includes you," Conn said, looking at the halfling.

"But mine are hidden, why should –" Ty's protest was cut short as Conn raised his voice.

"Because I said so, Ty; now take them off and leave them on the table. They will be delivered to you at dawn," Conn concluded.

"Just leave them, Ty, and let's get out of here," Kern said.

"Can't see any reason why I should; it isn't as though people can see them." Ty complained unceasingly under his breath as he reluctantly unfastened his arm holsters while the others waited.

"That's all I can offer you for now. Solomon will explain more once you get underway. Good luck, and bring back the King's gold. All of it." Conn heaved the massive double-doors open and gave orders to the guards outside. The guard hurried off, but soon returned with their old weapons – and their old, but freshly-washed, clothes.

"Put these back on; you won't stand out as much in the tavern," Conn insisted. The expensive fabrics and exquisitely tailored clothes had served their purpose, he mused – the trio had been knocked ever so slightly out of their comfort zone, awed and distracted by the trappings of wealth. However, Conn had no intention of letting them run off dressed like lords – time enough for their new wardrobes after they had completed his task.

Donning once more their familiar clothes and weapons, the party said their farewells to Conn. They walked along the corridor and down the centre stairs that led to the front door. Galandrik walked out while Kern stopped to examine one of the tapestries, depicting a battle between orcs and men many moons ago. In the centre of the picture was a paladin seated on his mount, both wearing bright silver-plate mail armour. The horse was on its two hind legs, rearing up, and the paladin held the reins tight in one hand and lifted his sword aloft in the other. Many orcs surrounded them, and Kern pondered the paladin's fate.

Ty stood next to Kern, examining a golden vase that sat on a plinth. As if reading Ty's mind Kern whispered, "You even think about trying to steal that and I swear I'll –"

"As if I would," Ty chuckled, and the pair walked out the main door, catching Galandrik up and heading for the Orc's Armpit.

Chapter Three: Mistaken Identity

The party walked towards the tavern in the cool evening; summer was coming to an end and the autumn chill was just starting to set in.

Ty crossed his arms and rubbed his shoulders. "I hope there's some warmer clothes with the supplies and horses."

"I'm sure there will be; he won't want us to freeze before we get his precious gold," Galandrik reassured Ty.

Ty shivered. "Yeah, I guess so."

Within the hour they could smell the food and hear the hustle and bustle of Raith's most popular drinking hole: The Orc's Armpit. As they entered through the main door, the smell of pipe tobacco filled their nostrils. Through the cloud of smoke hanging over the room, they saw three men playing instruments in the corner of the tavern: One on a flute, one on a crude banjo, and one banging a cowskin drum. A handful of townsfolk danced in front of the musicians; the music was old folk tunes from years gone by.

Kern pointed to an empty table and they quickly claimed it. They called over a busty maid, and soon they were all drinking pints of mead. Ty looked down at the leather wrist straps concealing his daggers – his old ones, with no release mechanism – and sighed.

Galandrik looked around the inn. There were races from all over the world of Bodisha: humans, halflings, wood elves, dwarves, and even the odd half-orc, all telling tales of high adventure and long-lost legends, or just stories of their day's events.

"Well, at least we have some decent work for a change," Ty commented, feeling glum about the temporary loss of the new dagger straps.

"Not that we had much choice in the matter," Kern replied.

"It still doesn't look right to me," Galandrik said. "Something just seems strange, sending us to get two chests of gold. Why is the king troubled over two chests' worth? He has more gold than Grimnoss Mountain has rocks!"

"Who cares?" Ty said, shrugging his shoulders. He filled his long bone pipe with stonecrop leaf, a common tobacco in Bodisha. "As long as we get what they want and we get our one thousand gold, what does it matter?"

"That stuff will kill you," Kern remarked, eyeing Ty's pipe.

"Yes, and so can a giant bat in Gateford Forest, but we're still going there!" Ty answered, blowing a smoke ring as his companions laughed.

"Right, who's for another?" Ty asked, standing. Galandrik and Kern both nodded. Ty walked over and stood in line at the bar; he was ordering the three pints of mead when a big fat human clumsily knocked into him, nearly bowling the halfling over. The fat man turned around and looked down at Ty. Without even a hint of an apology, he straightened his oversized pointy hat and turned back to his friend, a human who looked like he had been rolling in dirt all morning: Mud covered his clothes and face, with the odd piece of hay stuck in his straggly greying hair.

Ty was about to say something when he heard the fat man mention hill giants in the south killing his livestock. Being the inquisitive type, Ty edged closer to listen.

"Bloody hill giants've killed five cows, two horses, and eleven sheep so far this year! You just can't stop them. Bloody huge they are, and them clubs they carry are massive – the size of an ox!" the fat farmer said to his grubby friend.

"So where exactly do they come from?" his companion asked, picking a lump of mud from his neck and dropping it on the floor.

"I think they come down from the Eastern Mountains, and camp in the hills near Praise. They know our livestock is an easy meal." The first farmer paid for one jug of ale and another of what looked like red wine; Ty watched as he put the few coppers' change he had been given into a leather pouch hanging from his belt.

Ty didn't give it another thought. He quickly looked round the inn. No eyes were on him, and most importantly *Kern's* eyes were not on him. *I'll teach you to barge into people without saying sorry,* he thought as he drew a tiny double-bladed dagger from his belt. These were used much the same as scissors; thieves called them strap-cutters. As soon as the maid placed the three pints onto the bar, making enough noise for a smokescreen, he made his move, slicing the pouch's leather straps in one smooth, swift motion and catching the bag in another.

He slipped the pilfered pouch inside his tunic, as if searching for his own coin-pouch to pay the bar girl. Pulling his hand free from his tunic, he dropped some coinage on the bar. Noticing that there were only a few coppers left after she had collected the price of the mead, Ty said, "Keep those, my love, a gift from me to you," with a wink. The maid's face reddened; a tavern like the Orc's Armpit didn't attract big tippers. This little display caught the eye of the newly-poor farmer, but he turned back to his conversation without sparing a second thought for the cause of the maid's delight; he didn't even see Ty as the halfling walked away.

"What took you so long? We nearly died of thirst over here," Galandrik jested.

"Just listening to a tale of hill giants eating a farmer's livestock," Ty said, looking cheerful.

As Kern and Galandrik talked about battles of their forefathers, Ty discreetly checked the pouch. *Not a bad piece of work,* he thought; five gold pieces, over thirty silver, a handful of copper, and a nice ruby encrusted gold ring that looked small enough for a child – certainly too small for even his smallest finger. Still, Ty was pleased. *It's not the loot, it's the looting,* he thought, smiling to himself. He placed the gold pieces into the hidden pocket inside his tunic on the left. It was an old habit – he kept silver and copper coins on the right side and separate from his own until the money had been there long enough for him to forget where he'd stolen it from; then and only then he'd mix it with his own.

Eventually, Kern stretched his arms above his head. "I suppose I'd better go speak with the innkeeper about the rooms, make sure that's all sorted out."

Ty reached into his backpack and pulled out a bag; loosening the drawstrings, he emptied five bone dice onto the table. "Time to take your money, dwarf."

"You'll be lucky I'm skint!" Galandrik said, leaning back into his chair.

"That's all right, you can owe me." Ty answered with a wink.

The innkeeper was a large bald man wearing the filthiest apron imaginable. He confirmed that the rooms were paid for, then quizzed Kern as to what his business was in the town. Typical innkeeper questioning: One man's honest work is another man's dishonest opportunity to hijack it, and gossip was gold in any inn. Kern knew that telling the innkeeper of their quest would only lead to his selling the information to some other group, who might find the gold first and collect the reward for themselves. Thinking quickly and remembering Ty's remark, he replied, "Giants."

"Giants? There are no giants here in Raith, my good friend. Well, unless you count Tom the pig farmer's son – Big Will – but he's as soft as goose feathers." Throwing his grimy cloth over his shoulder, the innkeeper rested both hands on the counter.

"No, not in Raith – half a day's ride to the south. We intend to slay the foul beast and be back by tomorrow night, to spend our reward here in your…" Kern glanced around the inn. "…*Fine* establishment," he finished with a smile.

The innkeeper forced a smile, knowing full well that Kern had just insulted him and his precious inn.

"Any chance of getting drunk in this shithole?" a man shouted from the other end of the bar, trying to get the innkeeper's attention.

The innkeeper straightened. "I'll be seeing you, then," he said as he turned and walked to the waiting customer.

"Indeed you will, sir," Kern laughed to himself and returned to the table.

Several pints later, Kern looked fondly across at Ty. "Do you know, Rat, this is the first time since I've known you that we've been in a bar for more than an hour and you haven't gotten caught trying to steal from someone, or started a fight over a game of dice. You're always making trouble in the Orc's Armpit. I'm quite impressed."

"See, Kern," Ty replied smugly, "I know when to steal and when not to!" With that, he made a crude announcement and headed off to the toilet.

After a few minutes, Galandrik nudged Kern and pointed to the bar, where two humans were talking to four town guards. One man, wearing a pointy hat, was waving his arms and showing the guards two cut purse-strings hanging down from his overstrained leather belt; he seemed very angry indeed.

Kern looked back at Galandrik. "Rat!" he said, through gritted teeth. "I bet you a gold piece he had something to do with this, I just know it," Kern raged.

"Don't be too hasty, Kern. There are plenty of thieves about, and you're overlooking something else," Galandrik answered.

"Like what?" Kern asked, puzzled.

"Whoever stole that man's pouch… *didn't get caught*."

"Good point, my friend." Kern sighed. "I guess we'll find out soon enough, whenever Rat comes back from the toilet."

"Can you imagine Conn's face if we ended up back in the cells tonight for stealing – *again* – and missed the dawn meeting?" Galandrik laughed.

"I don't think we'd ever leave the cell if we did," Kern replied.

Bok and Joli sat at the bar, looking at the busty barmaid. "So how are we going to pay for the room?" Joli said to Bok.

"I don't know. You lost the card game, you figure it out," Bok replied.

Joli was the smaller of the two men. Long greasy hair covered his weasel-like features; a pointed nose, bad teeth, and a crooked right eye didn't make him pretty viewing. By comparison, Bok was the opposite – a heavyset man with a huge jaw line, scars cut across the left side of his face from a knife fight many moons before, with long grey hair twisted into a ponytail hanging down his back. He was not a handsome man by any means – except when he stood next to Joli.

Suddenly Bok grabbed Joli by the arm. Joli let out a painful cry and pulled his arm free, rubbing it exaggeratedly. "Ouch! What was that for?"

"I think our troubles are over," Bok said in a low voice, now grinning from ear to ear. "Look over there and tell me who you think you see."

Joli looked around the bar. "Just a load of rabble dancing, some dwarves and elves chatting, and a couple of fat humans at the bar. Why?"

"Next to the two fat humans, you idiot," Bok said, slapping Joli across the back of the head. Joli stared at the small figure next to the humans, squinting through the haze of pipe smoke that hung like morning mist over the bar.

"Well, well! If it isn't that little shit, Ty 'The Rat.' How much is he worth now?" Joli asked, having forgotten his arm and now rubbing his head.

"Not a great deal, but if you'll remember, we aren't exactly welcome back to Phebon ourselves, are we? We can't collect the reward if we can't show our faces. Stupid." Bok raised his hand, threatening to slap Joli again.

"What are we going to do, then?" Joli kept a keen eye on Bok's raised hand, ready to duck at the slightest sign of movement.

"Well, *he* doesn't know we aren't welcome back at Phebon. So we'll just corner him and threaten him: If he doesn't pay up we'll turn him over at Phebon – simple."

"But you said we *can't* turn him over," Joli whined. "You said they'd arrest us too!"

"No, stupid; we threaten to do it, not *actually* do it!" Bok was on the verge of losing his temper. "Now, don't let him out of your sight, and try not to let him spot you."

"He's taking three pints back to that table. Damn!" Joli exclaimed, observing the table. "He has friends, a dwarf and a human, and they look armed as well."

"It's only been a few years since he was forced to run from Phebon. I can't see him being any different from the fool he was then. And I say the only people who would hang out with a fool, are fools. They'll be no trouble, trust me," Bok said reassuringly.

The pair of thieves sat at the bar and watched the three men at the table across the room, drinking and chatting. After what seemed like an age, the human got up from the table and headed towards the bar. He chatted with the innkeeper, while Bok stared at the dwarf. "Go on, get up and leave the little maggot to us," he muttered to himself, but the dwarf didn't budge; it looked like they had started a game of dice.

"Any chance of getting drunk in this shithole?" shouted a man standing at the bar next to Bok. The innkeeper turned toward his customer, and the human returned to Ty's table.

"Blast the gods above," Bok said, slamming his fist on the bar in frustration and glaring at the man next to him. Bok and Joli watched, waiting impatiently for their next opportunity, until eventually Ty stood up and moved towards the toilet.

"Right; now's our chance. Let me do the talking, and be careful of his wrist daggers; as I recall, he was right fond of them," Bok warned Joli.

"Okay, let's do it," Joli answered, picking up his cloak from the chair and wrapping it around his shoulders.

As Bok and Joli neared the main entrance, they spotted four guards entering the inn; one of the humans at the bar was beckoning them over.

Bok turned to Joli. "Perfect." He spat onto the floor. "Ty won't want to cause a scene with those pigs in here."

The pair carried on towards the toilet. They walked past Ty's two companions, then strolled by the four guards talking to the two humans and squeezed through the dancing locals before passing through a small doorway. The corridor branched immediately to the left, where they saw three doors and a dead end. One of the doors had the common sign for male toilets. The pair drew their swords in the corridor in readiness.

Slowly Bok squeezed the door open and they both entered on tiptoes, being as quiet as possible. They could hear someone whistling. Carefully they looked round the corner. They could see Ty, doing his duty against a wall. There was a crudely cut groove in the floor, angling the flow out into the street through a rat-sized hole.

Bok and Joli quietly pointed their swords at their victim. Ty finished his business and turned round, still whistling – only to find himself face-to-face with two rusty blade tips. Immediately his hands went up. "Whoa, easy there! What is it you want?" he stuttered.

"Well, that's no way to greet old friends, now is it, Ty 'The Rat' Quickpick?" Bok said, smiling.

Ty stared for a moment at his two 'old friends.' "Well, blow me over – it's Jok and Boli," Ty answered, a newfound air of confidence in his voice.

"It's *Bok* and *Joli*, actually!" Joli said angrily.

"He knows our names, Joli; he's still just a fool – same as he was back then, same as he always will be. That is, until we get him back to Phebon where *certain people* will pay us handsomely for handing him over, then lock him up and throw away the key," Bok said, watching Ty's face change from confident to edgy. "And don't try and cause a scene, either; there are four guards at the bar – some complaint by a couple of humans, looks like. Those guards would be just as interested in your story as we are."

Ty's brow lifted slightly and his eyes widened. He was thinking frantically. Finally he said, "Listen, Bok and Joli, old friends," making sure he said the names correctly this time. "Why don't we cut a deal here? We *are* old friends, after all, and surely we can sort things out without going back to Phebon. That place was a shithole," he said calmly, "and I like being free, like a bird in the sky."

"What do you call a deal, then?" Bok said, prodding Ty's hands further up above his head.

Ty kept his hands as high as he could. "Well, I have some coinage you can take, and you can go on your way and let me go free."

Bok couldn't believe his luck – Ty had fallen right into his trap, before Bok had even mentioned the possibility of a payoff. "Where are these coins, exactly?" he asked suspiciously.

"Inside my tunic on the right side, there is a pouch; it has over three gold in silver coins and copper coins – take it, then let me go in peace," Ty said, hoping Galandrik would walk in any moment now.

"Joli, reach in and get the pouch while I keep my blade on him," Bok commanded. Joli did as he was told, lowering his weapon and retrieving the pouch from the folds of Ty's tunic. He quickly opened it and started counting the coins.

"He's right, Bok – there's the coins he talked about, and a nice little gold ring that might fetch some gold, too!" Joli said delightedly.

Ty shut his eyes in disgust, kicking himself for not putting the ring into another pocket. Before he could open them again, Bok had stepped forward and whacked his forehead into the bridge of Ty's nose, forcing him back against the wet wall.

Sliding down, Ty sat against the wall, holding his nose and trying to stem the sudden flow of blood. His head pounded with pain, and his vision had all but gone. "Have a nice life, fool," Bok said, looking down at Ty as he snatched the ring from Joli.

Ty didn't answer.

Bok and Joli left the toilet and headed back out through the bar. They walked past the dancing townsfolk again, and headed cheerfully for the door. As they came level with the guards Joli threw the pouch into the air and caught it. "That wasn't too bad for five minutes' work, if I do say so myself," Joli said, looking quite pleased with the results of the robbery.

There was a sudden shout from behind them: "My pouch!" Bok and Joli spun around to face the two humans and the guards, their faces in shock. The fat farmer was staring at them and pointing. "And there's my ring!" the farmer added, spotting it crammed onto Bok's finger. The guards drew their weapons and pointed them at the thieves.

"Give me the pouch and ring," a guard said, pointing a repeating crossbow at the caught thieves. Bok turned to Joli with a face like thunder and raised a hand in a threatening motion. Shaking his head in disbelief as Joli cowered beside him, Bok lowered his arm without swiping his companion and said, "You fucking idiot," through gritted teeth.

Joli handed over the pouch and Bok dropped the ring into the guard's hand. Quickly the farmer held the pouch next two the cut strings; the match was unmistakable. He then opened the pouch and emptied the contents into his hand. "The gold is missing," the fat farmer wailed.

"There must be some sort of mistake here; we just got given that pouch from Ty… Ty the Rat!" Bok protested.

"Yeah, yeah – I know him; he's the one with big ears and eats loads of cheese," the guard said, pushing Bok towards the door. Another guard followed, still holding a sword to Bok's back, closely followed by Joli being held by the last two guards; last came the two fat farmers plodding behind.

"But it's true, he's in the toilet," Joli argued.

"Yeah, because – don't tell me – that's where he lives, this rat friend of yours," the guard laughed. "Too much mead, this one," he said, to the laughter of the other guards.

Bok looked back at the toilet doors and saw Ty standing at the door pinching the bridge of his nose. Cheekily, Ty blew Bok a kiss.

"I'll hunt you down, Rat," Bok shouted across the packed inn.

Ty waved back.

Eventually Ty made his way back to the table; he had cleaned all the blood from his face, but couldn't hide the cut across the bridge of his swollen nose.

"Where have you been and what in hell's name happened to you?" Kern said, spotting the halfling's cut nose.

"Whatever happened, it looks like he lost," Galandrik chuckled.

"And why did that big fellow – the one the guards just led out of here – shout 'rat?' Nothing to do with you, I trust?" Kern asked, raising an eyebrow.

"Let's call it a case of mistaken identity. Anyway I'm tired and in pain, so no more questions. I'll tell you both in the morning; I'm off upstairs," Ty said, smiling and wincing at the same time. Without another word he got up from the table, gingerly walked round to the other side of the bar towards the stairs leading to the upstairs rooms, and disappeared through the door.

"Don't even ask." Kern said, cutting Galandrik's question off before it was fully formed. "See you at dawn."

"Aye lad, see you later, O ranger from the North," Galandrik said as

Kern made his way to the stairs. Kern waved, but didn't turn around.

"Bring me another pint of your finest ale!" Galandrik shouted to the barmaid, and settled into his seat with a comfortable sigh. It was going to be a long night, if he had anything to say about it.

Chapter Four
The Early Start

Kern stretched as he opened the wooden shutters to his window. His room overlooked a marketplace – a smaller one than where they had been arrested by Conn's men, but no less busy. Kern looked idly at the stall owners setting out the day's wares and building makeshift shelters against the weather. There was a knock at the door, and around a yawn, Kern called, "Who is it?"

"Open up, ranger! It is I, King Moriak!"

Kern recognised Galandrik's rough dwarven tones and laughed as he unbolted the door. "Come in, my friend. You're early," he said, yawning again and making Galandrik yawn in return.

"I couldn't sleep. I think it's the thought of smashing some orc skulls that woke me," the dwarf said, hitting his great axe against his chest, a dwarven gesture frequently made before battle.

"Well, I'm ready, Galandrik; shall we wake Ty? It's nearly dawn." The dwarf nodded, and Kern plucked his weapons and armour off the wall hooks, spaced out equally in a row behind the door. Lastly, he picked up his cloak from off the bed and settled it around his shoulders, checking that the fabric wouldn't impede him if he needed to quickly nock an arrow to his bow. Once Kern was fully dressed and armed, they headed down the corridor to Ty's room.

Galandrik knocked, and as he did, the door creaked open slightly.

Without saying a word, both men both drew their weapons. Kern glanced at Galandrik and, at a nod from the dwarf, slowly pushed the door open. When it was about half open, Galandrik peered into the room. He saw nothing out of place, and the narrow bed against the wall held a halfling-shaped lump.

Lowering his weapon, Galandrik said, "The idiot forgot to lock his door. Wake up, fool," as he walked over to the bed. When Ty didn't stir, Galandrik grabbed a corner of the bed linen and pulled it down. "Wake up, we got orcs to kill!"

The bed contained blankets and pillows, but no halfling. Before Galandrik could say another word, he felt the cold blade of a knife pressing against his throat.

"You should be more careful who you try to wake up, Galandrik Sabrehargen," Ty said after a tense moment, then withdrew the dagger from Galandrik's throat.

"Why would you *do* that?" Galandrik said, turning to sit on the bed with hands on knees.

"Just keeping you on your toes, dwarf. You should know that no thief worth his salt ever sleeps in his bed, unless it's with a nice dwarven girl," Ty joked, looking over to Kern, who was watching and shaking his head.

"Even so, you put the wind up me; I thought I'd had it! And if ever you even think about sleeping with a dwarf girl –" Galandrik stood up, taking deep breaths.

Kern sheathed his sword. "Too early for these games," he said sourly. "I'm going to get my gear from the stable," he said turning and walking away.

"Come on, dwarf, let's go kill us some orcs!" Ty said, offering his hand to Galandrik. They followed Kern down the outside stairs and into the barn.

When they got there, they saw four horses standing proud, all saddled and ready to mount. Two of the horses were Choctaw stallions, tall warhorses ridden mainly by humans or elves. The other two horses were a smaller breed called Bodishian Warmbloods; these were hard-working horses, ridden by dwarves, halflings and the other shorter races, as well as by women and children. Kern was standing next to the horses and talking to a tall young human wearing a black robe and hood, not too dissimilar to the outfit Conn favoured.

Ty and Galandrik approached the horses. Ty rubbed the nose of the closest; the horse never budged, seeming to instantly accept Ty as a friend.

"Ty, Galandrik, this is Solomon, our guide," Kern announced.

"Hello Solomon, I am Galandrik Sabrehargen, from –"

Solomon cut his sentence off. "Conn has told me all about you, Galandrik. Very pleased to make your acquaintance."

"Well, I won't bother introducing myself, then," Ty said, turning to Solomon, only to stop in his tracks and stare at the young man.

"I have heard about you also, Ty 'The Rat'," Solomon said, smiling.

"Where do I know you from?" Ty said, moving closer to get a better look.

"You maybe saw me at Conn's, or you may be mistaken," Solomon said, walking away and grabbing two backpacks from the top of a bale of hay. He handed one to Kern and one to Ty. "Here are your packs for the journey; there should be everything you need." He grabbed the last pack and passed it to Galandrik. "Ty, your horse is the white Warmblood; his name is Flight. Galandrik, yours is the brown – he's called Preacher; and Kern, yours is the black Choctaw named Trophy. Your weapons and armour are on the horses along with bedding and warm clothing. Is there anything else you can think of before we leave?" Solomon said, eying the three adventurers up individually.

"What about a nice breakfast?" Galandrik said, rubbing his belly.

"Praise is only two days' ride. You can feast when you get there. Nothing else? Good, then let's mount up," Solomon said with authority.

"Hang on, I have a question," Ty said, dropping his backpack to the ground and folding his arms. "Are you a guide, or the leader of this group?"

"I'm a guide," Solomon said, mounting his Choctaw.

"Then start acting like our guide, and not our leader," Ty said, picking up his pack, just as Solomon kicked his horse.

"Fine, now mount up! Come on, Fire!" The horse flew from the stable, lightly brushing Ty – just enough to knock him onto the seat of his pants. Hay and dust kicked up by Fire's hooves filled the air. When the dust finally settled, Kern and Galandrik both sat mounted, looking down at Ty as he spat out a piece of hay and wiped dust from his face.

"You know," Ty said, getting to his feet and holding his still-swollen nose, "I don't think I like him."

The party spent the next day riding south from Raith towards Praise. The path they followed was a dirt track made by wagon-wheels from hundreds of years' trading between the two towns. Solomon spent most of the day telling the others about his work for Conn, buying spell reagents from all over Bodisha. The trading routes were etched into his memory, he said, as a result of the endless days he spent searching for weird and wonderful herbs.

"So what sort of herbs do you gather?" Kern asked.

"All sorts; I travelled to Lake Fortune in western Bodisha for the watercap root, which we used for protection spells. The southern marshes are good for sagebrush herb, for healing potions, and I've gone as far as the Volic Islands for the prickly ash leaf that we use for cure spells. To name but a few," Solomon boasted.

"Sounds interesting. What's the most highly sought after?"

"It has to be the milk thistle. It's basically only ever found in the dingiest, darkest caves. It's white – through lack of sunlight – and once you cut it, it never grows back. We have been looking all through the eastern mountains, but can we find any?" Solomon spat.

"What's it used for?"

"Well, when mixed correctly with yellow evening primrose and witch hazel, it creates the most powerful invisibility potions."

"No wonder it's sought after," Kern agreed politely.

Ty stole frequent covert glances at Solomon as they rode, trying to pin down where he knew the guide from; try as he might, though, he just couldn't place him.

Night was closing in, and Kern announced they should look for a place to bed down. Solomon told them that halfway to Praise, there was a rocky outcrop just northeast of Deaths Wood. It had been used by traders for centuries and was often called the Traders Toe, due to its shape; it was an ideal place to shelter and sleep. Ty couldn't help but ask how Deaths Wood had gotten its name, and Solomon explained that traders heading to and from Praise suffered frequent ambushes near the forest; traders who tried to go through the wood tended to never come out.

Eventually they reached the Traders Toe, situated just to the east of the path. Solomon led them around the south side of the outcrop to a clearing, its black and charcoaled centre offering proof of many campfires made here in the past. There was rocky face to the north and trees dotted the ground all around. It was not a heavy wood; just enough to protect a camping party from the winds, yet open enough to spot any ambush that could be sprung. These features – combined with the fact that the area was hidden from the road – made it an ideal camp site. Once the party had agreed that the site met all their requirements for a night's rest, they dismounted.

"If it's all right with *everyone*, I'll feed, water, and tend to the horses." Solomon took a sneaky glance over his shoulder at Ty, who ignored the remark and examined the camp site.

"You do that, Solomon. I'll make a fire." Kern knew where Solomon's comment was aimed, but decided to ignore it.

"I'll get the food prepared," Galandrik said with a smile of anticipation.

"And I'll check out the surroundings and make sure this 'ideal spot' isn't an ambush waiting to happen," Ty said, with a swift glance at Solomon to make sure his barb had hit home, then disappeared into the woods.

It wasn't long until the horses were fed, watered, and resting. The fire was burning bright and an iron pot hung over it, full of potatoes, cabbage, carrots, and rabbit, all covered in mixed herbs. Dinner was bubbling away nicely, Galandrik thought, and smelled marvellous. Kern was examining the bow given to him by Conn back in Raith, while Galandrik stirred his stew.

Ty sauntered back into the clearing. "All seems okay. Some movement on the path to the south; looks like a caravan trail headed this way. I've set up a few traps which should announce any intruders; other than that, it all looks fine and dandy. Anyway, what's for eating? I'm starving," Ty said, sitting on a log near the campfire.

"*Rakib Stum,*" Galandrik answered.

"*Rakib Stum?* What the hell is that?" Ty asked, looking into the pot.

"That's dwarven for rabbit stew," Galandrik explained, ladling out an ample serving into a wooden bowl.

"I hope it tastes better than it sounds," Ty laughed. He handed the first bowl to Kern, who thanked him and asked for some bread.

"Want me to eat it for you, too?" Ty replied with a wry smile on his face, but threw him a chunk of sweet honey bread. Soon they were all eating the *Rakib Stum,* mopping their bowls with the bread, as the light darkened and stars sparkled in the night sky like pinpricks in black silk.

"How are we doing watch tonight, two hour intervals?" Galandrik asked the party. Ty shrugged his shoulders and refilled his bowl; Solomon nodded and Kern said, "Sounds good to me. I'll take first, if you like?"

"I'll do second watch," Ty volunteered. "Solomon, you can do third and Galandrik last, if that's all right with everyone?"

"I'm glad you said that, because I'm bushed," Galandrik replied, putting his empty bowl down and laying out his bedroll.

"Is everybody happy with that rotation?" Kern said, standing up. Galandrik and Solomon both indicated their agreement. "That's sorted then."

Once they had agreed on the order of night watch, their weariness seemed to settle in all at once. "Gods, I could sleep for a week," Ty said through a yawn. He wasted no more time and rolled out his bedding with one hand, holding his second bowl of stew in the other.

"I thought you said any thief worth his salt doesn't sleep in a bed?" Galandrik said drowsily, tossing a small stone across the campfire. He sat on his bedding holding his new axe, stroking the blade as if it were a puppy.

"Go to sleep," Ty answered as he finished up his stew.

Galandrik was soon snoring peacefully. Ty was almost asleep after finishing off his second bowl of stew, while Solomon stood to have one last look at the horses before lying back down. Kern climbed the rock face and watched for anything untoward. Once the rest of the group had fallen fast asleep, Kern walked back through the encampment to put out the fire; the moonlight made it easy to see and he didn't want the crackling of the flames or the smell of woodsmoke to attract any attention. He paced back and forth, checking each noise that caught his ear, but nothing eventful happened.

Nearing the end of his shift, he picked up his backpack and looked through it. There was food – hard rations which wouldn't spoil on the road – some healing balms, flint and tinder, and other basic survival items that might be needed by an adventurer. *Conn's certainly done his homework*, Kern thought.

Lastly, he pulled a wooden box from the bottom of the pack; it was about the size of a plate mail helmet with a wooden lid on two brass hinges. Slowly and with great interest, he opened it. The interior was divided by little wooden slats, creating four separate compartments, each one containing a glass bottle cushioned securely in a bed of hay. Kern carefully lifted one out; it was a typical-looking potion bottle with a bowl bottom and a long neck leading to a little cork stopper. Inside this one was a red liquid, swishing about like a sparkling glittery wine. Kern studied the bottle and saw the letters 'STR' engraved; immediately he thought, *Strength*.

The next bottle was identical, except that the liquid was a dull green, and a teardrop shape was embossed on the side of the glass. Kern placed the bottle back into its compartment. As he lifted the third potion, he heard a noise coming from the south. Quickly he placed the bottle back into the box, closed the lid, and slid it back into the safety of his backpack.

He grabbed his bow and nocked an arrow with a practiced movement. Aiming the bow downwards, he headed swiftly but silently towards the edge of the clearing, kicking Galandrik as he passed. Galandrik woke fully and immediately, and grabbed his two headed great-axe. Rising stealthily to his feet, he made his way over to Kern and whispered, "What is it, ranger?"

"There are voices coming from the south – quite a few of them too," Kern replied, peering through the black-on-black shadows of the trees.

"Should I wake the others? We can't leave them asleep."

"Yes, go wake them," Kern said, still looking intently to the south. Galandrik made his way over to Ty and Solomon and shook them awake.

"What is it?" Ty asked the dwarf, rubbing his eyes.

"Kern heard voices from the south, lots of them," Galandrik answered.

All three slowly moved southwards through the trees, bending low and keeping as quiet as possible; every now and then Galandrik would tread on a branch, and Ty would look over his shoulder to scold him with a frowning glance.

Eventually they reached a rocky mound and climbed up so that all four were at the top and peering over. Deaths Wood was only a few yards away, but between them and it was a dirt path. It branched off from the road, heading westwards towards the northern marshes. About forty yards away, they could see a band of orcs marching towards them. In the middle of the band were four orcs carrying a large log on their shoulders, and tied to this log hands and feet was what looked like a human, stripped bare apart from his leather leggings.

"I count ten, maybe twelve," Kern whispered to the others. "Right – Ty, you go down with Galandrik and hide on the other side of the path. I'll attack from up here. As soon as I fell the first orc, jump in," he said before turning to Solomon. "Can you help, Solomon, or not?" Kern asked the guide.

"Sure, I can do some ranged damage," Solomon whispered back.

"Good. Get going, you two, and wait for my attack," Kern said urgently.

But Ty balked. "Just let them go past on their way."

"Don't be stupid," Kern said in disbelief. "There is a *human* tied to a *log* down there, and it's our duty to help him."

"Plus there are twelve orcs to kill!" the dwarf added.

"There will be plenty of time to kill orcs later, and the human may be already dead," Ty argued.

"Don't help, then! But that means you don't get to help when we loot the orcs," Kern smirked.

Ty was silent for a few heartbeats, then said, "Okay, but this is the last time."

Kern winked at Galandrik.

Ty and Galandrik darted between trees, and soon they were on the other side of the path. Galandrik held his axe close to his chest and crouched down behind a massive bush, while Ty climbed a small tree and waited patiently. "Yes *sir!*" Ty whispered to himself bitterly.

Soon the band of orcs was just yards away. Up on the mound, Kern notched an arrow to his bow as Solomon held up his staff and whispered an incantation. Kern waited until the band of orcs was directly below them. He nodded to Solomon and stood, letting fly his first arrow. It thudded into an orc's neck, felling him instantly. Kern notched a second.

Solomon held out his staff; from its head flew a bolt of blue lightning that hit another orc square in the chest, consuming him in flame. The orc screamed and fell, rolling on the ground in agony.

Galandrik leapt from the bushes, swinging his axe wildly into the bulky side of an orc, slicing through his arm and into his torso. The orc dropped. Ty jumped down from his vantage point, drawing his daggers as he went. He landed behind an orc and rammed the duelling daggers into both sides of the orc's back, then withdrew them and struck again, twisting as he did so. The orc toppled forward, dead before he hit the ground.

The four orcs carrying the log dropped it instantly, and the human let out a tortured cry as he hit the ground with a thud. One orc turned to face Galandrik and swung his sword, but Galandrik blocked the blow with his axe, then swung himself. He hit the orc in mid-thigh, the blade cutting deep to the bone. The orc screamed in rage and pain as he fell, holding his leg as blood poured from the gaping hole.

Another orc ran at Ty, swinging his sword in blind fury. Ty rolled under the first attack, but the orc followed up with another swing that Ty only just managed to avoid. He backed up against the tree he had jumped from, and the orc raised his sword above his head, looking down at Ty with fury in his eyes. Ty couldn't do anything but raise his daggers, as if they could block the inevitable sword blow – but that blow never came.

The orc's eyes rolled back in his head as he fell down dead next to the tree, face-first in the dirt with an arrow quivering in his back. Ty heaved a sigh of relief and gave Kern a tight nod.

Galandrik faced another, but before the orc could manage much more than a half-hearted attempt at swinging his sword, Galandrik had beheaded his attacker; his head bounced a few feet away while his body slumped gracelessly down to the ground.

Two more orcs died trying to run up the slope towards Kern and Solomon; an arrow to the chest made short work of one, and the other was engulfed in flame by the magic erupting from Solomon's staff. The remaining two orcs, at the rear of the band, ran for the forest – they knew the battle was over and further fighting was pointless. Galandrik started to give chase, but stopped, knowing he could never catch them – and even if he could have, he didn't want to enter Deaths Wood.

Ty picked himself up from the ground, bushing dirt from his clothes. Kern and Solomon loped down the slope as Galandrik walked back to the group. The human on the ground spoke in a hoarse voice.

"Bravo, my good fellows, my brave rescuers. I am forever in your debt," he said, somehow dignified even while lying nearly naked in the road, tied by the hands and feet to a log.

"What makes you think we're going to untie you?" Ty answered, rummaging through the packs and pockets of the dead orcs.

"Even if you don't release me, it's better for me to die here than be eaten by those foul creatures," the log-bound captive replied.

Ty rolled his eyes as Kern said, "Of course we're going to untie you! Ty, what are you waiting for?"

Rifling through the belongings of the last corpse, Ty said shortly, "Busy." He came up empty-handed other than a couple of leather necklaces, each one with a tooth threaded on the thong. He threw one of the cords to Solomon. "Here, a special present to commemorate your very first orc battle." He made no effort to hide the mockery in his voice.

"Thanks, I'll treasure it always," Solomon replied drily, slipping the necklace into his pocket.

Kern finished retrieving his arrows from the dead bodies, then gave Ty a glare as he hurried over to the captured man and cut the ropes that bound him.

"Thank you, good sir," the human said as Kern helped him to his feet. "I am Nuran the paladin. My party was ambushed by those evil creatures, and only I survived," Nuran said, sadness lacing his voice. He was a tall man, at least 6'5", with a handlebar moustache and a courtly air.

"Come back to our camp and tell us all about it. I think there's some rabbit stew left, though it may be cold now," Solomon said, walking back towards the camp. Nuran walked to one of the orc bodies and retrieved a cloth sack containing his possessions.

"Good idea, Sol. Right – Ty, Galandrik: start shifting the dead off the road – and if they're not dead, make it so," Kern ordered.

"So Solomon can swan off to the camp and babysit some strange human, while we have to clear the mess up? How is that fair?" Ty argued, planting his hands on his hips.

"Life isn't fair, so just do it. Why the attitude all the time?" Kern snarled back, kicking an orc's head into the thicket.

"He's the damn guide, and he works for us! He should be here and *I* should be babysitting!" Ty shouted back, dragging a corpse by the arm.

"He's our guide, not our slave – now come help. Grab this big one with me." Kern and Ty dragged the dead orc off to the side of the road and into the bushes, lightly covering it with leaves.

"Well, whatever he is, he should be helping," Ty said truculently. "And I am *not* digging any holes."

"No one's asking you to!" Kern snapped, rolling the log Nuran had been tied to into the bushes.

"And furthermore, *he* should be rolling his *own* log!" Ty continued.

"Listen to me, Ty: He has been beaten, his party are all dead, and he has been tied to that log for gods know how long. The least we can do is roll a bloody log into a bush and offer him some rabbit stew!" Kern spat back.

"Why don't we just offer dinner to every waif and –"

"Shut it! Enough," Galandrik said, stepping in between them. The bickering stopped and there was a tense silence.

Once the bodies were all off the track and covered, they all walked back to camp and sat talking around the fire. Nuran was part of a group of humans fighting the orcs to the east – not for the King's army, but for simple pleasure… and, of course, riches. After hungrily gulping down the last of the rabbit stew, Nuran quickly fell asleep; Solomon covered him with a spare blanket.

"Whose turn for watch?" Galandrik asked.

"Whoever's turn it is, they'll need to keep a close eye on our new *friend*," Ty said suspiciously. "Personally I don't like sleeping this close to strangers."

"I'll take it, then; I'm not exactly tired now anyway," Solomon interrupted. They all agreed and bedded down for the rest of the night; the crash after the adrenaline rush combined with the warmth of the campfire left them all feeling sleepier than they would have expected.

Galandrik looked at his axe in wonder, smiling with the memory of the way it had cut through bone and flesh. He cradled it close to his chest, and soon drifted into a satisfied slumber.

Just before they fell asleep, Ty nudged Kern with his foot, and muttered, "Thanks for that… thing… earlier."

"Go to sleep, fool. You would have done the same," Kern replied.

The group was soon silent and sleeping, and Solomon kept an uneventful watch.

Chapter Five
The Giant on the Slope

The next morning they were awakened by the smell of eggs and bacon sizzling in an iron pan. Solomon had been busy cooking. They all ate heartily, Nuran more than the rest. After breakfast they broke camp, tidying away their bedrolls and stowing the cooking gear in their saddlebags. Nuran was dressed in his rather dirty plate armour and now looked like a paladin, Ty thought; a dirty one, perhaps, but a paladin all the same. The crest on his cloak was the emblem of the group Truelight, a renegade group of paladins who had broken away from royal duties many years ago.

"Solomon, why didn't you wake me for my watch? And what was that blue flame thing you done yesterday against the orcs?" Ty asked as he saddled his Warmblood mount.

"I told you, I wasn't tired. The 'blue flame thing' was just an offensive staff spell, a basic lightning spell, that's all," Solomon replied, trying to play down his magic skills.

"Is there such a thing as just a basic spell?" Ty said, raising an eyebrow. "Tell that to those orcs you fried," he added with a chuckle.

"So, Nuran the paladin, what are you going to do now?" Kern asked, picking up his bedroll.

"Well, to be honest, I have no plans," the paladin replied. "My group all perished; as I am still in your debt, perhaps I can travel with you, sir? My sword is yours if you will kindly allow it," he offered.

Kern looked at Ty and Galandrik; both seemed happy enough to allow the paladin into the group. "If there are no objections," Kern said as he mounted his horse, "we shall see how it goes, paladin. You can ride with Solomon."

"Thank you, sir," Nuran answered, grinning from ear to ear and twisting his moustache. Kern smiled privately; this was an enthusiastic reaction indeed for a member of an organization known far and wide for its courteousness, formality, and devotion to matters of faith.

Nuran mounted up with Solomon, and the party set off back down the road between Raith and Praise. From here, the city was only one day's ride away; if they kept up a good pace they could probably get there before dark. Soon they were level with Deaths Wood to their right.

It was easy to see how the forest had gotten its name. The uninviting trees looked as though they had died years ago, yet somehow retained their greenery. Shadows seemed to move among them, like people darting about playing hide-and-seek. Ty often thought he could see red eyes staring out through the trees. They kept a fair distance from the wood as they carried on towards Praise.

After a few hours' ride and one more food stop – to quiet Galandrik's constant moaning about his hunger - they finally passed beyond the straggling southern edge of Deaths Wood. Although none of them remarked on it, the mood of the group was noticeably lighter.

Praise was nearly in sight, about an hour's ride away. It wasn't a massive town, and didn't have much of a militia. The town was mostly used as a stop-off point between Raith and the trading towns to the south.

"Where were the orcs taking you, Nuran?" Solomon asked, glancing over his shoulder at the paladin.

"I don't know – I couldn't understand a word they said, but wherever it was I don't think it would have been good for me to be there. I think I would be in a massive stewing pot by now." They both laughed.

Suddenly Galandrik drew back on his horse's reins, coming to an abrupt stop. "Are my eyes deceiving me, or is that smoke rising from the town?"

THE KING'S GOLD

The party stopped and stared. Thick black smoke rose in the distance, swirling into the clouds.

"Quick – we'd better ride!" Kern lurched into a fast gallop towards Praise, followed closely by the others, with Solomon and Nuran lagging slightly behind. As they drew closer to the town they could now hear a great commotion, and could see that the smoke was indeed coming from Praise. Kern kicked his horse into a gallop and rode towards the town.

As they reached the main gates of the town they could see the townsfolk rushing about in all directions. Two people broke from the tumult and came running out towards them. The first man shouted, "Please help us, a hill giant is tearing up the town! You must help us, please!" But the second man shouted, "Just turn and run – you'll never stop it!" The two men ran on past the mounted party.

Entering the town, they could see a slope leading down to the River Narv where the town's mill was. A hill giant stood in the pathway, wildly swinging a massive club. Six of the town's guards were battling him, trying to get close enough to stab the giant while avoiding his weapon. The dead lay all around; most appeared to be town guards, crushed by the giant's huge club.

Kern dismounted from Trophy and quickly pulled his bow from his back. Galandrik and Ty both jumped down.

"Is this really our fight?" Ty shouted.

"Please yourself," Kern replied, running towards the giant and releasing two arrows as he went. Nuran and Solomon joined them on the slope and dismounted.

"This should be fun," Nuran said, drawing his long-sword and kite shield.

Galandrik followed Kern down the steep slope towards the giant. Kern fired another arrow as he ran but it had little effect, merely smashed against the giant's leather amour then split into pieces. Kern let the bow slip from his shoulder and left it on the ground next to his quiver.

Drawing his long-sword as he went, Kern ran directly towards the giant. The enormous creature smashed his club into another guard, sending him flying into the stone mill wall. The guard died instantly.

Kern reached the giant and swung his sword. Using one enormous hand to parry the blow, the giant knocked the sword from Kern's grasp. The sheer size and power of the giant amazed Kern; the force of the parry was unbelievable. The giant swung his club towards Kern. With no time to react or defend himself, Kern braced for the impact. Just then Galandrik reached Kern's side and swung his double-headed axe – not at the giant but at the club destined for Kern. The axe blocked the blow, embedding itself deep into the wooden weapon and sending impact shudders through dwarf and giant alike.

Solomon extended his staff and released a lightning bolt towards the giant, but it just fizzled out on the giant's armour, much as Kern's arrow had done. Solomon started talking up another spell.

The giant raised his club once more, the axe still embedded in it. Galandrik refused to let go of his weapon, and held tightly to the axe shaft as he was swung into the air – only to be shaken free and thrown several yards. He smashed into a wagon-wheel, losing consciousness instantly.

Nuran reached the fight and raised his long-sword, slicing into the giant's forearm. Blood gushed from the wound, but only seemed to anger the beast instead of actually hurting him. The giant brought his club down at Nuran; Nuran parried the blow with his shield, but the impact sent him flying backwards, his shield badly dented by the blow.

Kern saw Galandrik's axe come loose from the giant's club when it struck Nuran's shield. Dashing in quickly, Kern retrieved the axe from where it had fallen. Another guard ran in to attack the giant, but was swatted away like a rag doll.

Watching the fight unfold from his vantage point upon the slope, Ty knew his daggers were useless. His gaze swept the mill yard, and he saw a builders' wagon filled with rocks. It had apparently been abandoned, the team still in its traces, when the giant attacked. Ty thought for a second, then jumped up on the wagon's seat.

"Yah!" he shouted, snapping the reins. The horses turned – far more slowly than he would have liked – and headed toward the giant. When Ty reached the top of the slope he reined in the horses and jumped down, chocking the wheels with a fist-sized stone from the wagon. Then he released the horses from their bridles; he shouted and slapped their rumps, and the horses fled back into the town. As he quickly fastened the traces and reins to the tongue of the wagon, Ty shouted to Solomon. "Solomon, can you hold the giant?"

"Yes, but…" Solomon started to ask.

Ty jumped into the back of the wagon, saying, "No time to explain, just hold him, then release the stone from under that wheel." He pointed down to the chocked stone.

Solomon nodded and held his staff out, shouting "*Webfuska bethola!*" A burst of white flew towards the giant, covering the giant's legs and the ground at his feet with a white sticky substance, like strands of a spider's web.

Just as Kern hefted Galandrik's fallen great-axe, he saw the white goo fixing the giant to the earth. He swung the great-axe down upon the giant's foot, and the giant screamed horribly as the blade of the axe sliced through his toes.

Trapped by Solomon's spell and unable to move his legs, in a blind rage the giant swung his club wildly. Luckily for Kern it struck his legs, and not his head – still, the blow was forceful enough to send him spinning. His world turned upside down, then he thudded to the ground, landing on his back. The wind was knocked out of him, his vision full of stars swirling all around.

Nuran rose from where he had fallen and attacked again. The giant parried the blow, then swung his free arm, backhanding the paladin. Once again Nuran's shield took most of the impact, but he still went flying face down into the dirt. Nuran was also seeing stars.

The hill giant turned his attention back to Kern, who was still lying on his back struggling to get his breath. He grabbed his club with both hands and slowly raised it above his head, savouring Kern's helplessness.

Ty was standing on the seat on top of the cart full of stone. "Pull the stone out, quickly!" Ty shouted. Solomon wasted no time in knocking the stone away.

Nothing happened.

"Push it!" Ty screamed.

Solomon ran to the back of the cart and placed his shoulder against it; placing his feet firmly into the dirt, he pushed with all his might.

Nothing happened.

Two fleeing townsfolk saw Solomon struggling and ran over to help. The three men heaved and strained together, and slowly the cart began to move. With the wheels creaking along at a snail's pace, the men pushed for all they were worth, veins straining from their necks and temples.

All at once, the wagon was over the top of the hill and rolling freely down, picking up speed as it went, the heavy load of rocks pushing it along. Soon it was flying down towards the hill giant. Solomon fell to the ground as he watched the wagon roll off at speed. Ty stood on the seat, desperately trying to keep the wagon on target. His arms aching with the strain of the reins, Ty saw the giant raise his club.

Shaking his head to clear his vision, Nuran reached down and pulled a dagger from his boot. "Kern," he shouted, and threw the weapon. Kern turned in time to see the dagger land on the grass, inches from his hand. Seizing it swiftly, he looked up at the giant.

The hill giant was momentarily distracted by the noise he heard coming down the hill; he looked up in surprise at the oncoming cart. He tried to move but Solomon's web-spell still held him tightly. Arms still holding his mighty club above his head, the giant stood transfixed, looking straight forward at the oncoming cart.

Best chance, Kern thought, and launched the dagger up towards the giant. Not waiting to see where it hit, Kern rolled out of the way of the oncoming wagon before it rolled over him.

Nuran's dagger struck in the soft, unprotected spot right under the beast's chin. The giant dropped his club behind him and reached for the dagger, trying desperately to pull it free.

Ty saw the dagger strike the giant as he aimed the wagon, pulling on the reins with one last enormous heave. He jumped clear, landing on his shoulder, and rolled, ending up next to the still-dazed paladin. Ty quickly spun round, just in time to see the wagon strike the giant full on.

The wagon shattered on impact; wood and rock flew in all directions. The giant was knocked backwards from the impact. But Solomon's spell kept the giant's legs fixed to the earth, and they snapped with a sickening crunch. After an instant of shocked silence, the giant began screaming loudly enough to be heard from the other end of Praise.

Kern hunched down with his arms over his head. He heard the impact and felt its vibration; splinters of wood and chunks of rock rained down over him. Then it was quiet.

Kern looked up cautiously, and saw the giant laying on his back, the white ends of bones sticking out from his broken legs. Springing quickly to his feet and shaking his head trying to clear the stars, Kern grabbed Galandrik's great-axe. After a moment his vision regained its focus, and Kern jumped onto the giant's chest, raising the weapon above his head

The giant tried to scream and reached up for Kern, but it was over. Kern swung Galandrik's great-axe, striking the beast square in the forehead and splitting the enormous skull in two. The giant lay still, blood and brains flowing from his skull.

Kern stepped off and slumped to the ground.

Ty got to his feet and held out a hand for Nuran, which the paladin gratefully accepted. Ty heaved him to his feet as Galandrik pulled himself out of the broken wheel and sat up with his back against the wagon. The dwarf removed his helmet and felt an egg-shaped lump on his temple, blood trickling down his face.

Kern struggled to his feet and walked over to the dwarf, kneeling down beside him.

"Thank you, Galandrik, you saved my life." Kern looked at the dwarf's injured head. "Come on, friend. Let's see if we can't get that head patched up in the town," he said, helping Galandrik to his feet and steadying the dazed dwarf.

Kern held the dwarf's arm as they made their way over to the dead giant and looked down at the beast. Ty and Nuran came up next to them. Solomon slipped quietly into the group and stared at the monster.

"Big fellow, wasn't he?" Ty remarked.

"Far too big for my liking," Nuran answered.

Galandrik pulled his arm away from Kern and walked to the giant's head. Reaching out, he grabbed his axe and ripped it free, then wiped the blood and brain matter on the giant's bearskin jerkin.

Ty walked around to the other side and picked up Nuran's dagger, which had fallen to the ground when Kern had struck the fatal blow. As he bent to retrieve the dagger, he noticed a leather thong with a large golden medallion hanging around the giant's neck. Ty surreptitiously cut the strap and slipped it into his sleeve, then turned and handed Nuran his dagger.

By now, some of the townsfolk were slowly trickling back to the slope. The news was spreading that the beast was dead. The townspeople found stretchers for the injured guards and raced them back up the hill to the houses of healing in the town. The dead were simply covered where they lay.

A commotion began at the top of the hill; the companions turned to see a massive gathering of townsfolk coming towards them, cheering and celebrating the party's gallant victory. The cheering mob gathered all around the party, and a group of men hoisted Kern up onto their shoulders and carried him up the slope, cheering and shouting all the way. Throngs were gathered around the giant, kids probing with sticks and adults staring at the fallen beast in shock and revulsion.

Other townspeople beckoned the rest of the party to join them; one woman grabbed Galandrik by the hand and pulled him up the hill towards the town, and moments later Solomon and Nuran found themselves in the same position. Soon they were up the hill and being led through the town, cheers ringing out around them as they went. The celebrations reminded Galandrik of the solar moon carnivals he had enjoyed in Grimnoss when he was younger.

The party made their way through the town, surrounded by the cheering crowd carrying Kern aloft – all except Ty. He trailed behind, alone, at the ragged end of the crowd. No one led him along, he thought; no one lifted him up, no pretty girl held his hand and smiled. Had everyone missed his heroic cart ride? Did they not see the broken legs, snapped by the force of the impact, rendering the giant helpless? Had they not seen his jump from the moving cart at the last possible second? No, all they'd seen was Kern's kill, Ty thought, and the anger burnt inside him. He felt sick.

Chapter Six
The Ferryboat Man

Bok looked across the cell to Joli. "I can't believe that idiot fooled us like that. If it takes me the rest of my life to find Ty and gut him like a fish, I will wait."

"You and me both. Where do you think he was heading?" Joli answered.

"No idea, but someone in the Orc's Armpit will know. Trust me, a few copper pieces and tongues will wag," Bok growled.

Just then a red-headed guard walked down the corridor and stopped at the bars to their cell, staring in at the two captives. "This Ty you speak of – was he short with a red top-knot haircut? Had a big mouth, a couple of friends with him, a dwarf and a human?"

Bok stood up. "Yeah, that's him. Why you ask? Do you know him?"

"Let's just say I met him once." The guard's mouth twisted as he remembering being tripped into manure in the marketplace, and the humiliating incident in the bathing room. "And I may be able to tell you where to find him. Are you serious about having your revenge?"

Bok placed his hands on the cell bars, staring at the guard. "I hate him. I won't rest until I cut him open, spilling his guts onto his feet."

The guard believed him. "Right, listen up. At nightfall tonight, I'll come back and release you. Don't worry about the consequences; I'll sort that out," he said menacingly. "He was heading south to the town of Praise, to cross with the ferryman there. That's all I can help you with, but I'm sure a couple of resourceful characters such as yourselves can pick up his trail." He sneered and spat on the floor; having to cooperate with such lowlifes left a bad taste in his mouth.

"I'm sure we will, never fear. What did he do to you?" Bok asked.

"Just kill him." The guard turned and walked back up the stairs.

Joli turned to Bok. "Praise it is, then."

"Yeah, and this time I won't go easy on him. He won't know what's hit him," Bok said coldly. They settled in on the rickety bed and waited for nightfall; for Bok, it couldn't come soon enough.

The party was led through the town, past the massive fire-warning towers that sent up the smoke-alerts. All smaller towns in Bodisha had these towers, and had used them during the orc wars to alert other towns of an attack. The warning system was not used much in these days, but Moran, the Lord of Praise, had thought it necessary to keep them standing.

They were brought to a large barn at the far end of the town. Tables were being set up outside and the group was invited to sit. Townsfolk brought jugs of ale and water, along with wooden cups.

A lively atmosphere was building all around the town, and the comfortable hustle and bustle of normal street life had been replaced by a sense of urgency. People hurried through the streets carrying chairs and tables, musical instruments, crockery and tableware, and all the other items one would need to make ready for a street party.

Kern stopped a young girl hurrying past with a large bucket of red apples. "Hey, what's going on?"

"Lord Moran has ordered a celebration for your bravery, and because you killed the giant!" she exclaimed, seeming a bit starstruck. "Just wait here, sir, while we prepare the barn. It will be a feast to surpass all feasts," the girl exclaimed, then skipped off.

The group exchanged glances, but made no comment. Instead they relaxed and drank the ale, and amused themselves watching as the townsfolk scurried around them, fetching and carrying. The occasional girl stopped to fling her arms around Kern's neck, thanking him for his great service. Ty looked on in disgust.

They had just finished the first jug of ale when Solomon stood and stretched. "Well. Before we get too comfortable," he said, "I'm just going to untie the horses and get them to a stable, fed and watered."

"No need, take a look over there." Galandrik pointed to a barn across the street where their horses were being led in.

"Hm. Even so, I'd better just pop across and make sure," Solomon said, and walked off across the busy street.

Kern was looking at Galandrik's wound. "What about your head? You need to get that looked at," he said.

"Ah, it's nothing, just a scratch. I've had much worse. Pass that ale again, would you?" Galandrik said,

They rested for a couple of hours, which passed quickly enough with the help of several jugs of ale. From time to time, one or another of them would get up and peer through a window into the barn at the preparations. Huge tables had been carried in, in sections, and now filled the most of the centre of the room. Dozens of small tables dotted the edges of the barn and chairs were being brought in by the townsfolk, along with every sort of food and drink imaginable. The townspeople ran back and forth, filling the central tables with platters of freshly cooked meats, fruit, bread, and vegetables. Jugs of ale, wine, and water filled the gaps. At the far end of the barn on a raised dais sat a smaller table with two throne-like chairs behind it.

"That girl was right; looks like the feast to end all feasts," Nuran said, returning from a peek in at one of the windows.

"Yes, looks like we're heroes!" Galandrik added cheerfully.

"Kern is," Ty mumbled under his breath.

Solomon turned to Ty. "What was that?"

"Nothing, just talking to myself," Ty snorted.

Solomon looked at Ty speculatively. But just then a young man came out of the barn and stood in front of them, looking a bit nervous. "We are ready for you now, sirs," he said, bowing and gesturing with his free hand for them to enter the barn.

"At last! Come on, let's eat," Galandrik said, and walked into the barn.

"Don't have to ask me twice," Nuran said, following the dwarf into the barn. As they crossed the threshold, a riotous chorus of cheers, clapping, and whistling broke out. A dignified-looking couple sat at the small table at the far end; given the way they were dressed, Kern thought, these must be the nobility of the town. The human male wore a massive golden necklace like a mayor's chain of office, and the lady at his side wore a red dress fit for a queen, topped off with a tiara. Their applause was more decorous than most, but the relief and happiness on their faces was unmistakable.

Kern looked at Ty as they stood at their table, basking in the town's gratitude before taking their seats. "Hm. I forgot to tell you, but well done today. Without that cart of yours I don't think we could have beaten him," he said under the noise of the applause.

"No problem – we're even now," Ty said shortly, walking past Kern and taking a seat next to Nuran.

The cheering, clapping, and foot-stomping continued for a few minutes, then the man at the head table stood up and raised his arms for attention. The barn went quiet, and he said into the hush, "That's enough. I shall save the speech-making until we have all enjoyed the magnificent feast laid out for us." He gestured to a group of men and women still making final adjustments to the groaning food-laden tables. Another round of applause, slightly less enthusiastic, broke out, and the speaker raised his voice to declare, "Let us eat and drink our fill!" The music started again, and with a loud cheer, everyone joined in the festivities.

Before long the entire group had filled their plates and were eating to their hearts' content. The barn was full; even the outer tables were crammed with townsfolk. Outside was the same: If they couldn't find room in the barn they ate outside, where music played and people danced. Inside, minstrels sang and played their instruments.

After the group had all eaten more than they should have and drunk their fill of mead and wine, the room fell quiet; even the areas outside grew still as the music stopped. The important-looking man at the head table rose once more; within seconds there was absolute silence both inside and out.

"Welcome all, old friends and new. For the benefit of our new friends who have joined us here today, I am Moran, cousin of King Moriak, and Keeper and Lord of Praise." Moran looked around the barn with a regal gaze. "Today we were attacked by a monster, a monster that has been terrorizing us for weeks. I have no doubt that without Kern and his brave party we would have lost many more people today before this evil creature had finished. They displayed remarkable courage and skill. Therefore, I want to offer Kern and his fellows a permanent job here in Praise, as my personal guard."

A brief rustle filled the barn as the townsfolk gasped in surprise and shifted to whisper to their neighbours. All eyes were fixed on Kern and his party. Kern never took his eyes off Moran, and simply gave a slight smile. After a few heartbeats silence descended once more.

"Don't answer just yet – have a night's rest to sleep on it. I'm sure you will think more clearly after a good night's slumber. But know this: Even if you do not wish to stay with us, you will always be welcome here, all of you, and will have the freedom of the town and all that goes with that."

Moran picked up his golden goblet. "Friends, new and old, join me now in a toast to our new heroes. Drink, for they have saved this town from destruction." Moran raised his goblet and shouted, "Heroes!"

Everyone in the barn raised their drinking cups, goblets, and glasses; the masses outside joined in the celebrations and cheers as well. "Heroes! Heroes!"

Moran took his seat, holding his wife's hand on top of the table as the music and hubbub resumed. Kern looked in Moran's direction until he caught the Keeper's eye, then nodded. Moran nodded back, lifted his goblet and smiled.

The celebrations went on deep into the night, but not for Kern and his company. They were escorted to an inn – at no expense to them, of course. Their horses had been tended to, baths sat ready for the group to soak their aching limbs, and a nurse was sent to look at Galandrik's head and all the others' bumps and bruises.

Soon all the party were fast asleep, aside from Ty; he had crawled under his bed, a habit he'd had for many years. As a young man in Phebon, he'd wound up under his bed instead of in it after a night of drunken carousing. When the man who'd been buying the drinks snuck into Ty's room with a blade and began slashing at the rumpled covers and pillows, Ty had been able to reach out and slice his would-be murderer's hamstrings. Even a man's closest friends, it seemed, could be hiding secret motives, and Ty considered an uncomfortable night's sleep a fair trade in exchange for the element of surprise.

This night, however, it was more than physical discomfort keeping him awake. The cold wooden floorboards creaked beneath him as he reached into his pocket and pulled out the Giant's medallion. It seemed to shimmer from gold to silver, though maybe that was just the candlelight. He placed the medallion in his secret pocket, along with the gold coins stolen from the farmer. *One medallion for me, while Kern gets the keys to the town*, he thought; *typical*. Ty slowly drifted off to sleep.

Kern swung his sword in a wild arc in front of him, "Come out and fight me, you little whore!" He spun around, his sword again circling and slicing through the air. "Show yourself, you bastard," he cried as he swung his sword wildly, turning round and round like a blind man.

Ty woke with a jolt; banging his head on the wooden slats under the bed. With a wince he rolled out, crossing the room to sit in the chair next to the window. Rubbing his head, he wondered what the dream might have meant.

He stood up and stretched, trying to work out how long he had been asleep. He looked out the window and down into the street. A few people dawdled and wobbled home; he could still hear music playing from the barn. *I couldn't have been asleep for long*, he thought as he tore off a piece of his bedroll and wrapped it around his face, leaving only his eyes showing.

Reaching into his pack, he pulled out a pair of gloves – not from a set of armour, but a lightweight leather pair, like those used by acrobats and climbers. Pulling a coil of rope from the bottom of his pack and draping it over his shoulder, he cautiously opened his window and climbed out onto the windowsill. He looked around at the other windows to make sure no one was watching.

Looking up, he saw the edge of the roof; with a quick spring he grabbed it and pulled himself up. Squatting down, he looked into the street and across to the other houses. When he felt sure he was unobserved, he scurried up and over the rooftop. Most of the houses were connected, and where they weren't, it was just a jump down onto a wall, then across and up.

After scrambling across a dozen roofs he found a spot to sit and stared down at the quiet town. The moonlight lit up the buildings well. Ty had always liked to sit on rooftops; he knew nobody would disturb him there and it kept his climbing skills fresh. He'd lost count of all the nights he'd spent on rooftops in Phebon – mostly because he was hiding, but sometimes just to sit and think, like tonight.

The party was awakened in the morning and asked to join Moran for council after breakfast. Solomon and Ty restocked their supplies and readied the saddlebags. Soon everything was ready for their departure. They ate breakfast in the inn, then followed a town guard across the street to Moran's house. They were led to his study, where they stood in a line in front of his desk to wait for Moran's arrival. Just as Ty began to shift and fidget, Moran joined them.

"Good morning. I hope you all slept well."

"We did, and thank you for your hospitality, Lord Moran," Kern answered.

"Say no more of it. Considering what you did for us, it was nothing," Moran replied. "Did you think about my offer?"

It was an uncomfortable few minutes while Kern explained the group's mission from King Moriak. Kern's manner was eloquent and courtly as he explained that even though Moran's offer was tempting, they were pledged to find the King's missing gold.

After an awkward silence, Moran nodded his acceptance of their decision, then asked if they needed anything else. Their only request was for a horse for Nuran.

Moran bid them all farewell and thanked them again; soon they were mounting up. The party rode out of the town's southern gate, followed by scores of townsfolk who had been waiting to see them off. As they left the town, the people cheered and shouted their goodbyes. After twenty minutes the town was far behind them, and they rode southwest towards the river crossing called the Ferryman.

After a few uneventful hours they eventually reached a log cabin. They didn't see anyone outside the structure, but smoke curled up from the chimney. A ferryboat jetty was built out into the river. They could see the ferry heading to the other side, about halfway across.

"Typical; just missed it," Ty huffed.

"It'll be back in an hour," Nuran soothed.

"More like three hours! Look how slow he's going," Galandrik argued.

"He's pulling it by hand!" Kern had noticed the rope that was tied around a massive wheel, stretching into the water and across the river.

"It's a five-hour round trip; he does it twice a day, and when he returns he will not be going back until dawn," said a woman's voice, coming from the open window of the log cabin. They whirled around, startled, and saw a human woman with thick golden hair tied back in a long, wavy ponytail. A few strands formed ringlets that she had tucked behind her ears.

"She is gorgeous," Nuran whispered under his breath.

"You can say that again," Kern added quietly.

"We have rooms to rent out the back, and there is food in the pot if you have the silver to pay for it. Or, you can sit your mounts until dawn. The choice is yours," the woman offered, along with a smile to melt a man's heart. Before anyone had a chance to answer, she pulled the window shut.

"I suppose we might as well go in; we haven't got much choice," Solomon stated.

The entire party dismounted, and the front door of the cabin opened and the woman stepped into the sunlight. She wore tight leather leggings paired with leather boots; leaves were embroidered in golden thread down the sleeves of her white blouse, and on the edges of her collars and cuffs was a golden weave. Her blouse was tucked in, showing her slender figure. She stood over six feet tall, and from her belt hung a long hunting knife. Her features had a slightly elven cast, but overall she appeared human. The men stared as if she was the first woman they had ever seen.

"We have a little barn out back. Your horses will be well looked after. My brother Jay is already there."

"Thank you, that would be wonderful," Solomon said, bowing to the woman.

"You're welcome. And you can pay my brother for the horses' keep," she added before she disappeared through the doorway, smiling.

Soon Flight, Preacher, Trophy, and Fire, as well as Nuran's new mount, Thunder, were all unsaddled and in the shelter of the barn, and were being fed well. As Jay began brushing down the first of the horses, Solomon counted out the payment, then picked up a brush to help.

Jay was of slender build, like his sister, with short spiky golden hair; he stood a good five feet tall even though he seemed barely ten years old. His features also seemed almost elven, but Solomon noticed that the boy's ears were definitely human.

Kern knocked on the front door. "Come in," they heard the woman inside answer. Kern grabbed the handle and pushed; the door was heavy and very well-made. As they entered the room they saw a massive table with eight chairs surrounding it, and at the far end of the room was a huge open fire, with flames crackling, leaping and licking at the air. Around the fire sat large comfortable-looking leather chairs. The room was very homey and the kitchen area was full of pots, pans, vegetables, hanging rabbits, and herbs and spices. The woman turned to the group and said, "You can place all your weapons on that table next to the door; you won't need them in here. My name is Annabella, but you can call me Bell." She turned back around and carried on dicing onions. "Make yourselves comfortable," she added.

After Kern had introduced everyone, Nuran, Galandrik, and Ty settled into the chairs near the open fire.

"I take it you all want feeding?" Bell asked.

"Yes please, Bell," Kern answered for the party, pulling out a chair from the great table and making himself comfortable.

Bell turned, wiping her hands on a towel. "And I suppose you would like a drink also?" she said, bending down to pull a keg out from a small kitchen cupboard, then taking four wooden mugs from the worktop.

They all thanked Bell and happily accepted the beverage – all, that is, apart from Nuran. He had fallen asleep within seconds of sitting down, his handlebar moustache flapping gently as he snored quietly.

Bell sat at the round centre table next to Kern. "So, where are you heading, O slayer of hill giants?" Bell asked with a wry smile.

"News travels fast, I see," Kern answered.

"We hear most stories here. Was he really twenty feet tall with a club the size of a cow?" Bell asked sardonically.

"Oh, at least," Kern replied with a smile. "I would say more like twenty-five feet tall."

"Whatever it was, the town was truly grateful for your help. That giant had been terrorizing farmers for weeks – months even," Bell said as she got up and poured another drink for herself and Kern. "So where are you boys heading?"

Kern thought for a moment before answering. "We're looking for a party of orcs that ambushed some of the King's guard a few weeks back. We should pick up their trail on the other side of the river, just north of Gateford Forest," Kern explained.

"Oh, I see. What did they steal?" she asked, rising to stir the huge pot of stew.

"Just a couple of chests of gold," Kern revealed casually, taking a mouthful of ale.

"Hasn't the King got enough gold chests to accept the loss of a few?"

"That's exactly what I've been saying all along," Galandrik interrupted in a quiet voice; Ty had fallen asleep in the chair next to him.

"That's neither here nor there," Kern replied. "We were in a position where we couldn't really say no. It doesn't really matter how much gold he has or hasn't got, we are still pledged to find the gold that was stolen," Kern said, looking pointedly at Galandrik.

"My father will be back soon; I'd better get ready to serve dinner," Bell said, moving back to the kitchen area.

"Your father is the ferryman?" Kern asked, surprised.

"Yes, he is – and I should warn you, he doesn't like strangers," Bell said with a half-smile.

At that moment the front door opened, and in walked the biggest man Kern had ever seen. He stood easily seven feet tall, and nearly as wide. His forearms were bigger than mead kegs; it must have come from pulling the ferry every day, Kern thought. A huge black beard, greying slightly with age, hung down halfway to his belt.

The Ferryman walked into the kitchen and Bell stood on her tiptoes to kiss his cheek. "More strangers?" the huge man said, in a deep and rumbling tone.

"Yes Papa, these are the ones who slayed the giant," Bell said excitedly, hoping her father would pick up on her enthusiasm.

The Ferryman looked critically at the four strangers, two of them snoring gently. "This bunch killed a giant," he said in a disbelieving tone. "Well, best they tell me all about it over dinner," he chuckled as he walked to the sink to wash the dirt from his hands.

Bell placed the huge bubbling pot onto a stand on the table and added two loaves of freshly baked bread and a pot of freshly churned butter. Galandrik woke Nuran and Ty and they all took their places at the table, while Bell called Jay and Solomon in from the barn. Kern introduced them one by one to the ferryman, and the room was soon full of dinner-table chatter. Nuran twisted his handlebar moustache and began telling the tale of the giant's defeat in his best story-telling voice.

Kern studied Jay and Bell; they looked almost perfect in complexion, not a blemish marking their faces. Bell's skin in particular was like a sheet of shining silk. In the massive frame of the ferryman Kern saw years of hard work, and etched in every line across his ageing face. He looked every inch like the last survivor of a particular tribe of humans who lived in the eastern mountains, massive people who had been formed by nature and from years of hard work, carrying rocks out of the heart of the mountain when building their homes deep underground. Legend held that the tribe had moved on or died out many aeons ago, a result of the constant warring between dwarves, humans, and orcs. They had been forced out of their homes, but stories of this tribe of massive men and women were still told in towns and villages across Bodisha. *There is no way he's their father,* Kern thought, but kept his views to himself.

Nuran finished the story with a flourish; Ty thought privately that the events seemed slightly more interesting now than they had at the time.

"That's a very good story," the bearded man rumbled. "So where are you heading now?" He used a chunk of bread to wipe clean the bottom of his wooden bowl. Kern gave the same response he had given Bell.

The ferryman stroked his massive beard, thinking deeply; at length he spoke. "I bet you that gold has been taken to the orc town in the southern mountains. The name slips my mind at the moment, but that's where their loot is usually taken. If your gold has been taken there, I doubt you will ever see it again. Getting into that stronghold would be like climbing into hell itself. Apparently they store all their loot there in great piles until their Queen Valla visits. Then she picks what she wants, and dishes out the rest. And if she's not happy with the selections, she throws her orc captains into the gold-melting pots," he finished, ladling out another bowl of stew in the awed silence. "Stew's lovely, Bell; a little more pepper would have been nice, though," he said, smiling.

Bell slid the pepper pot across the table. "Add it to your own, father, not everybody likes it!" The ferryman chuckled as he added more than enough pepper to his bowl.

Galandrik shook his head slightly to dispel the image of flesh in a vat of bubbling, molten gold. "I hope the gold is there; we can crush some orc skulls!" he said, hitting his chest with his fist.

Ty looked across the table at the dwarf and shook his head. "What are you going to do, knock on the front door?"

Nuran chuckled as Galandrik answered angrily, "Maybe I will, thief!"

"Look, we don't know where it is. That's only what…" Kern looked at the ferryboat man with dismay. After being introduced only twenty minutes earlier, his name had already slipped Kern's weary mind.

The huge man smiled at Kern's embarrassment, and quickly put him out of his misery. "Call me Finn."

"It's only Finn's suggestion," Kern finally finished, nodding his thanks to the huge man.

"Even so, it sounds feasible," Ty said. "If it is true, what will we do?" Ty added.

"Go tell Conn he needs an army for his precious gold?" Kern shrugged.

"Or a dozen dwarves!" Galandrik chuckled.

They had each finished off two bowls of stew and a few jugs of ale by the time Bell began clearing the table. "Would you like a hand, Bell?" Nuran offered gallantly.

"No thank you, I can manage. Jay, please show the men to their rooms."

Around huge yawns, they thanked Finn and Bell for their hospitality, and left the payment for the meal and lodging on the table. Then, picking up their weapons, they followed Jay out the back door and across a small field full of vegetables to another wooden building. Jay opened the door and gestured for them to enter. Entering, they saw a square room with eight sets of bunk beds, laid out like a military barracks. At one end of the room was a washing bowl and towels; at the other, a large window faced east, showing the moonlight bouncing off Lake Col in the distance.

A slight wind rippled the calm water of the lake, and an occasional fish broke the surface to snatch up low-flying insects, making widening rings on the water's surface. It was just possible to make out the black shadows of the Eastern Mountains beyond the lake, rising up in the darkness like mighty black fingers with snow-white nails.

Solomon went for one last check on the horses, while the others bedded in for the night. "Are we doing a night watch?" Galandrik asked around a yawn.

"You can if you want. I'm hitting the sack. If anybody gets past that monster of a man to get to us, *we* aren't going to stop them," Ty said as he lay back onto a bed.

"It was him I was thinking we watch for!" Galandrik quipped.

"Oh. OH! I'll take first!" Ty said, leaping up as they all laughed.

They sorted out the watch order, and Ty did indeed take the first sitting. He sat looking out the window, but before long the view got monotonous. *Lovely, but boring,* he thought, looking around the darkened room. His gaze fell on the backpack at the foot of his bed. Idly looking through it, he found the same type of box Kern had – unbeknownst to Ty – found in his own pack. Slowly he opened it, finding four potion bottles, each in its own separate compartment, filled with hay to prevent any damage en route. Carefully picking one out, he examined it closely. It was a glittery blue liquid in a bowl-shaped bottle, the long neck plugged with a cork stopper. On the side of the bottle was an inscription. Angling the bottle this way and that in the faint moonlight, he could finally make out what looked like a string of bubbles, starting small at the bottom and getting larger towards the top of the potion bottle. Ty couldn't make heads or tails of it, and he placed it back into the box.

Just then, a movement caught Ty's eye from outside the window. Placing the box back into his backpack without looking, he kept his gaze fixed on the view outside. He saw movement again – a mammoth black bear running towards the lake. *That bear would make an impressive wall trophy or rug,* he thought to himself, *but killing it would be harder than killing the giant.*

Suddenly the bear stopped and turned, looking straight towards Ty. Even though the distance between them was great, he still felt it was staring right through him. The bear stood up on its hind legs and roared, rattling the glass on the window. Ty slipped down on the floor in fright, pressing his back to the wall, the window just above his head.

The bed closest to Ty was Solomon's, and he was awakened by the noise. He swung his legs out of the bed briskly, then stood looking down at Ty.

"What was that, and why are you sitting down there?" Solomon asked quietly, so as not to wake the others. Ty didn't answer, just pointed a shaky finger up towards the window. Placing both hands on the windowsill,

Solomon stared out. "There's nothing there," he said, looking down at Ty and shrugging his shoulders.

Ty turned on his knees and slowly rose up until his eyes were just visible over the sill. He looked out the window, eyes darting left and right. "There was the biggest bear, Sol, and he was staring right at me. I swear he knew I was here," Ty said, and Solomon could see the honesty in his face.

"Maybe you nodded off and dreamt it?" Solomon suggested. "Or maybe there was a bear, and he's gone to the lake to get some fish for supper," he smiled.

Ty stood up and stared out of the window.

"Yeah, maybe, Sol. You're probably right," Ty agreed. With a friendly slap to Ty's shoulder, Solomon went back to bed.

Ty stared out the window but saw nothing for the rest of his watch. As the time neared for Galandrik to take his turn at watch, he risked a quick look through Solomon's backpack. He found nothing of interest there, and finally went to wake Galandrik. He never mentioned the bear.

They were all awakened in the morning by Solomon, who'd had last watch. "Bell is doing up a breakfast before we leave, if anybody fancies some. I would recommend it because we won't get any more good ones for a few days. It'll be hard rations only, or whatever we can kill."

"Let's eat. I'm starving!" Ty said, grabbing his leather jerkin from the bottom of his bed.

"You're always hungry – you should be twenty stone by now!" Kern jested from across the room.

"I burn it all off; that's why I'm so slim. Input, output," Ty answered, glancing in Galandrik's direction.

"All dwarves have a belly!" Galandrik said, frowning at Ty.

"I never said anything!"

"You didn't have to; I could read your little mind! But one must feed a furnace," Galandrik said, putting on his armour as the others left the cabin chuckling.

Soon they were all seated around the table in the main cabin. Bell placed a large dish in the middle, heaped with eggs, bacon, and last night's leftover stew. She brought out loaves of bread, wrapped in paper for freshness, a small crock of freshly churned butter, and a dish of fruit preserves.

Soon the whole table was eating heartily. "Your horses are ready for you, and the ferry is too. As soon as you're finished, father would like to get on his way," Bell said, placing a pot of hot lemon tea on the table.

"We'll leave as soon as we finish, Bell; your generosity has been more than we could have asked for," Kern said. When they all had finished breakfast and thanked Bell, Ty slipped his hand inside his secret pocket, making sure no one was watching. He slipped out a gold piece from the pocket hiding the farmer's money, deliberately tossing the coin onto the table to make maximum noise.

"There you go, my good lady. That should cover breakfast with some left over to buy yourself and Jay something nice."

Everybody knew that the gold piece would cover far more than breakfast, dinner, the rooms, *and* the horses, but no one said anything. Bell picked up the coin and bit it, then slipped it into her pocket.

"Thank you very much, you are more than kind," Bell said with a smile.

She stood on the doorstep and waved them off as they led their horses towards the ferry. Finn was untying the mooring ropes as they approached him. Without turning he said, "There are slots for your horses to keep them calm as we cross; lead them on one by one."

After the horses had all been secured, Finn climbed aboard. The huge man stood on the side of the ferry, where a rope was threaded through two snatch blocks at either end of the wooden vessel. He seated himself on a chair at the left side of the deck and started to pull; slowly the ferry started to move forward.

Standing at the front of the barge, Ty saw a wooden rack, nearly as tall as Kern, with ropes hanging down; every six inches down the rope was a fish hanging from a hook. *There must be fifty fish there,* Ty thought with surprise. Kern walked over to him and stood staring at the fish. "They're fresh," Kern observed. "Pity we're not staying for tea."

Ty stared at Kern, thinking about the fresh fish and remembering what he had seen the night before. He studied the huge man pulling the ferry across the river. "When do you think he caught them?" he asked.

"I don't know, maybe he got up early," Kern answered.

"It must have been bloody early to catch fifty!" Ty said, crossing his arms.

"Maybe he went night-fishing," Kern said with a laugh, not realizing that Ty was thinking the very same thing.

"I think maybe he did," Ty said softly.

"Oh come on, Ty, I was joking. Pulling this all day, then spending all night fishing? No one could do that," Kern said, shaking his head.

"What about if he could..." Ty stopped mid-sentence, knowing how stupid he would sound.

"Could what?" Kern asked.

Ty turned and walked away, muttering, "Never mind, you wouldn't understand." He stood leaning on a barrel, then took out his dagger and started scratching the wooden lid.

Shaking his head, Kern walked over to Galandrik. "I think Ty is losing the plot," he said. "Right, so if you think a king wouldn't miss two chests full of gold, why do you think he has us looking for it?"

"I don't think we *are* looking for gold," Galandrik explained. "I think we're looking for two chests, but what's in them may be a different matter."

"Yes, that's a good point. I guess we'll have to wait and see," Kern said, patting the dwarf on the shoulder as he walked away. Further down the barge, he saw Nuran and Solomon playing dice on a barrel lid. "Count me in next hand," he said.

"Five silver pieces a go?" Nuran answered.

"Is that all?" Kern said with a smile, and placed a bag of coins on the table.

Ty glanced up at the ferryman and after only a moment Finn turned, as if he had sensed the thief's eyes on him. Ty turned away without meeting his gaze, and did not look at him again.

Two hours and many dice rolls later, they reached the far side of the bank. Waiting there was a fat man sitting on a cart; in the distance they could see the fringes of Gateford Forest. "Is he a friend of yours?" Kern asked Finn.

"Yes, he buys my fish every third day," Finn answered.

"You do a lot of fishing?" Kern asked idly, looking up at Finn.

"You seem to want to know a lot. Can a man not put a few nets out and make a few silver coins?" Finn said in his gravelly voice.

"You are right, sir, it is none of my business. I didn't mean to offend you."

The ferry finally stopped at the bankside. Finn jumped down and tied the mooring ropes to the jetty poles. "Your nets, I see, have been catching nicely, Finn," the man on the cart said, climbing down.

They led the horses off the ferry and bade Finn farewell – all except Ty, who did not even look back. Before they mounted up, Solomon and Kern unrolled a map and began tracing paths across it with their fingers, heads bowed in concentration. When the pair were finally in agreement on what route to take, they all set off southwesterly towards Gateford Forest.

After a good three hundred paces, Ty finally turned back to look at Finn, knowing that even if the ferryman was what he suspected he was, he could never catch him now. Finn had been loading the fish on the cart with his back to the traveling group, but at that precise moment the ferryman stood up straight, turned, and stared. Ty could feel the fierce gaze burning through him, just as the bear's had done the night before. Shivers ran up his spine and he looked away quickly, wrapping his cloak tightly around him.

Something dug painfully into his chest, and he reached inside his jerkin. It was the medallion he had stolen from the giant. Slowly he pulled it from his pocket and studied it closely. The centre of the medallion had three crystals - blue, red, and green - with runes carved all around the rim. Turning it over, he saw that there were also delicate engravings covering the other side. Ty couldn't make heads or tails of any of it, but he liked the look of it and thought it might be worth a gold coin or two. Glancing up, he saw Kern craning his neck to see what Ty was looking at, so he quickly slid the medallion back into his pocket.

"What're you looking at?" Kern asked, still trying to see what it was Ty was inspecting.

"It's a thank-you gift from your wife! She gave it to me when I left Leopard's Town," Ty quipped. The party all started laughing, except for Kern, who shook his head and trotted forward next to Solomon.

"Idiot. I haven't even got a wife," he said, which made Solomon chuckle all the more.

Chapter Seven
Deep Down

Bok and Joli looked down from the ridge at the town of Praise. "What are you thinking?" Joli asked, looking over at Bok.

"It stinks of Rat. He came this way." He spurred his horse and trotted off towards the main gate; Joli caught up after a few moments and rode next to him.

Traders were leaving and arriving at the town in steady streams. "This is a busy little place," Joli said, eyeing the traders. They reached a tavern called the Pig's Tail, and tied the horses up outside. After ordering a jug of ale each and chatting for a while, Bok finally called the innkeeper over. "Excuse me, sir. I was supposed to meet three friends here, but for some reason they haven't turned up. I don't suppose you might have seen them?" Bok said, keeping his expression as honest as he could.

"Might have, what did these friends of yours look like?" the innkeeper replied suspiciously.

"One is a dwarf, one is a human, and the other is a small one. He has bright red hair that he wears up in a knot."

"The only people like that that I know of are the group who slayed the giant, but there was five of them - the three you said, plus another two humans, one in robes and one looking like a paladin," the innkeeper said.

"What do you mean, slayed a giant?" Joli interrupted.

The innkeeper told the story about the battle – though in his version the giant was bigger and the fight much longer. When he finished his talk, Bok thanked him with a silver coin and an order for another jug of ale. As the innkeeper moved away, Bok turned to Joli.

"It must be them. It's way too much of a coincidence for two parties to be traveling south at the same time, with the same descriptions," Bok said.

"He said there were five, though."

"Maybe the other two were meeting them later, or maybe they picked them up on the way. But this is the only lead we have, so I say we carry on south. The guard told us they were heading towards Gateford Forest so even if it wasn't them who slayed the giant, we may pick up a better trail down there," Bok said, thinking out loud.

"Sounds good to me, Bok, but the stakes are higher now that there may be five."

"Like I said, it may not be them anyway," Bok said decisively. "Now get the ale in!" Bok said, banging his empty mug on the bar to get the innkeeper's attention.

Solomon pointed to a pathway that led close to Gateford Forest, running east to west, parallel with the north end of the forest. He explained to the group that this was the path the King's guards had been ambushed on. The ambush site was a bit further on, between a rocky outcrop to the north and Gateford to the south.

"I sense a strong presence of evil," Nuran announced.

"You will do," Solomon explained. "That forest is pure evil. Some of the stories about are legendary."

Galandrik quipped, "It's probably just Ty he can sense," but the halfling ignored the comment.

Soon they reached the rocky outcrop. Just off the path they saw the wooden cart turned on its side, the King's emblem still visible on the wooden slats now facing skywards. The two front wheels were completely smashed; otherwise the orcs would surely have taken it, Nuran thought.

Kern dismounted, squatted down and studied the ground.

"Maybe twenty orc prints, and half as many human prints. There was definitely a skirmish, but there's been much traffic through here since then, so it's hard to make out what exactly happened. Impossible for me to tell if the orcs went east, west, up or down," Kern said, walking bent over and studying the ground.

"What way should we try then?" Nuran asked, lifting both hands in frustration.

"Southeast to the orc temple, where Finn said Queen Valla will be!" Galandrik suggested.

"Right. Because that won't be too hard, will it?" Ty said, shaking his head.

"Well, *they* might help us decide," Solomon announced. Everyone turned to look at him.

"What are you talking about, Sol?" Ty asked with a frown.

"Orcs!" Solomon said, pointing west.

There were at least twenty orcs thundering towards them. "There's more over there!" Ty shouted, pointing towards the east, where another score of orcs were galloping in their direction.

"Get into the forest," Kern shouted, kicking his mount into a gallop as the others followed him towards Gateford Forest.

"That place is evil," Ty screamed from behind, trying to get Kern's attention over the noise of the horses' hooves.

"You'd rather fight?" Kern shouted back, turning his head.

"We could outrun them!"

"No chance, the forest is our only option!" Kern looked for an opening in the wall of trees.

"Over there!" Nuran shouted, pointing towards a path leading into the forest.

Solomon turned to look at the army of orcs behind them. "Quickly! They're gaining on us!" he shouted. They spurred their mounts into one final sprint, just as arrows started to fly past their heads.

They were within twenty feet of the forest opening when an arrow struck Galandrik in the shoulder blade. He dropped the reins and fell forward with a shout. Nuran, seeing the arrow hit home, leaned over, grabbing the loose reins from the dwarf's left side as Kern held Galandrik up from the right. "Hang on, Galandrik!" Kern shouted at the dwarf. They flew through the gap in the trees and crashed on, deeper into the forest, until they were sure no orcs had followed them. Slowing as they approached a small clearing, Solomon and Nuran supported Galandrik as Kern slowly eased him into their arms. They laid him on his side, and the group gathered around.

"How bad is it?" Ty asked, concerned.

"I don't know yet; I'll have to pull the arrow out and see. It doesn't look like it's struck anything nasty. It's only in an inch or so," Kern answered.

Galandrik's eyes rolled and he looked pale. "He doesn't look good, for such a shallow wound," Nuran said. "I think it's poisoned."

"If it is, he's in big trouble," Kern sighed. "Right, hold him down and I'll pull this bloody thing out." Kern grabbed the shaft of the arrow as close to the wound as he could manage. The others knelt down and held the dwarves head, legs, and arms steady. "One… two… three!"

Kern ripped the arrow out and tossed it to the forest floor. Galandrik shuddered like a fish on a riverbank but they contained him well. Kern fumbled in his pack and pulled out the healing balm and bandages Conn had supplied. After rubbing the balm into the wound, Kern bandaged it the best he could. When they rolled Galandrik onto his back, his skin was deathly pale and his eyes had rolled back into his head, sweat beginning to drench his face and neck.

"What now?" Nuran said.

"We sit and wait," Kern answered, looking Nuran in the eye.

"Wait? He's drifting in and out. He'll be dead within hours! What about taking him back to Praise?" Nuran urged.

"It'll take a day to get back, at least, and that's *if* the ferry is there waiting to take us. We'll have to literally carry him in. He's in no shape to ride, and even if we tied him to his saddle, we'd have to guide his horse – and stopping him falling off would be nearly impossible."

Nuran walked away, kicking a fallen branch off into the trees. Solomon sat with his back against a tree, holding his head in his hands.

"What about a spell, Sol?" Ty asked the guide.

"No good. I can heal wounds, but I can't fight poison. Sorry. I wish I could help."

Ty punched the ground, then rose and stalked off, shaking his head and muttering. He couldn't bear to look back at Galandrik sweating and shaking, helpless on the ground.

Kern sat back and began tidying away the remaining pieces of bandage, tucking them into his open backpack. At the bottom of the pack, he spotted the wooden box. "Potion!" he shouted, lifting the box from the backpack.

He opened the box quickly, and pulled out the bottle with the green liquid inside. "Look – a drip with a red cross on it; that must be anti-poison!" Kern said excitedly.

"What if it isn't?" Nuran asked, dashing back and kneeling next to Kern and Galandrik.

"He's dying anyway. Sit him up and pass me the water canteen," Kern said, steel in his voice.

Ty, who had come running back when Kern shouted, passed him the canteen; Sol and Nuran propped Galandrik up, his head flopping forward to rest on his chest.

Kern lifted Galandrik's chin with his left hand and slapped him in the face with his right. "Galandrik, it's Kern! Wake up," Kern shouted at the delirious dwarf. Galandrik's eyelids fluttered as he tried to focus, but it was not nearly enough. Kern splashed water from the canteen onto his face; it seemed to have some effect as Galandrik mumbled something incoherent.

"Drink this potion, it will make you better!" Kern carried on shouting, slapping the dwarf once more.

"Better… I must… d…d…riink," Galandrik slurred.

"Hold his head back," Kern said through gritted teeth. Sol and Nuran tipped Galandrik's head back as Kern uncorked the potion bottle. Slowly he poured the liquid into the dwarf's mouth, trying not to spill a drop. Galandrik drank it down well, considering the circumstances. When the bottle was empty, they laid the dwarf back down and waited, anxiously watching and waiting. You could have heard a pin drop in those moments; even the forest was eerily silent.

After several nerve-wracking minutes, Galandrik's eyelids flickered, then slowly opened, his eyes trying to focus. "Wh… What happened to the orcs?" he asked.

Kern collapsed in a heap next to his backpack and heaved an enormous sigh of relief. Nuran punched the air and spun round on his heel, shouting "Yes!" and Solomon placed his hand on the dwarf's shoulder. "Welcome back, friend," he said.

"Back? I haven't been anywhere!" Galandrik said, sitting up. Then he felt the pain in his back and let out a groan.

"Oh, stop your moaning, it's only a graze," Ty said, smiling widely at the dwarf. "Glad you're fine," he quickly added.

"Of course I'm fine, it'll take more than a blasted orc arrow to stop me! Now help me up," Galandrik said angrily, disgusted by the thought that orcs might have gotten the better of him.

Kern smiled to himself as Nuran and Ty helped the dwarf to his feet.

They rested briefly and then Ty and Solomon went on a quick scouting mission back to the entrance of the forest. They saw a few orcs camped there, waiting for them. Realization set in that they had no choice but to press on – through the forest. When they returned to the clearing, they talked through their options, and there was only one.

"There's no way we can take the horses through here. It's far too dense," Solomon added to the list of problems already facing them.

"No, you're right, Sol. What do you recommend we do with the horses?" Nuran asked.

"I know some animal lore; I could instruct them to go to another meeting spot."

"What about Finn? He would remember our horses, and maybe look after them until we returned," Kern mused.

Ty turned to Kern as if to say something, but then looked away, silent.

After some more discussion, they all agreed that Finn was their best option. Solomon whispered secret words to the horses, stroking each one as he did, while the rest of the group stripped the horses of the gear and baggage that would be needed on the rest of their journey. Still, the horses stood placidly, showing no signs of departing.

"Why haven't they left, Sol?" Ty asked.

"I told them to wait a day. That should give the orcs time to realize we are not coming out, and move on."

"Hm. Good thinking."

After the group had gathered up their equipment and said their goodbyes to the horses, they moved on through Gateford Forest, following the only track available. It had grown over many lifetimes ago, so they used their weapons to hack their way through the dense forest growth. Strange animal noises followed them as they moved cautiously forward, and red eyes peered at them from deeper within the trees.

After what seemed like hours, they reached a large circular clearing. At the far side stood a stone chair, moss climbing up one side. The clearing looked as if it had once been a gathering spot for the ancient forest people; it was easy to imagine the leader of that lost tribe seated regally on the rough-hewn throne, looking down at his or her followers as they bowed respectfully. Around the edge of the clearing stood a circle of stones, also covered in moss. These rocks had been carved into head-shaped figures, each one different from the next. All had seen damage over time from wind and weather, and some had lost parts of their once well-crafted faces.

"This looks like a good enough spot to camp," Galandrik said.

"I don't think the owners are coming back any time soon, do you?" Ty said, standing next to the dwarf.

Kern peered at the ground and after several moments said, "No one has been here for years. There are no tracks, apart from the odd fox, warthog, or deer. No human tracks at all."

"I'll start making a fire then," Solomon offered.

"Plenty of wood around," Kern joked.

"How's the shoulder?" Nuran asked Galandrik.

The dwarf rotated his arm round and round, "Feels fine."

"That's good – then you can make dinner!" Ty said, jumping up onto the stone chair and shouting, "I am King Ty, your illustrious leader: Now make my lunch!" He stood with his arms folded, trying to look imperious.

Nuran chuckled. "Very nice," Kern laughed, "now get down before you fall down."

Ty leaned on the high back of the chair, still enjoying his pretence of being King. He shouted, "How dare you mock King – arrgggh!" as the chair tipped backwards, sending Ty flying.

The chair had locked in place, angled back horizontally to reveal a circular staircase opening up underneath it, leading underground. The cobwebs and moss that had covered the entrance broke away to reveal the stairs, and the void below seemed to suck the air down into it, making a sort of vacuum noise. A swirl of dusty white smoke whooshed up and out as the underground compartment filled itself with fresh new air. It was plain to see that this hadn't been opened for ages. The light from the forest glade illuminated some twenty steps before the staircase fell into complete darkness.

Ty rolled to his feet as the others gathered round to peer down the stone staircase. "Didn't see *that* coming," he said, brushing dirt from his shoulder. Kicking a stone down the newly-opened stairwell, he listened as it clattered down into the darkness, echoing as it bounced down the stairs.

"Like tossing a coin into a well," Nuran muttered as the noise finally faded away. "I wonder what's down there," he said, kicking another stone down the stairs.

"A dungeon full of monsters?" Galandrik offered hopefully, ever eager for a fight.

"It's none of our business," Ty scoffed. "It'll just lead us completely off track. Now, what's for lunch?" He dusted his hands off as he walked away.

Kern glanced back at Ty. "You're right, Galandrik. Probably *loads* of monsters, guarding all their monster treasure."

Ty stopped abruptly. "Well. That is. Now that you… I suppose we could have a *little* peek down there; what harm could it do?"

Kern smiled to himself.

They forgot about lunch and gathered up their equipment. Nuran and Kern both lit torches; Kern led the group into the stairwell, with Nuran bringing up the rear as they slowly made their way down the stairs. The walls were carved of solid blocks of stone, damp to the touch; the smell was horribly stale, like swamp water left standing for decades. At the bottom their progress was halted by a stout wooden door.

"What do you think, Ty?" Kern said, raising the torch at the door.

"Let's have a look," Ty said, bending down to study the lock. "Hmmm, it's an old one, only three core barrels. Should be easy enough to do." Ty reached down to retrieve his bone-handled thieves' tools and went to work. After about two minutes they heard a soft *click*.

"Bravo! Nice skill, that," Nuran commented.

"Don't start him off!" Kern laughed.

Ty stood up and waved an elaborate bow in the direction of the door, inviting them to go through. Kern listened briefly for any sounds from beyond the door, then pushed it open; behind it was a square stone room with two more exits, a wooden door to the east and a barred metal gate to the west. In the centre of the room was a large stone pillar with a red ruby set in the top.

Ty examined the wooden door. "No lock on this, just a star-shaped hole. I guess we need a star-shaped key," he said, standing up and wiping his hands on his leather leggings.

"This metal door hasn't got anything, just bars," Nuran said, looking closely at the metal portcullis.

Kern looked through the bars and spied a lever on the other side. Getting the rope from his backpack, he tied a noose and began trying to flick it over the lever. After several tries, he finally made the shot, but just couldn't get the leverage to pull it downwards.

Solomon, who had been watching closely, groaned in disappointment. "Unlucky," he said, quickly adding, "Good idea, though."

Meanwhile, Ty's attention had been captured by the ruby in the centre of the pillar; drawing his dagger, he stealthily began prying it out of its setting.

"What about bending the bars, or lifting the gate?" Galandrik suggested.

Nuran laid his two-handed sword on the floor and said, "Let me have a go." He spat on his hands and had just grasped the bars, when suddenly a huge clanging noise reverberated throughout the chamber. The floor moved under their feet, and torches fell from their metal brackets on the wall. Dust and dirt sheeted down from the ceiling all around them, accompanied by the same vacuum noise they had heard earlier.

As one, Galandrik, Nuran, Solomon, and Kern spun around, hands flying to weapons, instantly ready to do battle with whatever new threat they faced.

Ty stood wide-eyed in the centre of the room, ruby in one hand and a dagger in the other. Dust sifted onto his shoulders from where it had fallen onto the hood of his cloak.

"What? What'd I do?" he said innocently.

Solomon grabbed the torch from Kern and ran up the stairs to look. After a few seconds they heard him say, "Damn!"

He walked back into the room. "When the ruby was removed, it must have locked the chair back into place above us. We're trapped."

Kern glared at Ty and turned back to the barred gate. Ty slipped the ruby into his pocket next to the medallion. Nuran spat on his hands again, and grabbing the bars with all his might, heaved and strained until, slowly, the bars began creaking and cracking. Gritting his teeth, Nuran strained again as Galandrik cheered him on with cries of "Go on, Nuran!" and what sounded like dwarvish battle cries.

After several more minutes of effort, Nuran sagged against the wall, resting his hands on his knees. "That's all I can manage," he said between laboured breaths. "I'm done in."

Kern turned side-on to the bars and pressed his shoulder against them, trying to squeeze through.

"You won't get through those bars, Kern," Galandrik laughed. "Your shoulders are much too big."

"You're right, I won't – but I know someone who will," he replied, turning to look at Ty.

Ty took a quick step backwards. "Not a chance. No way. Not me. I am *not* going through those bars," he said, waving both hands at Kern and shaking his head vigorously.

"It's your fault we're trapped in here!" Kern shouted across the room. "In fact, it's your fault we ended up in that prison in the first place! We wouldn't be here at all if not for you!"

Ty's shoulders slumped in resignation; he shook his head sadly, then begrudgingly took off his equipment and armour, dropping it on the floor.

He walked past Kern, jostling him slightly as he passed. Slowly he stretched one leg through the bars, followed by his head and one arm. His limbs seemed to dislocate as he squeezed the other shoulder through the incredibly narrow gap between the bars.

"That doesn't look possible," Galandrik admired.

"I know. He definitely has a gift," Kern replied. Holding the bars with one hand for balance, Ty placed the other on the floor; finally he lifted his other leg through. "Now pull that lever on the wall," Kern said, pointing through the gate at the lever.

"Really? Who would have thought of that?" Ty grabbed the lever with both hands and used what little weight he had to pull it down. When it finally clicked into the downward position, the gate began to lift up. Kern quickly stepped back, retrieving his arm from between the bars.

Holding the torch out in front of him, Kern led the others down the corridor. On the walls were mounted torches, which the group lit as they passed, keeping the area well-illuminated.

As they approached the end of the corridor, they spotted another wooden door. Ty once more brought out his tools and picked the lock, then pushed the door open. It revealed another square room with a door on the far side. The door was positioned several feet off the ground, and the floor seemed to shimmer in the torch light.

Kern moved as if to step forward, but Solomon stopped him with a hand on his shoulder.

"Hang on, Kern," Solomon said; he brought his staff forward and down onto the floor of the room. With a ripple, the end of his staff disappeared from view. "No floor – water," Solomon said, turning to Kern.

"Don't even think about it!" Ty said at once.

Kern handed his torch to Galandrik and took off his backpack, armour, and clothes.

"Stand still a moment," Solomon said, then extended his staff and started to chant something. A shimmering light flowed forward to surround Kern, then disappeared just as quickly.

"What was that?" Kern asked.

"Just some light for you to see by, when you're under that water."

"Thanks," Kern said, sitting on the threshold's edge with his feet dangling in the water. "Water's freezing; I'd better be quick," he said. Bracing on his arms, he twisted and dropped his lower body into the water. Taking a deep breath, he lifted himself up so the water was at his waist, then dropped down into the darkness and up again. Shivering, he hoisted himself out and sat on the edge with his legs still dangling in the water. "Pass me the rope, Nuran." As he tied the rope around his middle, he continued, "If I'm not up in five minutes, or if I give two quick tugs on the rope, pull me out," Kern said.

Nuran held the rope as Kern dropped back into the water.

"Good luck. Take this," Ty said nonchalantly, handing down a dagger. Kern took it silently but gratefully. He lifted himself up out of the water, taking in one last deep breath, then disappeared under.

Holding the dagger between his teeth, Kern swam close to the wall, following it deeper and deeper, until he eventually came to the floor. He was pleased to find that the spell Solomon had cast upon him was working well, and he could see all around. On the north wall there was another portcullis with a lever next to it; no other notable features could be seen on the walls or floor.

Aware that he couldn't hold his breath much longer, he pulled down on the lever. With a clunking, sliding noise, the iron gate began to rise. Kern looked beyond the gate and saw that it led further down another watery corridor. He squatted down, then pushed himself off and up, back to the surface.

"What do you think is down there?" Ty asked Galandrik.

"I don't want to hazard a guess," Galandrik answered.

"One thing's for sure, I wouldn't want to be down there. He is one brave man," Solomon said, looking into the water's darkness, which was broken only by a few small bubbles popping on the surface now and again.

"There's a thin line between bravery and stupidity," Ty quipped.

"Where does *cowardly* come into it, then?" Galandrik said, shooting a dark look at Ty.

Ty was spared answering by Kern splashing up through the surface of the water. As he lifted himself up onto the edge, Solomon tossed him a blanket.

"It's about fifteen feet deep, and there's a portcullis at the bottom. There's a lever to open it, but it heads on down another corridor. There's no way I could hold my breath for that long," Kern said, shivering.

"What about weighing you down so you get down quicker?" Ty suggested.

"Weigh him down with what, exactly?" Galandrik asked.

"What about… you!" Ty spat back.

"Leave it, you two, it's not helping matters," Nuran lectured.

"What I need, Sol, is a massive bubble!" Kern said, smiling at Solomon.

"Hang on!" Ty said, swinging his backpack off his shoulder. He reached in and pulled out the wooden box from the bottom, then opened it and handed the blue potion bottle to Kern. "You want bubbles? You got 'em," he said, feeling rather smug and proud of himself.

Kern examined the potion bottle and saw the bubbles etched on the side. "Certainly looks like potion of waterbreathing. What do you think, Sol?" Kern asked, handing him the bottle.

"It looks like it, but I don't make the bottles, so I can't say for sure." Shrugging, he handed the bottle back.

"There's only one way to find out." Kern uncorked the bottle and swallowed the liquid down. "Ew, that's disgusting," he said with a grimace. He handed the blanket back to Solomon and turned around, saying, "See you all in a bit," before taking a deep breath and lowering himself back into the water.

He swam down to the open gate and looked down the corridor with trepidation. The potion seemed to be working, so he swam along until he felt the rope go tight. He knew he had reached the end of his tether, and there was no length left. After a moment's hesitation only, he untied the rope, then watched as it floated to the roof of the corridor before he resumed his exploration.

After a minute or so, he reached an open doorway. He saw no obstacles, so he continued into another open room with another lever on the far wall. Hoping to find an air pocket, he swam up to the ceiling, but water filled the chamber entirely. He swam back down and placed his feet against the wall for leverage and pulled down on the lever. It was stiff and moved slowly, but after a slight struggle Kern heard a clunking noise as if from far away. The noise was distorted as it travelled through the water, and it seemed to echo ominously in his mind.

Glancing at the floor, he noticed holes beginning to appear, about the size of dinner plates. Not waiting to see what might live inside, he swam upwards and out to the corridor, towards the rope.

"I wonder what this place is all about," Galandrik said into the silence.

"What do you mean?" Ty replied, frowning as he tossed a pebble into the water, watching the ripples expand and disappear.

"Well, being a dwarf, we are always building places underground – but we either live in them or we mine them. We wouldn't do it otherwise. This place seems to have no actual reason for being."

"I don't know, really – I have heard stories about wizards setting elaborate traps and things to stop grave robbers and adventurers stealing their gold."

"All seems a lot of hassle to me," Galandrik said, mimicking Ty and kicking a little stone into the water.

"I guess the potion of waterbreathing is working," Solomon interrupted. Just then the group heard a grinding noise and watched as wooden blocks began to protrude from the east wall. Twelve of them jutted out, each about two feet long and a foot wide, making a stepping-stone route around the room and up to the door on the opposite wall.

"Bravo! Kern must have done it!" Nuran celebrated.

"I'll go check out the lock," Ty said excitedly.

"Shouldn't we wait for Kern?" Solomon said in a discouraging tone.

"I'm only going to look, I won't open it," Ty said, leaping onto the first step.

Suddenly, Nuran shouted, "Help!" He stumbled forward, nearly falling into the water. He only just kept his footing, and the rope was nearly pulled from his grasp. "Help me! It's Kern!" he shouted again, pulling the rope up as fast as he could, trying to stop the moist hemp from slipping through his grip. The others gathered behind Nuran and grabbed the rope where they could, working together to pull Kern to the surface. "Pull!" Nuran yelled, "Pull harder!"

As Kern swam down the corridor towards the rope, he felt a sharp pain in his calf muscle. He looked down to see a dragonfish locked on to his leg, blood seeping out into the water.

An adult dragonfish could measure up to a meter in length, with wings like a dragon, a yellow lion-like mane, and big black eyes set in a completely red body. They looked nasty, and more than lived up to their look.

Kern reached down and grabbed the dragonfish's head, squeezing it as hard as he could. The fish released his leg and swam off, retreating from his grasp. Kern swam backwards, watching the water billow red, his blood swirling like crimson smoke.

He saw the fish regain itself; it came towards him with lightning speed and attacked again, this time aiming straight for his face. Kern seized the devil fish with both hands, holding it at bay as it twisted and snapped in frustration. Its multiple rows of razor-sharp teeth were a mere six inches away from Kern's nose, and its incredible strength was already overtaxing his arms. With his right hand, Kern grabbed the dragonfish by the mane, struggling to keep it clear of his face. It thrashed about, snapping jaws coming ever closer to Kern's face. He pulled the dagger from between his teeth and stabbed at the dragonfish's body, and the creature thrashed even more wildly. Still holding it by its mane, Kern stabbed again and again until the thrashing stopped and the creature's black blood began filling the corridor. Kern let go of the mane and watched the dragonfish sink slowly to the bottom, giving only the odd twitch as it went.

In a daze, he looked at the still-bleeding wound on his leg and knew that only the coldness of the water was keeping the pain at bay. Slowly he swam up towards where the rope floated, resting against the ceiling; catching a flash of movement from the corner of his eye, he turned to look back down the corridor.

A school of dragonfish was swimming down the corridor towards him.

Kern pulled on the rope as hard as he could, but it hung slack in the water. He pulled himself along until the rope finally went tight, then tugged twice. Not wanting to wait around for his rescue, he began hauling himself along the length of the rope until he felt the rope being pulled from above.

He glided through the water; as he neared the doorway of the room, Kern realized that the rope would be running tight along the roof before heading up to the ledge where his friends were standing. He gritted his teeth and felt his knuckles rub against the rough stone of the roof as he passed into the open room. As he let out a watery scream, he looked down to see that the dragonfish had nearly caught him up, so he drew his knees up to his chest and began swinging the dagger as wildly as the water would let him. Fortunately for him, many of the dragonfish stopped to feast on their dead friend, gaining an easy meal. Kern struck one as it bit into his foot, then another as they began swarming all over him.

When he broke the surface of the water, Solomon and Galandrik pulled him clear and onto the stone floor, a dragonfish still attached to his leg and flapping madly. Ty forced his dagger into the creature's head until it stopped moving, all but a flinch now and again.

Kern sprawled out on the stone floor, trying to recover his breath. Blood oozed from his wounds; because of the blood-tinged water puddling around him, it looked much worse than it really was. Solomon grabbed the blanket and, with Ty's help, sat Kern upright. They wrapped the blanket around him. Solomon began bandaging the wounds on Kern's leg and right hand, where the scrape along the wall had removed most of the skin.

"What the hell happened?" Nuran asked after Kern finally got his breath back. Kern told the story while getting back into his dry clothes and they, in turn, told him about the wooden blocks that had appeared out of the wall. All agreed that the appearance of the blocks must have tied in with the cranking noise Kern had heard.

While they talked, Solomon dished out some meat jerky and bread. They ate and dozed in the first room; after a few hours, Kern was dry and warm again.

Ty stood and stretched. "Shall we head on then?"

The others agreed, so Kern, standing up, stretched his aching leg and walked a few paces back and forth, trying to hide the limp as best he could. "Just a scratch," he muttered.

They made their way back to the wooden "steps" and Ty skipped from block to block, finally kneeling next to the door above the water. He unwrapped his tools and plied his trade until the lock clicked open. Gently, mindful now of the risk of hostile creatures on the other side, he pushed the door open to reveal another square room. There were no other doors in the walls of this room, and in the middle was another pedestal, this one with a telescope on top. They climbed up the blocks and entered the room. The far wall was covered with scribbles of coloured chalk; amongst them sat a diamond, embedded into the wall.

"Can you read that, Sol?" asked Ty. Neither Solomon nor any of the others could make out what the scribbles said. Kern aimed the telescope at the wall and peered through; the writing was magnified, but he still couldn't make any sense of the manic scribbles.

"What you think, Solomon?" Kern asked.

"Still no idea," Solomon answered, examining the telescope as Ty walked around the edges of the room in a search for hidden doors.

"Don't touch the diamond this time, Ty! Last time the door locked behind us," Nuran said, looking down at the gem in the wall. Ty shot Nuran a dark look and carried on searching.

"There's something missing from this telescope. It looks like there should be a lens on the end," Solomon said.

Galandrik and Nuran both looked around, as if the lost lens might be lying on the floor.

"What would it look like?" Kern asked.

"Well, the one in Conn's study had a golden rim with three clear gems in the middle: green, red, and blue, if I remember rightly," Solomon replied.

Upon hearing Solomon's words, Ty spun around. "How big are we talking?"

"Sized to fit the end of the telescope," Solomon chuckled. "They all vary."

Turning away from Sol and Kern, Ty reached into his jerkin and pulled out the giant's medallion. Turning back with his hand open, he asked, "Like this?" The medallion sat in the centre of his palm.

"Where in Hades did you get that?" Solomon asked, astonished.

Nuran and Galandrik stopped their searching at this commotion. Solomon took the medallion from Ty and fitted it onto the end of the telescope, where it clicked into place perfectly.

"You little belter!" Nuran said with delight.

"He's full of surprises," Kern agreed.

"But where did you get it?" Solomon asked again.

"I just… found it, and thought it might be worth something," Ty mumbled.

"It's worthless. They are just glass eyes embedded in a metal shell, and coated in gold leaf to match the telescopes, that all," Solomon said, to Ty's disappointment.

Kern looked through the telescope at the wall; the colours from the lens deciphered the scribbles. "Not so worthless after all," he said. "The wall says, 'Water the diamond'." Reaching into his backpack, he took out his water canteen and splashed its contents onto the diamond. It fizzled, spluttered, and started to melt, until finally it had disappeared entirely, leaving behind a hole in the wall.

Kern peered in. "Look," he said, reaching in and pulling out a star-shaped key.

"I bet I know where that fits," Galandrik said. They headed back to the first room, being careful not to slip from the wooden blocks, and Kern fitted the key into the lock until they heard a click.

The door opened inwards. Beyond it was another corridor, sloping slightly downwards. They walked down the stone tunnel, lighting the wall torches as they went. This corridor was wider than the others had been, and felt strangely warmer. After some ten minutes of walking, they reached an arched opening; beyond this was a huge circular room, its wall lined with sarcophaguses. In the middle of the room stood a massive statue of a skeleton warrior; there were no visible exits. The room was well-lit by wall torches all around its perimeter.

"I sense evil," Nuran said once more, passing the torch to Solomon and drawing his two-handed sword. Kern drew his bow and notched an arrow, and Galandrik hefted his axe.

Kern, Nuran, and Galandrik walked cautiously into the room, mindful of Nuran's warning. But just as they crossed the threshold, a portcullis dropped, trapping the three in the room with the statue, and locking Ty and Solomon out.

"Prepare to die!" bellowed a tall cloaked figure from across the room. He had appeared from nowhere and was holding a black staff; his cloak was purple and deeply hooded, and they couldn't make out a face. Kern reflexively fired an arrow, which hit its target smack in the chest – but the arrow went straight through, as if it had pierced nothing but purple smoke.

"You dare fight me? You fools!" The ghostly figure lifted his staff. White lightning shot out from it at every angle, some bolts hitting the sarcophaguses. Where they struck, the stone lids shattered into hundreds of pieces; out of each one climbed a skeleton.

"Undead," Nuran muttered under his breath. "I *hate* the undead."

Solomon pushed, pulled, and rattled the bars as Ty searched fruitlessly for hidden levers; the pair could only watch as six animated skeletons attacked their friends.

Galandrik stepped forward and swung his mighty two-handed axe, shattering the nearest skeleton into hundreds of bony fragments. A second skeleton warrior swung his sword at the dwarf, who parried the blow with the head of his axe. Kern dropped his bow and drew his sword just in time to fend off a blow from another skeleton, and riposted with a swinging blow to the skeleton's legs, sending it crashing to the floor. Without a second thought Kern slashed downwards, crushing its skull, then twisted and blocked a blow from the side. Nuran raised his sword and swung a fierce blow at the two skeletons attacking him; the force of his swing ripped through the first and crashed into the second, splintering both of them into pieces.

The ghostly purple-robed figure sent out another blast with his staff, breaking open eight more sarcophaguses, and the skeletons flooded out into the room. "Hahahahaaa!" his laughter boomed out, "you cannot defeat my skeleton army!"

As Galandrik finished off his last foe, he turned to Kern, who was being attacked by three skeletons and was barely able to keep them at bay. Nuran was fighting off three attackers of his own, even as more skeletons moved towards them. They heard another crash and saw more sarcophaguses being blown open.

"Bring them around to me!" Nuran bellowed. Kern fended off his three attackers, blocking blow after blow, slowly walking backwards until he was next to Nuran; from the other side of the room, Galandrik did the same. When the three companions at last stood back to back, there were at least twenty skeleton warriors surrounding them. Nuran took a blow to the forearm as Galandrik caught a blade tip in the face, cutting his cheek open. Nuran swung his mighty weapon at his attackers, sending them reeling backwards.

"Whatever you have planned, Nuran, do it quickly!" Kern shouted as he smashed through a skeleton's midriff. Another took its place and lunged at Kern, but he parried the blow. A skeleton attacked Galandrik; the dwarf only just managed to shield himself but the creature then aimed another blow at his head. Nuran scattered his three attackers with one massive swing, then pointed his sword straight upwards towards the roof, holding the pommel with both hands. His voice rang out above the melee.

"By the holy light of God Christianos, be thou gone!" A bright white light seemed to beam outwards from the paladin's sword, illuminating the entire room and blinding Kern and Galandrik. On the other side of the grate, Ty and Solomon covered their eyes. The light appeared to swell in intensity, until all at once every skeleton shattered into dust. When the glow had faded away, nothing remained of them but the tattered rags of their clothing and armour, and their weapons.

Nuran fell to his knees, then collapsed completely on the gritty floor, coughing and gasping for breath. His sword laid next to him, dull and devoid of any colour other than a lifeless grey.

A wild, furious scream broke out; the purple-robed man was enraged by the destruction of his skeleton army. "You will never win!" the ghostly figure shouted, pointing his staff at the statue standing in the centre of the room.

Ty had opened his backpack and pulled out the wooden box of potions at the height of the battle against the skeletons. Now, as Solomon watched the purple-robed man raise his staff towards the statue, Ty looked over the three remaining bottles. He pulled out the glittery red concoction and peered at the 'STR' embossed on the side of the bottle.

"Oh well, what harm can it do?" Ty said to himself, uncorking the bottle and swallowing the contents in a single gulp. He quickly rose and grabbed hold of two bars. He took a deep breath and heaved, pulling them in opposite directions. Slowly they started to crack and creak.

Light emanated from the purple-robed mage's staff and swirled round the massive carved shape of the skeleton warrior. Colour slowly filled the statue as it was brought to life. "Come, Kraven! Come back to me," the mage chanted.

In moments the monstrous warrior was fully animated. Kraven brandished his shield on one arm and a sword in the other, and a second smaller sword was sheathed on his hip. He let loose a mighty war cry before jumping down from the pedestal. When he landed, the whole room shook;

the imprints of his feet dented the concrete floor.

Kern grabbed the drained paladin under the arm and tried to lift him to his feet, but it was no use. Nuran slumped back to his hands and knees.

Galandrik looked at Kern with a shrug. "Shall we?"

Kern stepped forward. "We shall."

Galandrik attacked with a swing meant for Kraven's thigh, but it was parried by the giant's huge shield; he came back with a blow which Galandrik only just managed to dodge by rolling out of the way. Kern ran in and jumped, bringing his sword down towards Kraven's head, but Kraven simply raised his shield to block the blow, and swatted Kern off to one side. The giant skeleton looked down at the two attackers in front of him and released another deafening battle cry. Galandrik thought he could almost feel the dusty breath. Kraven threw his shield down and drew his second sword.

Kern and Galandrik gathered themselves and prepared to defend once more against the giant's onslaught. Kern rolled under one of Kraven's attacking swords, striking at the skeleton as he went. His blade smashed into Kraven's thigh, bringing him down onto one knee. Galandrik's axe stuck Kraven's other sword, knocking it from the giant's hand. Kraven brought the hilt of his remaining sword sharply down onto Kern's back, knocking him flat to the floor. The ranger was laid out and winded, fighting to find a breath. The skeleton rose and placed one massive foot in the centre of Kern's back, forcing out what little air Kern had regained.

Kraven's free hand seized Galandrik's head, his giant skeletal grip covering the dwarf's entire metal helmet. Extending his arm and raising Galandrik high into the air, Kraven inspected the dwarf dangling in his grip. Reaching up, Galandrik grabbed hold of the bony arm as he was lifted ever higher, his metal helmet creaking under the immense pressure. Kraven brought his sword level with Galandrik's head, aiming the vicious point towards the helpless dwarf's eye.

"Kill, Kraven, kill!" the robed man shouted gleefully.

Ty kept straining at the bars until at last he had opened a gap just big enough for him to squeeze through. He looked to the centre of the room and saw Galandrik suspended from the skeleton's grip, a sword about to be thrust into the dwarf's face. Ty ran forward past Nuran, who was struggling to get to his feet.

"Just borrowing this," Ty said as he grabbed Nuran's great two-handed sword. Ty raised it high above his head, something he could never have managed before drinking the strength potion. He ran towards the giant skeleton, springing from a broken sarcophagus up onto the pedestal the giant had occupied. With Nuran's sword raised high above his head, Ty jumped, bringing the sword down with all his new-found strength. The blade struck true and sliced straight through Kraven's shoulder, severing the arm that held Galandrik aloft.

The dwarf fell to the floor with the giant arm still attached to his helmet. Kraven let out a blood-chilling scream of pain and turned round, swinging his sword at Ty.

Ty tried to duck under the attacking blade, but the skeleton's speed was too great. The sword ripped across Ty's shoulder, spraying blood into the air. Ty fell to the floor and dropped Nuran's sword, clutching his wounded shoulder.

Kraven loomed above Ty. Galandrik stood up behind Kraven and removed his crushed helmet, blood from his ears seeping down his neck. As he grabbed his axe, he saw Kraven raise one foot in the air, poised just above Ty. Galandrik swung his axe blade into Kraven's standing leg, shattering it into pieces. The skeleton fell to the floor and Ty rolled out of the way, still holding his shoulder.

Galandrik swung again and the blow this time was fatal; Kraven's skull was smashed into pieces.

"Noooo!" The ghostly figure screamed in disbelief and ran towards an exit on the far wall, which had appeared from nowhere. As he ran through the opening, it disappeared, closing up behind him.

Solomon had been watching the battle helplessly, still trapped on the other side of the gate. Now he heard a distant grinding noise, and the barred gate slowly lifted. He ran into the room, hardly knowing whom to assist first.

Nuran had just about gotten to his feet but was still wobbly, leaning on Ty's good shoulder. Kern was on all fours, breathing normally at last, and Galandrik sat with his back against the centre pedestal, wiping sweat from his brow and blood from his face. Kern crawled over to Galandrik and sat up next to him. "Thanks again, my friend," Kern said, looking at Galandrik. The dwarf managed only to nod back in appreciation, too tired to speak.

As the others recovered, Solomon walked around the room. Only the pedestal in the centre and several empty sarcophaguses remained. The exit through which the ghostly figure had escaped was now a solid stone wall.

After clearing a small area of dust and debris, they all rested and healed, covering each other's wounds with healing balm and bandages. Food was shared out once more, and the group ate in silence.

"Who do you think the mage was?" Galandrik asked, to no one in particular.

"No idea. I'm sure we'll meet him again soon enough," Kern answered.

"I hope this strength potion lasts until then," Ty said, flexing a bicep.

"Nearly as strong as me now!" Kern laughed.

Solomon examined some of the sarcophaguses, looking closely at the detailed designs and ancient markings along their sides. On one of them he found a pair of rubies embedded in the side, marking the eyes in an elaborate depiction of a king. He pulled out his dagger and pushed in under the ruby, prizing it free.

He caught the first ruby as it fell and slipped it into his pocket. As he pressed his dagger under the second ruby, to his surprise, the tip of the dagger went straight through the wall of the sarcophagus. It seemed to be hollow behind the decorated facing. He carried on and eventually the other ruby fell inwards. Solomon started poking at the side of the sarcophagus, making the hole ever larger, until he could have poked his head in if he so wished. Taking up his staff, he said something in an ancient tongue, and the end of his staff began to give off a bright light. He angled the light from his staff into the hole and looked in. He saw a chest inside, and after knocking in some more of the outer wall, he dragged it out into the room. Picking up the second ruby, he called to Ty, "Look at this; you think you could open it?"

The others, intrigued, clustered around Solomon and the chest. Ty bent over the lid, feeling a stab of envy that he hadn't been the one to find the chest, and went to work. Within seconds they all heard a click.

Solomon opened the chest and reached inside, then pulled out a quiver full of arrows.

"Are these any good for you?" he asked Kern, passing his find to Kern. Kern accepted the quiver and pulled out a single arrow. The feather fletching shone bright red, and the ashwood shaft looked exquisitely made. Runes were etched all around the shaft, down to the metal arrowhead.

"These look magical. I'm sure I have seen this rune before – the one for fire, I think. Thank you, Solomon."

Solomon reached into the chest again and pulled out a bottle full of a green liquid. 'Hemlock' was written on its side. "I have no idea what this is," Solomon said, shaking the bottle.

"It's poison, and not a nice one," Ty explained. "If you ate one or two hemlock leaves, it would be enough to kill you. It causes a weakening of the muscles and intense pain; eventually your muscles deteriorate and die. You lose your sight but not your mind… until death, that is. It's very popular in the trade."

"Sounds delightful!" Nuran said.

"I can remember when the thieves' guilds battled for control of cities and towns," Ty mused, "and they would feed hemlock to quails. The birds are immune to the poison, but the flesh from just one quail that's eaten hemlock seeds will paralyze a man. They would arrange to have the quail served to whoever it was they wanted to remove from power."

"Well, next time we come up against a band of orcs we'll offer them a quail salad!" Galandrik chuckled.

Ty shook his head. "Anyway, that bottle's full of concentrated hemlock; one drop applied correctly to a blade or arrow tip will kill anyone, even if your little axe can't."

"You better keep hold of it, then," Solomon said, passing Ty the bottle.

Next he pulled out some parchments, covered in writing. "These should come in handy," Solomon declared, shoving the scrolls into his backpack without further explanation. Under the scrolls sat a shining bronze helm and some wrist bracers. He passed the helm to Galandrik, and the bracers to Nuran.

"You could use a new helmet, after yours was squashed," Solomon said to the dwarf.

"Thanks, it fits like a glove," Galandrik answered as he slipped the new helm on.

"These bracers feel light," Nuran said; "I think they're mithril. Top quality armour, thanks," as he admired his gift. Solomon picked some gold coins from the bottom of the chest and slipped them into his money pouch. The chest was empty.

After resting for a couple of hours Ty finally stood up and stretched his arm out, feeling his wound tighten as it sent a sharp pain down to the tips of his fingers. With a slight grunt he began feeling his way along the wall, searching for secret levers, buttons, or anything that might open up a door. After several minutes, he stopped. "Here we go," he said, pulling a dagger from his sleeve and using it to scrape away the mortar from between two stone bricks. When he had gouged out enough, he wrapped his bony fingers around the brick and pulled it out, dropping it to the floor. He reached in gingerly, feeling for anything, pressing his arm in right up to the shoulder blade.

A few seconds later they heard the click-thunk of a lock being opened, and a door swung slightly open – the same door the purple-robed mage had run through. Ty withdrew his arm and rubbed off the cobwebs. He looked through the door and saw another corridor leading on.

"Bravo, young man," Nuran said, looking over Ty's shoulder and down the corridor.

"Speaking of 'bravo,' Nuran, how did you destroy all those skeletons?" Kern asked.

"A skill you learn when training as a paladin. The power to destroy undead."

"Seems like it takes a lot out of you," Solomon observed.

"Yes, and I can't do it again for a good while. It all depends on how much I use. That time I used everything I had."

"Well, whatever you did, I'm glad for it, otherwise I would have had to kill them all myself!" Galandrik boasted.

"*All?*" Kern laughed, "I was three ahead of you when Nuran stepped in!"

"Rubbish you were," Galandrik argued.

"Without me, he would have squashed *your* head in his hand, and broken *your* back with his foot!" Ty interrupted, pointing at Galandrik and Kern in turn.

"It's a good thing we all work as a team then," Solomon quipped, defusing the tension.

"Let's move on," Nuran announced, lighting up a torch. Ty pulled out his pipe and filled it with stonecrop leaf, as Kern felt the spot on his leg where the dragonfish had bitten him. It was much improved.

They moved cautiously on down the corridor, and within minutes they reached another door which was slightly ajar. Nuran pushed the door and it opened wider, revealing a circular room which was empty except for a rope hanging down in the centre. A bright light shone down from above, and a rat scurried into a crack in the wall as they entered. The room resembled the bottom of a dry well, and Ty searched the circular room for more hidden passages, but found nothing.

"I guess we need to climb up. Ty, you go and see what's up there; after all, you're the quietest, and the best climber," Kern said with a smile.

"The sooner we are out of this place, the better," Ty answered, taking hold of the rope and tugging to test its strength.

"Don't pull too hard, lad; that potion may still be working. We don't want you pulling the world down onto our heads," Galandrik said with a wry smile.

"This is the thanks I get for saving your life, typical!" Ty hoisted himself upwards. The rope went up a good thirty feet before he finally reached to top. It was exactly what it had looked like from below – an abandoned well.

Ty pulled himself up onto the side wall and looked around. He was in a clearing which obviously hadn't been used for many moons. Still in

Gateford forest, he thought, but the trees did look thinner now. He shouted down to the others it was clear to come up. Eventually they all made it up, although Galandrik did need a helping hand.

"That's better; the dank smell down there was hideous," the dwarf said, taking a deep breath.

"I'd have thought you would've liked it, reminding you of home," Ty said cheekily.

"That's completely different, where we live is –"

"Don't bother, Galandrik. He's making fun of you," Kern said, shaking his head at Ty.

"Right – which way's south?" Solomon interrupted, studying the map, and Nuran chuckled.

Chapter Eight
To Catch a Fish

Bok looked at Joli and pointed towards a house in the distance. "That must be the Ferryboat man's house."

"Yeah, and the ferry is in too," Joli answered.

"I don't think they can cross at any other point, unless they rode around Lake Col - and I doubt they would be doing that," Bok said as he kicked his horse into a canter.

"No, I think you are right," Joli said to Bok's back.

They made their way down to the ferry and found a huge man standing there.

"Can I help you?" Finn rumbled.

"Yes, we need to cross the river. Are you the ferryboat man?" Bok asked.

"I am, and it will cost you. No ride is free in Bodisha," the man said, throwing a bale of hay onto the wooden ferry.

"Yes sir, of course not," Bok agreed.

"You are very lucky, as I am just now leaving. Walk your horses on; there are slots for them to keep them calm."

Bok and Joli walked their horses onto the ferry, then watched as the massive man finished loading straw and barrels. He then clambered up onto a chair and began heaving on a rope, and slowly the boat began to move.

Bok leaned on a barrel and looked out over the river. "Do you think we should ask him if Ty and his party have been across here?" Joli whispered to

Bok.

"We don't need to," Bok said, smiling to himself.

"Why's that?" Joli asked, a puzzled look upon his face.

Bok pointed to the barrel top. Joli peered closer and saw the words 'The Rat' carved into it.

"I told you he was an idiot," Bok said, smiling at Joli.

"It looks like he did this not long ago, either," Joli said, picking a fresh splinter out of the barrel top.

"We're not far behind them, and if they tried to go through Gateford Forest we will probably overtake them."

"I doubt if even the Rat is that stupid," Joli laughed, "but then again…"

"We'll pick up their trail on the other bank. The tracks should still be fresh."

"Wherever they've headed, we should still be able to find them and kill that little toad."

"Don't worry, we'll find him, and we *will* kill him. Trust me," Bok said with a slight snigger.

Kern and the others were on the move, headed south, using the sunlight that managed to penetrate the trees as a compass. The trees were definitely thinner here, so their progress was easier, and the moss-covered ground seemed damper underfoot. Eventually, the tree canopy spreading over them thinned out like a threadbare cloak, allowing shafts of light to penetrate to the forest floor. They could hear the sound of running water in the distance, and a few minutes later they found it.

The group stood on the bank of a large pool; a waterfall on the far side flowed majestically from over a ledge and down into the pool. Gushing and splashing down onto the rocks jutting out of the water, it sprayed mist into the air, creating a beautiful rainbow.

"There is a keep just south of here, the Norse Keep; we can get supplies and restock there," Solomon suggested.

"Sounds good to me, but first I think I'll wash here to get the stink of that dungeon off me," Kern said, lowering his weapons and backpack to the grass.

"Good idea," Galandrik answered, and joined Kern in stripping off his armour.

Before long they were all washing and cleaning their gear and clothing in the pool, using the waterfall as a makeshift shower. Using the churned-clean sand from near the bottom of the waterfall, they scrubbed away the dirt from the dungeon and forest. Nuran finished first, and he sat on the bank eating a slice of dried beef and joining in the joking and gaiety.

They all felt better for the wash, and after a brief pause to eat they headed south. They walked until nightfall, until they finally left the confinement of the forest behind them and were on open ground. They found a wagon path, made from years' worth of traders moving between Marsh Town and the towns of the north.

A few hours more brought them to the top of a hill where, in the brightness of the moonlight, they could see Norse Keep below them in the distance. It was a good mile away; beyond that they could just make out a mountain range, rising up out of the earth like a tidal wave of stone. Cheered that their destination was in sight, they headed down the slope towards the Keep.

As they neared the Keep, Ty grew uneasy. "This looks far too quiet for my liking," he said.

"Yes, I agree. There are no lights or activity," Solomon said.

"Are you sure they still use this place then?" Galandrik asked.

"Traders have used this Keep as a halfway point between the southern and northern towns for centuries," Solomon explained.

"Indeed they do; they restock here or rest for the night," Nuran added.

"Not any more, by the looks of it," Ty said as they approached in the bright moonlight.

The Keep was a big place with two massive towers at the front, holding up the two huge main gates. A wall surrounded the Keep, with another tower built at the far end.

As they approached the main gates, they could see that one of them was only just hanging upright; the bottom hinge had been smashed off, and it looked as though the massive gate could fall at any moment.

"It looks like someone attacked the place and smashed straight through these gates," Nuran said.

"I agree. This place didn't hold much militia – maybe ten or twenty guards, maximum," Kern said, looking at the marks of violence on the gate.

"I think it was recently, as well," Ty said.

Kern knelt and examined the ground. "By the looks of these tracks I would say orcs – and quite a few of them."

They walked quietly and carefully into the courtyard. As they stood just inside the doorway, they could see the once-thriving shops were all empty, doors and windows smashed; some were even razed to the ground. A small marketplace had once been situated on the far eastern wall; now there were only the remains of smashed tables and carts.

"Try and find some clues, and grab anything that could come in handy," Kern said.

"I feel a heavy presence of evil; be on your guard," Nuran said, drawing his sword.

"Should I check out the inn? Maybe we could sleep there – if we're lucky there may be some food and drink left in the cellar," Galandrik asked.

"Good idea. I'll come with you, but the orcs have probably raided everything," Nuran said as he followed the dwarf.

Galandrik and Nuran walked further into the courtyard, in the direction of the inn, when suddenly the floor seemed to spring to life all around them, lifting them off the ground and filling the air with dirt and dust. They were caught up in a net, the sides of which drew up as it was lifted off the ground. From all directions, orcs attacked.

Kern quickly fired two arrows at the first two oncoming orcs. As the arrows soared through the air, they changed into little firebolts, thudding into their targets and engulfing them in flames. The orcs dropped to the ground, rolling and screaming. Ty and Solomon both drew their weapons and turned to face the orcs, but from the towers above them came nets with weights tied all around the edges. Hundreds of small fish hooks were stitched into the net, so that the more the captive struggled, the more firmly he was caught. Ty and Solomon tried frantically to cut through the net that held them, but as they struggled it only got worse – the hooks made it impossible for them to get free.

Some thirty orcs stood surrounding Kern, who now held his bow with two notched arrows, the runes around their shafts flickering with fire, awaiting release. The orcs had their weapons drawn. Glancing up, Kern saw orc archers filling the tower windows above, and he knew fighting was pointless. Slowly he lowered his bow.

From behind the ring of attackers stepped forward the orc leader. He carried a massive club, and his face had two white lines painted across it; his helmet boasted a red plume of ostrich feathers, and his black leather armour shimmered dully in the moonlight. He stood in front of Kern, looking down at the human.

"Drop your weapon," the orc demanded. Kern didn't take his gaze from the orc as he let his weapon fall to the ground. The orc looked over at Ty and Solomon caught in the net, then up to Galandrik and Nuran hanging above him. "Like little fishes caught in a net!" he shouted. The orcs all laughed and jeered, banging weapons onto shields, then without warning the orc leader swung at Kern with the back of his hand, knocking the ranger to the ground. Blood trickled from a cut on Kern's lip as he tried to push himself back to his feet, but he couldn't find the strength. His arms went weak and his world spiralled down into darkness.

Hodash approached Grig, the orc leader. "Sir, the prisoners are ready for transport to Sanorgk."

"Well done. Where did you put their weapons and equipment?"

"All put on the back wagon, sir. Oh, and we did find these, on the two fishes caught on the ground." He held out the necklaces Ty and Solomon had taken off the orcs they'd killed while rescuing Nuran.

"Orc reward necklaces, for bravery. Hm," Grig said with a fierce scowl. "Take the others to the mines, but send those two to the upper cells. We need to find out where they got those from."

"Yes sir, it will be done," Hodash said, turning back towards the prisoners.

The orcs made ready to leave. Six saddled horses stood at the front of the orc troop, and at least twenty orc soldiers were lined up behind them. Then came the cart, where the captured party sat or slumped with hands tied up behind their backs. After the cart came another group of twenty or so soldiers. Finally, bringing up the rear were two wagons full of equipment, boxes, barrels, sacks, and weapons.

Grig walked forward and mounted the lead horse, followed shortly by the five orcs who rode with him. Grig turned in the saddle to face his troop.

"*Uglul kuk forged,*" he shouted, then kicked his mount into a canter and led his band out through the smashed gate of the Keep.

Kern sat up, dried blood staining his shirt and face. His hands were tied, as were his feet. Looked around at the other members of the party, the moonlight revealed them all to be disheartened – especially Galandrik, with a black eye and a deep cut across the bridge of his nose and cheek. The cuts had been inflicted by the dungeon skeleton, but had opened again and fresh blood dripped down his cheek onto his shirt. He must have put up a quite fight after being let down from the net trap, Kern thought.

Ty and Solomon met his eyes; each of them tried to force a smile but it wouldn't come to either face. Nuran laid on his side, either asleep or unconscious; he too looked as though he had taken a beating from the orcs.

Ty glanced behind him, past the band of walking orcs, and could make out their backpacks on another wagon, along with their weapons. How stupid of him to walk into an ambush like that, he thought. The danger had been so obvious. They *knew* the Keep had been attacked recently, and *still* they walked into the trap. He bit his lip and closed his eyes.

Solomon edged closer to Kern and whispered. "Where do you think they'll take us?"

"No idea. I'm sorry for getting you into this," Kern mumbled back, looking down.

"It's not your fault, Kern," Solomon answered, sincerity in his voice.

"Thank you. You are a good friend."

"Just try to keep it together; we may yet get out of this. We need you," Solomon said, just as an orc walked alongside the wagon, looking in.

"No talk!" he shouted, spitting into the cart. Kern gave the most encouraging smile he could muster, though he thought it was probably not very convincing.

The troop marched until dawn, then finally stopped and made camp. To the south was the mountain range, and to the west was the edge of the southern marshes. The party were dragged off the wagon and their hands were bound to each other. After being given stale bread and a small drink of what tasted like dishwater, they were then further secured by being tied to the trunks of the trees scattered around the campsite.

"This doesn't look good, old friend," Ty said, craning his neck in the direction of the tree where Kern was tied.

"No, I'm afraid it doesn't. Even if we could get free, there are way too many of them for us to try and fight our way out."

"How are you two?" Ty said, flicking a foot out in Nuran's direction.

"Aching a bit from where they stuck the boot in, but I'll survive," Nuran said, forcing a smile.

"Let me have my axe and we will see who's wearing the boots!" Galandrik roared.

"I don't think they will be handing it back, unfortunately for us," Kern replied.

"I think Kern is right. We just need to sit tight and wait for our moment to either attack or run," Solomon said.

"Tight is the word I would use," Ty said as he tried to wriggle his hands free.

"Why do they march through the night?" Solomon asked.

"I think they move in the darkness for more cover," Nuran answered. "Northeast of these mountains is human land, and orcs are hunted there. A few half-orcs mix in with the humans, but they are never completely welcome. When we cross this mountain range and get further south, we will be the hunted." A chill skittered down Ty's spine at the thought of entering orc lands as prisoners.

The orcs slept until dinner time, then broke camp and prepared to move on. The party were pushed and shoved back onto the cart with no more food or drink offered, much to their disappointment (and Galandrik's slight relief. He was hungry but the food was so terrible, and any meat cooked by orcs might – *best not to think about it*, he decided with a shudder).

The orc troop picked up a path that led through the mountain ranges to the south. It wasn't as clear a path as the trader's roads they had been on, but it was good enough for them to travel at a fair speed. After a good few hours of marching, the light was beginning to fade; on either side of them the mountain peaks rose higher and higher. Every now and again, rocks would tumble down, narrowly missing the troop and their captives.

As dawn broke, they came to a halt. The previous day's procedure was repeated, except this time the prisoners were tied back to back, apart from Solomon, who was tied to one of the wagon's wheels. Again the food given to them was bread and water, which they forced down despite the taste. Their wrists and ankles were sore and chafed, and blood covered the ropes that bound them; but the more they moaned, the tighter the ropes got. Their bodies ached and exhaustion nagged at them, but every time one drifted into sleep, an orc would promptly wake him up with a slap of his sword or a fist. They did their best to stop each other from drifting off.

The path through the mountain range grew ever steeper as they progressed through the pass. Eventually the path levelled out, then started descending; they could see they were at the highest part of the pass. The mountains arched round in a horseshoe shape; sitting in the middle and surrounded by the soaring peaks was a massive black tower – Sanorgk.

Lights shone through many windows around the tower, and thick black smoke rose from many smaller huts clustered at its base. In front of the great tower was an enormous hole in the ground. It appeared to be at least a hundred feet wide, with vicious-looking black, red, and white smoke swirling upward from its depths. The prisoners could make out the noises of anvils being struck, fires being stoked, and whips being cracked.

Sanorgk... This must be the place Finn was talking about, Solomon remembered, *where they store the goods and wait for Queen Valla to take her spoils.*

When they reached the massive hole, the path they were on forked. One branch led down into the pit, the other up towards the massive temple. The troop stopped at the fork and Grig ordered six of his troop to take Kern, Galandrik, and Nuran downwards into the hole. "Enjoy your stay," Grig shouted behind them, laughing.

Galandrik was drawing breath to return an answer when an orc guard pushed him forward down the path, sending him falling head over heels, rolling twice. Kern and Nuran, their wrists still bound, couldn't help him back up, but an orc hauled him to his feet, and they continued down the slope. The wagons and the rest of the orc troops carried on towards the black tower, Ty and Solomon carried helplessly along with them.

Chapter Nine
The Black Tower

The slope led down and around, slowly twisting its way underground. The air was full of dust and smoke; Galandrik, Kern, and Nuran could see humans, dwarves, and elves, all working under the watchful eye of orc guards, who carried whips and other weapons with which to beat the prisoners. Some of the slaves were shovelling coal into furnaces; others were digging, blacksmithing, or just carrying and fetching.

The trio were led down to the far side where lines of men dug away at the walls; others lugged full coal buckets to the furnaces. They were shackled by metal ankle restraints joined together as a threesome with a heavy length of chain between them, eventually connecting to a stake that was anchored to the ground.

"Dig, you pigdogs!" an orc guard snarled, cracking the whip above Nuran's head. They grabbed pickaxes from the ground around them and started to work. They looked around at the other prisoners for clues as to what they should be doing, and tried to blend in as quickly as possible. The guard moved on, cracking his whip at another human further down the line.

"This is hell! We need to get out of here, and fast," Galandrik shouted across to the others, raising his voice to be heard above all the other noises surrounding them.

"How do you intend on doing that, exactly?" Kern answered, swinging his pickaxe half-heartedly.

"There must be over fifty guards down here, and they all have big sharp weapons. Furthermore, we are shackled to each other; I think the odds are in their favour, don't you?" Nuran said sarcastically.

"I don't care! Even if I have to chew through my own leg and fight a hundred and one of them, I am not staying here!" Galandrik smashed his pickaxe into the rock.

"They will have to let us out for air and food, surely?" Nuran said, thrashing the ground with his own pickaxe.

"Yes. We will have to see how the land lies later and work out an escape plan," Kern replied. "And at least they didn't separate us – that improves our chances considerably."

The three captives fell silent and bent resentfully to their work. After an hour or two a tall elven male approached them. A short chain between his ankles limited his stride, and he was carrying an empty sack. "Hello," he said cheerfully, "I haven't seen you three before. Just been caught?"

Nuran grunted. "Yes, they caught us a couple of days ago at the Norse Keep. We arrived today."

"A little tip from me – keep working when you're talking, otherwise a guard will belt you," the man said as he opened the sack.

"I'm Kern. How long have you been here?"

"About two months. You need to be strong, so eat whatever they give you. A weak slave is a dead slave. Keep your spirit and strength up the best you can. Do as you're told and one day you might get a chance to escape. Personally, I have only heard of five attempts – but that doesn't mean any succeeded." He nodded meaningfully to the side of the slope near the entrance. Five poles stood there, each bearing a head speared onto its upper end.

"I see." Kern gave Galandrik a meaningful nod. The dwarf scowled and turned away.

"I am Nuran," the paladin said, "and our dwarven friend here is Galandrik. He's in a bad mood. He hates orcs." Galandrik's pick thudded into the rock floor, and he didn't look up.

"We all hate them. Wearing yourself out hitting the ground like that will only get you whipped once you're too tired to work anymore. And don't think breaking your tools will help," the elf said as Galandrik rained violent blows on the rocky earth. "They'll just punish you for that too! Remember – a weak slave is a dead slave. Keep working steadily, but conserve as much energy as you can. I'm Jarrow," the elf added as he filled his sack with coal.

"When do they feed us?" Kern asked.

"Three times a day. The first two are down here and the last one is when you finish and they take you out of here. They swap you out for the night shift. The food is terrible and we dread to think what it is, but they need to keep us fit enough to work. Our beds are in the little huts at the base of the big tower," Jarrow explained.

"Heavily guarded?" Kern continued with his line of questioning.

"Not really. Where you going to run to? If you haven't noticed, there's mountain on three sides; the only open side is a marsh that leads to the sea. Mix that with the fact that you're shackled to two other prisoners, I'd say the chance of actually escaping is slim." Jarrow smiled to soften the words a bit as he put the last of the coal into his sack.

"Even so, we can't stay here like this. I'd rather take my chances in the marsh shackled to these two," Kern snapped.

"Good luck then! Here comes a guard, speak again soon," Jarrow answered as he dragged the sack of coal away towards a furnace, getting a kick from the guard as he walked past.

"I hate to say it, but we really need Ty and his lock-picks," Galandrik admitted.

"Would be handy, I agree, but these shackles look rusty," Kern said. "Maybe we could smash them open."

"I wonder why they took Sol and Ty away," Nuran pondered.

"Not exactly the burliest of people, were they? Maybe they've set them doing something else," Galandrik muttered. "Cooking our dinner or something."

"Maybe they *are* our dinner!" Kern grinned, trying to lift their spirits.

"Don't even think that! I hate the taste of rat," Nuran laughed half-heartedly, but Galandrik only scowled more fiercely.

"I'm kidding," Kern said. "They're probably cooking or doing something less physically demanding, but just as horrid as this."

"I doubt that very much," Galandrik grumbled.

"Look out, another guard," Kern warned the others.

The orc guard stopped behind the trio. Dressed in filthy dark brown leather armour, he was a fearsome sight. His fangs protruded from his mouth, curling upward towards his crooked nose, which was adorned with a ring. The light green skin of his hefty arms and legs bulged with oversized muscle. The whip he carried in his hand dragged along the ground.

"A little dwarf, how sweet," he grunted in broken Human. Kern glanced over at Galandrik, who ignored the comment and slammed his pickaxe into the stone.

"Rubbish at digging, dwarves," the guard continued conversationally. Galandrik carried on, trying not to let the guard bother him. "Even the elves put more into it." At this, Galandrik stood up straight and took a deep breath.

"Easy, Galandrik," Nuran said.

"Shut it, human filth!" The orc's whip cracked inches away from Nuran's head.

"Dig, dwarf!" the orc jeered. "We had a girl dwarf here last week. She was fun," the orc goaded Galandrik. "We *all* liked her!"

With that Galandrik turned and charged towards the orc. Before he was even close, his chains tightened and he fell face-first into the dirt and stones. Nuran's ankle shackle was yanked by Galandrik's fall, and Nuran toppled over too. The orc placed his foot in the centre of Galandrik's back, and the dwarf writhed under the pressure.

"She screamed when I gutted her, too," the orc continued, then stepped away from the three of them as he shouted, "DIG!" His whip cracked once more, and Galandrik felt it rip across his back. He and Nuran got clumsily to their feet, and picking up his pickaxe, Galandrik struck blindly down into the dirt as the orc watched. He could feel blood trickling down his arm from the sharp rocks the orc's foot had ground him into.

"Don't stop again, or I'll gut you like I did her," the orc finished, and walked on to the next line of captives.

When he was a safe distance away, Galandrik spoke without breaking his rhythm. "Sorry, Nuran. He knew what buttons to push."

"That's okay. Just try to take it easy – they can make our life even more of a hell than it already is."

"Yes, it won't happen again. Fucking orcs."

The guards did their rounds every thirty minutes or so, and the time passed without further commotion. The whip cracked a few times, but it was more a gesture of power than an attempt to actually cause any damage. Even orcs knew an injured man couldn't dig.

They were given three water breaks, which seemed to come in roughly two-hour intervals. As the time approached for what they thought should be the fourth water break, anticipation made them feel even thirstier – but the fourth water break never came. Instead, after what seemed like hours, the day-shift slaves were lined up and led out of the pit, up the slope toward the huts. Lines of slaves, all shackled in threes, trundled up into the cold open air of the night. The sweat that had formed during their hours of labour was instantly chilled nearly to freezing, and they shivered in the moonlight. The silvery light shone down on them, revealing the massive black tower and the hundreds of smaller structures all around its base. The prisoners were herded to various different huts as other slaves were led past them in the opposite direction – down into the pit, to continue the night's work.

The three prisoners were led to a small hut, barely large enough to accommodate four slaves. Their guard shoved them into the single cramped room. Four straw beds lined the floor, and in the middle of the hut a metal cauldron hung over a smoking fire. Smoke rose towards the hole in the tapered ceiling, wafting away into the night.

The chain between them was long enough to let them each occupy a bed. Four battered tin bowls were scattered on the floor; Kern dished out the stew. It was the first meal they'd had since before their capture, and their hunger far outweighed their concerns about the taste or who had prepared the food. Against one wall rested a jug of water and four wooden cups; green leaves floated on top of the water.

They were about to wash the horrid taste of the stew out of their mouths with the equally horrid-tasting water, when the iron-barred door of the hut opened and Jarrow was pushed into the room.

"Well, we meet again. Saved any for me?" Jarrow picked up the last bowl and spooned out his share.

"Have you ever thought about escaping?" Nuran asked Jarrow, not wasting time with any small talk.

"Nope, not yet – but I am up for a try," Jarrow answered. "I won't do suicide runs like some have, though."

Kern poured himself a cup of water and picked out a floating leaf, throwing it onto the floor. "What are the leaves for, in the water?"

"We don't really know. Some people say it's to make you work harder; some say it makes them sleep. I think it's just to disguise the taste of the crap water," Jarrow said, finishing off his meagre bowl of stew.

Nuran lay back onto a straw bed and drifted off into a much-needed sleep.

"He has the right idea," Jarrow said, nodding at the slumbering paladin. "You'll need to sleep hard to work hard, trust me." He scraped the last spoonful of stew from the bottom of the cauldron.

"I agree. We'll talk again tomorrow and work out a way to leave this prison," Kern said, lying back and shutting his eyes. Galandrik lay awake, cursing the orcs and all they stood for as he listened to the steady breathing of the others; then his eyes, too, slowly closed.

Hodash and Grig marched Solomon and Ty to the main door of the Sanorgk Tower. The tower guards nodded at Grig as the four climbed the staircase leading up to the door. There was a guard standing at either end of every fifth step, each with a tall spear and large tower shield. Ty counted at least six pairs of guards as they climbed, their armour brighter and cleaner than the armour worn by the orc troops. This tower was clearly home to someone or something powerful, he mused.

The massive tower doors swung open and the prisoners were pushed in, their hands still tied behind their backs. The room they found themselves in was bigger than they might have imagined. In the centre, standing some thirty feet tall, was a statue of a tall, slim orc woman. A crown rested upon her head and her right hand bore a massive staff capped with a crystal orb. Her gown was regal and clung to her curves, a golden belt around her waist, golden tassels dangling. Gold and silver leaf covered her shoulders and arms. In the privacy of their own minds, Ty and Solomon both thought, *This must be Queen Valla.*

On the far side of the statue were doors – and lots of them. Orcs buzzed about everywhere. Opposite the captives, a set of stairs led up to a second-floor balcony; how high these steps went they couldn't tell, but they seemed to go up forever. Ty could smell food cooking; a glance at Solomon showed that the guide was clearly just as hungry as he was. To either side of the stairs sat two great wooden lifts. Thick ropes descended from the dizzy heights of the tower to attach to the tops of the lifts, and the walls of each were made of no more than wooden slats and iron bars.

The orcs pushed their captives towards the lift on the right. Their rope restraints were cut away, replaced by locked metal wrist bands, joined by a chain. As they entered the rickety-looking lift, they each received a blow to the back, sending them sprawling down to the floor.

"No need!" Ty winced through gritted teeth, his eyes squinting with the sudden pain. The orcs stood above them, swords drawn. Just outside the lift, a massive orc pulled down the lift gate, then turned to the side, nodding to someone they couldn't see. Slowly the lift began to move upwards, rocking and swaying as it did. As they ascended through the heart of the tapering tower, the levels got smaller and smaller. Some levels revealed four or five doors going round in a circle; some had a lone set of double doors. Other levels seemed to have no rooms or doors at all, only an open circular walkway with small slits for windows, probably used by archers many moons gone by. The lift eventually creaked to a halt, and Ty thought they must be near the top.

A burly orc guard opened the lift door from the other side. Ty and Solomon were hauled to their feet and ushered across onto the walkway.

Once the lift was empty, the big guard closed the lift door and shut the handrail; the lift then started moving slowly downwards. Ty glanced over the handrail and watched as the lift slowly descended, until a slightly less enormous guard prodded him roughly forward.

Solomon looked around the level and counted five iron-barred gates locking the rooms beyond. *Prison cells,* he thought immediately. The rooms spanned one half of the circular level, and an enormous set of wooden double-doors occupied most of the opposite half.

As the rising lift approached eye level, Ty was able to see all their possessions stacked inside it, along with two more orc guards. The lift carried on upwards and out of sight. He looked at his wrists, where his daggers used to be, and bit his lip. Grig and Hodash prodded them to within a few feet of an iron-barred door, and they all waited as another orc fumbled for his ring of keys. Eventually he found the correct key and unlocked the door, and the prisoners were pushed inside.

The prison cell was spartan. Two wooden beds sat opposite each other against the walls, three or four thin blankets heaped on each with a couple of stuffed hempen sacks acting as pillows; Ty didn't like to think about what the stuffing might consist of. Completing the room's décor, a wooden bucket sat against the far wall, and a sparse layer of straw covered the floor.

As they looked around, they heard the door lock shut behind them.

Hodash and Grig moved along to the next door, followed by the other two orcs. Ty and Solomon could hear the door being opened and some words being exchanged; they watched as a human prisoner was led out with hands chained together in front of him. He was led around to the far side of the level and through the double doors. One of the orcs stood guard outside, while the other made his rounds of the cells, inspecting all the rooms and their prisoners.

The sounds of screaming and shouting came from behind the double doors. Ty waited for the guard to pass by their cell before looking to Solomon. "When do you think we'll be dragged in there?" He raised an inquisitive eyebrow.

"I don't know, but let's hope we're not. By the sounds of that, it doesn't bode well."

"Tonight we escape," Ty said, looking around the cell as if looking for another way out.

"I admire your enthusiasm, dear friend, but how do think you can do that? We're at the top of a tower with hundreds of orc guards all around us, locked in a cell – oh! and shackled!" Solomon's sense of defeat was clear in his voice.

Ty glanced around discreetly, making sure the guard was well clear before pulling a small leather pouch from his boot. "Well, *this* is a start," he said, slipping the pouch under the hemp-sack pillow.

"Your thief's picks?" Solomon whispered, hopeful enthusiasm tinging his voice.

"No, these are my tools, *dear friend*. No prison can hold me, which is why they call me The Rat," Ty said arrogantly.

They both fell silent as one of the orc guards made another sweep of the landing. When he had passed by, Ty retrieved the pouch and unrolled it.

"What do you intend to do, exactly?" Solomon asked, keeping a watchful eye on the guard.

"For now, I'm just going to practice unlocking these," Ty said, working on the wrist restraints. "It's difficult with one hand. Then we have to hope he doesn't drag us in there tonight."

After a couple of hours, the double doors on the far side opened and the two guards entered the room beyond. They reappeared in a few moments, dragging the human back to his cell. One orc held him up on either side; his head sagged as his feet slid across the stone floor. They heard the cell door open and a groan as the human was thrown in forcefully, then the sound of the door being slammed shut and the key locking it.

The guards resumed their patrol as Hodash and Grig emerged from the far room, closing the double doors behind them. Grig patted one of the patrolling orcs on the shoulder as their paths crossed, and joined Hodash to wait at the lift gate. When the lift arrived, the larger guard secured the lift door behind them, then resumed his watch.

"So what's the plan? I don't think we are getting dragged into that room tonight," Solomon whispered.

"I think you're right. We must act tonight. If we wait, we risk getting butchered by those monsters tomorrow."

"So what is The Rat's master plan, then?"

"You see the lift rope? That's my way up."

"And then what?" Solomon kept his voice low, one watchful eye on the patrolling guards.

"Hopefully find a window or some other way to leave this foul tower."

"What about me?" Solomon added to Ty's ever-increasing list of problems.

"Well, I saw our equipment go up in the other lift. If I can find it and retrieve some weapons, we could fight these two down here – then we both go up and escape."

"Grab my backpack if you see it. I have something in there that could get us down safely if we need to jump from a height," Solomon said.

"OK, but for now we wait. I can't see these two just walking round and round all night. They must sleep or change shifts or something."

Ty and Solomon bedded down and waited. After what seemed like forever, the sound of footsteps got quieter and the scant daylight filtering in from the tower's windows faded to gray shadow. Ty rolled over and looked beyond the bars of his cell door. One guard sat on the floor with his back to the wall, seemingly in a deep sleep; the other guard walked aimlessly, kicking at thin air and marching in circles. Ty rolled off his bed and crept over to Solomon's. He whispered, "I'm going to need all the spare blankets you have and your pillow. I'll stuff it under the covers, so if he does look in he will think I am sleeping." Without another word Ty had all of Solomon's spare bedding, and heaped it up under one thin blanket, into the shape of a body.

"Ty, here he comes," Solomon said as loudly as he dared. Ty rolled silently under his bed and held his breath. The guard reached their cell door and stopped to look in. Solomon slitted his eyes, pretending to be asleep, and could just make out the guard's bulk standing in the doorway. Solomon fought to keep his breathing steady and calm – then the guard moved on.

"It worked!" Ty whispered, rolling out from his hiding place.

"Yes. He definitely stopped and looked in."

The guard made his way around to where his partner slept on the floor, and sat down beside him. Before long, his head was nodding too; he eventually fell into a deep sleep, his snores echoing around the landing.

Ty knelt down in front of his locked cell door and went to work on the lock. He held a scrap of cloth over the lock to muffle the noise. Because the lock could only be opened from the outside he had to do it blind and backwards; this skill was practiced by higher-level rogues. Ty'd had to teach himself after being kicked out of the Guild, and the many occasions he had been locked up had provided him with valuable practice.

Eventually the lock clicked.

"I'll be as quick as I can, Sol," Ty whispered, looking back at Solomon with a cheeky smile.

"Be safe – and come back with my backpack and staff." Solomon gave Ty a thumbs-up gesture. Ty paused at the door, then stepped over to Solomon's cot and unlocked his hand restraints.

"That's just in case I don't," Ty said, turning back to the door. Slowly he crept through and gently closed the door behind him. Crouching low, he moved quietly to the handrail that circled the walkway. The lift rope was just on the other side. Ty tested the handrail first for its strength, making sure it would hold his weight; the last thing he wanted was to fall to his death because of a schoolboy's error.

With one hand on the handrail he leaped up, landing with the ease of a gymnast. He held his position on the handrail for a few seconds, making sure the guards didn't stir, then leapt again, this time catching the rope. It was further away than he had anticipated; it had looked a lot closer when he'd stood next to the handrail and sized it up. Getting back would be slightly harder, he thought, but he was sure he'd be able to manage. He wrapped his legs tightly around it, and carefully edged his way upwards. Solomon watched from his cot as Ty's feet slowly disappeared from sight.

Ty climbed until he could see the floor of the next level; it was smaller than the one below and had only two doors, one on either side. A sleeping guard was slumped on the floor next to one of the doors, his head bowed and arms folded; his sword was propped up against the wall next to him and his helmet lay in his lap.

After pausing for a brief moment to rest, Ty pulled himself upwards until he could see the floor of the topmost level. It was again smaller than the last, with only one door – but sitting outside this door were three guards, playing a game of bone dice. Ty breathed a silent sigh of relief that they were on the opposite side from where he dangled on the rope.

Ty eased back down the rope, hand over hand, until he was level with the penultimate handrail. Stretching his foot as far as he could, he just managed to grab the railing with his toes, giving him enough leverage to pull himself over to the railing and jump down. He squatted quickly with his back against the railing. This was a crucial moment, he knew – if the guards above or below were to notice the rope's movement, he was done for.

He watched the sleeping guard for any movement, but there was none. Moving silently, he padded towards the doorway and slowly reached for the hilt of the guard's sword. The orc snored gently as Ty brought the sword into position, inches away from his chest.

Nah, he would still scream, Ty thought. He turned the sword and held the blade horizontally over the guard's head, ready to bring the flat of the blade down sharply. *But if I don't knock him out in one, he'll scream blue murder. Damn!* He held the hilt with both hands and held it straight over the sleeping orc's head. *Right through the skull,* he thought, and took a deep breath.

Suddenly the guard's head rolled back, and he opened his mouth in an enormous yawn. Ty seized the opportunity and forced the sword straight down the orc's throat. The orc's eyes flew open in astonished pain as Ty heaved on the sword with all the weight he could muster.

The guard reached up with eyes wide, grabbing for the blade – but just like that it was over. With one final push, Ty sank the sword hilt into the orc's mouth with a sickening crunch, snapping bone and muscle. Ty stepped back and watched as the dead orc slumped to one side.

The helmet rolled from the guard's lap onto the floor, making an almighty clatter. Thinking quickly and moving even faster, Ty reached down and pulled the guard up by the shoulder, propping him upright. Placing one foot in the guard's groin, he heaved the blade free, and the guard's head dropped forward. Ty slid the blade between the guard's arm and side, then pulled it out. *Clean as a whistle,* he thought as he propped it back up against the wall. Ty folded the guard's arms across his chest, then placed the orc's helmet on the floor next to his leg. He ran round the level until he was under the orcs above, out of their line of sight, and waited.

"Fraksh!" Ty heard someone shout from above, barely a second later. "Wake up! Grig will have your guts!"

Ty waited anxiously, but there was nothing more. The voice from above had nothing more to say, and apart from the faint sounds of chatter and skittering dice from above, there was silence. Slowly he eased back around to the door next to the dead guard, keeping a close eye on the handrail above.

He crouched there silently, waiting to hear any noise from the guards, but no alarm was raised. After several moments, he moved slowly forward to the closest door and went to work with his picks. The lock soon clicked open and, as slowly as he could, Ty pushed the door open and peered inside.

The room was a semi-circle, one large table filling the back wall. On the table were weapons – swords, daggers, bows, arrows, axes – and piles of armour that had been looted by the orcs. Ty slipped silently across the room; he found their weapons straightaway, as they had been thrown on top of the pile. Soon his precious daggers were back on his wrists, his boot daggers and small crossbow back in their places. He wrapped his cloak around him, hiding anything that might glisten in the darkness.

He gathered up the rest of the party's weapons and laid them out on an old blanket he found lying on the floor. Taking a leather drawstring from a backpack, he tied his friends' equipment up into a neat bundle, making it easier for him to carry. Then he set the bundle down next to the door. Looking around the room once more, he spotted Solomon's staff on the floor under the table. He snatched it up and laid it across the bundle.

Ty edged the door open and stepped onto the circular walkway, quietly closing the door behind him. He made his way over to the second door, keeping as close to the wall as he could so the guards above had less chance to spot him – if they were even looking. After a few moments' work with his tools, the second door clicked open – but as it did, one of the bone lock-picks snapped in two. Cursing under his breath, Ty entered the room – then immediately forgot about his broken pick. This room was a mirror image of the first one, except for the fact that this table was glittering and sparkling. Gems, diamonds, small caskets of gold, necklaces, rings, goblets – everything a dragon would need to make a comfortable bed, piled high and unattended.

Eyes wide as a child's in a sweet shop, Ty walked towards the table. He spotted his party's backpacks, tossed carelessly against a wall. When he inspected his pack, he found it had been looted; the potions had gone, but he didn't care. He tipped what was left out onto the floor – a couple of torches, flint and tinder, a blanket, and some old stale rations. He moved over to the table and began stuffing the pack with gems, gold – everything he could reach. When the pack was stuffed full, he tried to lift it, to swing it over his shoulder – but he couldn't budge it. *Damn,* he thought frantically, *how am I going to carry it? Ah! Solomon!*

He cast a look at the riches still piled on the table, wondering if he should fill another backpack. He picked a diamond out of the pile, bigger than any he had seen before. He studied it for a minute, then popped it into his mouth. After three attempts he managed to swallow it; picking up a handful of gold coins and trinkets, he distributed them over a few pockets. His mind was scrambled by the lure of the gold. He couldn't focus – his mind was swirling, trying to work out a way to take *everything*.

Then he heard a noise from outside, and snapped back suddenly into reality. He inched the door open and saw that the rope he had climbed up on was swaying – someone was using the lift. Ty stepped out into the walkway and gently closed the door behind him. Looking over the handrail he saw the lift moving up – without another thought, he vaulted over the rail and onto the rope. He slid down as fast as he could, his palms burning from the rough rope. When he came level with the handrail below, opposite his cell, he tried to catch the railing as he had done before, stretching his leg out and straining to reach the rail, but the speed of his descent ruined any chance he had of gaining a sure footing. He could see the guards, both propped up against the wall and still sound asleep.

He climbed down the rope until he was a bit lower than the handrail on his level. He knew this was the last chance he would have; the lift was only feet away and rising. As soon as he was level with the handrail he sprang from the rope. He misjudged the distance by a fraction, and his foot caught on the top of the handrail. He tumbled over the rail and landed gracelessly, rolling twice and ending up with his back to his cell door. It creaked and opened slightly; then a hand reached out and grabbed him, dragging him into the cell.

"Quick, into your bed!" Solomon whispered, closing the cell door. Ty handed Solomon his staff, which Sol quickly slid under his blanket as Ty scurried to get under his own.

The thief's noisy landing had wakened the two sleeping guards, and they sprang to their feet just as the top of the lift came into view. Unknowingly, by waking them Ty had spared them a whipping from Grig.

"Hurry up, you fool, it's our shift change! You go that way," the bulkier orc guard said to the other as he rubbed his eyes, trying to bring himself fully alert. He walked quickly to the lift door, hoisting it open just as the second guard moved into position.

"Everything OK?" Grig said, stepping out of the lift, followed by his companion Hodash.

"They're all sleeping like little mice," the guard said, yawning. After giving a brief report, both night guards entered the lift. Once they were inside, Hodash pulled down the door and secured it, and the lift descended. Within a few seconds it was out of sight.

"Let's wake these soon-to-be-dead prisoners up, shall we?" Grig said, looking at Hodash with an evil smile.

"Yeah, let's have some fun."

They walked to the nearest cell, drew their swords and rattled them across the bars as they walked, like children clattering a stick down the length of a fence. They were clearly enjoying themselves, making as much clamour as possible.

"If they hit our door, it'll open, and I can't lock it now!" Ty whispered to Solomon.

"Get ready to fight," Solomon replied, pulling the covers over his face.

The two guards reached their cell door and as Grig's sword pushed against it, it swung open. Ty's heart was beating fast and his entire body seemed to tense.

"Those stupid guards left this one open! They'll get thirty lashes for this," Grig said disgustedly. "Lock it up, quickly."

Hodash stepped forward, producing a large ring of keys from his belt. He pulled the door closed and had just put the key in the lock when Ty flung off his thin blanket, sat upright on his bed, and threw a dagger.

His aim was true. The blade struck Hodash full in the throat. Dropping the keys, the guard staggered back, grasping the dagger. He managed to pull it out of his throat, and a fountain of blood pumped from the gaping hole. He fell to his knees as blood fountained out on to the cell floor.

"No!" Grig roared, kicking open the cell door. He raised his sword and lunged at Ty. Solomon rolled out from under his covers and swung his staff into Grig's solar plexus with all his might. Grig pitched forward as the air whooshed out of his lungs.

As Grig doubled over, Ty drew his second dagger and stood up, thrusting the blade deep into the guard's chest. With one hand on Grig's back, Ty ripped the dagger upwards towards the dying orc's throat.

Grig stopped moving and fell to the floor, lifeless. His blood pooled on the floor.

"Lift them onto our beds," Ty said, taking charge of the situation. They lifted Grig and Hodash's corpses up onto the beds and covered them up. They scuffed their feet around the cell, kicking at the hay on the floor and doing as much as they could to absorb or cover the blood on the floor. Ty crawled under the beds to pull out any straw lurking there, while Solomon emptied the rags and hay from their pillowcases. Satisfied they had done their best to disguise the scene, Ty grabbed the ring of keys and left the cell with Solomon, locking the cell door behind them.

"We need to climb up to the next level," Ty said.

"What about the other prisoners?" Solomon whispered.

"Not my problem. We need to get out and find the others. We haven't got time to save everybody," Ty said with a shrug. They crept to the handrail and looked over; the lift hung unmoving, its rope only a few feet away.

"Happy?" Ty asked.

"Yes, let's go."

They jumped from the handrail, Ty going first and making it look easy. Solomon struggled at first, but eventually, with Ty's help and whispered advice, maneuvered up the rope and over the handrail on the floor above. They quickly slipped into the room with the weapons.

"Take all this; the others'll be no good without their weapons," Ty ordered. They gathered all they could manage, then stealthily made their way over to the other room.

"Now, take a look at this!" Ty said, pushing the door open to reveal the table full of gold.

Chapter Ten
The Escape

Solomon walked over to the table, eyes roving over the haul of gold and jewels. "They must be here," he said, as if to himself.

"What must be here?" Ty asked. Solomon didn't seem to hear him, and was spreading the loot about, shoving the larger items out of his way. Coins and trinkets dropped to the floor.

"Be quiet! Do you want to wake the world?" Ty hissed.

Solomon froze, then lifted out a small chest, about the same size as the potion boxes they had carried. He reached back into the pile of treasure and pulled out a second. With one in each hand, he turned to Ty.

"The King's Gold," he said, with absolute delight.

"*That's* the King's gold? You couldn't get a hundred gold pieces in those!" Ty eyed the two little chests. Despite their small size, they did look very expensive and regal, covered as they were in gold leaf and glittering with gems and diamonds. The hinges of solid mithril gleamed in the torchlight. Solomon stooped to pull a blanket out of his backpack. "I'll explain later," he said. He wrapped the chests and placed them in his backpack. He pulled out the scrolls he had found in the casket hidden in the sarcophagus and fixed them in his belt, then tied Kern's longbow and quiver to one side of his pack.

"Why not now?" Ty asked suspiciously.

"I'm not going to try to explain everything while we're in this much danger," Solomon explained, standing up and donning the pack. "Now is not the time."

"Yes, you will, Sol! Now is a perfect time! King's Gold my arse – if there's gold in those chests then I'm a bloody elf!"

"We'll need as much armour and rations as we can carry," Solomon said, sizing up the other packs and ignoring Ty's outburst.

"Fine," Ty fumed. "What about the gold, then?"

"Leave it. You'll be richly rewarded by Conn anyway."

"*Leave* it? Are you *mad*?"

"King Moriak is a very generous man," Solomon said soothingly, "and this is a pittance compared to what's stored away in his vaults."

"'What's in his vaults' – that means nothing unless he's willing to share it with me!"

"After I tell him what you've done, he will be *very* grateful."

There was a small pause. "How grateful?" Ty quizzed.

"Listen, the King treats me like a son," Solomon said, rather boastfully. "I'll tell him of your bravery and cunning, and he will make you very rich."

"The king sends you on missions to orc temples because he thinks of you like a son?" Ty scoffed.

"No, I requested to go. I wanted to repay the King's generosity in some way," Solomon lied.

"He must be generous indeed, to inspire someone to *want* to come here!"

"Trust me – he is very generous to those he favours."

Ty packed as much of the armour and rations as he could into Kern's backpack, leaving Nuran's heavy breastplate and leggings behind. He looked down at his gold-filled pack and sighed.

"We'll never carry these climbing. Leave them outside the door, near the railings. I'll climb up and drop down a rope, and we'll pull them up – but first we need to deal with the three guards." Ty was still angry about the two small chests and Sol's refusal to explain them. He was beginning to suspect that they had been tricked.

"What's the best way?" Solomon asked.

"I could probably sneak up on one and do some damage, but after that

I'd really be depending on your backup," Ty said, waiting to see if Solomon would step up to help solve the triple problem.

"Could you attack one and get away without being hit?"

"Of course. But two would chase after me straight away."

"Okay. Hit one, then run back round towards me. By that time I could do some crowd control, leaving just the last one for you to deal with?"

"What about if I attack one with my crossbow and you do whatever it is you are going to do to another, then we *both* deal with the last?"

"Sounds like a plan. Just try and do it quietly. We don't want to wake the world," Solomon replied.

"Quiet is my middle name," Ty said, leaping onto the rope.

"I thought it was 'The Rat'?" Solomon chuckled.

Ty looked back at Solomon and gave a quick grin. He shimmied up the rope to the topmost level, and jumped off over the handrail. The three guards on the other side were still at their dice game, kneeling over the dice tray and watching the tumbling cubes intently. Ty looked over the railing and beckoned Solomon up.

Solomon jumped for the rope. He didn't manage it as smoothly and adroitly as Ty had done, but he managed to grasp the rope firmly and started climbing up. Ty gave Solomon a thumbs-up, and got a nod back in reply.

Ty squatted low, and slowly moved round towards the guards. Just before the arc of the handrail, where he was still not quite in view, he pulled out his small crossbow and cocked a bolt. It was a small enough crossbow to fit inside a thief's cloak, but powerful enough to render crippling damage in the right hands. Add hemlock poison to the arrowheads and it was certain death, but without the hemlock Ty would have to trust to his aim.

Ty held the crossbow to his chest and took a deep breath. As he breathed out, he leaned forward and fired a bolt into the threesome. It struck the furthest guard in the collarbone and threw him backwards to the floor, reeling in agony. The other two guards jumped up and grabbed their weapons, which were leaning up against the wall next to them.

Solomon saw Ty's attack, and wriggled a foot or two up the rope to get a better view of his prey. Wrapping his legs around the lift rope, he extended his staff, pointing it at an orc.

"*Blaxon forchaloo!*" His shout was accompanied by a burst of white light from the end of his staff, aimed towards one of the guards. The ball of energy stuck the guard straight in the face, and he immediately dropped his weapon, bringing both hands up to his face and shrieking in pain. Still running but now directionless and unable to see, he screamed blindly straight towards the handrail.

Ty dropped the crossbow and drew his daggers. The last orc advanced, raising his sword to shoulder height. Ty, watching every movement the orc made, braced himself as the sword swung downwards; at the last instant he rolled to the orc's right.

The blow missed Ty's left shoulder by mere inches, and the sword crashed against the floor. Ty rolled and stood up, lashing with his dagger at his opponent's ribs, but the orc was too quick. He parried the attack with a swing of his sword, sending Ty's dagger flying down the walkway floor.

Ty stood with his last remaining dagger in his left hand. The orc lunged forward; Ty barely managed to sidestep the blow, slicing the orc's arm with his dagger as he did, but his strike cost him his balance. Falling down to one knee, his back against the wall, this time he feared the worst. Relentless, the orc raised his sword once more to deliver the killing blow.

But just at that moment, the screaming orc, blinded by Solomon's magic, plunged into the handrail. With his hands still covering his face as he screamed, his forward momentum carried him over the railing. He plummeted through the cavernous central emptiness of the tower to his death, his screams waking every orc in Sanorgk.

The orc above Ty was distracted momentarily by the commotion, giving Ty just enough time to roll, spring to his feet, and prepare himself to attack. The orc lunged, but Ty was ready. He dodged under the blow and thrust his dagger into the orc's stomach. Without pausing, he ran to retrieve his other dagger. The orc dropped to his knees, then rolled over, both hands clutching Ty's dagger. Ty dashed back to the orc brandishing his retrieved dagger. Without hesitation, he forced the blade through the orc's eye socket and into his brain. The orc twitched and was still.

Ty looked around for Solomon. He had climbed over the railing, but stood there frozen with fear, watching the fight.

"Thanks for the help!" Ty shouted as he pulled his dagger from the orc's eye socket.

"But... but..." Solomon stuttered.

"But *what*, exactly? The plan was for *both* of us to take on the third, not just me. If that orc hadn't gone over the railing I'd be dead!" Ty snarled, wiping his daggers on the dead orc's leather armour.

"It was all over so soon! Anyway, we haven't got time to argue – look." Solomon pointed at the lift ropes, both rising.

"'Be quiet,' you said," Ty said sarcastically.

"I didn't know he was going to run blindly over the edge! He could have just as easily run into the wall, or just stayed where he was," Solomon argued, pulling up the backpacks from the level below.

Still shaking his head, Ty ran to the big window and looked out at the ledge below. "The window, Sol," Ty said, "it's our only hope." He looked over the smashed handrail and added, "And we'd better be quick, too!" Without waiting for Sol's response, Ty turned to the dead orc and picked up his sword. Taking a step back, he hurled the sword through the window, glass flying inside and out. Ty used his dagger to knock out the remaining pieces of glass, and hastily threw his backpack on.

While Ty was frenziedly working on their escape route, Solomon asked, "What if we cut the lift ropes?"

"No time," Ty said. "Plus we'd be lucky to cut through even one. They're thick, and they're moving too fast. Come *on!*"

Ty scrambled up onto the ledge, Solomon following close behind him. Looking around for their next move, they realized there was no escape, just one huge drop. They stood on a windowsill with no way up or down. They could see the mountains all around, and the lights from the little huts below them seemed like stars flickering in the night's sky. The soft moonlight flowed over them and through the smashed window.

Ty looked back inside. "...I guess it wouldn't hurt to *try* cutting the ropes," he said.

"No time!" Solomon echoed Ty's earlier words, pulling out one of the scrolls tucked into his belt. "I knew these would come in handy," he added as he unrolled it.

"Be quick – I can see the top of the lift! What is it?" Ty asked.

"Scrolls of Featherfall. When I say 'jump,' jump straight up, as hard and as high as you can," Solomon ordered. Ty swallowed hard and nodded.

"*Flex Foucam Folly,*" Solomon shouted. With that, a red light covered them both, swirling and circling around them, then disappeared as quickly as it had come.

"Now… jump!" he shouted, and Ty jumped.

The feeling was incredible – he felt he was floating like a feather, drifting on the night air towards the side of the mountain. The wind rushed against his face as he looked back at the tower; he could see figures at the window, gesturing wildly.

They drifted for a good sixty seconds, then Solomon shouted, "Brace yourself!" above the noise of the rushing wind.

Ty saw the mountain looming ever larger as he floated slowly towards it. They came to rest some fifty feet above ground level on the mountainside. Small stones scattered and fell as they got their footing.

"Look down there," Solomon said, pointing to a small ledge below them. He jumped again. The spell was still working and he landed on the ledge with ease; Ty followed. The ledge led inwards to a small cave, just big enough for the two of them to sit comfortably. Once inside Ty turned to Solomon, grinning.

"That was by far the strangest thing I have ever done. It felt like I was floating, flying, *and* falling," he said.

"Me too. I had heard about it, but never done it."

"How long does it last?" Ty asked, crawling over on all fours to peer over the ledge towards the many small towers below.

"Not sure. Why?" Solomon replied.

"We need to rescue the others. My guess is they're in one of those small huts," Ty said as he stared at the ground below. Then in one smooth motion he spun round and brought his dagger to Solomon's throat.

"What the hell are you doing?" Solomon squawked, dropping his staff and raising his hands.

"You can't trust anybody, Sol," Ty said, stony-faced. "Now tell me about these chests."

"Okay, okay, I'll explain," Solomon said, his eyes crossing as he tried to focus on the dagger at his throat.

Ty withdrew the blade a few inches. "Yes. I think you should," he answered.

Solomon took a deep breath. "Well, remember the thief in the marketplace?"

"The apple thief? Yes, why?"

"That was me," Solomon said with a smile.

Ty sat back and thought for a moment. "I knew I recognised you from somewhere when we met," he said, "I just couldn't place you."

This revelation put Solomon in a completely different light, and Ty was thinking hard while Solomon talked. "We needed a couple of thieves to retrieve our chests," he continued. "We knew the orcs would have them here, and we knew only a talented thief could have located them." As he talked, Solomon lifted a chest from his pack and unwrapped it.

"It's starting to make sense now," Ty nodded.

Solomon placed the chest on the cave floor.

"I thought these were magically locked?"

"No, magically protected from damage," Solomon answered as he placed four fingers on four separate gems. He pushed them all at once and the lid clicked open.

"Ingenious," Ty observed.

Solomon carefully opened the lid and Ty peered in.

"It's an egg!" he exclaimed angrily. "We risked everything for a damn *egg*?"

"No, not just any 'damn eggs,' two white dragon eggs! Ty, you don't understand – these are possibly the last two in Bodisha!"

"Where is the mother dragon?" Ty asked after a tension-filled pause.

"She nests in the mountains northwest of Tonilla, why?"

"Because that's where we are taking them, not back to Conn for pets."

"You think he wants them for pets? They won't be *pets*, man! They'll be trained by the dragonriders and used in the great wars against the orcs, not *pets!*"

"I don't care! I am not sending the last two white dragons in Bodisha to their deaths!" Ty said angrily.

"You're more worried about two animals than the orc army overrunning Bodisha and enslaving us all?" Solomon asked incredulously.

"The king does not need two dragons to defeat an army of half-brained orcs!"

"It doesn't matter what he *needs*, it's what he *wants*," Solomon argued.

"Well, what the king *wants* and what the king *gets* just might be two completely different things. If you want to go back and crawl up to your precious king and tell him Ty said that, please do!"

"You would go against your king? Take the side of a dragon before your king?"

"Listen, Solomon – if that is even your name?" Ty said scornfully.

"Yes, Solomon is my name. I never wanted to lie or keep secrets from any of you. My orders are to get the eggs back to Conn. I follow orders and *I do as my King says.*"

Ty stared at Solomon for a few seconds. "Well, *Solomon,*" he said, "he isn't *my* king, and *I* take orders from no man."

"Of course he's your king!"

"Who says so? Who said he has the right to tell you or me what to do?"

Solomon gaped at Ty, thinking about the thief's words. "That may be so," he finally managed, 'but these dragons belong to King Moriak."

"There you go again, Sol. They don't *belong* to anybody! They are dragons and they were here long before that fool King Moriak!"

"Yes, but –"

"No *buts*, Sol. He doesn't own the mountains or the forests, nor dragons or men! We are free, and those who follow a fool king are bigger fools."

"But who would we follow? Who should we –"

"Solomon," Ty said, placing a hand on his shoulder, "you will follow your own dreams and make your own legends. You don't need a king to tell you what to do. You are a free man, make your own decisions in life. Life isn't a destination – it's a journey, and one that *you* must travel." Solomon bowed his head, and Ty continued, "On *my* journey with *my* decisions, I will take the dragons back to where they rightfully belong. These dragons are sacred animals. They shouldn't be enslaved by humans."

There was a silence; Solomon stared down into his lap while Ty waited. Finally Solomon raised his head and nodded.

"OK, I'm with you. What shall we do?"

Ty flashed Solomon a grin, then tucked his dagger away and dropped to all fours again, looking down at the huts below.

"First we need to find out which hut the others are in, then get them out somehow," Ty said. Then he felt a stunningly heavy blow to his head, and his world went black.

Solomon leaned over Ty's limp body. "You're right, Ty. You just can't trust anybody."

He dragged Ty inside the cave and stripped off the halfling's cloak, wrapping it around his own shoulders. He pulled a tiny box from his pack and opened it. Inside was a scrap of tissue-thin paper. Solomon cupped the tissue in his hands and, bringing them close to his face, whispered into them.

When he opened his hands, a tiny bird flew out and away into the night sky. Solomon smiled. "Fly, my baby, fly."

He tied up his backpack again and swung it over his shoulder, then jumped from the ledge of the little cave down to another outcropping a few feet below. He knew the Featherfall spell would fade out soon so he had to move fast, jumping from ledge to ledge and away from the tower. After a while the commotion from the tower got quieter, and Sol knew he needed a good head start to keep ahead of any following orcs.

Solomon was only about ten feet above the ground when he spotted a lone orc below him, walking alongside a limping horse. Solomon saw his chance.

He grabbed the biggest rock he could lift, and waited until the orc was directly below him. Then he jumped, smashing the rock into the orc's head as he landed. The orc fell instantly and Solomon quickly down and seized the reins before the horse could bolt. He touched the tip of his staff to the horse's foreleg and muttered a few arcane words as a soothing pale green light swirled briefly around the hoof the horse had been favoring. Then he jumped into the saddle, leaned forward to whisper into the horse's ear, and kicked it into a gallop. The horse ran like the wind, faster than it had ever gone before.

Solomon rode towards the mountains due north, searching out the path that had brought them here.

Kern woke up to the noise of shouting from outside their hut; he heard footsteps running back and forth along with sound of horses' hooves.

"What the hell's going on?" Galandrik asked, startled into wakefulness.

"I don't know. Sounds like the orcs are going to war," Kern answered.

Jarrow looked out through the bars. "Something's badly wrong here," he muttered as hordes of orcs rushed by.

An old man led an orc horse past their cell door. "Jumbo!" Jarrow shouted, recognizing the man. "Come over here."

The old man looked around, making sure no orcs were watching, and quickly moved over to the door, leading the mount behind him.

"What is it, Jarrow? Be quick before you get me whipped!" Jumbo had to shout to be heard over the noise and commotion.

"What the hell is going on out there? Are they going to war?" Jarrow shouted back.

"Yes, against two thieves!" Jumbo replied.

Kern heard the comment and his blood chilled. He joined Jarrow at the door.

"What do you mean, old man?" Kern demanded.

"Apparently the two thieves that were brought in yesterday killed a few orc guards, stole some of the queen's gold, and disappeared into the night!" Jumbo answered with a laugh. "Good for them, I say! Now I must go, here comes a guard," and he quickly walked on, dragging the horse behind him.

Kern sat back on his straw bed. "I can't believe that good-for-nothing, cheating little thief has left us here to die!" he raged.

"He could hardly have helped us," Nuran answered.

"But he could have *tried*," Galandrik chimed in, agreeing with Kern.

"Typical of him, to steal some gold as well. I should have known better than to trust that toad," Kern said, still furious.

Galandrik sighed. "Best we work out a plan to escape ourselves, then," he said, lying back on his bed.

"I agree. Wasting energy moaning about it is not going to help us any right now. We're digging tomorrow," Nuran said as he turned over in his bed.

"They're right, Kern," Jarrow offered. "Your friends may have deserted you, but your time will come. Now get some rest. Remember," he reiterated, "a weak slave is a dead slave."

Kern lay on his bed, cursing the day he'd met Ty 'The Rat' Quickpick.

All the times I helped him, he thought, and his stomach twisted with helpless rage.

Chapter Eleven
The Headache

"Where do you think they went?" Joli asked.

"I don't know, but if we follow this path between Gatewood and Blame down towards the Norse Keep, we can't be far away from them. We may even meet them coming out of the forest to the south."

"Maybe we shouldn't have gone to Blame."

"Well, I thought he would've headed there. Now we know they didn't, so they must have gone through the forest or down this path. Either way I think we should eat; we've been traveling all night." Bok guided his horse off the track towards Gateford Forest. He could see a little circle of trees, perfectly placed for travellers who needed shelter from the wind and rain, not too far off the road. They set up camp and settled in to eat some of their dried hard rations.

"I think they went through the forest," Joli said, biting into a piece of dried beef.

"Really. Why on earth would you think that?"

"I don't know, just a hunch," Joli answered sombrely, spitting a piece of fat onto the dirt.

Bok rolled his eyes, then got to his feet. "Can you hear that?" he asked.

"Hear what?"

"I hear a horse," Bok said, peering out through the trees to the south. "I don't believe it," he said triumphantly.

"Don't believe what?" Joli asked, finally spotting the horseman in the distance.

"That is, without a shadow of a doubt, Ty 'The Rat' Quickpick!" Bok drew his sword.

"I can't see that far; how can you be sure?" Joli asked.

"The cloak, I recognise his cloak: black hood and brown bottom," Bok answered, looking over his shoulder at Joli.

"He's far too tall for Ty."

"He *looks* taller because he's on a *horse*, you idiot. It's him, I can *smell* it!" Bok scolded.

"All right, then, if you're sure. Let's do it."

"Quick, over there – on the highest part of the bank near those trees at the side of the road. We can jump him from there. You go to that forward tree," Bok ordered as they left the clearing, "and I'll sit behind the far one. When you jump out from behind the tree, the only thing he'll be able to do is swerve straight into me." Joli followed obediently and they waited behind their respective trees, ready to put Bok's plan into action.

The rider was flying towards them, his head down as he rode his lathered mount as fast as he possibly could. As horse and rider reached the ambush point, Joli jumped out, launching a throwing axe at his mounted target.

Solomon never even saw his attacker; the axe thudded into his shoulder, breaking his collarbone. Smelling blood, the horse reared in a panic, and did exactly what Bok had predicted it would. Solomon, now in agony from the axe embedded in his shoulder and struggling to stay upright, veered straight towards him, helpless to control the horse. Bok jumped out as the mount drew level, and struck.

The blow caught the rider in the side, slicing a devastating path through his rib cage. Solomon fell from the horse, landing face down in the dirt. The horse reared up on its hind legs, flailing its forelegs at Bok before galloping off up the path. Solomon's backpack, loosened from its fastenings, fell from the saddle to the ground. Bok stood above the felled rider, raised his sword. "Payback, fool," he said, bringing his sword straight down and piercing Solomon's neck, with a sickening crunch as the sword cut through the spine. Solomon's body twitched once.

"That was a lot easier than I thought it would be," Joli said, walking over to the corpse, "but he definitely looks taller laying down."

"I told you it would be easy," Bok said, ripping his sword free. He leaned down to wipe it on Ty's cloak, then replaced it in its scabbard. He snatched up the backpack lying on the ground next to the body and turned back to the clearing.

"Drag him off to the side, out of sight, then meet me back at camp."

Joli cursed under his breath at the task ahead. He grabbed the body by the arm, dragging it off to the side of the pathway. He had already started to walk away when he remembered his throwing axe. Returning to the body, he tugged and pushed until he succeeded in rolling it over.

Solomon's eyes stared sightlessly up at him.

"Bok! I think you'd better come see this!"

Bok set the pack down and came jogging back over. "This better be good or I'll… oh." There was a long silence. "I don't believe it," Bok said, staring down at the lifeless face of Solomon.

"I think we murdered someone. I told you he was too tall," Joli said, looking at Bok.

"But, but – this is definitely his cloak!"

"I think we better get the hell out of here," Joli said, tugging to retrieve his throwing axe from Solomon's shoulder.

"For once I think you're right," Bok agreed, hurrying over the wagon path towards the clearing on the other side. Once they got to the clearing Joli saddled up the horses while Bok emptied Solomon's pack out onto the ground. He kicked through the bits and pieces, then saw the corner of one of the chests poking out of its covering blanket. Picking it up, he unwrapped the protective swaddling.

"Look what we have here." He turned the casket to admire it from all directions, greedily adding up the worth of the gilding and gemstones, the mithril hinges; he was practically drooling at the thought of how much this piece of treasure would bring him.

"Nice. What's in it?"

"How should I know?" Bok said, shaking his head in disgust at Joli's naiveté. Then he spotted another blanket-wrapped shape on the ground, and pointed it out to Joli. "Unwrap that, see if it's another."

Joli drew back the fabric to reveal another chest, as richly decorated as the one Bok held.

"There you go! Lucky dip!" Bok said, holding his up and shaking it vigorously. Joli mimicked the motion with his own casket. After a few moments of twisting and turning the coffer in all directions to examine and admire it, Bok sat on a tree stump.

"Right then, let's see what's in it." He went to work with his picks, and Joli did the same.

Ten minutes went by, in which time both had gotten the same result.

"This is a tricky little sucker," Bok declared. "I wouldn't be surprised if it's full of platinum pieces! I have heard about these tiny chests holding a small fortune."

"Mine's the same. I'm going for the smash option," Joli said, placing the chest he held on a tree stump. He walked over to his mount and got his axe out, then went back to the little chest on its tree-stump perch. He rested the axe against his legs and spat on his hands, rubbing them together.

"Platinum pieces, here I come," Joli said, swinging the axe high above his head and bringing it down with all his might. He hit the chest plumb centre. Bok, watching from a few paces away, was amazed at what he saw.

When the axe connected with the chest, there was an explosion like a massive lightning strike, sending Joli flying backwards. When the smoke cleared, the chest sat intact on the tree stump, but nothing of the axe remained. Joli lay on his back, moaning and groaning. Bok walked tentatively over to the chest and poked it with one finger. It looked the same as before – untouched, unmarked, unscathed. He picked it up, looking closer to where the axe blow had landed. Not even a scratch, dent, or chip marked the casket's surface. It looked as good as new.

"I don't believe that," Bok muttered.

"I do!" Joli said, sitting up with another groan, looking at his blackened, burnt hands.

Bok placed both chests back in their blankets and slipped them into his backpack.

"I think whatever is in those chests doesn't want to come out in a hurry," Bok said, slinging the pack over his saddle and strapping it on.

"Tell me about it!" Joli said as he searched for the remains of his axe.

"Right, then – mount up and let's get going," Bok ordered the still-shaken Joli.

"Where are we heading?"

"To Forkvain, to see Xioven the mage."

"Xioven?" Joli frowned at the suggestion. "But we still owe him, and we have *well* exceeded the time he allowed us to get him the money."

"Exactly. When he opens these for us with his magic, we'll just slip him some platinum to pay what we owe him and everyone's happy!"

"Sounds good to me," Joli replied as they rode off heading south.

Ty groaned, his eyes blinded by the daylight shining into the small cave. Gathering his muddled thoughts, he finally remembered the events of the previous night and gingerly felt the lump on the back of his head. *Solomon, you sly old dog,* he thought.

He realized how cold and hungry he was and reached into one of the backpacks, pulling out a blanket and wrapping it around his shoulders. He wondered briefly where his cloak was, then came to the conclusion that Solomon had robbed him as well as assaulted him.

He was relieved to find that Sol had left some of the rations, at least, and he pulled out some salted meat and ate mechanically. After his hunger pangs had abated somewhat, he looked down at the small towers and rubbed his eyes, still slightly dazed from Solomon's blow. He searched his pockets, but didn't find anything else missing, apart from his cloak, Solomon, and the pack containing the chests. Ty leaned up against the entrance to the cave, staying low and keeping out of sight.

Right; where are you, Kern Ocarn? He waited for hours, dozing occasionally. Finally around midmorning, judging by the sun, he saw movement down below. Groups of slaves were being chain-ganged down towards the slope of the pit, as another line of chained slaves came up and out. Squinting, he tried to spot Kern, Galandrik, or Nuran. Eventually he found them – all three of them, and someone else.

They were being led to the south of the Black Tower of Sanorgk. Not directly under him, but close enough; he thought he could get to them without being seen. He watched as they were herded into a meagre hut with a plume of smoke coming out of the top.

He gathered his gear and wondered if he could lower it all down together. He found only enough rope to make one lift, and he knew he could never get back up for a second. He decided to wait until it was fully dark, when the guards would probably be sleeping.

Everything below was quiet and still, apart from the patrolling guards that circled around the huts. They shadowed the perimeter and occasionally wandered in amongst the huts – but seemed to be paying special attention to the hut that held Kern and the others. After Ty's escape with Solomon, it seemed the rest of their party was under close scrutiny. He slowly lowered the weapon-filled pack down the mountainside. It wasn't as hard as he'd thought it would be; the pack touched down on the ground below without incident. Then he edged himself over the lip of the cave entrance, easing down from ledge to ledge, finding footholds as best he could. His light frame didn't disturb many rocks, but the odd loose stone fell down the mountainside, making more noise than he would have liked. He froze for a few seconds each time, before carrying on with his descent.

Eventually he stood next to the weapons and backpack. He grabbed Galandrik's axe, Kern's longbow and arrows, and the sword he'd picked up, not entirely certain that it was Nuran's. Slightly encumbered, he trudged on, keeping behind the little huts and close to the mountain.

When he reached his companions' hut, he waited until the patrolling guard walked past, then made his move and darted to the front door. Crouching down, he peered through the iron bars of the door, and saw four beds with four sleeping bodies.

He could hear Galandrik's familiar snore, and saw Kern sleeping fitfully in the nearest bed. As quietly as he could, he poked the hunter's bow in through the bars and tapped Kern on the forehead. Without waking, Kern swatted the bow away as if it were an annoying fly. Once more Ty tapped Kern on the head, slightly harder this time.

Kern opened his eyes and looked at the thief. One finger to his lips, Ty cautioned, "Shhhhhh." Kern grasped his bow and Ty pushed the quiver through, followed by the sword and axe.

"I thought you escaped?" Kern whispered.

"No, but Solomon has."

"Why didn't you go with him?" Kern asked.

"I didn't get an invite. I'll tell you after we get the hell out of here," Ty said. Reaching through the bars, he passed Kern the ring of keys he had stolen from the tower guard. Ty went to work on the hut lock, which opened in seconds.

Kern tried a few keys, and eventually found one that unlocked his ankle restraints. He moved swiftly to the others, waking them and unlocking their restraints – including Jarrow. He handed around their recovered weapons; Jarrow, of course, had none.

Ty opened the door and they followed him single-file around to the back and the rest of their equipment, closing the door behind them. Ty had brought all the armour and equipment he could carry, and as they retrieved their gear, Galandrik and Nuran thanked him.

"No time for that now, people. You can pat him on his back until he bruises when we are away," Kern said, swinging his bow over his shoulder. "Jarrow," he asked, "do you know a quick way out of here? We came in to the west, through the mountains."

"That way will be crawling with orcs, looking for your friend. I've heard stories about a secret passage to the east, around the back of the tower?" Jarrow offered.

"Secret passage it is, then," Kern said, looking around at the others for their approval.

"Let's get the hell out of here," Nuran said. Galandrik smashed his axe against his chest and added, "Please let us meet a few on the way!"

"I'm sure you will get your revenge, Galandrik," Kern said with a smile.

Deep inside, he was glad they were back together again, but he didn't know how to show it. With a furtive glance at Ty, he regretted having cursed him the night before.

But now wasn't the time for it. Now was the time for leadership.

They headed towards the tower, keeping to the shadows behind the buildings and hard against the mountain's southern inner wall. Once around the back of the tower, they spotted a pathway leading towards the eastern curve of the inner mountain. Troublingly, it led straight through the heart of the garrison's campsite – some fifty tents that were situated directly in their path.

Each tent looked big enough to house ten orcs, Nuran thought, and he did the math. "There could be five hundred orcs here."

"Damn!" Ty hissed.

"We've not finished yet," Kern said tightly.

"Over there!" Galandrik pointed to a stable.

"Perfect," Kern said, then told the others, "Head to the stable. Keep low."

The group snuck over to the stable, crouching behind barrels and tents as they went. When they were within about twenty feet, they could see four orcs sitting around a makeshift table playing cards at the right end of the stable. Two more guards stood talking at the other end, some distance away – the stable was huge, long enough to house thirty horses. Outside were carts lined up, three filled with ore from the mining and three filled with hay for the horses' feed.

"What's the plan?" Ty whispered.

"We need to split these up, make them easier to control," Kern said. "Ty and Galandrik, go make your way around the back of the stable. See what you can do to distract them, so we can get a bit closer. And," he added, "whatever you're going to do, try to do it quietly. We don't want to wake the world."

"Don't even think about aiming that comment at me," Ty growled.

"I'm just reminding you to keep it down." Ty shook his head and nodded for Galandrik to follow him. Kern and the others stayed low and watched.

"I'll give you *keep it down*," Ty muttered to himself as they made their way around the tents and behind the stable. Finding a likely spot behind a cart full of barrels, Ty squatted down and waved Galandrik over.

"I'll make a noise," he told the dwarf. "Keep low and behind the barn. When he turns the corner you take him down – and make sure he goes down the first time. We don't need any screaming."

"What if there are two?" Galandrik asked.

"I'll deal with the second one."

"Three?"

"Will be a crowd."

Galandrik stepped behind the back of the shed, and Ty crouched down, making sure he was well-hidden. Galandrik was only a few feet away; the orc would have to walk right between them. Ty picked up a fist-sized stone and threw it halfway up the barn wall, towards the four orcs. All four stood up and looked towards the back of the barn, and one shouted something in Orcish.

Kern, Nuran, and Jarrow watched tensely as all four orcs rose from the table and immediately grabbed their weapons. One of them shouted down the side of the barn. Then he whistled at the other two orcs, and gestured for them to walk round the far side of the barn.

"Shit," Kern whispered. "You go after those two, and I'll back up Galandrik and Ty." Without another word Nuran and Jarrow slipped after the orcs, making their way between barrels, carts, and tents – anything they could hide behind.

Kern pulled two arrows from his quiver and notched them, pulling the string back tight. He carefully turned his bow so both arrows were lying side by side, and aimed them at the orcs.

Ty shook his head and held up four fingers as he mouthed the word "four" to Galandrik; the dwarf nodded and held his axe ready.

When the first two orcs reached the end of the barn, Galandrik swung his axe straight into the midriff of the closest. The second orc stepped forward, trying to gain advantage over the back of his dead companion; as soon as his head was turned Ty pounced, and sinking his daggers deep into the orc's sides. He twisted the blades, then pulled them out and struck again. The orc fell sideways to the floor, pinning Ty beneath him. Ty's dagger was still stuck in his victim's side.

The remaining two orcs rounded the corner behind their comrades and saw the ambush. One of them leapt forward and swung his sword at Galandrik, but the dwarf parried the attack. The second stood over Ty, who struggled to pull his arm free from the weight of the dead orc lying on it. He could see the delight in the orc's eyes, like a spider preying on a fly caught in its web. The orc's mouth opened and he took a deep breath, preparing to bellow a battle cry. In the surreal slowness of the moment, Ty stared in fascination at the sharp, elongated teeth inside the orc's mouth and a line of saliva dripping from his bottom lip. Then time snapped back to normal as an arrow head appeared between the orc's teeth, having penetrated from behind through the back of his neck. A second arrow struck Galandrik's attacker in the side of the neck, and both orcs fell forward to crash on top of Ty.

Nuran and Jarrow followed their orcs around the far side of the barn and hid behind a wagon, watching as the guards looked round the end wall. Though they couldn't know what the orcs were seeing, they guessed it was Galandrik and Ty defeating the other orcs, because after these two guards had crouched and watched for a few seconds, they began quietly backing away. Nuran kicked a shovel on the ground and Jarrow gladly picked it up as the two orcs retreated ever closer.

Nuran watched as the two orcs turned and ran – straight towards them. He gave a nod to Jarrow and they waited until the orcs were level with them, then pounced. Nuran's sword beheaded the closest in one swing. Jarrow swung his shovel at the legs of the second, who immediately tripped, pitched forward, and dropped the sword he was carrying. Standing above the orc, who was crawled frantically on his stomach reaching out for his lost sword, Jarrow brought the shovel down into the exposed back of the orc's neck. His first blow only managed to make a slight cut in the crawling orc's flesh, so down he thrust again and again, dark blood splattering on the shovel until the orc was beheaded. Jarrow threw the shovel down in the dirt.

"This way," Nuran said, running past Jarrow towards the back of the barn. When they turned the corner they could see Galandrik dragging an orc by the arm. They ran over and helped uncover Ty from the pile of orc corpses.

Kern joined the group and rushed everyone into the barn, "Quickly, everybody mount up. We need to be gone before any patrolling orcs alert the world."

"Agreed, Kern, but should we cause some chaos first?" Nuran suggested.

"What did you have in mind?"

"Fire. The wagons outside are full of fresh hay," Nuran said as he led a horse from its stall. "If we set them alight, I'm sure the horses would do the rest?"

"I like it!" Galandrik smiled.

"Are all paladins as evil as you?" Ty quipped.

"Evil? I am good, killing evil!" Nuran answered. "Now bring more horses."

Keeping as quiet as possible, they quickly attached two horses to each cart, including each of the ore carts. The horses were surprisingly good-natured, and didn't offer any resistance. Aside from two patrolling orcs – both dispatched silently in less than a second – everything went quietly and smoothly. When their mounts and the carts were ready, Nuran grabbed a handful of hay. The others moved around to the side of the barn so they could mount up while staying out of sight from any orc tent.

After a thumbs up from Kern, Nuran raced over to the metal fire bin next to the orc's card table. It stood waist-high, circular and filled with wood and coals. The bottom had holes cut all around, allowing air in to feed the fire. A crude tin container hung above the bin, but its contents were anybody's guess.

Nuran dipped the handful of hay into the fire bin, and it lit immediately. Keeping low, he ran over to the carts and lit the bundles of hay. It was only moments before the panicked horses were racing through the orc tents, trailing the fiery carts behind them. Before Nuran ran to join the others, he kicked over the fire bin, sending hot coals and embers into the barn. The large wooden pillars that supported the front roof section were ablaze before he had even mounted his waiting horse.

"Go!" Kern shouted, and they set off at a wild gallop along the edge of the camp, towards the eastern path. The camp was a welter of absolute chaos and noise, shouts and screams. Tents were burning as the horse and carts ran wildly through the camp; some orcs were trying to douse the flames while others ran to stop the horses. The barn was engulfed in flames and this sent off the horses harnessed to the three ore-filled carts, trampling orcs and tents as they fled the heat and flames of the barn.

No one noticed the prisoners escaping.

"There it is!" Nuran shouted as he pointed at an opening in the East Mountains. Two orcs stood guard at the entrance, distracted and alarmed by the sounds and sights coming from the garrison camp. The party's horses bore down on them from out of the darkness, but they heard the hoofbeats too late. Before they could draw their weapons, Kern's sword had decapitated one; Galandrik's axe split the skull of the other.

They flew past the bodies and into the tunnel. Gouged out of the pure stone of the mountain, it was wide enough for a cart to travel through – easily wide enough for two mounted men to ride abreast. Their pace slackened a bit, as they didn't want to overtax the horses, but they kept moving steadily onward.

Chapter Twelve
Old Friends

Conn sat in his study, talking to Belton, his faithful friend and companion.

"Any news of Solomon and the dragon eggs?" Belton asked.

"No, but it's only been just over a week, so it's early days," Conn said, looking across his cluttered desk at his friend. Scrolls, parchments, and random pieces of paper lay strewn all over his table.

"Where were King Moriak's men taking those eggs, when the orcs stumbled across them?" Belton asked Conn.

"To be sacrificed to the gods," Conn answered coldly.

There was a small silence. Belton said tentatively, "I support King Moriak one hundred percent, but I… I just don't know if I agree with the deliberate extinction of white dragons, just to appease the gods."

"You know how ill he is; he thinks it is the ultimate sacrifice. He thinks the gods will bless him with eternal life or something. And don't let anybody hear you say you disagree with anything the king does, or he'll have your head on a pole before you can say 'dragon'."

"He may be ill, but I don't think it's any sickness of the *body* that's making him kill dragons."

"Something is twisting his mind?"

"I think it's his son, Hordas," Belton ventured. "He's evil, that's all there is to it. Rumours are he fills the king's head with these pathetic stories about gods and killing dragons."

"Maybe he does, but that doesn't change things. You just can't speak against him."

"Still doesn't make it right, either."

"Listen, friend, I am not saying I agree – but it's the king's wishes, and what he wishes for, he gets. It's too far gone now anyway. We've killed every white dragon from here to hell, and those last two will go the same way, whether it be the king's wish or his son's. They only kill the farmers' livestock, anyway. They're vermin, a bloody nuisance!" Conn argued, as he opened the study window to let in some fresh morning air.

"Nonsense and you know it! They were here long before we were, and all we have done is hunted them. I'm damn sure they killed sheep, cows, and wild horses before we stuck a fence round the beasts and declared ourselves their owners," Belton said, clearly angry.

"We don't know if these are the last two *existing*," Conn said placatingly. "Just the last two we can *find*."

"Well, that's okay then," Belton said sarcastically.

"I know, friend – it's not right… but that's life," Conn said, putting an end to the conversation.

Just then, Solomon's messenger-bird landed on the windowsill, then fluttered into the office and onto Conn's cluttered desk. He gently scooped the bird up into his hands, wrapping his spindly fingers round it, and held it up to his ear.

"Well, my friend, I think you have talked the dragons up," Conn said, opening his hands and sprinkling bits of paper, like tiny feathers, onto the floor.

"What's the news?" Belton asked.

"Solomon has the eggs, and he rides back. He should be here in four days. Kern and the others are dead," Conn said rising to gaze out of his study window.

"That boy is full of surprises," Belton said, standing up to join Conn.

"Aye, he is; he has come up in leaps and bounds. I just wish my sister were here to have seen his progress," Conn said.

"Yes, such a shame. Childbirth is a cruel thing; one second giving life, the next moment life taken away," Belton said, placing a hand on Conn's shoulder in consolation.

"Very true," Conn agreed with a sigh. He picked a little piece of tissue paper from his pocket and cupped it in his hands. He whispered into his grip, then opened his hands to release a little green-speckled bird which flew off and away, into the air. "Fly, my baby. Fly," he whispered.

The party slowed their pace in the tunnel, confident that no orcs had followed them. Kern turned in his saddle to speak to Ty.

"So what happened with Sol then?" the ranger asked.

"Well, remember that apple thief we helped in the marketplace?"

"Yes, the one *you* helped that landed us in prison. Kind of hard to forget," Kern laughed.

"He and Solomon are one and the same."

"What are you saying, it was all planned?"

"Yes," Ty said bitterly. "There is no 'king's treasure' or one thousand gold in reward. Never was."

"I told you! What did I say from the start?" Galandrik exclaimed.

"You did, friend, indeed you did," Kern sighed. "So what was it he wanted us to do, then, if there were no chests full of gold?"

"Oh no, there *were* two chests; we found them in the Black Tower. They were just not full of gold," Ty explained.

"I don't understand, to be honest," Kern said as he shook his head.

"In each chest was a white dragon's egg. Maybe the last two in Bodisha."

"Bloody dragon's eggs?" Kern said, surprised. "So we travelled all this way for bloody *dragon's* eggs?!"

"King Moriak wanted them to use against the orcs in the great war, apparently," Ty said with a shrug of his shoulders.

"Strange, I thought dragons took years and years to mature," Nuran chipped in.

"No idea," Ty said. "I'm just telling you what Solomon told me, before knocking me out and stealing my cloak." He ran his hand over the lump on the back of his head.

"Solomon knocked you out?" Galandrik asked with a doubtful chuckle.

"Yes, you want to feel the lump? I really didn't think he had it in him."

"So what are you going to do now, then?" Jarrow asked of no one in particular.

"Who *is* he?" Ty asked, frowning at Jarrow.

"I am Jarrow. I have been a slave to the orcs for the last two months, and you have released me from that life. I am very grateful for what you've done for me."

"Don't mention it."

"As we all are, Ty," Kern said awkwardly, then hurried on, "and the answer to your question, Jarrow, is I have no idea."

"Head to Forkvain and think about it," Galandrik said.

"Well, we can't catch Solomon up, and I wouldn't think Conn wants us dead now that we've done his dirty work," Kern mused. "So it looks to me like we are free to do whatever we want, to be honest."

"We are officially free!" Galandrik cheered.

"True," Ty said dryly, "apart from the five hundred crisped orcs who want us dead, we should be fine!" He sighed, weary from the night's exertions. "Let's get to Forkvain, like Galandrik said, and sleep on it. Maybe we can find work."

"Have we any money to buy a beer?" Galandrik asked.

"Yes, I took the liberty of borrowing some gold," Ty said. "I wanted to take a sackful, but Solomon convinced me that Conn's reward would be just as profitable. He really was good," Ty admitted ruefully.

"I bet he led us into the Norse Keep on purpose, so the orcs would take us to the tower," Galandrik said.

"Probably. They had it completely worked out, I guess," Kern said. "But let's just forget it now and get to Forkvain." He glanced over his shoulder, looking back down the tunnel.

"What I don't understand is why he knocked you out," Galandrik queried. "Why not just let us accompany him back to Conn? It didn't matter to us whether it was gold or dragon's eggs in the chests."

"Probably so they never had to cough up the gold for your reward,"

Nuran said.

"Well, actually I think that could have been my fault," Ty admitted.

"Go on," Kern smiled. "This should be good."

"Well, I told him that we were going to take the eggs back to the mountains north of Tonilla and give them back to the mother dragon," Ty elaborated.

"That is very honourable of you, sir," Nuran said soberly.

"Thank you. I was so angry about being tricked and having no reward, I just thought 'sod Conn – we'll do what's right, deny him and the King's wishes, and hand the eggs back.' But all it got me was a lump on the head," Ty said, rubbing the sore knot again.

They proceed down the tunnel until it came to a dead end. They dismounted and looked around, Ty checking for any signs of hidden levers or switches, but no one found anything promising.

Then Galandrik said, "Feel this, there is a draft here."

Nuran walked over and held out a hand. "You're right," he said. "I think this is a door more than a wall. Let's give it a push." He placed both hands on the wall and planted his feet. Jarrow, Ty, and Kern all squeezed in to help.

"One, two, three… push!" Nuran ordered.

They strained to dislodge the giant stone block. At first their efforts seemed fruitless, but then they could feel it starting to move. They managed to push the block just enough for them – and the horses – to squeeze through the opening. They could feel the wind through the doorway and stepped out into the open air. They found themselves in an open field; apart from a few scattered trees, the land was empty, just miles of lush green grass.

"I think we'd better keep on moving," Nuran said.

"Yes, we kicked a massive ant's nest back there," Kern agreed. "I don't think it'll be long before they put out the flaming tents and want to know whose boot it was."

The party moved on, heading east towards the town of Forkvain. Ty shared out what little food he had taken, and they ate as they rode, thinking it better to keep moving except for brief stops for water and rest for the horses. Morning came and went; still they pressed on, though they were confident that no orcs had followed them.

Eventually they saw Forkvain in the distance, and the mood changed.

"Thank the gods for that," Galandrik said into the silence.

"Aye, I am starving," Kern admitted.

"Me too," the paladin added. "And to have a bath would be a delight," he said, lifting his arm and sniffing.

"I could sink a pint of mead!" Jarrow laughed.

"Excuse me, but as far as I am aware you lot haven't got a pot to piss in between you. So how exactly are you paying for food, baths, and mead?" Ty asked as they trotted along.

"I have some money in Forkvain," Jarrow replied.

"You know I'm good for it!" Galandrik chimed in with a wink. Ty revelled in the fact that he was the only one with money, that they would have to rely on him to pay. They rode on towards Forkvain, spirits rising.

Forkvain was a large city, nearly as big as Raith. A massive wall surrounded the city, as was common for most towns and cities in Bodisha. Orc attacks were a constant threat, especially in the eastern lands. Forkvain catered to adventurers and traders, boasting shops selling weapons, armour, magical items, and adventuring equipment. A small marketplace with a row of workshops at one end completed the town. The militia's presence was greater here than in other places around Bodisha. The King's Army trained to the south of Forkvain, and this town served as the new recruits' first training post.

Kern rapped on the massive gate with his fist. The wooden slide in the door opened and a set of eyes peered out.

"What's your business in Forkvain?" the voice behind the door asked.

Before Kern had time to answer, Jarrow stepped forward and in a confident and assured voice said, "Lord Jarrow and his companions wish to enter," as he looked through the door slit.

"Well, why didn't you say?" the voice replied.

"*Lord* Jarrow?" Kern asked, raising his eyebrows.

"Why didn't you tell us?" Nuran asked.

"You didn't ask," Jarrow replied, walking his horse through the open gate and into the town.

"Now there's a turn-up for the books – someone more important than *you*," Ty said as he moved past Kern.

They rode through the town's streets until they reached an inn called The Bull; they tied the horses up outside and entered. It was a large establishment, but quite empty. They settled in at a round table. Jarrow spoke to the innkeeper, then joined the others. Five flagons of ale were soon brought to the table, and before long the table teemed with bowls, plates, and cutlery. The barmaids scurried about bringing trays of roast pig, breads and cheeses, a saucepan full of chicken stew, and fruit.

"Tuck in, lads, this one is on me," Jarrow said. Their relaxed chatter fell silent as they devoted their attention to the first real food any of them had had in days.

After they'd all eaten their fill, Kern leaned back into his chair. "Where shall we start, Lord Jarrow?"

Jarrow chuckled at his remark. "I'm not a Lord. I don't wish to be one and I have no land," he explained. "All it signifies is that I have acquired some antiquities on my travels and amassed some wealth, but I am no Lord. The title is merely honorary, and was given to me when I donated some gold to Forkvain, that's all."

"So how did you end up in the orc mines?" Nuran asked.

"I was ambushed just south of here, overrun as I rode," Jarrow replied.

"That's what happened to us, overran," Galandrik said. "Couldn't fight that many, plus it was a trap."

"How long has that tower been there?" Ty cut in.

"Not long; it's the iron ore. They mine for it, make the weapons, then ferry them to whatever war they need them for," Jarrow said, picking up a chunk of bread and stepping away from the table. He walked over to the innkeeper and they had a brief and whispered conversation. Jarrow shook the innkeeper's hand, and returned to the table.

"I thank you again for your help. It was greatly appreciated. If there's anything I can do for you, come and see me. I live at the far end of the town in a farmhouse. There's a big tree just outside the front door. The locals call it 'The Dead Man' because of the way the gnarled bark has fashioned a face that looks distinctly like an old man. There are two large branches which never grow leaves; they say those are his arms, and there is even a split in the base of the trunk making it look like his legs are underground. Some say it moves a bit towards the east every year." Looking around at the faces of his friends, Jarrow laughed self-consciously. "That's the historian in me, I'm afraid. Anyway, you really cannot miss it," he said, then went around the table, shaking their hands one by one.

"Again, I am truly grateful for the help, but I must bid you farewell now," Jarrow said. "I have been away for some time and I am eager to get back to my business. Please excuse me," then, with a slight wave and a nod to the innkeeper, he was gone.

"What a nice man," Nuran offered.

"Yes, and him being a Lord was a surprise," Kern added.

"We break him out of hell itself and he buys you a bowl of stew!" Ty burst out. "That squares it just because he's a Lord – excuse me, because he *calls* himself a Lord?"

"What did you want, fourteen horses?" Galandrik said, polishing off his flagon and waving the innkeeper over.

"Yes! That would have been a good start!"

The innkeeper reached the table. "More ale?" The innkeeper was a portly man, and his red cheeks glowed in the firelight.

"Yes please, good sir," Galandrik answered. Moments later, he returned with four full flagons.

"How much is that?" Galandrik asked, with a sideways glance at Ty.

"Lord Jarrow has paid for anything," the chubby innkeeper answered, "all the food and drink you want, your rooms for the night – oh, and breakfast, as well."

"Say, what do you know of Lord Jarrow?" Ty asked the innkeeper.

"Not a lot, really. He moved here a few years ago and has shown us nothing but kindness. Some people say he has slayed dragons and stolen their gold. In his house he has a dragon's head on the wall, and he says it was his first ever kill! But it's all old wives' tales, if you ask me." He waddled off back to his place behind the bar.

The group chatted as they drank, catching up on the time they'd spent apart. Ty told of the fight with the tower guards – adding a few more orc guards to the scene for good measure. He told of the window jump, and how they'd floated down to the mountain with orc arrows whistling past their ears as they went. The inn was filling up now; the party were all merry and the stories were flowing with ease.

"Nuran Iffes," came a booming voice from the direction of the bar. "I thought you were dead?!" Nuran turned, and his face lit up with pleasure.

"Haydar! You old dog, you," Nuran replied, going over to the man. They greeted in the old paladin way, grasping each other's forearms.

"What the hell you doing down in Forkvain?" Haydar asked, still gripping Nuran's forearm with one large hand, the other coming to rest on Nuran's shoulder.

"Well, to be honest it's a long story. How long have you got?"

"Actually just until tomorrow morning. That's when we leave to go to Tonilla."

"Heading to Tonilla? Why Tonilla?"

"That's how far the orcs have come – well, nearly that far. They're coming from the east; Tonilla should be under attack in three weeks," Haydar explained.

"Really, that's bad news. You know about the tower just west of here?" Nuran asked.

"We have heard rumours about an orc tower that makes the weapons and uses humans as slaves."

"The Horseshoe Mountains west of here, it's hidden in there. They are digging for iron ore and making weapons. If you put a stop to it maybe it would hinder their advance?" Nuran suggested.

"Sneaky little buggers, on our turf too! We heard about people disappearing and skirmishes between humans and orcs," Haydar replied, "but put it down to renegade orcs on personal conquests – didn't realize they had settled in!" He paused, twisting his moustache, apparently in deep thought. "We've got a thousand camped to the east, ready to advance north; we could split some and take a few hundred to the Tower," Haydar said, thinking out loud.

"It might be worth your while. I know a hidden entrance to the west, under the curve of the mountain."

"I'll speak to my superiors and tell them of your story. In fact," Haydar asked, "why don't *you* come and tell them?"

"Well, I haven't been with the paladins for a while, since I joined the Truelight," Nuran answered sheepishly.

"That's all in the past, Nuran. Plus, with the information you are going to give them, they'll welcome you back with open arms. We cannot find enough good men these days," Haydar replied, pressing the point.

"All right, I'll come with you and talk to them - but only because it's the right thing to do, not because I'm joining up again."

"Good, good," Haydar answered, finishing off his flagon of mead.

Nuran went back to the table and explained his plan to the others. "So I'll be back either tonight or first thing in the morning," he finished.

"No worries," Kern answered.

"See you later, big guy!" Ty's cheeks sported a reddening glow from the mead that coursed through his body.

"It must be your round, lad!" Galandrik slurred in Nuran's general direction.

"It's free, you great bearded fool!" Nuran laughed back at the dwarf, patting his shoulder as he left the pub with Haydar.

"I'll get these, I need the toilet anyway," Ty said as he rose, slightly unsteady on his feet. He approached the bar and called to the innkeeper, "Here please!"

"Would you like the same again, my good man?" he asked.

A man next to Ty at the bar turned and shouted to the innkeeper. "Oi, I was here first!" he complained angrily, and loudly enough to make Kern and Galandrik turn their heads.

The innkeeper found himself in a slight predicament, but ignored the human and kept his gaze focused on Ty.

"Yes please, I'll take three ales," Ty said, raising his voice as though he were the victor in an argument.

"If you serve this little pig dog before me I will not be best pleased," the human said, looking directly at Ty.

"Pig dog?" Ty said taking a step back. "Did you call me a pig dog?"

"No, I called you a *little* pig dog!" the human answered, bending down to Ty's eye-level.

Kern got up, empty flagon in his hand, pretending to be carrying it back to the counter. It was plain that the confrontation was getting a little too heated, and he tried to smooth things over. "Look, let's all just get some ale and calm down," he said evenly.

The big human swivelled his head to look at Kern. He drew himself up to his full height, towering over Kern by several inches. Out of the corner of his eye, Kern also noticed three of the human's friends, each getting ready to join the fracas. "And you must be Pig Dog's dad?" the human said, folding his arms. Galandrik made his way over to stand next to Kern. "And you must be Pig Dog's mummy!" The human began laughing heartily, and all his friends joined in on his joke.

"I think she's going to cry, Drigo," one of the men said.

Kern turned to the dwarf. "Mummy?" he said out of the corner of his mouth.

"Shall we?" Galandrik muttered back.

"We shall," Kern answered.

With that, Kern swung a fast right hook, smashing Drigo square on the jaw. Drigo's head was jolted backwards and he took a step back, then turned back to Kern. With a bellow of rage he launched a punch of his own, hitting Kern on the side of the face. Kern was knocked sideways and down to the floor. Galandrik easily ducked an awkwardly-aimed punch from one of the other men and landed an uppercut, knocking that opponent out cold – but another blow hit him straight on the jaw. The force of impact knocked him backwards, but he managed to stay on his feet. Ty picked up a barstool and brought it crashing down on Drigo's back, knocking him to his knees.

Another human ran at Kern, delivering a powerful kick to the stomach as Kern was getting up. Kern was knocked back down, and he rolled onto his back. Drigo turned, still on his knees, and swung a punch at Ty, hitting him in the ribs and sending him crashing into the bar.

Galandrik managed to parry another oncoming punch, then sent an elbow cracking into the attacker's face, knocking him backwards to the floor. Kern blocked another kick to the head, grabbing his attacker's foot. With a sharp twist he spun his assailant off-balance, and a sickening crack was heard as the man's ankle dislocated. Screaming and sobbing, he fell to the floor and rolled around there in agony.

Drigo – now standing above Ty – drew a dagger from his belt. Ty looked up and spotted the blade, then shouted, "He has a weapon!" Hearing this, Galandrik charged at Drigo and jumped onto his back, covering and gouging at his eyes.

Drigo swung his dagger blindly behind him and managed to stab the dwarf in the shoulder. With a howl of pain, Galandrik fell to the floor; Drigo spun around, sneering down at the injured dwarf, and raised a foot.

Ty rolled away from the bar and in the same movement drew his dagger and sliced it across the back of Drigo's supporting leg, severing the tendons there and sending the big man plummeting backwards screaming. His head slammed into the bar, knocking him out cold.

Kern regained his feet an instant before his attacker did. Kern stood his ground. The man drew a dagger and lunged at Kern, thrusting forward, then swinging left to right, Kern managed, barely, to sidestep the attacks. Then, grabbing a metal bowl from an abandoned table, when his attacker thrust forward again Kern seized the advantage, stepping forward into the space created by the other man's lunge and smashing the bowl into his opponent's face, sending him reeling, staggering, and finally toppling over, unconscious.

The last man gingerly climbed to his feet behind Kern, raising a rusty blade above the hunter and preparing to plunge it into his back. That was the last thing he did as a living man; Galandrik's hand axe thudded into his back, knocking him forward into Kern. Kern turned and gripped the man's arms, not knowing a strike from the rusty blade wasn't to come. The man's eyes rolled in his head and he dropped the weapon, pitching to his knees. Kern let go and his assailant fell face-first into the floor as a corpse.

At last, six town guards burst in through the front door. The innkeeper rose from his hiding place behind the bar and grabbed a guard by the arm. Waving his arms about his head and gesturing at the four men on the floor, he volunteered a disjointed and spirited account of events, explaining how Drigo and his men had started the brawl, though the others had very thoroughly finished it.

The guards took down the innkeeper's story and the three unconscious men were dragged out to be carried off to the guard house; the dead man was tossed onto the back of a cart. Barmaids came round from their hiding places behind the bar, buckets and brushes in hand to clean the blood from the floor.

After thanking the innkeeper, Kern, Ty, and Galandrik sank back down into their seats, nursing their wounds.

"Like the good old days, eh?" Kern said, glancing at Ty.

"Yes, but they hurt worse now than they did then," Ty replied.

"You can say that again!" Galandrik rubbed his bruised and bearded chin.

"What a pointless death, though. All that over waiting for a jug of ale," Kern reflected.

"Not that pointless!" Ty answered, dropping a money pouch onto the table.

"You stole his money?" Kern asked, sounding aghast.

"I don't really consider it stealing. More like compensation for the injuries," Ty said, his hand pressed to his ribs.

"You are one sneaky little pigdog," Galandrik laughed. He winced as he tested his shoulder's movement, then relaxed, realizing the wound wasn't as bad as he had first thought. Kern ordered another round of ales.

The next morning the group was sitting eating breakfast and discussing what to do next, when Nuran came in through the front door, and sat down at the table. He was acting sheepish, and Kern suspected something was afoot.

"Morning, Nuran," Kern said tentatively.

"Hm. Depends on how you look at it?" Nuran answered. All three looked up from their breakfast at the paladin. "I… uh… I have something to tell you all," Nuran said, clearing his throat once or twice and not meeting anyone's eyes.

"You found us some work and it pays a king's ransom?" Ty said, uncomfortable with the sudden tension in the room.

"No, I am afraid not – unless you want to ride to war with me," Nuran answered without lifting his gaze from the table.

"To war?" Kern echoed his words. "You're re-joining the paladin ranks?"

"Yes, I am afraid so," Nuran said. "Haydar said I could help lead the attack on the orc tower, then they want me to re-join the others at Tonilla," he explained.

"Maybe we *should* join you," Galandrik said.

"Maybe *you* should!" Ty said snidely, with a sideways glance at Kern.

"It's a worthy cause, Nuran. Our blessing goes with you," Kern said sadly.

"Thank you. I'm sure our paths will cross again someday. I will always be in your debt for rescuing me from the orcs," Nuran said as he rose from the table, "and one day I may repay you."

"Stay for breakfast at least," Ty asked.

"Sorry, we must leave right away," Nuran said. As he began to walk away from the table, he muttered, "Maybe it's better this way. I'm no good at goodbyes."

Kern quickly stood up and blocked his way, then reached out to clasp Nuran's hand. "Goodbye, friend," he said simply.

"Goodbye, all," Nuran said, shaking Kern's hand in the paladin way. Then he turned and left the inn.

"Then there were three," Ty said as he stabbed his fork into a sausage.

"I liked him," Galandrik mumbled. "Very honest and trustworthy, a true gent."

"Paladins are like that," Kern agreed.

"Right, let's go find another tied to a tree then!" Ty laughed.

"Oh come on, you liked him as much as we did," Kern replied.

"You liked him because he saved your bacon when he destroyed all those skeletons."

"Rubbish," Galandrik chipped in. "We had it completely under control."

"Really? It looked different from where I stood," Ty laughed.

"Hiding behind that gate, I guess it would look different!"

Ty frowned at the dwarf. "Hiding? If I remember rightly I –"

"We *all* did well," Kern interrupted, and shook his head.

"Yes, he was a good man," Ty agreed, "but with or without him, we need to sort out where we are heading next."

"I've been thinking – we should sell those orc horses and buy some normal ones," Kern suggested. "Restock our equipment and maybe head south."

"What about north, back to the ferryman to see if our horses are still there?" Galandrik suggested.

"Could do," Ty said, scratching his stubbly chin. "Then push on to Praise and pick up some work."

Kern stretched. "But if the horses aren't at Finn's," he said, "we'd have to ride the orc horses all the way. The brands on them would stand out a mile and I don't think we need any more attention." He moved to a window and stood looking out at the hustle and bustle of the traders as they prepared for the morning market, pushing barrows and driving carts filled with all manner of goods. He seemed to be deep in thought.

After a brief silence, Ty spoke up. "What about getting some new horses here? Then, if our horses *are* with Finn, we can sell them at Praise for a profit."

"That might be a better idea," Kern agreed.

"Right – here's some gold, courtesy of Drigo and his pals," Ty said, dropping four gold pieces onto the table. Galandrik and Kern each took two of the coins.

"We'll get equipped and meet back here at midday. I'll sort the horses out later," Kern said.

"Sounds good to me," Ty said. "Think I'll go for a bath and a shave."

Galandrik sniggered. "Bath sounds very good, then maybe some female company."

Kern and Ty shared a glance and a smile at the dwarf's eager tone, then they went their separate ways.

Chapter Thirteen
We Meet Again

Bok and Joli sat on their mounts watching the smoke rise from the town in the distance. The near-total lack of cover, aside from a few scattered trees, made this an ideal vantage point: The view was clear for miles. To the west stood the mountain range that surrounded the temple of Sanorgk, and to the east was the town of Forkvain, home of Xioven the mage.

"I have a quick question." Joli said, turning in his saddle to look at Bok.

"What is it now?"

"If Xioven is there, what if he opens the boxes but there is nothing inside? Then we still owe him money and we still don't know Ty's whereabouts."

"They won't be empty. Trust me, magically-sealed boxes always hold something valuable," Bok reassured him.

"I hope you're right. We're low on supplies," Joli whined, "and we only have enough money for one comfy night's sleep in an inn. And I don't want to go back to pick-pocketing."

"I said *trust me*." Bok glared at Joli, who clamped his lips shut and kept any doubts to himself.

The pair rode on and reached the gates of Forkvain just after midnight. After convincing the night watchmen on the main gate that they were coming into the town to work as personal guards for a very private but important businessman, they were inside and riding their horses through the town.

"It's too late to go see Xioven tonight," Bok decided. "We'll have to go in the morning."

"Good," Joli answered. "I'm starving. We've been riding for days without a decent meal or rest," he said dispiritedly.

"Look, there's the Bucket of Blood Inn. Let's head in." Bok tugged on the horse's reins and gently kicked his horse in the direction of the Inn.

After an uneventful but enjoyable evening of ale and food, the pair paid for a room and bedded down for the night. In the morning over breakfast, Joli was thoughtful.

"If there *are* a few platinum pieces in these boxes, are you still going to look for Ty?" He wiped his plate with a chunk of bread.

"No, I'll put a platinum piece on his head and let others fight over him," Bok answered.

"I'll double it," Joli said, laughing.

"To be honest, I think he's dead already," Bok continued.

"Why do you think that?"

"Because of his cloak on the other man. Why would he give it up?"

"True. Maybe that fellow stole it?"

"Maybe. Whatever the truth may be, he'll either turn up or he won't." Bok said, standing up. "Let's go see Xioven."

"Can our horses stay here until later, good man?" Joli shouted across the bar to the innkeeper. The innkeeper nodded his approval, and Bok and Joli left the Bucket of Blood Inn headed for Xioven's shop. The streets were busy with people scurrying about on their morning business. After walking aimlessly for ten minutes, Bok stopped a young man walking past. "Excuse me, could you tell me where I could find a magic shop around here?"

"There's only a couple. You have *Fire and Water* and *The Quarterstaff*. Just carry on along this road and you'll walk right by both, one on either side of the road."

"Thank you."

"No worries," the man said and went on his way.

After only a couple of minutes Bok saw the hanging sign, rocking gently in the breeze, "There it is," he said, pointing across the street. "The Quarterstaff."

They crossed to the shop, pausing outside the window to look in. Potion bottles bubbled, jars and vials of ingredients lined shelves, and boxes of books were stacked everywhere. The place looked more like a jumble sale than a shop.

When Bok pushed the door open, it brushed against a bell hanging just above and set it to jangling. A voice from the back of the shop shouted, "Two seconds," as they closed the door behind them.

Before long a short bearded man walked through from the back room and through a curtain made of long strings of beads.

"What can I—" Xioven stopped short and stared at the customers. Then he placed his fists on his hips. "Well, well! I hope you've come to pay me what you owe?" he said sharply.

"Yes, old friend! You didn't think we would forget about it, did you?" Bok answered with a smile.

"Would we do that to you?" Joli quickly added.

"Well, you're here now. Let's see it," Xioven answered. Bok quickly took off his backpack and reached in, pulling out the two bundles of cloth. He placed them onto the counter and slowly removed the coverings; the two little chests looked as shiny as new.

"This is your payment?" Xioven asked, bending down to examine the chests.

"Well, not exactly. We need you to open them," Bok said, smiling ear to ear.

"I see. You've stolen these and think there is something of value inside, so you want me to open them. If there is, you will pay me back, and if there isn't, you will make some excuse and leave town again. Is that about right?" Xioven said with a wry smile on his face. Bok looked at Xioven and frowned with a disbelieving look.

"I'm hurt," Bok answered, shaking his head.

"So I'm right then?" Xioven replied, folding his arms.

"Hmm, yes – sort of," Bok admitted. "But even if they are empty, the gems on each box should be enough to cover our little debt," he added quickly.

"Considering that you probably won't pay me otherwise, the boxes will do as payment," Xioven admitted, picking up one of the boxes. "Looks finely made, for sure, and the mithril hinges alone should be worth a good bit." He picked up the other chest and gave them both a gentle shake.

"Let me get a spell for these," Xioven said, slipping through the hanging beads to the back room.

"See! I told you he could do it," Bok said, turning to Joli.

"I hope you're right. We'll be rich!" Joli answered

Xioven returned with a scroll, then placed one of the boxes onto the counter, clearing off a space around it. He unravelled the scroll and began reading aloud, in a language that neither Bok nor Joli had ever heard. As he finished reading the scroll, it vanished in a tiny puff of red smoke; a circle of red light seemed to spin and whirl around the box before it also disappeared.

"That, my friends, is *open sesame!*" Xioven said, spinning the box around towards him. He rested his hands on the chest for a moment, as if to draw out the suspense. "Let's see what you've got," he said, and attempted to lift the lid.

The lid wouldn't budge. Xioven lifted the box for a closer examination.

"Strange," he muttered. "Must be a higher level than that – probably a magical lock. Hold on," he said, walking to the back again. This time he returned with a hollowed-out elephant's foot containing dozens of wands. Some were wooden, twisted like the fingers of old trees; others were metal, sleek and shiny with pointed ends. There were thick wands and thin ones, long and short, fancy and plain – each one different from the next.

Xioven rummaged through the wands. "Magic missile, wand of wonder, identification, fireball, teleportation… Ah, here it is!" he exclaimed. "A high-level open-locks." He pointed the wand at the chest on the counter.

"*Cori porrt flal,*" Xioven shouted, and a green flash of light erupted from the wand. It engulfed the box, spinning around it in all directions before suddenly disappearing. Xioven tucked the wand into his belt and, with a grunt, tried to lift the lid – but to no avail. It was still locked tight.

"Damn, this lock is more powerful than I thought," Xioven said. "I'll need to go see my old friend Donovan. He will have something that will open this." He placed the two chests on the shelf behind him. "Come back tonight just before dark fall and I'll have them open," he said.

Bok reached across and grabbed the shopkeeper by the collar of his robe, dragging him halfway over the counter. "Don't even think about cheating us, mage," Bok said, nose to nose to Xioven. "You know what will happen if you cross me."

"Don't judge everybody by your standards, rogue," Xioven answered with a splutter.

"Just as long as we are perfectly clear," Bok said through gritted teeth, and released his hold on Xioven's robe.

"As I said, be here tonight just before dark fall and you can have the contents of your precious chests. And the next time you lay hands on a shopkeeper, remember what sort of shop you are in," Xioven said darkly as he straightened his robe.

"See you later," Bok answered, walking to the door of the shop. The bell jingled again as they left.

Xioven stood at the counter for a long while, until he was sure the two thieves were long gone. Then he turned and picked up a chest.

"What's in you?" he whispered, studying the chest thoughtfully before placing it back on the shelf.

Ty walked through the town's marketplace, looking at all the trinkets and bric-a-brac the market sellers had to offer, but nothing really took his eye. Keeping his coin pouch hidden away from the town's pick-pockets, he wandered around looking in shops and at stalls. He saw many different items but nothing was of particular interest until one of the stall-keepers shouted, "Blow pipe and darts! For you, sir, only a few silver coins." The dirty market seller waved a bamboo blowpipe.

"Let's have a look at that," Ty said, taking the pipe and looking through it.

"I will even throw in these ten darts!" the market seller said eagerly, scenting a sale, and rolled the darts out onto the table.

"This couldn't kill a cat!" Ty scoffed, dropping the pipe next to the darts and turning away from the stall.

"But the darts are coated in the finest mandrake money can buy! They would drop a dragon," the seller exclaimed. Ty stopped in his tracks and looked over his shoulder, then turned back and picked up a dart.

"If these can penetrate dragonscale, then my name isn't Ty the Rat," the thief said, scoffing.

"Dragonscale, no – but a cloth shirt they would," the seller replied.

Ty picked up the pipe again. "Ok, how much?" he asked.

"For you, only five silver pieces, with the darts," the trader stated.

"Three and we've got a deal," Ty said, holding the pipe out to the trader.

The stall-keeper continued to barter. "Four and I will throw in a bag for the darts. Shall we shake on it, my friend?"

With a smile, Ty agreed. "You got yourself a deal." He shook the trader's hand and paid him, then tucked the pipe into his belt.

"Thanks and good day," Ty said nodding to the trader.

"May the gods bring you luck this very day."

"I need some," Ty smiled. He wandered around the market a bit longer, and eventually decided to head to the bath house for a clean-up. He had to ask another trader for directions, and wound up having to buy a cooked lizard on a stick for the information.

Ty leisurely made his way along the street, pausing often to look into the windows of all the different shops. They boasted armour, weapons, fine clothes, and everything else that might tempt a person with money to spend. As he carried on towards the bath house, he glanced in the window of a magic shop, a sign that read '*The Quarterstaff*' hanging above its doorway. He had stopped to gaze through the window when his heart jumped into his mouth. He couldn't believe it: Bok and Joli stood inside the shop.

Ty ducked slightly to conceal himself and looked closer. They were talking to a little shopkeeper with a long grey beard. Then Bok shifted to the side and Ty's heart stopped beating completely. His jaw dropped – the shopkeeper was holding two chests that looked identical to the ones

Solomon had shown him.

"It can't be possible," Ty whispered to himself. He saw the shopkeeper place the chests on a shelf behind him and turn back to the pair of thieves, when suddenly Bok grabbed the shopkeeper and dragged him partway over the counter. Ty ducked down even further and watched as Bok let the shopkeeper go with a shove, then turned towards the shop door. Ty quickly backtracked a few steps and disappeared into a shadowy alcove. He watched from his hiding place as Bok and Joli left the shop and walked off down the street.

Pulling his hood up over his face, he quickly crossed to the other side of the road and followed the pair until they entered the Bucket of Blood Inn, then he watched through the window as they sat at the bar and called for two flagons of ale. Ty turned and ran back to the Quarterstaff.

Entering the shop he heard the bell ring and the shopkeeper shout "One second!" Ty approached the counter and spied the two chests on the shelf. They were definitely the ones Solomon had shown him. His head was spinning – how had Bok and Joli gotten their hands on the chests, and how could he possibly get them back? He knew he couldn't attack a mage in his own shop – that would be suicidal. He had nowhere near enough gold to buy them, and stealing them would prove difficult to say the least. Then the mage stepped through a beaded curtain. Without even looking at Ty, he went straight to the chests and placed them into a sack before he finally turned to face Ty.

"How may I help you, good sir?" Xioven said, smiling at Ty and placing the sack with the chests on the counter.

For a split second Ty thought about grabbing the chests and running, but he knew he wouldn't even make it to the door. He tried to think of something the mage would have to go into the back room to fetch, giving him time to snatch the chests and run.

"Have you any… ah… rings of invisibility, good sir?" Ty asked with an innocent smile.

"I do indeed! As it happens, someone came in just yesterday and sold one with five charges left." The mage turned around to look through the clutter and mess. "Now, where did I put the damn thing?" he said, scratching his white beard. "Oh, I remember!"

To Ty's disappointment, the mage reached into his pocket and pulled out a handkerchief. He unfolded it and let the contents fall into his cupped hand, then extended his arm to Ty; in his palm sat a shiny gold ring.

"Lovely!" Ty said, reaching to take the ring.

The shopkeeper closed his hand quickly. "Pay to touch, my friend, pay to touch, especially with invisibility rings," he said with a smile.

"Of course, of course. How much would you like, my good sir?" Ty asked.

"That will be fifty gold coins for every charge," the shopkeeper said, rewrapping the ring and placing it back into his pocket.

"So that will be… two hundred gold, then. It's a deal – I'll just go get the money from my friend and pop back tomorrow," Ty replied.

"Very well," the mage replied. "I will be here, and so will the ring – and by the way, it's two hundred *fifty* gold," he chuckled.

"Oh yes, so it is," Ty smiled and bowed. "My math was never that hot," he said as he made his way to the door. The bell rang as Ty left the shop; he headed straight across the road to a weapons-shop called The Golden Axe. He paused in front of the weapons-shop's window, not looking through the glass at the display, but watching the shopkeeper behind him, reflected in the window-glass. *Just my luck – the one item that he didn't keep in the back of the shop was in his damn pocket!* Ty thought.

He watched as the mage locked the door and headed off up the street, leaning on a walking-stick. After a few moments, Ty put his hood up to cover his face, then turned and followed the mage at a cautious distance.

Every imaginable thought was going through Ty's mind: Should he mug the mage? Try to render him unconscious? Maybe just explain the situation, that the chests were actually his? His heartbeat had gone crazy. Usually he was calm in these situations and his training took over, but right now he felt more alive than ever before. With a thrill, he remembered the blow pipe he'd purchased. Not wanting to risk pricking his finger on a mandrake-coated dart, he quickly slipped on his light leather gloves. He fumbled for the leather bag and pulled out two darts, then pulled the pipe from his belt. He dropped one into the pipe and held it ready, carefully holding the other dart in his other hand.

The mage walked on and on through the streets until he turned and walked down a small alleyway. Ty waited, then stepped into the alley behind the mage.

Seeing that the end of the alley was getting closer, Ty quickened his pace; he knew he had only seconds, and might not get another chance as good as this. As his pace quickened, so did his carelessness – he stepped on a small twig, which broke under his weight with a faint crack. The tiny noise was enough to alert the mage, who instantly turned round to look back down the alley at the thief. With a shrewd gaze, the mage quickened his own pace.

Ty cursed himself silently for the schoolboy error. Moving silently was bread and butter to any practicing thief, and Ty took pride in the fact that he was a master at the technique. *Just not today,* he thought ruefully. Even so, he was quicker than the limping mage and quickly made valuable ground. When he was within shooting distance, he quickly squatted for stability, raised the pipe to his lips, and blew.

The dart struck Xioven in the back of his right leg, stopping the mage in his tracks. He spun around with surprising speed and agility, and lifted his walking-stick to point at Ty. A bolt of white lightning burst from the end of the stick, hurtling down the alley towards him. With nowhere to go, Ty flattened himself against the wall in an attempt to dodge the magical blast.

He was almost successful. The bolt of light glanced off his shoulder, shredding his skin and sending pain flashing down his arm. Ty released his daggers into his palms and sprinted towards the mage. Xioven, now bracing himself on one knee and one hand in the dirt of the alley, aimed his staff again. Another lightning bolt flew towards Ty, striking him in the leg just above the knee and ripping straight through his light leather leggings. The smell of burning flesh filled the alleyway, and the blow sent Ty spinning through the air. He landed on the ground in a heap, and knew that one more bolt would kill him.

Ty struggled to get back to his feet, but the pain in his leg was crippling. He fell onto one knee and looked hopelessly at the mage.

"Make that five hundred gold!" Xioven said, raising his staff once more. Ty shut his eyes, one hand out as if he could block the oncoming blast of lightning – but it never came.

He opened his eyes and saw the mage lying facedown in the muck of the alleyway. Slowly Ty got to his feet and hobbled towards Xioven, blood coursing down his leg with every step. He knew his wounds badly needed treatment. Bending over the mage's body, he retrieved the chests and placed them into his own pack. He rifled through Xioven's pockets until he found the handkerchief with the ring.

Xioven groaned and tried to lift his head. Ty grabbed the mage's staff. "Here's a down payment," he said, and struck the mage on the back of the head, silencing him.

At that precise moment, three men – sellers from the marketplace, by the looks of them – walked around the corner into the alley. They froze at the sight of Ty bent over the mage, but their hesitation was brief.

"Stop, thief!" one shouted, and they began running towards Ty and Xioven. Ty tried to run in the opposite direction but fell to the ground. The pain in his leg was too much for him.

The men were halfway down the alley by now, shouting 'Murderer!' and 'Thief!' Just in time, Ty remembered the ring in his hand. Even in such a dangerous moment, the potential for drama tempted him. He dragged himself to his feet, faced the oncoming men, and shouted "Be gone!" With that, he slipped the ring onto his finger and disappeared.

The onrushing men stopped in confused amazement. Ty turned and hobbled away down the alley with as much speed as he could muster, leaving the puzzled fruit-sellers and fishmongers behind him.

Soon he was in front of The Bull, and he leaned against the front of the inn trying to think. His head pounded with pain from shoulder and leg; he felt faint and his eyesight wavered in and out of focus. Ty knew if he entered like this – in the shape he was in – he would attract too much unwanted attention, so he stayed invisible and waited until someone approached and opened the door. He quickly followed them in and slipped up the stairs to his room. He closed the door behind him then took off the ring, carefully placing it in his hidden pocket. He felt he had aged decades in the past few hours, as though his life force had been drained. He strapped his wounds up as best he could and fell back on the bed, exhausted. Within seconds his world was in darkness.

Bok and Joli walked along the busy street just before sundown. "What do you think he found?" Joli asked excitedly.

"Hopefully something worth a fortune," Bok answered as they reached The Quarterstaff. The doorbell rang out as they entered the shop and closed the door behind them. "Xioven!" Bok shouted out. "Tell us some good news!"

There was no answer.

"Hello?" Joli said, looking through the beads, just as the mage came out from the back room, holding a towel to the back of his head.

"What the hell happened to you?" Bok asked.

Xioven pulled the towel from his head with a grimace, showing the pair the blood-stained cloth, then placed it back on his injured head.

"It seems that your chests are of more interest than you thought," Xioven said, sitting down in a chair behind the counter.

"What do you mean?" Bok asked, folding his arms and frowning.

"After you left here, a halfling came in asking to buy an invisibility ring, then followed me when I left to go see Donovan. He attacked me and robbed me of your precious chests – and *my* invisibility ring," Xioven explained, throwing the dart onto the counter.

"What's that?" Joli asked.

"That, my friend, is the dart he used to drop me. Find the owner and you will find your chests," Xioven said, wincing as he rubbed his head.

"Damn it!!" Bok said, turning angrily to look out the window.

"If you want to settle our debt, find him and torture the little whore!" Xioven growled.

"What did he look like?" Joli asked.

"Just like any other halfling, short, cloaked, and skinny," Xioven replied.

Bok walked over to the counter and picked up the dart. "I don't know if I am angrier at you for losing my chests or getting you a bump on the head," Bok said, examining the dart.

"Ask around the market place, they always sell these sorts of things." Xioven turned and walked through to the back of the shop, signalling an end to the conversation.

The door closed behind them and the bell rang out. Bok and Joli hurried to the marketplace, but it was half-empty, some vendors just closing up shop and others loading carts to take their goods away. Bok stopped an old trader pushing a wheelbarrow full of silks. "Where could I find blow darts?" he asked the old man.

"Go right at the end; there is a stall for those. Be quick though, he's shutting up shop," the trader replied.

Quickly Bok and Joli walked through the marketplace and eventually found the stall; a dirty, skinny human was packing his items away. "Excuse me," Bok said, tapping on the stall counter.

The man turned to the pair and then went back to what he was doing. "I'm closed, come back tomorrow," he replied.

"Is this one of your darts?" Bok said, holding up the dart.

The man turned to face them and took the dart from Bok. "Yes, I sold it this morning," he replied.

"May I ask to whom?" Joli inquired.

"Hmmm… I just can't quite remember," the human said, exaggeratedly scratching his chin.

Bok tossed two silver pieces onto the table. "Has that jogged your memory?" he said with a small grin.

"I think it is beginning to come back to me now," the trader said, picking up the coins.

Exchanging glances, Bok and Joli placed their hands on the hilts of their swords, ready to draw.

"You better answer me wisely now," Bok said through gritted teeth. "I'm going to ask once more, and if you 'can't remember' I will cut you from ear to ear."

The trader knew he wasn't going to get a better offer, and decided to tell all. "Yes, I remember – he came this morning, short fellow," he said hurriedly.

"We know that already. What did he look like, this short fellow?" Bok said, leaning forward.

"A halfling, small, hooded. He said his name was, uh, Kay Fat or something."

Bok drew his sword a few inches. "This is your last chance."

"I'm telling the truth! He said something like, uh… 'Try the Cat,' I think it was," the trader blurted out, beginning to sweat.

"Let me kill him," Joli said, drawing his sword and advancing.

"No! Wait! I swear he said something like if those darts could penetrate a dragon's scale then his name wasn't Cry the Cat, or something like that," the trader said, holding up trembling hands.

"Wait," Bok said, placing one hand across Joli's chest, holding him back from the trader. "He didn't by any chance say '*Ty the Rat*'?"

"Yes! Yes, Ty the Rat! That's him, short halfling," the trader said, stuttering with relief.

"I don't believe it! That damn thief has our chests!" Bok said, giving the side sheet of the trader's stall a blow with the flat of his sword.

"How… how can he be…?" Joli faltered, more confused than ever.

"I don't know, but he's up to something! He doesn't rob mages in alleyways just for a hobby. He *knew* Xioven had those chests, and he took them," Bok explained.

"Then it *was* his cloak on the guy we got the chests from! Damn, this pig-whore is really getting to me now," Joli said, walking away from the stall.

"Getting to *you*? He's making my blood boil," Bok said, raging.

"Let's go tell Xioven who robbed him," Joli suggested.

They headed back to the shop and explain to Xioven that it was Ty who took the chests. The mage told them of the two lightning bolts he had fired, and described the damage they would have inflicted. "He must still be in town; the wounds will need treating," Xioven stated. "If not, he will be dead within hours."

"We will check the healers and Cleric houses," Bok told Xioven.

"Yes, do that. I will spread the news – someone will rat out the Rat!" Xioven said.

"Add a good price; he meant to kill you, too," Bok told the mage.

"How do you know that?"

"Those darts he purchased, he was told they would stop a dragon," Bok explained.

"That may be so. My resistance to poison is high, very high," the mage said, turning round and walking away.

Chapter Fourteen
Backdoor Exit

Kern was sitting at the bar in The Bull, enjoying an early-evening ale, when the front door opened and Galandrik walked in.

"Have you seen Ty?" the dwarf asked worriedly.

"No, why?" Kern replied, looking surprised at Galandrik's concern.

"It's all over town. Ty 'The Rat' wanted for mugging a shopkeeper down an alley," Galandrik explained.

"What? I know Ty and he's no mugger! He's a lot of things, but a mugger? Definitely not," Kern answered.

"Mugger or not, he's wanted for it!" Galandrik said, looking out into the street. The door to the bar opened and two town guards approached the innkeeper. After a brief chat they left. The innkeeper walked over to Kern and Galandrik.

"They are after your mate. I told them he left this morning after breakfast and hasn't been back," he said in a low voice. "Look, I don't want any trouble, but you're not welcome anymore. Just get your things and go quietly, please. I didn't say anything this time because you are friends of Lord Jarrow, but I can't risk my livelihood." The innkeeper took Kern's empty jug and walked off.

"Looks like Ty's gotten in some sort of trouble again," Kern sighed. "Let's get our stuff and go find him."

"Aye, we'd better go before the innkeeper changes his mind," Galandrik agreed. They walked past the bar towards the stairs.

"Thanks," Kern said to the innkeeper as they walked past. "We will get our gear and be on our way." The innkeeper nodded back with relief.

They walked through the back door and up the stairs to their room. When they entered, the first thing they saw was Ty, laid out on the bed and covered in blood.

"What in hell!" Kern shouted, running over to the bed. He immediately felt Ty's neck for a pulse.

"Is he… alive?" Galandrik asked, looking down at the battered body in shock.

"Yes, but only just," Kern answered. "His pulse is so faint I can barely feel it."

Galandrik lifted the bandage from Ty's leg and looked underneath. "He's lost a lot of blood. We need to get him to a healer; that wound is deep," the dwarf said, re-dressing the leg wound as best he could.

"We can't – you said he's wanted everywhere," Kern replied, examining the wound on the thief's shoulder.

"If we don't, he's going to die," Galandrik said. "And die soon he will," he added, glancing at the torn skin on Ty's shoulder.

"I got it! Jarrow!" Kern said. "We'll take him to Jarrow. He still owes us a favour, and maybe we can hide there, out of the way," he continued as he passed Ty's backpack to Galandrik. "You pack up our things as quickly as you can; I'll go saddle the horses."

Galandrik gathered their scattered belongings, pausing every few minutes to check on the unconscious thief. He was securing their packs when Kern returned. "Horses are ready," he said tersely, his face tense with concern. He moved to the bed, looking down at Ty uncertainly.

"Help lift him onto my shoulder," Galandrik instructed, and together they hoisted the motionless thief. Kern gathered their packs and led the way down the back stairs to the stable, where he quickly mounted up.

"Pass him up." They laid Ty in front of Kern.

When Galandrik had collected their packs and mounted his own horse, they headed off following the directions Jarrow had given. To avoid any confrontations with the townsfolk or militia, they kept to back roads and alleyways. Before long they hit the far side of the town. The houses thinned out here; although they were still inside the town walls, the homes looked like farmhouses, each one surrounded by ample land for grazing and small fields. Eventually they found what they were looking for: A farmhouse with an enormous old oak tree in front of it.

Jarrow was right, Galandrik thought, *that tree* does *look like an old man with outstretched arms.* Uncomfortably, he recalled his childhood listening to stories told by the elder dwarves, about trees that had walked the earth many moons ago.

Jumping down from his horse, Kern let Ty fall into his arms. The halfling groaned slightly and Kern could feel the sticky warmth of Ty's blood soaking into his shirt from the leg wound. Galandrik rapped on the door with his knuckles.

Upon opening the door, Jarrow beckoned them in without hesitation. "What on earth has happened to him?" he asked.

"I wish I knew!" Kern replied, carrying Ty into the safety of the house.

"Take him through the back and up the stairs," Jarrow said, pointing Kern in the right direction and calling for servants to assist. Kern didn't hesitate; he climbed the stairs as quickly as he dared, not wanting to jostle Ty's wounds any more than necessary. He laid Ty down onto the bed, then stood staring helplessly at the halfling's limp form. Galandrik and Jarrow entered the room followed by servants with clean towels and bowls of steaming water.

Jarrow studied Ty's wounds, then dressed them the best he could, causing the halfling to groan and thrash weakly. "His skin has been shredded, but luckily the heat from whatever caused the injuries has also sealed the wounds somewhat," Jarrow explained. "Otherwise I think he'd be dead by now. Even so, he's going to need medical help."

"We don't... Can you..." Kern hesitated.

"Yes. Look after him while I fetch a friend who's a healer. You must keep talking to him and keep a cool, wet towel on his forehead. That may help a bit," Jarrow ordered. "Try to rouse him; if fever sets in, he may go for good."

Kern and Galandrik took turns talking to Ty, intent on his every twitch. "Come on, buddy, don't let a little wound stop you," Kern said, dabbing Ty's forehead. Ty's eyes rolled, but he made no reply.

Galandrik leaned over, saying with forced cheer, "Remember the arrow I took from that stinking orc? Didn't stop me, and this won't you!"

"You can't leave us before telling us this little yarn."

"Must've been six of them, hey lad?"

They carried on like this for what seemed ages, changing tactics and topics several times before Jarrow returned with a white-robed man, who virtually shoved Kern out of the way to get to Ty.

"Excuse me, excuse me," the cleric said as he barged past.

"I think we should leave Prolumus to his work," Jarrow said, holding the door open.

"Is he going to be all right?" Galandrik asked Prolumus.

"Go!" Prolumus muttered. He dropped his bag onto the bed and began rummaging through it,

Downstairs, Jarrow led them through a kitchen where a woman in a white apron was bustling about preparing the evening meal. Her long grey hair was tied back into a ponytail, and she smiled as Jarrow led them into the main room and invited them to sit down.

The woman entered a few minutes later, carrying a tray of cups and a massive jug of red wine to the table. "Please, allow me," Jarrow said, filling three cups.

"Thank you," Kern answered taking a cup.

Jarrow sipped the wine and smiled. "This is the finest wine in the land. It's Verona, from Loft in western Bodisha. There's a monastery there and the monks have a vineyard, apparently have been making this wine for hundreds of years."

"It certainly is a fine drop of wine." Kern agreed. Galandrik also nodded in appreciation.

After a few more sips, Jarrow said quietly, "I think you'd better start from the beginning."

"There's nothing to tell," Kern said wearily. "We all split up this morning to go get supplies. We thought Ty went to the bath house. We had planned to meet back at The Bull and decide where we were going to head next."

"Then the next thing we know, they're saying Ty's wanted for a mugging, and the innkeeper told us we were no longer welcome at the inn," Galandrik chimed in. "When we went to our room to collect our things, Ty was sprawled out on the bed bleeding to death."

"I guess we'll need to wait for Ty to regain consciousness so he can explain," Jarrow said.

"I guess we will," Kern agreed.

"So did you decide where you're heading next?" Jarrow asked, taking another sip of Verona wine.

"Nope, we didn't get that far. We probably would've headed back up north, but I think that's changed now," Kern said. "Wherever we decide to go, we will have to do it very quietly."

"You are welcome to stay here for as long as you need," Jarrow reassured them. "Guards won't come here."

An hour or so had gone by, along with more than a few cups of Verona wine, when Prolumus walked into the room, drying his hands on a towel.

"Saved me any of your fine Verona?" he asked Jarrow abruptly.

"Of course I have, my good friend! How's our patient?" Jarrow asked, pouring the cleric a cup of wine.

"He will live, but he's very weak. It's not just the blood loss, either; there's something else. Has he been affected by anything magical lately?" the cleric asked after taking a deep draught of the Verona.

"Not that I can think of," Kern replied, turning to Galandrik. "How about you?"

"I can't think of anything either, apart from our friend, who fried a few skeletons with a *ward undead*," Galandrik answered. "Why?"

"It may be nothing, but… There is a certain strain of magic which causes those affected by it to lose the colour in their irises, and their skin develops a grey tinge, as if all the blood has been drained from the body." Prolumus scratched his beard, then admitted, "It could just be down to his blood loss."

"Who knows what he got up to?" Galandrik said, draining his third cup of Jarrow's wine.

"Whatever it was, he is not to be moved for at least twenty-four hours," Prolumus said, filling a second cup of wine.

"And *he's* getting done for mugging? He should get the other guy done!" Galandrik laughed.

The woman came in and set another bottle on the table, then spoke quietly to Jarrow. "Yes, Molly, bring another case up," he answered.

"It does seem strange that Ty came out worse. He gets up to a lot of things, but mugging people isn't one of them. Something is definitely strange here," Kern said, standing up and stretching his legs. At that moment there was a knock at the door. Jarrow got up to answer it, then walked back into the room with a young elven man.

"This is Ltyh, a good friend of mine who also serves as my aide," Jarrow announced, pouring Ltyh a cup of wine.

"Hello," Ltyh said, joining the others at the table.

"What exactly did you find out?" Jarrow asked.

"Well, it seems that your friend upstairs robbed a shopkeeper of his goods down an alley. He first knocked the man out with a blowdart, then clubbed him – with the shopkeeper's own staff," the aide told them.

"Ty never uses a blowpipe," Kern said emphatically.

"What exactly did he steal?" Galandrik asked.

"Two chests, apparently. The shopkeeper values them highly, and has put a mithril-piece reward on Ty's head, as long as the chests are returned. Furthermore, the poison on the dart was top strength. It should have killed the shopkeeper – he's very lucky to be alive, apparently. He isn't taking this lightly. He wants back the items Ty stole, and wants to lay robbery and attempted murder charges against him as well," Ltyh added, taking a sip of wine. "There was also a report of the mugger vanishing."

Kern stood up and turned to Ltyh. "Oh, he's good at that! Disappearing is his specialty. Let me check something – I'll be right back."

Kern left them, soon he walked back into the room with Ty's backpack. He sat back down and untied the drawstrings. Reaching into the pack, he pulled out two cloth bundles and placed them carefully on the table, then folded back the cloth to reveal two small chests richly encrusted in gems.

"I think we found the chests," Kern said, examining one of them.

"Didn't Ty mention two chests?" Galandrik reminded him. "The ones Solomon told him were the King's Gold?"

"Yeah," Kern replied, "but Solomon would be nearly back at Raith by now. There's no way they would have ended up here."

"Maybe it's just a coincidence," Jarrow put in.

"Coincidence?" Galandrik said, raising an eyebrow and picking up the other chest.

"Yes, I agree," Kern said. "It is weird, but I can't possibly see how these could be the same chests."

"How the hell do you open it?" Galandrik said, rattling the chest at his ear.

"Let me have a look," Jarrow said. Galandrik offered it to him, but after a few minutes Jarrow handed it back. "Magically locked, I guess," he concluded.

"It certainly looks that way. Maybe we could smash them open?" Kern said with a smile.

"I think we should ask Ty what's going on first, before we start smashing things up," Jarrow smiled.

"Yes, I guess you're right," Kern sighed.

"I shall get Molly to make up a couple of beds for you," Jarrow said, standing up.

Conn sat in his study when the paper bird landed on his windowsill. It jumped over to his desk and perched on his hand. With a smile he raised it to his ear. The smile didn't stay long; the good news he had anticipated was not the message the magical beast carried.

The bird told him of Solomon's body, dead on the side of the road for some three days, next to the blood-stained cloak of the halfling who had travelled with him. It told of the King's Gold, vanished into the world; and of Solomon's corpse, stripped of everything, including clothes and dignity. As the colour fled Conn's face and tears filled his old eyes, the bird told, mindless and heartless, of the feast the wild animals had made of Solomon's decaying corpse. *No hands or feet left*, it chirped or whispered in its secret tongue, *face and eyes eaten all up, all up.* Unable to bear the bird's message, Conn sat back in his chair; opening his hand, he sprinkled paperdust onto his desk. A tear ran slowly down his cheek.

Wiping the moisture away after several long, silent moments, he remembered his sister as a child playing in the garden, her curly blonde hair and bright blue eyes full of joy. Her rosy-red cheeks, her favourite red shoes that she wore even when their mother had forbidden it, saying they were for feast days only. Another tear fell onto his desk as he pictured her face when she had announced that she was having a baby, the joy that her first child was on its way.

He didn't bother to wipe the tears away as he remembered the day he'd gotten the message – her pains had begun and the midwife was alarmed; he hadn't asked why, could barely think at all during the panicked run to her home. The stricken look on the old herb-woman's face, the blood on her apron; the wailing of the serving-girl, the whiteness of the sheet pulled up over his sister's face. He seemed unable to form any thought besides *Too late, too late. I didn't get here in time.* Even the fifty lashes he'd given the messenger with his own hand, for being too slow with the message, didn't take away the grief and guilt he felt.

"If only I'd been there, I could have saved her," he murmured into the silence of his study. He remembered holding Solomon for the first time, wrapped in a soft blanket, so tiny and helpless. Kissing the child's head and making *that* promise to his sister and the gods – that he would take care of the boy, look after him and never let any harm come to him.

He had failed; he had let his sister down and he knew it. "I should never have let Solomon go out with those thieving fucking bastards."

Conn stood up and wiped his face again. He let out a sigh and paced the room trying to clear his thoughts. "Damn you, Ty the Rat… You are a dead man."

He stared sightlessly out the window, then strode with purpose to the cupboard across the room. He selected a bone map-case and, pulling out the map, unrolled it onto his desk.

"Guards!" he shouted.

The massive double doors to his study opened to admit Svorn, the captain of Conn's guard.

"Yes, my Lord," he said, bowing his head.

"Assemble twenty of your best men, and make ready to travel," Conn ordered, his voice harsh with anger.

"Where are we headed, Lord?"

"You will be going south, towards Blame, maybe as far as Forkvain," Conn said, standing up.

Svorn had never seen his ruler's face so distorted by anger; he quickly lowered his gaze. "Our mission is?" Svorn asked.

"To kill Kern Ocarn, Ty 'The Rat' Quickpick, and Galandrik Sabrehargen, and retrieve the King's Gold!" Conn shouted, placing two hands on the windowsill.

"Yes, my Lord. I shall leave immediately. Will that be all?" Svorn said, bowing.

"No. Release Draygore and Hellthorn," Conn said through gritted teeth, turning to face Svorn.

"Are you sure, my Lord? The wyverns may not be necessary. I'm sure my men and I can handle it," Svorn argued.

"Do as I say, man!" Conn stepped towards Svorn. "Question my orders again and I'll rip your heart out!"

"Yes Lord Conn," Svorn said, snapping to attention and looking up, trying to miss Conn's stare.

"Get the clothes they wore, their scent will be on them. Let the wyverns smell them, then release the beasts," Conn thundered.

"It shall be done, Lord. I will rally the men." Svorn asked, walking back to the door.

"One last thing, Svorn. If you get to them before the wyverns do… I want Ty brought back alive," Conn said menacingly

"Yes, my Lord." The double doors slammed shut behind the soldier, and Conn closed the window.

"Your death shall not be in vain, Solomon. I promise."

Svorn walked into the barn. In the middle was a metal cage that stood fifty feet high and just as wide in diameter. In the centre of the cage stood four massive wooden stakes; each the size of a beer barrel, they rose from the floor like huge fingers reaching up from under the ground. Two black wyverns sat inside the cage, their huge black wings curled up behind them, razor sharp claws and teeth, and dead black eyes. Bones and carcasses lay scattered all around the floor of the cage. Around the wyverns' necks were huge metal collars attached to chains that were anchored to the stakes.

Inside the barn were some twenty guards, who scurried about after Svorn's entrance and sharp commands. Just outside the cage door sat Merk, the wyvern trainer. Svorn stood by the table and waited. Merk was utterly absorbed in his writing, but finally looked up; seeing Svorn there, he quickly stood up, brushing off his chest and straightening his helm.

"Captain Svorn! What brings you here?" Merk asked, still brushing down his uniform.

Svorn dropped the bag of clothes onto the table.

"In that bag are the clothes of three thieves who Conn wants dead. You are to give Draygore and Hellthorn the scent as soon as possible, then release them," Svorn ordered. His eyes were fixed on the wyverns as he spoke.

"Yes sir, it will be done," Merk answered, then called over two men in long black robes. He gave them their instructions, and the two men walked away and unlocked the cage.

"What are they doing?" Svorn asked, curiosity getting the better of him.

"They will cast a provocation-control spell on the wyverns and then tell them what's to be done; then the wyverns will leave, find and kill their targets," Merk explained.

"I've always wondered - are wyverns not just a hybrid dragon?" Svorn questioned. "They certainly look like them."

"Definitely from the same family but no, they are not dragons," Merk answered with a smile.

"Then what's the difference?" Svorn said, feeling slightly stupid.

"Well, wyverns kill by biting and ripping their prey apart with tooth and claw. Dragons will burn you to a crisp," Merk said with a smile, "but they hardly ever eat human flesh."

"So dragons are the stronger?"

"Two fully grown wyverns against a young adult dragon would probably win, but yes, dragons have more fight. They say you can speak to a dragon, and they are just as intelligent as we are. Wyverns are slightly more animalistic, but both species can understand human, elf and many more languages," Merk explained.

Svorn glanced up at the beasts, as if to see if they were listening, then carried on with his questioning. "I guess that's why there are more wyverns then; nobody hunts them like they do the dragons."

"Wyverns are still hunted, but dragons have been hunted nearly out of existence. I think the tales of treasure never did them any favours," Merk said. "And now I hear we are apparently adding dragons to our army?"

"Are we really? It's the first I have heard of it," Svorn replied.

"That's what I was told," Merk said

"Really. And where did this reliable information come from, may I ask?"

"Svorn, you know how the troops gossip. It was just mentioned in a conversation over a jug of mead." Merk turned to one of the guards and ordered the roof to be opened, in what Svorn suspected was a deliberate attempt to change the subject.

Ten men on each side of the cage started pulling down on ropes connected to a complicated-looking pulley system. The ceiling slowly started to open and sunlight penetrated to the barn floor,

The bars of the cage were built flush to the roof, to prevent the beasts from acting on any thought they might have of grabbing a guard before flying. When the roof was completely open and the two robed men had calmed the beasts, they unlocked the wyverns' neck braces and held the bundles of discarded clothing up to the wyverns' snouts, whispering incantations as they did.

"What are they whispering?" Svorn asked.

"It's a sort of hypnotic spell. It keeps them under our control and brings them back here," Merk explained. "If we didn't do that, who knows where they would end up; they'd probably terrorize local villages until someone killed them."

The two men left the cage and locked the door behind them. "Are you ready, Sir?" one of the men asked Merk.

"Here we go, then," Merk answered, after receiving a nod of approval from Svorn.

One of the robed men pointed at the cage and shouted something. A red mist sprayed forth from his hand and covered the wyverns, the beasts screamed as they flew upwards, their great wings flapping and twisting with surprising gracefulness. The wind stirred by their flapping wings sent hay and dust swirling into the air as Draygore and Hellthorn disappeared through the roof and into the morning sky.

Once the wyverns were out of sight, Merk ordered some of the guards to clear the cage of carcasses, and he and Svorn left the barn together.

"I have always thought highly of dragons; beautiful creatures," Svorn said.

"Yes, they are," Merk agreed, nodding. "Unfortunately there are not many left."

"Not many that fly about waiting to be killed."

"What do you mean?" Merk asked.

"If you were a dragon, and as intelligent as you say they are, would you come out of hiding?"

"Maybe not. Never thought of it that way. I hope there are some more about."

"So do I. Thanks for the help," Svorn said brusquely.

"Always a pleasure to help the captain of the guard."

Bok and Joli walked into the Bucket of Blood Inn and spotted Xioven sitting at a corner table. They crossed the crowded room just as Prolumus was calling over the maid.

"Two more please." As they sat down, he asked, "What have you found out?"

"Nothing really, apart from the fact that one of the horses was left tied up at the inn's stable. We questioned the innkeeper and he told us that they'd all just left and the room was a bloodbath and left," Bok explained

"I knew I did him some damage. I'll be surprised if he actually survived; that alleyway was tiny, and I caught him twice," Xioven said, taking a celebratory swig of ale.

"Maybe you did kill him, and that's why they left the horse," Joli said, smiling.

"I hope not," Bok answered. "If he's dead we will never find those damn chests."

"He'll turn up again like a bad-smelling rat, just like he normally does," Joli said, draining his goblet.

"Well, if he is alive, he is still close by and someone is hiding him," Xioven said, taking a mouthful of ale. The barmaid placed their jugs of ale in front of them, then started clearing the table next to them.

"After the reward you offered for the chests, any rogue who knew of his hiding place would have told you by now," Bok stated.

"For a mithril coin they would rat out their own mothers," Joli agreed with a snigger.

"I guess we just wait and see if he reappears at some point," Xioven said, calling the maid over once more.

The maid – who had been listening intently to their conversation; gossip was as good as coin in the town's taverns – stopped cleaning the table and glanced over her shoulder. Making sure the innkeeper's attention was focused elsewhere and whispered, "My friend works over at the Bull Inn, and she said that the thief who robbed you came into town with a local man."

"I see, and who was this local man?" Bok whispered, leaning onto the table.

"I don't really know him, but his name is Jarrow. He lives at the far end of town somewhere; a big tree sits right outside his house," the maid informed the men as she pretended to wipe the table.

"Well done, my pretty, and here is some coin for the information,"

Xioven said with a smile, dropping some silver onto the table.

"Why, thank you, sir!" The maid giggled and headed back to the bar, and Joli shouted, "Bring us some bread!"

"That's a start," Xioven said. "You two head off and see what this Jarrow guy is all about. If you learn anything useful, let me know right away."

Bok and Joli finished their morning meal and headed off to find Jarrow's house. After an hour, they found what they were looking for.

"Looks like someone beat us to it, Joli." Twelve town guards were approaching the house.

"I guess the Rat is going to be forced out of his hole," Joli laughed.

"We'd better hide over here and wait," Bok ordered and they walked across the grass and sat under a small cluster of trees.

"I have an idea," Joli said, smiling. Bok raised an eyebrow in reply. "If they are in there, their horses would be in the stable."

Bok placed his hand on Joli's shoulder. "Good thinking. Let's go around the back and have a look, while the guards are busy elsewhere."

Chapter Fifteen
Eggs for Breakfast

Kern, Galandrik, Jarrow sat eating breakfast. "So, how long before Ty's good to be moved, do you think?" Galandrik asked Jarrow.

"Prolumus said twenty-four hours, and he's usually right," Jarrow answered.

"We can't go anywhere until nightfall anyway; everybody in the town is looking for him," Kern pointed out.

"Good point. Why don't we hand him in and take the mithril?" Galandrik said, trying to keep a straight face.

"Nah," Kern laughed, "it would be too boring without him around."

"True. Well, have we got everything ready to travel tonight, or do we still need supplies?"

"I think we are sorted. Jarrow has kindly offered us a horse for Ty," Kern answered with an appreciative smile in Jarrow's direction. "I very much doubt it will still be at The Bull where we left it. Other than that, we're ready," he finished.

"So if these are the chests that Ty told you about, are you taking them to their rightful owner?" Jarrow asked.

"God knows we're not welcome back the way we came," Kern replied. "I don't have a better plan – do you, Galandrik?"

"Nope," the dwarf said as he finished off the last of his breakfast. "We're running out of options. Why don't we head to Marsh Town and sail across to Lave?" Galandrik suggested. "Apparently there is a lot of work to be had there."

The dining room door suddenly opened and there stood Ty, one arm in a sling and Ltyh hovering just behind him. "Anybody for bone dice?" he said, forcing a smile.

"I'll give you bone dice!" Kern exclaimed. "You are supposed to be resting!"

Looking distressed, Ltyh helped steady Ty along. Ty moved somewhat gingerly, and was using a walking stick to keep the weight off of his injured leg. "I told him to stay in his room and rest, but he insisted on coming down," Ltyh spluttered, red-faced.

Kern and Jarrow stood up and helped Ty to the table. He sat with poorly-disguised relief, and looked around at the others. His face was a ghostly grey, and to Kern's eyes he looked surprisingly thin.

"Good to have you back, friend," Kern said, folding his arms and gazing sternly at Ty.

"Yes, indeed," the dwarf agreed. "How do you feel?"

"Like I've died and come back to life," Ty winced, stretching out his injured arm. "So, when do we leave?" he added, with a wry smile.

"We are not going anywhere, my friend. First, you need to rest and heal, and second, you need to tell us just what the hell happened," Kern insisted, leaning back in his chair.

Ty laughed. "You are not going to believe what happened."

"Try us," Galandrik and Kern said simultaneously.

"Well, remember the two rogues from the Orc's Armpit, Bok and Joli? Where that bully knocked me around in the toilets, then proceeded to get himself locked up for stealing the farmer's purse?" Ty began.

"Not *quite* what happened, but yes, we remember," Kern laughed.

"Well," Ty continued, "after we parted ways at The Bull, while I was looking for a bath house I looked into this shop window and saw those two – Bok and Joli – *and* the chests that Solomon stole from me! I couldn't believe my eyes, to be honest; I followed them to the Bucket of Blood inn, then went back to the shop," Ty said, taking a cup of water from Ltyh and sipping. "Thank you."

"So you stole the chests from the shopkeeper?" Galandrik asked.

"I was trying, but I couldn't find a way. So I followed him and tried to do it the old-fashioned way, but it went a bit wrong and… well, he nearly had me. How was I supposed to know he had a staff-of-lightning-bolt as a walking stick?" He swallowed a big gulp of water, only to start coughing.

"Easy, fellow, take your time," Jarrow said, leaning forward to place a hand on Ty's shoulder.

"Yeah, a magical staff is the last thing I would expect a magic-shop owner to have," Ltyh joked.

"Whatever," Ty groaned, wiping water from his chin. "I got the King's Gold back, didn't I?"

"Yes you did, Ty, and well done," Galandrik said.

"But where did you get the blowpipe from?" Kern quizzed.

"I picked it up in the marketplace that morning. The seller told me the darts would drop a dragon; it nearly got me killed instead."

"But – blow darts?" Kern asked. "How long have I known you? You *never* use blow darts!"

"I know." Ty smiled and then winced. "I don't really *know* why, to be honest. It was just a spur of the moment buy."

"So, tell us about these chests," Jarrow asked.

"Of course. Please bring them to me."

"Ltyh, fetch the chests, would you please?" Jarrow asked. Within moments the aide returned and placed the cloth-wrapped chests on the table.

Ty unwrapped one of the chests and placed it on his knees. He rested his bandaged arm over the top of the box as if to stop it falling from his knee. Using his arm to block his friends' view of the chests, he slid his other hand under the bandaged arm and pushed the four gems that triggered the lock. A slight click was heard and Ty placed the chest back on the table. Leaning back in his chair, he used his stick to flip the lid up. Jarrow, Kern, and Galandrik stood and peered into the box.

"Is that it? Is that what all the fuss was about?" Galandrik growled.

"It appears so, my bearded friend," Kern replied, reaching to pick up the egg.

"Not so fast!" Ty snapped. "Solomon told me to never, *ever* touch the eggs."

"Why didn't you mention that before?" Kern asked sitting back down onto his chair.

"I didn't think we would ever see them again, let alone have the opportunity to touch them," Ty answered breezily, closing the box with his stick.

"Why can't we touch them?" Galandrik asked.

"He said if we touch a dragon's egg, we'll get dragflu – dead in days, and painfully, too!" Ty said, with eyes wide.

"I have never heard of such a thing," Jarrow mocked.

"All right, I'll open the box and you can stroke them Jarrow, then the proof will be in the pudding," Ty said, reaching for the chest.

"No, no – I believe you, old friend. I was only joking; of course we can't touch a dragon's egg," Jarrow said, backtracking hastily.

Ty smiled to himself and placed the chests back into the backpack. "Right. I'm going back upstairs to rest," he said, getting to his feet with help from Ltyh.

"Take your time, friend, we need you fit," Kern added.

Ty paused at the door, but didn't turn around. "You would get lost without me," he said without looking back, and the door closed behind him

Galandrik stoked the fire and before long they were sitting in front of a comfortable blaze, rolling bone dice.

"I suppose we just wait, I guess," Galandrik sighed.

"We can't do a lot until he is fit enough to move on," Kern replied.

"I might even come with you," Jarrow laughed.

"You laugh, but you would be more than welcome, friend. Plus it would give me the chance to win some of my silver back!" Kern answered, rolling the dice again.

At that moment Ltyh came bursting into the room, the door bouncing off the wall behind him. "Jarrow!" he exclaimed.

"What the hell is it, lad?" Jarrow said, springing to his feet.

"There are loads of town guards outside, and they're heading this way," Ltyh said, pointing out the window.

"That blasted innkeeper!" Kern spat, dashing to the window. "I knew he wouldn't keep his mouth shut."

"Go warn Ty, help him to hide somewhere. Just make him disappear!" Jarrow told Ltyh, who ran out of the room; they could hear his footsteps pounding up the stairs.

"What about me and Galandrik?" Kern asked, grabbing his sword.

"Keep your weapons close, but try not to look like you're ready for a fight – they'll know something is afoot."

Kern and Galandrik placed their weapons at their feet, hidden under the long table cloth.

"I'll get the door, just be calm," Jarrow said, straightening his shirt as they heard a loud knock on the door.

Ltyh dashed back down the stairs and into the dining room, sitting next to Kern and trying to bring his breathing back to normal. "What's he doing up there?" Galandrik asked in a low voice.

"Not a lot. Looking for a suitable hiding place. I said I would help him, but he just muttered something about *the day he needs someone to help him hide he'll quit hiding.*" Ltyh shrugged.

"That's him all over," Kern said, shaking his head. "I'm sure if there is somewhere to hide, he will bend into it – wait, can he even bend…? You know, I think this might go bad."

Jarrow opened the front door. A guard stood at the door, helmet in hand; five others were ranged behind him. All six looked intimidating and severe. "Hello and good morning, sirs," he said, smiling.

"Morning. We have some questions," the guard stated. "When you came into town the other day, you were with four companions."

"Yes sir, that is correct," Jarrow answered.

"Where could we find them now?"

"Two have joined me for breakfast, and the other two have gone on their way. What is this about?" Jarrow enquired, trying to look suitably puzzled.

"We think one of them robbed a shopkeeper in town, nearly killed the poor fellow. We'd like to come in and look around – and to be honest, I am not really asking," the guard said in a stern voice.

"But of course!" Jarrow said. "I have nothing to hide, good sir." He stepped to one side, allowing the guards to enter his house. They spread out and began their search around the first floor of the house, checking in cupboards, under the stairs, lifting mats and chairs, looking for anywhere a hidden door might be.

Meanwhile, Jarrow returned to sit calmly at the table next to Galandrik. He picked up a jug of lime tea that was still just about warm.

"What about some lime tea for you and your boys?" Jarrow offered the guard.

"No thank you," the guard said. Turning his attention to Ltyh, Kern, and Galandrik, he asked, "Any idea where the other two went?"

Galandrik shrugged his shoulders but offered no reply. Ltyh looked down as Kern said, "No idea. We were only traveling with them to be safe from bandits and orcs – strength in numbers and all that."

"Go search upstairs," the guard shouted to the others.

Under the cover of the tablecloth, Kern carefully nudged a sword towards Jarrow's feet; Jarrow felt it bump into his shoe and gave a barely perceptible nod. Kern's heart felt like it was going to burst from his chest.

Ty looked down the stairs though the cracked door and saw the six guards enter the house, followed by Jarrow, who closed the door behind them.

Damn, he thought, and gently closed the door. Using his stick, he hobbled over to the window, leaned on the bed as far as his aching limbs would allow, and carefully peeked out. Three guards were searching though the stables, stabbing hay bales with their swords, and three more were directly under his window, searching the back gardens. *Impossible*, he thought; he'd never escape out that way. Even if the guards hadn't been there, he didn't think he could have climbed out of the window, so it was a bit of a relief not to have to try. He turned back to the bed and tried to bend down to look under it, but the wound on his leg stopped him. He tried again and felt the wound start to open up. Biting his lip he rolled onto the bed, holding his leg; he felt the warm blood beginning to seep through the bandages.

After a few moments he heard the sound of someone coming up the steps. Struggling to get to his feet, he limped to the door and slowly nudged it open just enough to peek through. Five guards were nearly at the top of the stairs. He closed the door and hobbled to the cupboard and opened it, but it was full of junk. Ty knew he wouldn't be able to hide in there without the noise and mess giving him away. He heard the sound of the door knob being turned and his heart stopped. Then he remembered the ring and desperately dipped a hand into his pocket. Fumbling, he pulled the ring out just as the door was pulled open, but he knew he'd never get it onto his finger in time.

The door swung wide and the guard entered Ty's room. Ty felt weak with relief when he realized the guard's head was turned to give instruction to the men behind him. Ty quickly slipped the ring on an instant before the guard turned and came in.

The soldier walked over to the bed, bent down, and lifted it with one hand to look underneath. "I knew this was a wild goose chase," he mumbled. He knelt on the bed, opened the window, and shouted down.

"Found anything?"

Ty couldn't hear the reply, but just then he spotted the water bowl on the floor filled with the blood-stained rags that Prolumus had used when treating him. Quickly he pushed it under the bed with his toe, praying it wouldn't make a noise on the wooden floorboards. Fortunately, just at that moment the guard closed the window, and the creaking and shuddering of the old wooden frame masked any other sounds.

"Searching for injured halflings, who cares?" the guard muttered to himself, walking past Ty to the cupboard. It was only a small back bedroom; Ty backed up against the wall and sucked his stomach in as the guard passed.

The guard only just missed standing on Ty's feet with his leather boots. He stood in front of the cupboard and opened up the doors with a sudden yank, as if to scare anyone hiding in there. The door nearly hit Ty in the leg, and he let out a soundless sigh of relief. Ty spied the guard's purse hanging just in front of his nose and fumbled for his scissors; unfortunately he couldn't find them and the chance had gone as swiftly as it had come.

The guard closed the doors and turned to face the injured thief. Ty's heart stuttered in fear until he realized that the man was looking at a picture that hung directly above Ty's head. He held his breath and felt for his daggers, but they were missing. The guard turned and looked up to the ceiling. Ty felt a warm trickle down his leg; he carefully glanced down and saw a drop of blood hanging from a corner of a bandage.

Please no, don't fall, Ty thought. The guard inhaled deeply, as if to shout for reinforcements – but then he sighed, and walked out of the room. "Clear," Ty heard him shout as the door slammed shut, and thought he might faint with relief.

Kern nudged Galandrik and nodded at the guards tromping down the stairs. "All clear, sir," said the guard who had searched Ty's room as his commander returned from outside.

The head guard turned to the table. "Thank you for your cooperation," he said with a nod in Jarrow's direction. "If you hear of anything, or remember anything, please let us know at once. Good day to you all." The guards all left the house and slammed the door shut.

Without a word amongst them, all four men sprang up from the table and ran upstairs, jostling each other in their haste to reach Ty's room. Jarrow opened the door, and they stared in disbelief to see Ty lying calmly on the bed.

Kern stepped in past Jarrow and folded his arms. "Care to share with us how they managed to miss an injured, bleeding thief lying on his bed?"

"Now, that would be telling," Ty answered smugly.

"Come on, thief, tell us," Galandrik said, perplexed.

"Just slipped into the cupboard is all," Ty said, waving his one good arm in that direction. "I covered myself in all the junk, no big deal."

"You simply hid in the cupboard," Kern replied, "right," then, shaking his head, he turned and left the room.

"Well... good to have you back, anyway," Galandrik said with a nod, and he and Ltyh followed Kern down the stairs.

Jarrow stood at the door and looked down at Ty. "That cupboard has been stuffed full of junk since six moons ago," he said seriously. Ty held Jarrow's gaze, a neutral expression on his face. "You never slipped in there, did you?" he asked the injured thief.

Ty stared silently back at Jarrow. "And you never slipped under the bed." The silence was deafening until finally Ty spoke.

"You know I can't tell you, don't you, Jarrow?" Ty answered, a depth of seriousness in his voice that Jarrow hadn't heard before. As the seconds ticked by, Jarrow studied Ty's face and could see he was never going to tell his secrets.

"Maybe you'll tell me another day, Rat," Jarrow said, smiling as he backed out of the bedroom shutting the door behind him.

Ty opened his palm and looked down at the ring. *Three charges left*, he thought, and slipped the ring into his secret pocket. Grinning to himself with the pleasure of having a secret, he shut his eyes.

"Maybe he did die after all," Joli said, watching the guards leave the house.

"Rubbish! I can smell him," Bok said through gritted teeth. "Plus, when Cronos named him the Rat, it was for a good reason."

"So what's our plan then?" Joli asked.

"Sit and wait it out, I guess. He'll turn up somewhere... and then we'll gut him."

Three moons had passed. Kern, Galandrik, Ty, and Jarrow were all seated around the breakfast table, and Ltyh was serving up a breakfast of eggs, tomatoes, and ham, along with freshly baked bread.

"How are you feeling this morning, Ty?" Jarrow asked.

"Good, thanks," Ty replied, stretching his wounded arm.

"When are we leaving?" Galandrik asked the table.

"I think we can go whenever you like, my good friend," Ty answered, looking at Kern for approval.

"Well, I'm up for leaving after breakfast, if you two are," Kern said, sitting back in his chair and rubbing his stomach, "I need to go soon, before Jarrow feeds me to the bursting point. I haven't swung a sword in days," he added.

"And you never swung it very well before," Ty retorted, grabbing some honey and raisin bread.

"I've kept you alive this far," Kern said, draining his goblet.

"Some things never change," Galandrik interrupted. "I can see that it's nearly back to normal for you two, so let's talk about getting out of here, shall we?" The dwarf wiped tomato juice from his beard with a napkin.

"What about the old hide-in-a-barrel trick?" Kern said, leaning forward to place his elbows on the table.

"What about you kiss my skinny arse?" Ty replied, grabbing another piece of bread.

"That sounds good to me! I'll grab him and you get the barrel!" Galandrik said, standing up.

"You come near me, dwarf, and I swear you'll go over!"

"Well, what do you suggest, then?" Kern asked the thief.

"Easy. Tonight we slip away in the darkness towards Breeze. Couldn't be any simpler," Ty answered, approaching the open fire and rubbing his hands

"It seems to me you three don't do simple," Jarrow said, standing up and taking their breakfast dishes through to the kitchen.

"What about our mounts, did you bring them?" Ty asked sitting down.

"We'll sort all that out; just make sure you have all your belongings packed and ready to go at midnight," Kern answered.

"I'll go into town to get some heavy rations; it's going to be a journey and a half, I fancy," Galandrik sighed.

"Grab some potions as well. Most of what we didn't use has been smashed or lost," Kern replied.

"If you buy them from the Quarterstaff, don't mention me," Ty said with a laugh.

"Don't worry, I won't!" Galandrik smiled back.

"I'll go get the horses sorted out," Kern said, resting his hand on Ty's shoulder.

"Thank you," Ty said, placing his hand on the ranger's.

"Any time, Ty, any time."

The night was bright, moonlight bouncing off the silvery leaves that surrounded Jarrow's house. The air was cold and the horses' white breath filled the stable's air. Jarrow looked out of his window.

"It's time we were going, friend," Kern said as he stood next to their host.

"I know, and although I am sad to say goodbye, I wish you all the best."

"Why don't you come with us, Jarrow?"

"No, Kern. I will stay here."

"But you don't suit this town! Come with us; adventure and let yourself feel alive again."

"I have fought too many wars and spilt too much blood, Kern. My fighting days are over."

Kern stared at Jarrow for a moment. "Thanks for all you've done for us, Jarrow."

"You saved me from orc slavery – it was the least I could do."

At that moment Ltyh walked in. "Horses are ready, Kern."

"Thanks, Ltyh. Go call Ty and Galandrik, please."

"Of course," Ltyh said, walking to the door.

"Well... so long," Kern said, shaking Jarrow by the forearm.

"So long, Kern Ocarn. Maybe we'll meet again."

"I'm damn sure we will."

At that moment Ty and Galandrik came into the room, and said their goodbyes to Jarrow and Ltyh.

"Give my thanks to Prolumus when you see him, Jarrow, and farewell," Ty said, shaking Jarrow's hand then pulling his hood up over his head.

"I will do that. Good luck on your quest."

"We'll need more than luck, I fancy," Galandrik grunted.

"I'm sure you'll find some," Jarrow answered.

All four walked through the house into the kitchen; Ltyh was cleaning up the pots and pans from their farewell meal. When he had finished, he walked casually out into the yard stretching his arms as he did. For the last few days he'd gone out each night and gazed up at the stars for several minutes; anyone keeping the house under surveillance would see only the same again tonight. But as he pretended to admire the full moon, he was actually scanning the area discreetly for any signs of movement or watchers. After a few moments he went back inside. "It's all clear."

"Right, I'll go. Grab the backpacks and pass mine up; I don't think I can manage it yet," Ty said.

After making his way with Ltyh stealthily to the stable, Ty paused to check over his horse's gear. "Thanks for everything, friend," he said to Ltyh.

"At least things have been more interesting lately," Ltyh laughed. Then in a more solemn tone, he said, "It's been my pleasure."

"Just as killing you will be mine!" Ty heard as Bok jumped out from his hiding place in a corner of the barn, launching a ferocious attack.

Ty jumped back, grabbing a pitchfork and parrying the first two blows from Bok's sword. A third blow swiped sideways straight for Ty's stomach, and only a swift backwards arch saved Ty from the attack. Bok took the initiative as Ty arched back. Dodging the vicious tines of Ty's pitchfork, Bok threw a vicious right hook, catching Ty square on the chin, spinning him round and felling him to his knees.

Bok stood above him and raised his sword. "Die, you scum," he hissed as he brought the sword down furiously.

"No!" Ltyh screamed, as he tackled Bok from the side, sending them both through of the barn stable doors and to the ground. Ty's leg was throbbing from the fall but he managed to get to his feet, and released his daggers into his hands. Through a haze of pain he advanced on Bok. Without warning, Joli lunged out from behind a water barrel, sword already in motion crashing down towards Ty. With a swift roll he dodged the blow and ended up sprawled on the ground, looking up at his second attacker. Joli's sword hit the barn floor inches away from Ty's left ear, sending sparks into the night.

Bok recovered swiftly from Ltyh's tackle; climbing to his feet, he grabbed Ltyh by the throat and hoisted him up from the floor. In his other hand he drew back his sword, ready to thrust it forward and up into the Ltyh's midriff. "You are one stupid fucker," Bok spat through clenched teeth as he savoured the moment. Ltyh looked at Ty trying to scream for help but Bok's grip succumbed his voice, terror flooded his ash-whitened face and wide eyes.

With a hoarse scream, Ty stumbled to his feet and scrambled towards Bok, forgetting his other attacker momentarily. Ty was knocked flat on his back by a swift kick to the face from Joli. Dazed, he watched helplessly as Bok forced his blade into Ltyh's stomach. With a sickening twist, Ltyh fell to his knees. A trickle of blood slowly rolled down his chin and he fell onto his side, his wide eyes still staring at Ty.

"Finish him," Bok shouted, pointing his blood drenched sword at the thief on the floor.

Ty tore his gaze from Ltyh's form and looked up at Joli; his vision blurred as stars spun, twisting and turning in front of his eyes.

"It'll be my pleasure," Joli answered as he raised his rusty sword above his head, grinning evilly down at the fallen thief. Ty tried to roll onto his side in an effort to get up, but the kick had disoriented him too much and he slumped facedown, waiting for the inevitable. He closed his eyes in resignation.

The blow never came. "Another time, Rat, another time!" he heard Bok shout, then running footsteps fading into the distance.

Ty roused to the sound of a familiar voice. "You okay?" Kern asked, helping the thief to his feet.

"Look after Ltyh, he's been hurt – badly," Ty managed, leaning on Kern's shoulder.

"We know. Jarrow and Galandrik are carrying the boy into the house. They will send a servant to fetch Prolumus."

"What about Joli?" Ty asked, rubbing his bruised chin, his vision slowly clearing.

"He has seen his last starlight," Kern answered, nudging something on the ground with his foot.

Ty followed the movement of Kern's foot; eventually his eyes focused on Joli's body slumped on the barn floor, a dagger protruding from his eye-socket.

Ty sighed. "Poor fellow never had the brains he was born with," he said. "Bok led him a dog's life."

Galandrik came back out. "We need to go now!" he said, his voice urgent but low.

"What about Ltyh?" Ty asked, as Kern helped him mount his horse.

"There's nothing you can do for him. Prolumus is on his way, but Bok isn't going to keep this quiet. There will be twenty town guards here before you know it. Jarrow is urging us to leave; he says he'll make up some cock and bull story about Ltyh catching burglars in the barn."

The three companions finished mounting up, and without even a single glance back they raced from Jarrow's house. Ty cringed as the horse's gait made him wince with every hoofbeat, but he held the reins tight and kicked on.

Jarrow looked sadly down at Ltyh lying on the leather chair, now ghostly grey. The older elf knew there was nothing more he could do.

There was a loud knock at the door, and Jarrow sighed.

Chapter Sixteen
Into the Mountains

After two hours' hard riding, the trio came across a rocky outpost. The landscape was slowly changing, growing hardened with more stone and rock and less grass; pathways of hard-packed dirt and mountainous terrain now replaced the green fields behind them.

"I think here would be a good place to stop and give the horses a rest."

"I agree, Galandrik; head up that rocky slope," the ranger answered, nodding at Ty.

They climbed up the rocky path leading up a winding foothill, the leading edge of the Eastern Mountains; soon they found a clearing amongst the last few trees that littered the rocky hillside.

"Here will do lovely," Ty said, swinging his leg over his horse's back and landing on the ground with all the grace of an orc.

"Still in a bit of pain?" Kern asked, dismounting his steed.

"Yeah, but it's a hundred times better than when he first struck me with that lightning bolt. I honestly thought I was going die or lose my arm. It ripped the flesh like no pain I have ever felt before. I don't think that fight in Jarrow's barn did me any favours either; it's killing me holding the reins," Ty answered as he rotated his shoulder.

"You were lucky to escape – and more than once," Galandrik pointed out.

"I think maybe Cronos should have named you *'The Cat'* instead of *'The*

Rat,' the number of lives you seem to have," Kern said as he tied his mount to a tree stump.

Soon the three companions were seated, eating a quick meal. "So, you think the dragon will accept the eggs back?" Galandrik asked.

"No idea. But even if she doesn't, I won't be taking them back to Conn," Kern answered with a smile.

"If she doesn't, she will probably just eat us anyway."

"Even dragons wouldn't eat dwarf," Ty laughed.

"At least I'd make a meal!"

"*And* afters!"

"I can see you're feeling better," Kern added.

"I think I liked him better tucked up in bed," Galandrik grumbled.

"Whatever the outcome, we shall find out soon enough, I guess. But we did what's right," Ty said.

"This is about the first time you've ever done the right thing in all the time I've known you," Kern grinned.

"Rubbish! What about in Glabow, when I helped the locals build their church? It was *days* I spent cutting, sawing, and nailing, wheelbarrowing rock and clay – my hands were red raw!" Ty snapped.

"Only because the priest who was running the job had a stash of holy loot that you wanted to get your hands on. Helping them build was the only way to gain his trust and get invited into his house!" Kern shot back with a laugh.

"Well…even so, I helped them!" Ty laughed and blow a smoke ring.

"I think we should move on. It's been a good three hours since we left Jarrow's and we need to be well into the mountains by morning," Galandrik said, stroking his mount's mane as the beast munched an apple from his palm.

The party gathered their possessions and left the clearing; slowly they picked their way over the rugged pathways up into the mountains. Low, rocky hills on either side slowly started to rise up like giant stalactites, the path between them widening as tree cover slowly disappeared.

"It's bloody bleak here," Ty said, wrapping his cloak tighter around his shoulders.

"And it's not going to get any better, either," Kern added.

"Rubbish, it's the best landscape in the world! The smell of the rock and the beauty of the mountains are like nothing else in Bodisha," Galandrik insisted.

"What beauty? What about the rolling hillsides and lush green forests? Now that's beautiful," Kern argued.

"I would rather be in the Orc's Armpit rolling bone dice," Ty said drily.

"Typical from you," Kern replied.

Just then a black shadow streaked across the moonlit landscape, covering them in darkness. A rush of wind surged around and through the party, and cold air engulfed them as their horses reared wildly. Then, as quickly as it had come, it was gone.

Kern struggled to regain control of his mount, then drew his longsword. "What the hell was that?"

"No idea; storm clouds?" Galandrik answered doubtfully, drawing his huge axe. "We are getting up on higher ground."

"You always draw your weapons when it's going to rain?" Ty said, spinning around on his mount.

"Good point," Kern replied, "but let's move on." He kicked his mount into a quick canter

A shriek from above suddenly echoed through the mountains; Galandrik's horse reared once more, sending the dwarf crashing to the ground. Kern, trying desperately to control his own beast, spun round, looking up to where the noise seemed to have come from.

"Wyverns! Quick, into that cave!" Ty shouted, spurring his mount on. Kern reached down and grabbed Galandrik's hand, pulling the dwarf up onto the back of his own horse.

The wyverns swooped. Galandrik watched in terror as the creatures dived towards them, wings flapping in the night sky and shrieks filling their ears. "Hurry up, they're gaining on us!" Galandrik yelled.

Ty reached the cave opening first. Jumping from his horse, he grabbed his backpack and then slapped his mount, sending it racing on upwards into the mountains.

Kern and Galandrik tumbled from their shared mount; taking a stance with drawn sword and raised shield, Kern faced the swooping wyverns. In his fear, Galandrik neglected to grab the backpacks from the side of Kern's mount, and instead dived straight into the cave where Ty stood watching and urging his companions on to safety.

Hellthorn spread its great wings to slow his diving approach. Fierce talons ripped into the haunches of Kern's mount, slashing flesh and bone. Draygore crashed into Kern's shield, teeth shrieking against metal, and sent Kern falling backwards towards the cave entrance, dropping his sword. Kern's horse, screaming in terror, crashed to the ground as Hellthorn ripped into its throat. Blood poured from the wound, and the horse thrashed briefly, then twitched and lay still.

Draygore, now standing in front of Kern, lunged again, swiping its head towards Kern's shield and knocking it from his hand. Scrambling to grab his sword, Kern settled into a defensive crouch, readying himself for another attack. Draygore's head snaked forward, biting and snarling. Kern rolled under the attack and lashed at the wyvern with his blade, cutting deep into the beast's leg. Thick black blood oozed from the cut, sending Draygore reeling back from the attack. With a flap of its giant wings, the creature flew up into the air, screeching in thwarted rage.

Hellthorn advanced from Kern's blind side, sinking razor sharp teeth into his shoulder. Thrown off balance by the impact and sudden pain, Kern fell forward, the weight of the wyvern pinning him facedown. The wyvern ripped into his armour, but Kern's scream of pain was cut short as he lost consciousness.

Rushing from the cave, Galandrik swung his mighty axe at Hellthorn's back. The blow thudded into the wyvern's shoulder with a sickening crunch; the wyvern turned, swinging its black wing into Galandrik and knocking him back into the cave entrance.

Abandoning Kern for the moment, the wyvern turned its attention to Galandrik, stalking forward with its mouth widely open in a hiss that showed razor-sharp fangs, blood-coloured spit oozing and frothing like a rabid dog. Galandrik braced himself for the oncoming attack – then suddenly a bottle flew from the cave entrance and smashed into the wyvern's chest, covering it in an oily liquid. Hellthorn reared its head back with a screech, fangs glistening like bloodied daggers in the moonlight. Enraged, it readied itself to lunge again at Galandrik.

Ty stepped from the cave holding a torch. He hurled it towards the wyvern, and his aim was true. The torch took Hellthorn in the middle of its chest, sending sparks and flames in all directions and igniting the liquid splattered on the wyvern's hide. Within seconds the wyvern was ablaze, spinning and thrashing, screeching as the flames burned into its flesh. Its frenzied movements only fuelled the fire and finally the creature fell to the ground, giant wings flapping feebly as the flames engulfed it.

"Burn, you devil," Ty muttered. Then, helping Galandrik to his feet, he said, "You all right?"

"It'll take more than a bat to stop a dwarf lad!"

"Good. Help me with Kern then."

As they grabbed Kern under his arms and dragged him into the cave, Ty glanced up and saw Draygore swooping back down towards them. Pulling Kern the last few feet to safety, he then retrieved Kern's sword and Galandrik's axe before stepping back into the cave. The burning wyvern was now motionless and silent, and the smell of burning flesh filled the cave and their nostrils.

Once safely inside, Ty lit another torch and they carried Kern back into the depths of the cave, propping him against a wall. Galandrik inspected Kern's torn shoulder; fortunately, the armour had taken most of the damage and the wounds were not as deep as he had feared. Ty helped Galandrik dress the wounds, and after Kern was patched up Ty pointed the torch towards the cave entrance. He watched as Draygore tried in vain to get its huge head into the cave opening. Scratching and snarling the beast tried to force its way in; after a while the wyvern disappeared and the noise stopped.

"It won't get in here; it's far too big to fit into the entrance," Ty said.

"Good, go set fire to it! Like the other one," Galandrik suggested

"I can't. That was the only oil we had, unless you want to go outside and get the other from the saddlebag," he answered, sitting down looking through his backpack.

"I'll give that a miss; I think burning its mate has probably made it a bit mad," the dwarf said with a wry smile.

"We'll wait until morning; it might have cleared off by then," Ty replied.

Kern opened his eyes blearily and, with a grimace, looked down at his shoulder. "Ouch," he whispered, shaking his head as if to clear it. "What happened to the wyverns?" he asked.

"Ty used the torch oil to burn one, but the other one is still about," Galandrik explained.

"Did we get all the belongings?"

"We managed to salvage one backpack, but the horses either bolted or perished."

"These were sent for us," Kern said, rolling his shoulder.

"You think so? Maybe their home is in these mountains and they saw us as a threat to their young."

"I don't think so. I think they were sent to kill us."

"You think we have made the King angry?" Galandrik said helping Kern to his feet.

"Most definitely, we are wanted… badly."

"Story of my life," Ty interrupted. "I think we'll have to go deeper into this cave," he continued as he squatted down, squinting his eyes trying to see into the darkness at the back of the cave. "Looks like there's a little passageway heading downwards at the back here."

"I don't think that beast is going anywhere, judging by the screams from outside," Galandrik agreed.

"We only managed to keep Ty's backpack, so rations will be in short measure," Kern said.

"We are short on everything!" Galandrik said, picking up his axe.

"That's a point. How're the chests?" Kern asked.

"Fine; I checked them. They're made of sturdy stuff. How's the shoulder?"

"Not too bad at all, to be honest," Kern answered, rolling his shoulder experimentally.

"Let's make a start, then, before that thing attracts more attention than it already has," Ty said, waving his torch down the passageway.

They walked cautiously deeper into the cavern. The stale air was stinking and the floor was slippery with water that trickled in downwards from the cave entrance. After ten minutes' walking, the passageway had still not changed; it sloped downwards at a steady decline, and the further they walked the worse the smell got.

"Is this damn corridor ever going to end?" Ty said, shaking his head.

"Dunno. Is your moaning?" Kern replied.

Ty opened his mouth to reply, but Galandrik interrupted. "I see you two are back to normal!"

The party walked on until the passageway opened into a circular cavern that was clearly more than just a natural chamber. A door sat at the far side of the room; barrels and crates lay strewn about the room, and the rotten fruit and meats that filled the crates gave off a nearly unbearable smell that permeated the room. Some of the leaking barrels still held mead that had gone off long ago, adding to the stench in the air. The party covered their faces with cloaks and hoods, trying to protect their nostrils from the stink.

"This must have been an old storage room," Ty said, gagging behind his hands.

"And not too long ago abandoned, by the looks of it," Galandrik answered, kicking over a crate and sending a nest of rats scuttling into the crevices in the walls.

After examining the door Ty got his lockpicks out and went to work on the lock. Within minutes the lock clicked; Ty smiled at the others, looking overly pleased with himself. As gently as he could Ty pushed the door but it seemed to be stuck. Setting his shoulder against the door he pushed harder, to no avail.

"Are you sure you unlocked it?" Kern asked smugly.

"You heard it unlock as well as I did!" Ty barked back.

"Maybe you're losing your touch," Galandrik chuckled. "Or your injuries may have weakened your lock-picking skills – or maybe the door has a magical lock as well?"

"Look, I know a magically-locked door from a normal door. This isn't locked with magic, it's just old and needs a good shove," Ty said, walking back to Galandrik,

"A shove, you say? Right – stand back," Galandrik announced. Dropping his axe to the floor, he spat on his hands and gave them a quick rub, then picked the axe up again.

"Won't this make more noise than a little?" Kern protested, stepping back a pace. "And who knows what's lurking around here."

"Any better ideas? We stay in here, that smell will kill us," the dwarf answered, holding the giant axe to one side, readying himself for a swing.

Covering his eyes, Ty shouted, "Hit it!" And with that, Galandrik's mighty axe swung round and into the door with a deafening smash.

They all peered expectantly at the door; Galandrik's blow had splintered the wood, removing a smallish chunk.

"Maybe I'm losing *my* touch?" Ty said, raising an eyebrow.

"I ain't finished yet, lad!" Galandrik swung and again knocked only a modest chunk out.

"Want *me* to have a swing?" Ty said, smiling and offering a hand.

"Just leave him to it," Kern said.

Galandrik swung his axe three more times before succeeding in making a hole large enough to climb through. Kern stepped up to see what lay beyond. "There's a boulder up against the door. Someone didn't want it opened," he announced.

"Maybe some*thing* didn't want it opened," Ty suggested.

After a few minutes they squeezed through the hole, after knocking away some remaining shards of timber, to find themselves in a corridor that led straight on ahead. They continued walking down for a few minutes, then arrived at the entrance to another circular room.

They look through into the room, it had another sloping corridor heading downwards to their left. The wall on the right featured a massive hole, probably ten feet in dimension. From beyond the opening, they could hear voices which seemed to float up from whatever lay below. They walked slowly to the hole, and stretching out carefully over a pile of rocks, they looked over and down.

Directly in front of them and about ten meters down was a massive room. To either side were two curving slopes leading down to the floor of the room. In the room's middle sat a stone table. At each corner of the table was a wooden post rising several feet, and on the table lay a man. He was spread-eagled, hands and feet each tied to one of the wooden poles. A pentagram symbol was scrawled on his bare chest, in what looked like blood, and he was nude except for a leather loincloth. Standing next to the bound figure, a tall figure wearing red robes and bearing a wooden staff was chanting. Perhaps two dozen men were ranged around the room, all in similar but drab-coloured robes, heads bowed and arms folded.

"Curse the humans, curse the humans, and curse the humans," the man in red shouted, raising the staff high above his head. Ty caught a glimpse of the head of the staff, and it appeared to have been carved into the shape of a bird's head. The ritual continued. "With my hawk's head I will pluck out your eyes; with my claws I will rip the flesh from your black human bones; and with my wings I will lift you into the heavens, then drop you into the pit of hell!" the red-robed man sang, as the men around the table raised their arms above their heads, as if on cue, and cheered.

"With the blood of this man we will steal the magic of men. We will use their magic against them, we will drive them back to the sea, and the land will be ours once more!" The robed man rested his staff on his victim's forehead, then dragged it down over his chest.

"It's going to be a sacrifice. Maybe we can sneak past without them noticing?" Ty whispered.

"What about the man on the table? We can't just leave him to these creatures," Kern replied incredulously, as they slipped quietly back down from their vantage point.

"This isn't our fight! We have to get through here, and fighting these will only end in disaster," Ty hissed back.

"Kern is right," Galandrik said, drawing his huge axe. "We can't leave him."

"With or without you, Ty, we fight!" Kern said, drawing his sword.

Ty shook his head and dropped his backpack to the cave floor while pulling out his crossbow. "What's the plan?" he asked unenthusiastically, still shaking his head.

Kern leaned forward, scouting out the surroundings. In a few moments he turned to the others, "We go down and around. Count to a hundred, then hit the leader, the one in the red robes, with your crossbow. Even you couldn't miss a target that size," Kern grinned, trying to lighten the mood. Ty just stared at him bleakly, and Kern sighed. "When you drop the leader, then we'll charge in. They don't look armed so it shouldn't be too hard," he finished.

"Ok, but don't say I didn't warn you," Ty said, lying down on the rocks and loading a crossbow bolt.

Kern and Galandrik slowly made their way down the slope, keeping low under the cover of the wall; eventually they reached a stone slab behind the tall man in red.

Once in position behind the man, they could see three other exits, corridors leading away from the room. The man on the slab was elven; not very old, Kern thought, but then elves always did hide their age well. He gauged the distance and thought he could get to the table within seconds, and braced himself for the attack.

Galandrik whispered, "Shall I concentrate on crowd control while you deal with the man in red?"

"Yes," Kern said with a nod. "Do it berserker style; they'll shit themselves!" Galandrik smiled and gripped his axe.

Ty sighted down his crossbow at the red-robed man; he could see Kern and Galandrik nestling behind a stone slab within feet of his target, "Always fighting other people's battles," he muttered. "We never learn. Always doing things for others for nothing, probably won't even get a thank you…" Ty held his crossbow steady, the lethal tip of the bow aimed directly at the man's chest. A minute passed as Ty counted under his breath.

"96, 97, 98 –" then he froze. He felt something cold and hard against the back of his neck.

"I wouldn't do that if I were you," he heard a voice say from close behind him – *too* close. Cursing to himself he dropped his crossbow next to him, then held his hands out in front of him and waited.

Xioven and Bok sat at their usual table in the Bucket of Blood inn. "Sorry for your loss, Bok," Xioven said, taking a mouthful of ale.

"Yeah, thanks. He was a good friend, Joli was. *Damn* that Rat! I will avenge Joli and get those chests back if it's the last thing I ever do," Bok vowed, slamming his jug of ale on the wooden table and spilling most of it.

"When are you going to set off on their trail?" Xioven asked the thief.

"As soon as my horse is readied. They shouldn't be hard to track; there's only one path through the Eastern Mountains this far south, and that's through the towers and into Breeze," Bok explained.

"He seems to leave a trail of destruction wherever he goes, so it shouldn't be too hard," Xioven said grimly.

"Yeah, he's a walking disaster. And I nearly had him! Standing above him, ready to strike, when some barn hand who wanted to be a hero stepped in. Well, I soon put paid to him," Bok smirked.

Bok's boasting was cut short by the sound of horses outside. Xioven and Bok turned and looked out the window Thirteen riders, all wearing the King's emblem on their breasts, were dismounting and tying their horses up outside. "I wonder what the hell King's men are doing here," Xioven said curiously.

"Yeah, I wonder what they want in Forkvain," Bok said.

The door swung open and Svorn entered the inn. He stopped and looked around walking from one end of the bar to the other, he walked back to where he entered "Barman, over here," he snapped.

The potbellied barman shuffled over to where Svorn was standing. "Yes sir?"

"I am Svorn, captain of the King's personal guard. Have you food here?"

"Yes, certainly – for you and your men, the finest food in Forkvain," the barman declared.

"I doubt that, but it'll do. Bring food and drink enough for thirteen men over to those tables," Svorn said, pointing at the table next to Bok and Xioven. He walked outside and then came back in followed by twelve well-armoured men. They all sat down after removing some of the armour that encumbered them. Before long, the table was lined with pots of stew, bread, fruit, and ale, and the men dove in hungrily, talking over one another as they shared stories of glorious battles in days gone by.

Bok got up and stood at the bar next to Svorn, two empty mugs in hand. Svorn looked the thief up and down with a steely gaze. Svorn turned back to the barkeep. "I'm looking for a party of three, a Human, a halfling and a dwarf. They go by the names of –"

Before he could finish his sentence, Bok interrupted. "Ty the Rat!"

Svorn looked suspiciously at Bok, his hand instinctively moving to the hilt of his bastard sword.

"No need for that, good friend! I am also looking for these thieves," Bok explained, holding both hands up in a gesture of innocence.

"Best you explain…*friend*," Svorn said menacingly, crossing his arms over his chest.

"I will indeed explain – but please, Svorn, captain of the King's guard, come join me and my companion," Bok said, taking a step towards his table and pointing to an empty seat. Svorn followed Bok over and sat down warily.

"This is Xioven, my good friend and the respected owner of the Quarterstaff Magic Shop, and I am Bok the bounty hunter," he said, giving Xioven a kick under the table.

"Good to meet you," Xioven said, that was replied by a nod of the head from Svorn.

"I have been following the trail of those you seek since Praise," Bok began.

"Why do you follow these men?" Svorn asked, leaning back in his chair.

"There is a bounty on their heads," Bok replied, "for theft and murder."

"Who did they kill?"

"They killed my associate Joli, not even two days ago!"

"But you said you have been following them since Praise. That is over five days' ride from here," Svorn said, picking holes in Bok's story.

"Yes, indeed it is," Bok said with a slight stutter, "but when we began tracking them, they were wanted for stealing horses in Praise. We caught up to them two days ago, and my friend died at Ty's own hand."

Svorn stared at Bok and frowned, contemplating his statement. "They have stolen two valuable chests from me as well," Xioven added.

"From *us*," Bok corrected quickly.

Svorn's attention turned to Xioven, and Bok's horse-stealing tale was forgotten in an instant. "Chests? What chests?" Svorn asked, gazing intently at Xioven.

"Two splendid, jewel-encrusted chests. I was on my way to go get them opened when he…that *Rat* ambushed me and stole them. I did some damage to him, but he got away in the end," Xioven explained.

"So where did, ah, *your* chests come from?" Svorn asked, leaning back into his chair and lacing his fingers behind his head.

Xioven looked at Bok for assistance but he said nothing; his eyes widened with a blank expression.

"Oh come now, tell me where these precious chests came from," Svorn said, leaning forward to rest his elbows on the table. "I'm interested in jewel-encrusted chests; it's a passion of mine."

Bok turned slowly to Svorn, "…I won them," he lied. Xioven closed his eyes and sighed heavily in disbelief.

"Oh, you won them, really! You won these jewel-encrusted chests," Svorn said with a knowing smile.

"Yes, I got lucky," Bok said, looking down at the table.

"Extremely lucky, I would say, luckier than the other guy. At what game or contest exactly did you win these *precious* chests?" Svorn asked. Svorn placed his sword and his forearms on the table and leaned in, lacing his fingers together.

"It was a game of… bone dice, in – up north near Gateford forest," Bok said, stuttering over his sentence.

"Bone dice, you say! And who did you win these off – or I should say, who lost?" Svorn asked. He lifted his hands, resting his elbows on the table and his chin on his clasped hands.

"I... I... didn't catch his name. He was a traveller and he stopped at our camp, that's Joli and I, the one Ty killed," Bok stammered. Svorn's restless movements were making him very nervous, and his gaze kept darting to the sword on the table between them. "We had a few ales and one thing led to another, and we ended up playing dice, that simple really."

"So what did you have to put up against these precious chests?"

"Just gold, the guy couldn't open them, the chests I mean, so he just wanted to be rid of them – I mean, well, that's what he *told* me anyway," Bok said with added enthusiasm, sensing a possible escape from his web of lies.

Svorn rested his hand on the hilt of his sword and learned back in his chair. His men had picked up on his body language and expressions, and they set down drink and food, readying themselves for action. A bead of sweat trickled down Bok's temple, but he dared not wipe it away; he just stared at Svorn and tried to look honest. Xioven's hand was trembling; he could hardly lift his goblet without spilling its contents.

Svorn suddenly leaned forward. "Right then!" he exclaimed. Bok flinched in his chair like a child expecting a smack, and Xioven spilled his ale. "What's up with you two?" he added.

"Nothing, good sir," Bok said with false cheer. Quickly recovering his posture, he lifted his ale and took a massive swig, his hand visibly shaking.

"So do you know where this Ty went with your chests?" Svorn asked, smiling.

"Yes, though the Eastern Mountains to Breeze," Bok said, confidence returning to his voice.

"As you are a bounty hunter, I suppose you can track him?" Svorn said, standing up from the table. Bok and Xioven clambered nervously to their feet as well.

"Yes sir, I'll find him," Bok said.

"It's settled, then. We will meet in the stables tomorrow at dawn and proceed together," Svorn announced. "You will get your chests, I will get my man and take him back to the King, and we will all be happy."

"We will, thank you," Bok said, extending his hand for a handshake. "May I ask why you want him?"

After a pause, Svorn answered. "He is a thief who stole two precious jewel-encrusted chests which belong to me. I will reclaim them and deliver his punishment - beheading."

Bok swallowed deeply as Svorn ignored his proffered hand. The soldier walked back over to his men, sat down and began to eat.

Bok and Xioven hurried out of the Inn. "Why did you mention the chests?" Bok hissed, once outside.

"Stealing horses, you said! He knew Ty wasn't a horse thief!" Xioven replied.

"Whatever. I think he bought my story about winning the chests," Bok said. He thought about the sentence of beheading, and scratched his neck.

"I'm not too sure," Xioven answered.

"I must go with him, even if he doesn't believe me. I will never get a better chance to kill Ty."

"Yes, but what about the chests though?"

"Don't worry about the chests. I'll keep a watchful eye on them and take them at the right time. It's what I do, remember?" Bok boasted.

"It's your choice, but stealing from the captain of the guard isn't the wisest thing to do."

"Maybe not, but they are more interested in Ty than in those chests. Besides, the King has more than enough gold already."

"Whatever you say, my friend. May the gods be with you."

"Fuck the gods; I want Ty."

Svorn settled into his seat at the table next to Tez, his second-in-command. Grabbing a ladle, he scooped a portion of beef stew into his bowl, then tore off a chunk of fresh herb bread and began eating with gusto.

"What was that about?" Tez asked. "At one point I thought you were going to kill them."

"I thought about it, yes. They killed Solomon," he said, seemingly unbothered as he dipped the chunk of bread into the stew.

"What? And…you let them go?" Tez said, frowning.

"Yes, that's exactly what I did, Tez. They told me some cock and bull story about winning the chests at dice and how Ty stole the chests from them," Svorn said, wiping stew from his chin.

"But, how, I thought…*Huh?*"

"I know; I don't understand exactly what went on," Svorn said, finishing off his stew. "But what I *do* know is that Ty still has the chests, and our new friends are going to lead us straight to them."

Tez smiled. "You want someone to watch them, make sure they don't leave town? You may have spooked them."

"Yes, send Jud and Alexon," Svorn said, grabbing some cake covered in sweet frost icing for dessert.

The next morning Svorn and his men readied their horses. His men, full from a hearty breakfast, donned their armour and saddled the mounts. Bok walked round the corner leading his horse. "Good morning," he said, yawning.

"Good day, Bok. Where's your companion?" Svorn asked.

"He isn't coming. He can't ride a horse and he has a shop to open; he would be useless," Bok answered.

"I thought he was your partner?" Svorn said, turning back to his mount and tightening the straps on his saddle.

"Well…sort of. I do the hunting and he does the…erm…selling."

Svorn looked at Tez and raised an eyebrow; Tez suppressed a smile.

Soon they were on the move, heading east. After a solid three hours' ride, the soldiers came to a rocky outpost. The landscape was slowly getting harder under foot and the luscious green grass was sparser. Bok raised his hand and called a halt. Sliding from his horse, he studied the ground for a moment, then picked up some dried horse dung and crumbled it in his hands, sniffing at it.

He walked up a rocky path through the rugged beginning foothills of the Eastern Mountains; soon he came to a clearing surrounded by a little sprinkling of trees. Svorn and Tez followed, watching intently as the 'bounty hunter' bent down to pick up a dried apple core, and something else that Svorn couldn't make out.

"What is it?" Svorn asked Bok, sounding slightly impatient.

"Lemon-leaf pipe tobacco. Three people camped here not two days ago – and this, my friend, is horse shit," Bok said, rising with his hand out, a piece of horse muck in his palm. Svorn looked at him without moving.

Bok slowly turned his hand, letting the horse manure fall nearly onto Svorn's boot. Then he dusted his hands off and walked past him back to the others.

"Remind me of this day just before I kill him, Tez," Svorn said, kicking the muck on the ground and turning.

The party moved on and eventually came to a cave entrance. Outside the cave was the corpse of a half-eaten horse; next to this was the wyvern, burnt and charred. Vultures scattered as the mounted men rounded into sight.

"What in the pit of Hades is that?" Bok said, jumping down from his horse and walking over to the wyvern.

"Looks like the remains of one of the wyverns sent by the King to kill your friend Ty," Svorn said, dismounting.

"I guess it lost that battle," Bok laughed.

"Yes, unfortunately it does. But maybe the other wyvern got them," Svorn said, walking over to the cave entrance and looking in.

"Maybe, but I think these footprints say different. I think they hid in this cave," Bok said, squatting at the entrance and peering in.

"Tez, where does this cave lead?" Svorn asked, turning to his fellow soldier.

"I think it's one of the old ore caves that lead all through the mountains," Tez answered. "I'm not sure where exactly they exit, but I should imagine somewhere near Breeze."

"Head through the two towers and look for the exit," Svorn said. "Take half the men. I'll follow Kern and his merry band through the tunnels and herd them out the other side, where you will be waiting."

"Yes sir," Tez replied. "Good luck, and see you on the other side."

Tez picked six men and headed up the main rocky path, towards the two towers that had guarded the entrance through the Eastern Mountains, many moons ago.

Svorn, Bok, and five of the King's guard stepped into the cave.

Chapter Seventeen
A Tricky Spot

Ty felt the tip of the blade push deeper into the back of his neck. "Get up slowly, and leave your crossbow there," he heard the voice say. As he slowly got back up on his feet, he tried to get a glimpse of his capturer – but every time he shifted his head the blade seemed to dig deeper.

"Walk down the slope, slowly." Ty didn't argue. As he moved down the slope, he glanced at the backpack on the floor and thought about the chests. He also thought there was more than one person behind him; the sound of footsteps echoed around him. Reaching the bottom of the slope, he turned into the main room. Looking over to where his friends were hiding behind the massive stone slab, he could just make out a slight movement in the shadows.

Ty's captor pushed him forward into the main room towards the table where the elven man was trussed. As Ty approached the table, the tall man in the red robes turned and looked at him. Ty could now see that he was a half-orc priest.

"What do we have here?" he hissed at Ty.

"I found him up there next to the old supply exit, pointing a crossbow at you," the voice behind Ty explained to the robed half-orc.

"I was actually pointing at the elf; I thought I'd help you out," Ty said with a smirk.

Ty felt a blow to the back of his head. It wasn't very forceful, but Ty seized the opportunity. He crumpled into a heap and, while balled up on the floor, slipped the ring from his tunic. He held it in his hand, poised between thumb and forefinger.

He was hauled back up to his feet by his captor, whom he could now see was another half-orc dressed in leather armour, his face scarred by many blades that had gotten too close for comfort. Next to Ty stood two more guards. The scarred half-orc behind him kept his blade pressed to Ty's neck. He yanked Ty around to face the orc in red; Ty's backpack was slung in a heap on the ground.

"What are you doing in my mountain?" he hissed.

"You may not believe me, but I'm on a mission from King Moriak. If you let me live, I won't tell him how you have mistreated me. If not…well, there will be one hundred of the King's guards flushing you out of *'your'* mountain before you know it!" Ty said confidently.

The red-robed orc stared at Ty for a second, then suddenly let out a bark of laughter, which prompted all the other robed men to laugh as well. Ty could even hear the two men behind him chuckling.

Ty looked down at the floor, his face reddening. Anger built up inside him at their mocking laughter, and he could feel the heat rising in his face. The sword that had been resting on his neck moved slightly away now, as the half-orc behind him laughed at his expense.

An uncontrollable rage raced through his body; shaking, he thought. *I hope you're ready for this, Kern.* He slipped the ring under his belt and released the daggers in his sleeves into his hands, took a deep breath and spun around, slicing through the throat of the half-orc guard behind him. Instantly the guard dropped his sword, both hands flying to his throat. Blood gushed through his fingers as he fell to his knees. Completing his spin until he was facing the red-robed orc, Ty released the dagger. His aim was true, but the orc parried the dagger with a swipe of his staff, like swatting away an annoying fly. Ty seized the dying guard's sword and assumed a defensive stance.

"Kill him!" the orc priest commanded, but before the guards could move, Kern and Galandrik had cut them down from behind.

The room dissolved into chaos. Most of the robed orc followers scattered, running through the openings in all directions. Three or four disciples ran at them to attack, but they were cut down with ease by Galandrik's huge axe; Kern barely had a chance to even join the fight. In moments, only the tall half-orc in red was left. Ty walked toward him, his eyes still ablaze with anger.

"Not so funny now, is it, you maggot?"

"Oh, that's a matter of opinion, my short soon-to-be-dead friend," the priest hissed walking slowly backwards.

"I think you will be sooner than I," Ty said, readying the dead guard's sword.

"I think not. Before you see the light of day again, I will have gutted you like the pig that your mother gave birth to. You come into *my* mountain, *Tovlok's* mountain, and kill my men? You will die! All of you!"

With those words Tovlok slammed the base of his staff down onto the stone floor; from its top came a blinding flash. Ty, Kern, and Galandrik instinctively brought their hands up to their faces to protect their eyes, but the light seemed to penetrate their flesh, and they were blinded as if they'd stared straight into the light.

Slowly their sight returned, and the room was empty. Even the dead were gone; it was as if they had dreamt it all. The only evidence remaining was the elven man lying on the slab, his eyes rolling in his head as though he had been drugged.

"What the hell are we going to do with him?" Galandrik asked.

"We'll have to take him," Kern answered, cutting the rope and hauling the man upright into a sitting position. He looped an arm over his shoulder, and grunted, "Get the other side, Galandrik."

They got the elven man to his feet, supporting him as Ty grabbed his belongings, Ty checked the dragon-egg chests quickly, then noticed another green backpack which sat next to the slab. Being careful to block the others' view of his activities, he swiftly picked it up and stuffed it into his own backpack.

"Which way?" the dwarf asked, straining under the weight of the elven man.

Ty ran to the exits. One by one he examined them, then finally turned to the others and said, "This one has a breeze coming up through the tunnel, but that's about all I can tell you."

Ty led the way through the damp corridor, it was lit by lanterns hanging on rusty brackets. He held the half-orc's rusty sword in readiness as he went, searching for traps every twenty paces. The tunnels turned east and west; they encountered two or three forks and guessed the way by following the breeze Ty had mentioned.

Eventually they came to a square room with three exits, Fragments of the doors lay around the cave, and the hinges hung at awkward angles from the jambs.

"Looks like these doors were smashed open quite a while ago," Ty said, examining the scene as the others set the elven man down as gently as they could, propping him up against a wall.

"Galandrik, light a small fire," Kern said, retrieving a water canteen from his backpack.

"I'll give him some water, maybe we can bring him out of his stupor."

As the fire was lit and rations shared out, Kern slowly trickled water into the mouth of the elven man. Two or three hours had passed when finally the man muttered something. "Ped…lyn… My na… is Ped…lyn." His fluttering eyelids settled and he seemed to fall back into a deep sleep once more.

"Well, he had a lot to say," Ty said, jumping to his feet. "Shall we go then?"

"Sit down," Kern commanded, shaking his head. "You know damn well we are not going to leave him, so stop being an idiot."

Ty sat back down in a sulk, crossing his arms and muttering certain disgruntled words under his breath.

Another couple of hours passed and Ty got to his feet, "You two can look after sleeping beauty here; I'm going for a scout about."

Kern stood up, rubbing his injured shoulder. "Is that wise? What if you get lost, or come up against a nasty little imp?"

"Ha, ha, you're so funny," Ty sneered, throwing his backpack over his shoulder. "If I do meet a 'nasty imp' I will tell him I know Kern Ocarn, the mighty ranger from the north!"

"Whatever, but don't come back bloody and bruised," Kern said.

"Shall I go with him?" Galandrik asked.

"No chance!" Ty said. "You make as much noise as an ogre dragging a bag of rocks; you would alert every monster for miles! I'll go by myself, and maybe I'll find a way through this shit mountain."

Galandrik cast Ty a frown but knew deep down that the halfling was probably right. After Ty had left, Kern raised an eyebrow to Galandrik. "He will be back – probably running, chased by forty goblins," Galandrik said laughed as the elven man stirred.

Kern held his head up as, his eyes still rolling in his head, the man looked around, trying to focus.

Eventually he spoke, rubbing his head as he did so. "What the hell happened? Who are you two? Am I dead, and where is my party?"

"Whoa, slow down, friend!" Kern said, offering the elf some water. "We saved you from being sacrificed by some half-orc in red robes. You were laid out on a sacrificial slab, remember?"

"No," the elven man said after a sip of water. "The last thing I remember is coming into the caves to gather some ingredients; the rest is a blur. Did you see anybody else?" the elven man asked, still rubbing his head.

"No, just you," Galandrik replied, shaking his head.

"Damn; maybe they escaped."

"May I ask your profession?" Kern said politely.

"Oh, magic really. Illusions, potions, spell-making; that sort of thing. We heard that some rare and unusual plants grew here and thought we would give it a look."

"No muscle, just cloth-wearers?"

"We had a hired hand, but he legged it the minute we were ambushed," the elven man said ruefully.

"That sounds right," Kern agreed. "You can never trust them; they are ruthless."

"Yes, this isn't the first time. Anyway, my name is Pedlyn and I owe you my thanks," he said, bowing his head as best he could. "You didn't happen to pick up my belongings, did you?" he added, looking around the room.

"Sorry, you never had anything with you that we saw," Kern said, tossing a piece of wood from a smashed door onto the fire.

Galandrik passed Pedlyn some salted beef. "You'd better eat, Pedlyn. You'll need your strength to get out of here."

"Thank you," the elf replied, biting into the dry chunk of meat and chewing thoughtfully.

Ty walked down the darkened corridors; the passageways were lit only by the odd lantern. He counted the steps between lanterns – roughly one hundred. He tracked his progress and his turnings with a small chalk mark on the wall every so often, and gauged the distance he had travelled by the number of lanterns he passed.

Eventually he sat and removed the green backpack from his own and opened it up. Inside were scrolls; leather bags full of leaves, berries, and other ingredients; a purse with some gold; an old stick, a robe, and hat; a couple of unmarked potion bottles; and a small spell book.

Ty slid the gold into his secret pocket and picked up the book. Oddly enough, it wouldn't open – no matter how hard he tried, he couldn't get the covers to part. After a few failed attempts, he slid the book back into the bag and set it on the corridor floor next to him.

Standing up he started off again down the corridor making marks on the walls under lanterns as he went. He reached a door made of oak, which seemed bigger and better-preserved compared to the other doors he had passed along the way. Slowly he bent down and looked through the keyhole, but saw only blackness. Pressing his ear to the door he heard the murmur of voices. Slowly he reached down for his lockpicks – then stopped, picturing the look on Kern's face if he were to come running back with angry pursuers at his heel. He tiptoed away and headed back to the party. *Twenty-four lanterns;* he thought.

Pedlyn was clearly feeling much better; the elven man was standing up talking to the others when Ty entered the room.

"She's awake then?" he said cheekily, looking at the elf.

"Oh, I forgot to tell you, Pedlyn. We have another *friend*. This is Ty – or, as he likes to be called, Rat," Kern announced with an introductory gesture towards the thief.

"Hello Ty," Pedlyn said, bowing his head.

"No *'thank you'* then?" Ty replied. Kern turned away, as if reluctant to witness what he knew would happen next.

"I was going to get to that, young Rat. I am indeed truly grateful for your assistance in saving my life, and anything I can do to repay you, I will do," the elf continued, bowing a second time.

"Whatever," Ty replied, squatting next to the fire and rubbing his hands together.

"Ignore him, Pedlyn. He can be tetchy sometimes, and doesn't like strangers," Galandrik said, walking past Ty and nudging him with his knee.

"I know *you* and I don't like you," Ty said with a sneer.

"So what did you find, Mr. Rat?" Kern said, smiling at Ty.

Ty explained the corridors, how they weaved left and right until they reached the big oak door and the voices behind it. The party decided to leave and after putting out the fire and packing their equipment they walked slowly down the corridor. Galandrik offered Pedlyn a dagger as they walked, which Pedlyn gratefully accepted.

"I am not very skilled with a blade, but will do my best if we meet anything along the way," he said.

"Try not to cut yourself," Ty laughed from the front, watching discreetly for his wall markings and counting them. They walked on, going further down the tunnels and deeper into the mountain with every step.

"Wait!" Pedlyn said in astonishment, pointing at a green bag on the floor. "That's my backpack," he explained. Walking swiftly over to it, he picked it up and looked inside. "All there, apart from the gold," he said a few moments later, smiling. "I wonder how it came to be left here," the elf mused, drawing out the robe and hat and donning both items.

"I wonder indeed," Kern said, glaring at Ty.

"I'm surprised you didn't trip over it when you walked past here earlier, Ty," Galandrik added.

"I must have missed it, walked right past it," Ty replied, avoiding eye contact with Kern, knowing the stare he would get. He rubbed the old wound on his shoulder uncomfortably.

They finally came to the end of the last corridor, revealing the big oak door. He listened carefully, then turned to Kern. He held up two fingers, then motioned as though he were throwing an invisible rock. Kern gave Ty a nod and a thumbs-up.

"What on earth was that?" Pedlyn whispered.

"There are two orcs behind the door," Kern replied, drawing his sword as Galandrik hefted his mighty two-handed axe. "Ty calls orcs 'rock-chuckers'," he added.

Ty pulled his tool pouch from his boot and unrolled it on the floor. Scratching his chin for a moment as he studied the tools, he finally selected two picks, then rewrapped his tools and replaced them in his boot.

Ty stopped, holding his picks in place, and nodded to Kern, who slowly walked over to Ty.

"Grab a rag and hold it around my hands to muffle the noise. I've got a feeling this might alert the orcs," Ty said in a faint whisper.

Kern nodded and pulled a cloth food-wrap from his bag. Carefully he held it around Ty's hands as the thief went to work on the lock. After a few moments Ty nodded, and Kern stepped back, holding his sword aloft. Ty nodded his head once… twice… and on the third nod, he turned the doorknob.

A muffled click was heard, but nothing as loud as they had expected. Ty stepped backwards and drew his daggers.

Kern reached forward and touched the handle to the door; then he turned to Ty and nodded again.

With a sudden yank he wrenched the door open. Inside the room were five orcs, two standing and three sitting and rolling dice. The two standing orcs lunged at Kern. A dagger flew through the air and took one down, catching him square in the throat; blood poured from the victim's wound. The second orc was felled as quickly as the first, by a slicing blow from Kern's sword.

"*Two*, you said!" Kern spun round and finished off the orc with a thrust to the chest.

Galandrik ran past Kern into the room. By this time the remaining orcs had overcome their shock at the sudden invasion. All three advanced towards the fearless dwarf. The closest one took Galandrik's axe straight in the chest, opening him up like a hog on a butcher's hook. The axe embedded into the orc's chest, and it pulled Galandrik down with the orc as he fell to the side. The next orc jumped over his dead companion and faced Galandrik, who still struggled to free his axe. The last orc charged Kern, screaming in a long-forgotten tongue. Kern, advancing to assist Galandrik, was forced to divert his attention to parrying a blow from the orc. "Ty, help Galandrik!" Kern shouted.

Ty knew he couldn't cover the distance in time, and raised a dagger above his head. Kern parried the attacking third orc, a sweeping blow narrowly missing his target. Ty's line of sight was hindered by Kern's movement and he could just make out the orc raising his bastard sword above his head for another blow.

Galandrik had one foot on the dead orc's shoulder, wrestling with his axe which was still wedged in the orc's ribcage. He glanced up and saw another orc looking down at him, drool dripping from his mouth onto Galandrik's chest. Galandrik reached for his belt dagger before remembering he'd given it to Pedlyn. Releasing the handle of his axe, Galandrik threw his arms up to cover his face, in some vain attempt to parry the downward strike; he shut his eyes and waited for the end.

Kern disabled his attacker with a slice to the leg, and followed with an upward stab to the soft, unprotected area under the orc's jaw. Blood geysered from the wound and covered Kern as he knelt to finish the orc off. Glancing over to where Galandrik battled, Kern saw the orc standing above the dwarf with sword upraised; Galandrik's arms were crossed – protectively, hopelessly – over his head.

Ty leapt forward with all the speed and dexterity he possessed; he dashed past Kern as the ranger jammed his sword deep under the orc's chin. Ty raised his dagger, but knew he was too late.

Suddenly something hit Ty in the shoulder, spinning him round and into Kern's dead opponent. Kern looked up as a lightning bolt stuck Ty a fleeting glance on its path to the orc above Galandrik. It stuck the orc in his side and knocked him flying to the ground; the orc convulsed uncontrollably as white lightning engulfed him all around. It crackled and sparked before slowly fading, leaving the orc's body lying motionless on the floor.

Galandrik quickly rose, finally yanking his axe clear. He stepped over to the orc that had been struck by lightning and raised his axe; it came down with a sickening thud and split the orcs head like a watermelon.

Ty rolled to his feet, patting his shoulder frantically. "What in Hades was that?"

Kern looked to the doorway and saw Pedlyn holding his book in one hand, his other hand extended, palm up.

"Sorry, Ty," Pedlyn said, lowering his outstretched hand. "You jumped in front from out of nowhere. I was aiming at the orc and had no time to spare."

Galandrik turned and walked to the mage. "Thank you, Pedlyn. You saved my life, and I am truly in your debt," the dwarf said as he bowed his head.

"You saved my life first; consider the scales balanced," the mage answered, nodding back.

"So you're a mage then?" Ty said, rolling his shoulder.

"No, he's a blacksmith!" Kern laughed.

"You know what I mean," Ty replied, bending down to search the dead orcs.

"Yes, I am a mage. My order is in Breeze, the Order of the Relentless."

"You could have warned us. I wouldn't have jumped in your way if I'd known," Ty said, slipping some silver pieces into his tunic.

"Not everybody accepts us; a lot of people think we practice the black arts."

"Well, we do accept you, and thank you for saving our friend," Kern answered. Looking around, they saw they were in a square room with only a little furniture – a small table littered with cups, dice, and some copper pieces; a few chairs. A cupboard and two closed doors finished the room. After listening closely at one of the doors, he knelt and peered through the keyhole, then searched for traps by running his hands over the door and its frame. "I think it's a store cupboard," he said, as if speaking to himself. He placed his hand carefully on the doorknob and slowly, quietly, opened the door.

After peering inside, he pulled the door fully open to reveal a food and armoury store. Inside were old rusty swords, shields, daggers and everything else used to arm up an orc for battle; boxes of hard rations, fruit, and wine sat on other shelves.

"Good guess," Galandrik quipped.

"I could smell the fruit." Ty smiled at the dwarf.

They salvaged what they could use from the store, and searched the rest of the room.

Ty turned to the main door and closed it. "What're you doing, Rat?" Kern asked. "Just locking this in case the guy who wanted to gut Pedlyn is following us. A little trap will help to hinder whoever may follow," Ty explained as he searched the room for likely trap-making items.

"I could help with that, Ty. A little magic in the lock always hinders," Pedlyn said.

"Be my guest," the thief answered, picking up a line of hemp thread from an old crate.

Pedlyn pulled the gnarled wooden wand from his backpack and touched it to the keyhole, reciting some old elven words: "*Shakran oy bolmak.*" The lock glowed red as waves of dancing red lights circled the lock, then vanished.

Ty look over his shoulder and saw the wand. Muttering to himself, "A stick," he shook his head. It would have fetched a good price, had he recognised it for what it was when he was sifting through the elf's pack.

"What stick?" Kern asked.

"I need one for this trap, that's all, nothing," Ty said, retrieving a dagger from a dead orc's belt.

After Ty had set his traps and the room had been fully searched, the second door was opened. It was an exit, leading to another corridor lit by lanterns.

The group moved on. They walked cautiously through endless corridors and old mine shafts, rats scurrying all around them. Galandrik got some menacing looks from Ty for kicking out at them.

The only real lead they had was the slight breeze that no one other than Ty could feel. Twice they paused to eat, and they stopped in an open room and slept, taking watch in shifts, but they continued to move on.

"We are going round in circles, Ty," Kern grumbled.

"No we're not," Ty argued. "Trust me, I said."

Kern looked at Galandrik and raised a sceptical eyebrow.

"We *have* been going for a long while," Galandrik ventured.

"Well, you're the dwarf that builds and lives under these wretched mountains; *you* find the way out!" Ty folded his arms and leaned back against a wall.

"All I was saying is…" and with that they heard a banging in the distance.

Ty looked at Pedlyn and in unison they said, "The traps at the door."

"We'd better move, and move fast," Ty said, stepping further down the corridor.

"Wait! Why run? They are looking for us; maybe we can ambush them?" Kern suggested.

"Good idea, but we need a better place than a corridor. Galandrik might just be spotted," Ty said, looking at Galandrik, who sucked his belly in.

"Okay, let's move forward and look for somewhere better," Kern said, pushing past Ty.

They moved on as quickly as they dared; Ty kept a lookout for traps as best he could. The corridors weaved east and west, slowly inclining. Their legs began ache from the steepness of the climb. Eventually they reached an archway that opened onto a large balcony; beyond that was an open room that seemed to go on forever. There were alcoves, arches, and ledges everywhere they looked, orcs hustled and bustled on every platform and ledge, pulling ropes up and down to lift or lower buckets filled with rocks and water. It was like the inside of an ants' nest. The commotion was staggering and the smell awful.

Kern gestured to the others to keep low, and they all crawled forward towards the edge of the balcony. Galandrik's movements sounded like someone dragging a string of pots and pans, which infuriated Ty, and he glared more than once at the dwarf.

Once at the edge of the balcony they carefully peered over, between the rungs of a wooden handrail badly tied together with tiger grass.

Below them the scene was the same. A stream of rushing water flowed through the bottom of the room and out under a massive opening which looked like a huge open mouth swallowing the flow of water. Orcs scurried about in every direction, digging and smashing rocks with shovels, picks, and axes. Ty nudged Kern and pointed; Kern followed the line of Ty's finger and saw Tovlok talking to three orcs at the bottom of the cavern, just above the mouth-shaped exit where the water rushed through.

Galandrik counted at least fifty workers and twenty armed orcs; he turned to Kern and whispered, "I think we could take them."

Kern shook his head and pointed up at the higher ledges, scattered with orc archers.

"Pedlyn, have you any magic that could help us here?" Ty asked.

"Sorry. I'm a mage, not a miracle worker."

"I guess we'll have to go back and face... wait, if he's down there, who's behind us?" Kern asked, looking back down the tunnel.

"I say we fight," Galandrik snarled.

Kern shook his head at the statement. "We wouldn't stand a chance."

"Whatever you decide, decide it quick. Look," Pedlyn said, pointing down the corridor to where flickering lights were coming into view.

"Shit! We'll have to jump," Kern announced.

"You *are* joking?" Ty frowned. "That's fifty feet, we'll be lucky to survive the fall!"

"What else should we do?" Kern snapped,

"Fight?" Galandrik asked hopefully.

"No!" Ty and Kern said together.

"Kern is right; we have no choice but to jump," Pedlyn said, fumbling in his bag. He finally pulled out a bag of green leaves, and passed one to each of them. "Chew this, it'll help you breathe under water. It will not last forever so don't think otherwise; it will aid us, that's all."

They chewed the leaves with grimaces and gags. "Tastes like cat piss," Ty said, trying to swallow.

"I'll take your word on that," Galandrik replied.

Kern drew his dagger and began to cut the tiger-grass bindings on the wooden handrail. The others followed his lead, not cutting completely through, but just enough that they knew a slight push would easily collapse the rail. The lights from the tunnel were growing brighter and now they could hear voices.

Suddenly an arrow hit the floor between Ty and Galandrik; at almost the same instant, a horn bellowed from up above, "Shit, they've spotted us!" Kern shouted. "No time to cut the bindings, jump NOW!"

The horn echoed around the cavern as arrows flew from all directions, one glancing off Pedlyn's backpack, another striking Galandrik's shoulder but failing to penetrate. Orcs began running up the slopes on either side. The companions scrambled up from the floor, trying to dodge the arrows that flew past. Kern swung a leg over the top of the handrail, but as he put his weight on it, it collapsed; he fell, very ungracefully, down into the water, Pedlyn following immediately behind him.

Ty looked over at Galandrik. "After you, my friend," Ty said, side-stepping an arrow.

"See you in hell!" Galandrik shouted as he plummeted down into the water, arrows following his descent.

Ty stood poised on the edge. Always one for the dramatic gesture, he ducked another arrow, then held his arms out from his sides, closed his eyes, and let himself fall forward.

He waited for the sensation of weightlessness, the wind whipping past his face, but it didn't come. He opened one eye, peeping down to see his feet still planted firmly on the rock. Something was holding him back. He tried to turn his head but could only manage a few inches in either direction. He waved his arms frantically as he felt himself rising into the air. His feet now clear of any solid ground, he felt himself slowly revolving.

Once he was fully turned, facing back down the corridor, he found himself face-to-face with Tovlok, who was holding him aloft by the scruff of the neck.

"Well, little one, it's time you died," Tovlok said, grinning. Ty released his wrist daggers and stabbed at the half-orc's wrist, but it was like striking metal. "Pathetic," the half-orc hissed, and raised a double-forked dagger up level with Ty's face, savouring the moment.

Ty struggled as options flashed around in his head: Invisibility, wriggling out of his tunic, kicking, punching – but it was too late. He knew his time had come. *Why didn't I just jump like Kern did? Why always be dramatic?* He watched, helpless, as the dagger was readied.

The half-orc's eyes opened wide and his glare turned to stone. Ty glanced down and saw the tip of a blade protruding from his stomach, blood beginning to pour down his robes. His jaw opened and slowly his eyes rolled in his head. He toppled forward, Ty still clutched in his grip. As they plummeted towards the water Ty could see, standing in the space behind where Tovlok had stood, an unexpected face: Bok.

Chapter Eighteen
Babysitting Fire

Ty hit the water back-first, with the half-orc next to him. The water was freezing and he was blind. Confusion, panic, and disorientation washed over him as he was swept along towards the giant mouth. He struggled to reach the surface for a breath, but arrows were striking the water all around him. He could hear the whooshing noise they made when they hit the water. Spinning and turning he was carried along, but he didn't struggle in the water; he seemed able to breathe without swallowing a drop.

He could just about make out the lifeless body of the half-orc being swept along next to him. As they went down into the mouth everything went dark. They rushed along, tossed and turned about by the rushing water, and then Ty felt himself falling. *A waterfall,* he thought, just as he was dropped again into another fast flowing stream. Ty struggled to see what was around him, trying to keep up with the water's direction – then his world went black, as a sudden thud on his head sent him into a lifeless haze.

Kern, Galandrik, and Pedlyn were swept along in the water until they went over a third waterfall. Kern struggled to adjust to the bright sunlight, squinting his eyes tightly as he landed in a calm pool. He felt the bottom under his feet and pushed himself to the surface. Still struggling with the sudden daylight, his eyes slowly refocused as he bobbed on the surface of the water. There were several men standing on the banks of the pool all around them.

All the men were dressed in the livery of King's guardsmen apart from one; that one was standing up front holding a large crossbow and dressed slightly more extravagantly, giving the impression of a higher rank.

"Don't even think about it, thieves," Tez said, cocking his crossbow. "Just swim over to that shore and lie still."

Too wearied to resist, they did just that, swimming over to the closest shore and scrambling up, throwing their weapons down to the grass. Once fully disarmed, the guards prodded them until they all sat back to back, then one of the guards secured them with a length of rope, tying it off with a handful of complicated knots.

Suddenly, the body of the red-robed half-orc came flying over the ledge above them and landed into the water. After a few moments, it bobbed to the surface face down. As it did, a shout was heard and four other bodies flew over the edge. These were very much alive, all thrashing and screaming.

After landing with enormous splashes, the four newcomers crawled out of the water, revealing themselves as Svorn, Bok, and two guards. They stood on the shore, catching their breaths and glaring at the roped men. "Where is he?" Bok shouted, struggling for breath.

"Where is who?" Kern answered with a knowing smile.

Bok turned to Svorn as if asking for permission, then swung a fierce backhand at Kern's jaw, knocking his head into Pedlyn's. A trickle of blood rolled down from Kern's lip onto his chin.

"You may regret that," Kern said calmly, licking his throbbing lip.

"I might, really? Right then," Bok shouted, "I will ask you once more, where is that fucking Rat?"

"Kiss my –"

Bok punched Kern full in the nose; the crunch of breaking bone and cartilage was clearly audible. Kern winced and his eyes began to water; blood now streamed from his nose and mouth.

"This is your last chance," Bok said, whipping a dagger from his belt and pressing it against Kern's neck. Another trickle of blood dripped onto his tunic.

"I don't know, we left before him. You saw what happened."

Bok drew the dagger back to strike, but Svorn caught his arm, stopping the fatal blow.

"You are not killing anybody," he said, and pushed Bok away. "You two, search them," he ordered two of his guards; he ordered others to drag the body of the half-orc out of the water. After a thorough search of the captives and the corpse had revealed nothing, Svorn glared at Kern. "Where are the chests?" he barked.

"We sold them," Kern answered.

"To whom?"

"The Fire and Water magic shop in Forkvain."

"Is that right," Svorn said, obviously sceptical.

"As I sit here now. They'd brought us nothing but trouble, so we cut our losses."

"So let me get this straight... Your friend went to all that trouble to steal them and then you just sold them?"

"Yes. We got them open expecting riches, but they were empty," Kern said, spitting a mouthful of blood into the dirt.

"You lie!" Bok interrupted.

"The mage must have grabbed the contents before our friend stole them."

"I'm going to kill him!" Bok stepped forward again but Svorn held out a hand, stopping his advance.

"Tez, send two men back to Forkvain and check out their story. The rest of us will wait here for the other one until dark, then we move on. Hopefully he's dead and we can go home; I'm sick of these damn thieves. We saw him drop with the half-orc; if he doesn't appear before dark, an arrow must have sunk him. There's nowhere else he could have gone; the water was way too strong for him to swim against it."

"Where's his corpse then, you fool?" Bok snarled.

Svorn drew his sword with lightning speed and spun around, the tip coming to rest against Bok's throat. "You ever question me again and I will cut your fucking tongue out!"

Bok held his hands up and swallowed hard. "Yes, sorry."

"You'd just better hope Kern's story doesn't turn out to be true and those chests are in Forkvain." Svorn stared at Bok for several long moments, then re-sheathed his sword, "Get out of my sight."

Kern managed a smile as Bok walked past, but he didn't see the ranger's jest. Seething from his dressing-down, Bok sat up against a tree watching Svorn's soldiers strip the half-orc's body of its richly dyed robe, and wondered if the shopkeeper had double-crossed him.

They waited until nightfall, but there was no sign of Ty. True to his word, Svorn gave the command to move on, and the prisoners were marched through the fields and paths until they hit a main road that led all the way to Breeze. Kern, Galandrik, and Pedlyn were crowded into the back of a wagon. It was a jolting, uncomfortable ride; Pedlyn's back was still sore from the bruising water landing. Cold, wet, and miserable, the party didn't speak as they drew ever closer to the town of Breeze, resplendent in the moonlight.

Breeze was the main town on the east-west roads through the Eastern Mountains. Everyone stopped here; it wasn't a huge trading town like Raith, but you could buy virtually anything you wanted. It seemed more geared to the traveller, with pubs and shops lining the streets, and dancing girls swaying provocatively in the windows.

They entered Breeze through the main gates. As they travelled through the streets, people ran alongside the wagon laughing and jeering; some even spat on them. Only common criminals were led through town in the back of a wagon.

Eventually they reached a massive house surrounded by an enormous wall, giant gates barring the entrance. Four guards stood watch at the gate; upon seeing Svorn, they unbarred the gates and the wagon was led through. Svorn and his guards dismounted near the front entrance of the house; Svorn handed his reins to a waiting horseboy, then started up the steps.

"Take them to the dungeons," he said, without turning back.

The captives were led from the wagon around the side of the giant house. House guards patrolled every thirty paces or so and trees lined the inside walls of the grounds. They finally reached a small, plain door at the back of the house. One of the guards unlocked it and led the trio inside, then along dark, damp corridors and down winding steps, until they reached a large underground room with six cells, three in a row along either side of the room. They were each pushed into separate cells, and the barred doors slammed behind them.

One of the guards undid his trousers and began pissing into Galandrik's cell. "I hate dwarves," the guard said, laughing as he aimed in Galandrik's direction.

"Surprising," Galandrik said thoughtfully. "With that little thing you should feel like you're family."

The guard finished off and turned round, walking out of the only door. They heard the lock click shut.

"Well, this looks familiar," Galandrik said, stepping over the puddle of piss as it flowed towards the drain in the centre of the room.

"Aye, they all have a tendency to look the same," Kern answered.

"You've been behind bars before?" Pedlyn asked.

"A couple of times," Kern said with a snort.

"This is how we met," Galandrik added.

"You met in a cell?" Pedlyn said with a smile on his face.

"Yes, we did," Galandrik replied.

"It was much like this one, to be honest," Kern said, looking at the hinges on the door. "It's at times like this I miss Ty the most," he added, rubbing his chin and gently touching his broken nose.

"Is he dead?" Pedlyn asked solemnly.

"Don't be stupid. Ty, dead? He will turn up all grinning and happy," Kern replied.

"Yes, I can see him now," Galandrik grinned. "But you're right – he would relish getting us out of here," the dwarf said, kicking at a rat as it scurried out of the drain.

Svorn entered the study, his usually bright and gleaming armour dirty and dull. He stood silent as Conn sat with his back to him, facing a roaring fire.

"Where are my chests?" Conn said without turning. Biting his lip, Svorn didn't answer. "*Well?*"

"We…" Svorn cleared his throat and started again. "We lost the Rat and the chests, my lord. We think he died under the Eastern Mountains. There was a battle with the orcs there; we lost three men of our own. Ty never came out, nor did the chests, my lord," he reported.

Conn spun round in his chair and stood up, his face like thunder and his eyes squinting in anger. "You know how precious they are?" Conn asked, thumping the table with his fists.

"Yes, my lord. We did all we could, I swear it."

"The King will not be happy about this, you know that," Conn added walking over looking out the window, His arms now folded, he rubbed his chin.

"I'm sorry; I have failed you and the King, my lord," Svorn said, bowing his head.

"Do we have the others?" Conn said, glaring at Svorn.

"Yes, there are three of them. They seem to have picked up a mage on their travels," Svorn said, trying to be as enthusiastic as possible.

"They need to be punished, and never let to see the light of day again. Make sure they suffer every day. Keep them locked up until they forget their own names," Conn snarled. "I travel back to Raith in two moons, and I will have to explain this ball-up to the King – *and* only one wyvern returned," he said, sitting back down in his chair.

"It will be done as you wish, my lord," Svorn answered, not daring to mention the burned wyvern carcass he'd seen.

"And clean yourself up," Conn continued. "You're the captain of my guard, not a beggar. Now be gone," he hissed, spinning back round to face the roaring fire.

Svorn closed the door behind him; taking off his helmet, he wiped his forehead. He headed along the corridor and down a spiral staircase, at the bottom of which sat Bok. "Thank you for the help," Svorn said, throwing the cutthroat a bag of coins. "Don't ask for any more; our business is complete," he added, nodding to another guard to see Bok out.

"Many thanks, but he's not dead. You know that, right?"

"I don't care, as long as he stays 'dead,' that's all that matters," Svorn replied, watching Bok walk to the exit.

"Don't say I didn't warn you," Bok said, walking down the path to the main gate, tossing the bag of gold in the air.

Two days had passed. The imprisoned trio had been given no food, and precious little water. They were routinely soaked with cold water during the day, which made them freeze at night; their morale was low. Galandrik had even contemplated killing a rat for food, but had refrained – so far.

"I wonder what rat tastes like?" he mused aloud.

"You'd eat your friend?" Pedlyn joked.

"No, not Rat – rat. A dirty, smelly, horrible rat!"

"Yes, your friend," Kern added to the banter.

"You know what I mean." Galandrik managed his first smile in two days.

"We could try one," Pedlyn said, squatting near the drain.

"I don't think it's going to pop out with you sitting there!"

"You wouldn't want to eat rat," Pedlyn said. "They carry horrible diseases – plus we have nothing to cook it on," he added, giving up on the jest and walking back to the wooden bed.

"Who said anything about cooking it first?"

"You're one sick dwarf," Kern said.

There was a long silence as they each busied themselves with their own thoughts.

"You think he's dead?" Galandrik finally asked Kern.

"Well, he was right behind us, and he didn't come out."

Pedlyn turned to Kern. "But before you said he would 'turn up all happy and smiling'."

"Indeed I did, and I hope he does, but… this time I'm not too sure. That water had a ferocious current."

"What about the eggs? Do you think those chests are waterproof?" Galandrik added.

"There's me, wondering if our pal is alive, and *you're* wondering about the eggs!" Kern laughed, and there was a despairing note under the amusement. Then he sighed. "Good point though."

"Well," Galandrik said, stroking his beard, "wherever he is, I bet the chests aren't far away."

Ty's eyes opened slowly. His head was pounding. Reality hit him like a thunderbolt – he was still in the water, his head barely clearing the surface, and his legs pointed in the direction of the current. He instantly started to cough, water spluttering out of his mouth. He tried to see what was holding him but couldn't. He knew his tunic was caught up on something but couldn't tell what. He was in total darkness, and the noise from the rushing water was deafening.

He carefully freed one arm from the strap of his backpack, and the force of the water's flow made the pack swing around to his other shoulder. He pulled his other arm free, then raised a leg out of the water and wrapped the backpack straps around it. Slowly he pulled one arm in to free it from the sleeve of his tunic. As he spun around in the current he felt around with his free arm, eventually determining that his collar was snagged on a piece of wood. He released his dagger and cut himself free.

Floating freely now, he was pulled along by the water towards an opening with sunlight bursting through into the darkness. Ty was flung out of the gap; he seemed to be in the air for ages, then landed in the centre of a pool with a splash.

Pedlyn's leaf had worn off and he struggled to hold his breath until he broke through to the surface. He bobbed there in the pool while he took stock of his surroundings. He was alone, apart from two wild dogs some ten feet away on the bank, greedily ripping flesh from a carcass. He treaded water towards the dogs until he could feel the sandy bottom of the pond under his feet. He continued moving slowly forward, bending nearly double to keep most of his body hidden under the water. At last, he leapt up, shouting and splashing the water with his hands; the dogs bolted.

Ty stepped out onto the grass, dragging his backpack behind him. He slumped to the ground and took off his freezing wet clothes. He wrung them out as best he could, and laid them on a rock to dry in the morning sunlight. Tipping the contents of his backpack out onto the grass, he saw that only the chests were intact; everything else was either smashed or waterlogged and ruined. He suddenly remembered his money pouch, and reached quickly into his tunic. With a smile he pulled the pouch out, intact and heavy with coin. He felt in his pocket for his ring, but it was empty; frantically he searched all his other pockets but the ring was gone. All he had left were his chests, his gold, and one dagger.

He sat on the grass to think, and spotted one of the dogs lurking nearby, next to a tree. He picked up a rock and threw it; the dog disappeared, but he thought it wouldn't stay gone for long. He stared at the thing the dogs had been eating, half submerged in the water.

It looked like a corpse.

He stood up to see better and moved stealthily forward. It *was* a corpse.

He grabbed a branch and poked the body's back, just in case it was still alive; it didn't move. Using the stick for leverage, he rolled the corpse over; even though the face had been mostly eaten, he knew it was Tovlok. He threw the stick down and walked back to his clothes. He knew he should have been triumphant that he had survived while his attacker was dead, but he felt nothing at all.

After an hour he felt warmer and his clothes, though still damp, were not half as wet as they had been. He shook off his stupor enough to get dressed. He stared down at the chests, then sat next to them and picked one up. Resting it on his knee, he placed four fingers on the gems and pushed. The chest clicked open; the egg inside looked as good as ever at first glance, but then Ty noticed something different. He gently lifted the egg out of the chest for a closer look. It was freezing to the touch, and steam rose from its shell like a morning breath on a winter's day.

Ty heard a noise from behind; turning, he saw the two dogs edging closer, getting braver by the second. He gently placed the egg down next to his backpack, then leapt up and ran at the dogs, waving his arms and shouting. The dogs hesitated briefly, then bolted. Ty chased them for a few steps, then stopped as the dogs retreated a small distance. It was obvious to him that as long as the body was there, the dogs were not going to be chased off.

He walked back to the corpse and stood above it. "Well, I'm not burying you, if that's what you think," Ty said to himself.

He grabbed one leg of the corpse and dragged the body into the shallow water, then used the stick to push the corpse into the pool. It floated lazily towards the centre of the pool, then gradually sank. Ty shook his head. *So much death,* he thought; *every day another death.* Distractedly, he walked round the bank to a higher point and studied the landscape, wondering to himself where Kern and the others would have gone.

From behind him he heard a squeak; thinking the dogs were back, he turned and ran, waving the stick and shouting "Be gone!" – but there were no dogs in sight. Again he heard the squeak. He looked around carefully, but saw nothing. *Ah well, time to go,* he thought.

He turned and walked back to his backpack. When he got there he saw that the white dragon's egg had split in two. "What the –"

Ty bent to pick up the empty shell; the inside was empty and wet. His expression changed to panic. "Oh, *fuck,*" he said loudly.

He stood back up, looking around frantically. *I've only gone and fed one of the last baby dragons to a couple of wild dogs,* he thought, running to where he had last seen the hounds. They seemed to be gone; he saw nothing but grass and trees. He looked up at the sky for a few seconds. *Maybe it flew away? Kern will never believe this.*

He walked back down to his backpack, shaking his head. *Can my luck get any worse?*

Kneeling down next to his equipment he heard the squeak again, and out of the corner of his eye saw his backpack move slightly. Grabbing a stick, he cautiously lifted the flap of his backpack.

The baby dragon inside squealed and snapped at his hand.

"Whoa, little fellow," Ty said, dropping the flap closed in surprise. After a moment he lifted it again for another peek. The dragon squealed again, opening its mouth wide; Ty let the flap fall again, and thought it was a good thing the little creature couldn't yet breathe fire, or he'd have been burnt to a crisp. It didn't appear to be very happy in its new surroundings.

Picking up a soggy piece of what had once been hard rations, Ty lifted the flap once more and held his hand out a few inches from the backpack. The dragon snapped again to bite, then saw the offering. It hesitated before stepping out of the bag, then took the food and swallowed it down greedily.

Looking around, the dragon stretched and flapped its wings, then folded them back and sniffed Ty's hand. Ty broke off another small piece of soggy beef and placed it on his knee. The dragon jumped up and gulped it down again, then looked up at Ty and started to sniff him, inspecting Ty as intently as Ty was inspecting the dragon.

Slightly bigger than Ty's hand, the dragon was a very dark green. Its skin was smooth, but Ty could see the impressions of the scales that would one day appear. Its head was lizard-like, with high bones above the eyes and bony spines down the side of its face. Its wings were tucked away like a bat's, and more spines protruded down the length of its back. It sniffed and wriggled, reminding Ty of the dogs he had raised as a child in the thieves' guild, training them to be guard dogs that would let only members of the guild pass in and out of the guildhall.

The dragon's curiosity was plain to see as it took its first tender steps into the new world. Ty watched it explore for several moments; then there was a noise from behind him and the dragon slid back into the backpack in a flash. Ty jumped up and looked around; the dogs were back and only a few feet away. Ty shouted and waved his arms once more, and the dogs backed off a few paces, but they were bolder now, and Ty knew they would not relent.

He carefully picked up the backpack and looked inside; the dragon was curled up at the bottom, its big round eyes looking up at Ty, almost sad. Ty arranged the two chests in the pack as best he could to give the baby dragon some space, then kicked through the contents of his backpack where they lay scattered on the ground. There was nothing worth taking – everything was ruined or smashed. He closed the backpack and swung it onto his shoulder, then walked along the bank up the path. He kept a close eye on the dogs, but they were now heading to the place the corpse had been, and showed no interest in Ty as he edged around them, making his way north towards Breeze.

Ty grabbed a lift on the back of a farmer's wagon headed for Breeze. As the wagon jounced along, he opened the backpack. The dragon was sleeping, tiny and helpless. He closed the bag and thought about the other chest. Was its egg ready to hatch as well? *One dragon will be hard enough to conceal, let alone two – but they should grow together, and if you have one, you might as well have two...* His mind was spinning with thoughts and ideas. Oh, how he wished Kern were here! He would know the solution. *What the hell am I doing babysitting a dragon?*

Finally they reached Breeze and entered through the tradesmen's entrance; Ty thought it would be safer this way. He flipped the farmer a coin and bid him good day. After searching the town he eventually found an inn – slightly more expensive than his usual haunts, but Ty thought it best to get somewhere less troublesome than the Bucket of Blood in Forkvain.

The Red Horse inn boasted massive stables, housing many horses of quality. This was a rather high-class inn, and Ty knew his story about being ambushed and robbed on the road – hence his shabby appearance – would definitely raise eyebrows within days. Even so, the innkeeper took enough of Ty's gold to cover a minimum stay of three nights.

Once in his room upstairs, Ty laid the backpack on the bed and checked on the dragon. It was still sleeping. He opened the cupboard door, then gently placed the bag on the floor, leaving the flap up. He closed the cupboard door quietly, and locked it. *Time to find the others*, he thought, *but first I need to get cleaned up and get some supplies.*

He purchased some new clothes, then headed to a bath house. He couldn't remember the last bath he'd had, so he paid for the full treatment – bath, shave, and haircut. Leaving the bath house, he had never felt so clean, and the aching in his limbs seemed to have disappeared. After eating his fill of eggs, bacon, bread and warm Lillie tea, he went to the marketplace and purchased cheese, biscuits, fruit, and five live mice. *A good variety,* he thought; *surely it must eat some of these things.*

He purchased a few weapons to replace those he had lost – particularly a dagger to fit his empty wrist holster – then, with his new hood raised, headed to some local inns where he listened and questioned. It didn't take long for him to find out that three men had been brought through here two days ago by the King's guard, and exactly where they were being kept.

He headed back to the Red Horse; it was now mid-evening and he needed a good bed; his companions would have to wait another night. Two days ago, the man in the inn had said. How long had he been stuck in that cavern? Two days, floating in the water? It didn't seem possible.

After locking the door to his room behind him, he threw his cloak and other new possessions onto the bed and unlocked the cupboard door. He opened carefully, and he saw that the dragon was sitting up on the backpack looking around. Upon seeing Ty, it made a tiny squeak. Ty knelt down and the dragon immediately jumped up onto his legs. Ty scooped the dragon up and held it up at eye level.

"What are we going to call you, eh?" he whispered.

Standing up he walked to the bed and set the dragon down on the pillow. He unwrapped the cheese from the market, along with the fruit and biscuits, and laid them out on the bed. The dragon came over, sniffed at the offerings, then walked away, "I guess not," Ty said. "All right, what about this, then?" He plucked a mouse from the box and held it up by the tail. With the hilt of his dagger, he struck the mouse on the back of the head. It fell still instantly. He dropped it onto the bed and the dragon sniffed at it, then flapped his wings and turned back to sniffing the bed and his new surroundings. "Really!" Ty said. *What the hell do you feed a bloody dragon, then?* he wondered.

As he pondered, another mouse jumped out of the box and ran along the bed. The dragon turned in a flash, spread his wings, opened his jaw wide, and squealed. Ty knew he was trying to breathe fire; the mouse seemed to draw the same conclusion, and it jumped down to the floor and scurried under the bed. Within a heartbeat the dragon followed, making Ty jump. He tried to catch the dragon but he was gone under the bed in a shot. Ty knelt down and lifted the bottom of the bed sheet just in time to spot the mouse's tail sticking out of the dragon's mouth – then with a gulp it was gone.

He reached up and grabbed another mouse from the box, letting it go on the floor. The mouse scurried towards the gap underneath the cupboard. The dragon gave chase and, with quite frightening speed, caught and grabbed the mouse. With a crunch and flick of his head the mouse disappeared.

Ty sat on the bed looking down at the dragon. "So *that's* what you wanted, some sport food," he said, smiling. The dragon returned to the bed and tried to jump up, but couldn't quite manage. Flapping his wings, he tried and tried until eventually Ty picked him up and sat him on the bed. Ty shut the box with the last two mice in it, and placed it in the cupboard. "Your breakfast," he said to the dragon, then laid back on the bed. With the dragon curled up next to him stealing his warmth, Ty pulled the cover up over them both. Within minutes they were asleep.

Kern swung his sword in a wild arc in front of him, "Come out and fight me, you little whore!" He spun around, his sword again circling and slicing through the air. "Show yourself, you bastard," he cried as he swung his sword wildly, turning round and round like a blind man. A small cloaked figure holding two daggers stepped out from behind a tree and crouched in front of him, ready to attack.

Ty sat up the next morning and let his eyes adjust to the morning sun that shone through the window while he cleared his mind. He'd had some troubling dreams, he thought, but he couldn't quite remember any details. He must have been truly exhausted; he couldn't believe he had slept so long – or that he had left himself so unguarded. Then he remembered the dragon and panicked briefly, until he lifted the covers and saw the creature there, still sound asleep. "That's what I will call you – *Sleeper*," he said.

Looking out the window he gauged the time as midmorning. He gathered his gear and stood looking at Sleeper uncertainly. *Do I risk leaving you here, or do I take you with me?*

He walked downstairs and headed to the bar, which the plump innkeeper was wiping down.

"Good morning," Ty said, acting as posh as he could manage.

"Afternoon, er…?" the innkeeper replied.

"Ravenhill, Mr Ravenhill – but you can call me Bill," Ty answered. "Now, just a quick question about my room, sir. I purchased some goods yesterday that I intend to take to Forkvain for resale. Do I have to carry the blasted things about with me, or are they safe in your establishment?" Ty said, folding his arms.

"Well, for a small fee I can make sure nobody interferes, if you know what I mean," the innkeeper said with an oily smile.

Trying to maintain his disguise as a wealthy merchant Ty didn't hesitate; he took out a gold piece and flipped it onto the bar. "Good man," he said; as he walked back to his room he was already scheming ways to steal the gold piece back.

He placed the still-sleeping dragon on top of a pillow in the bottom of the cupboard, then grabbed the two remaining mice by their tails and tossed them into the cupboard. He quickly shut the door, sealing their fate.

Ty left the Red Horse Inn and headed towards the house where his companions were allegedly being held captive. He wondered briefly if perhaps they were being treated as honoured guests – anything but prisoners – but he doubted it; just the fact that they had been carried through the town on a cart told a story by itself.

He strolled past the main gates and tried to gauge how many guards patrolled the grounds. He counted two at the gate, two on the main door, and two walking around the house. Once he was past the gate and out of the guards' line of sight he sprinted, trying to get ahead of the patrolling guards. After about fifty paces he came to a tree that grew outside the house's great wall, but overlooked into the garden. He stood at the bottom and spat onto his leather gloves out of habit. After rubbing his hands together and taking a quick glance around, he jumped up and grabbed the lowest branch. With a heave and a strain he pulled himself up; sitting on the low branch to catch his breath, he suddenly realized how unfit he was. He still felt a bit disoriented, and figured he must have taken a blow to the head while being tossed around the underground river.

He had another careful look around before going higher. Up and up he went, until he could clearly see the inner wall. The two guards patrolled in one direction and he could see another pair walking towards them, but there was no sign of an entrance along that side of the house. He climbed down and walked around to the back of the house where another tree was positioned perfectly. Once more he climbed up for a better view – and there it was: The back entranceway and, if the stories were to be believed, the door leading into the dungeon. Not many ever used it as an exit.

Guards patrolled the grounds in pairs. Ty counted; *maybe forty-five seconds to get down, over,* and *pick the lock, and that's if it isn't barred from the inside or guarded. I'm not a fighter,* he thought, *I'm a thief, a damn good thief but not a miracle worker; there must be another way in.*

Climbing down to the ground and pulling his hood up, he continued to walk around the wall of the house. "Think," he hissed under his breath. "Think, gods damn you, Rat!" Then he grinned. "That's it! *Rat!* Go in like a rat! Brilliant!"

Ty hurried round the house looking carefully at the ground, until eventually he came across a drain cover. It was in the open and he knew he would have to come back at night. He knelt down as if inspecting his leather boot straps, then flicked his dagger out and prized it under the lid of the drain cover. To his surprise it lifted easily. He flicked the dagger back into its holster and made his way back to the Red Horse, visiting the market on the way to buy suitable clothes, some weapons, rope, and more mice.

Chapter Nineteen
Rats and Sewers

Ty sat on the bed and fed Sleeper. The dragon ate three mice; Ty thought he looked bigger already, but dismissed the idea as being unlikely. Once Sleeper had fallen asleep he did the same as he had done the night before, settling the dragon into the bottom of the cupboard complete with the scurrying mice. He left two mice in the box up top.

Rat put on his newly purchased dark clothes and strapped three short swords to his back as tightly as he could without restricting his movement. Then he wrapped black leather bindings snugly around his wrists, boot tops, and neck. He had been down in enough sewers to know where the shit seeped in. He tucked a small torch into his belt and a waterproof pouch with flint and tinder in his pocket.

He left the inn and headed towards the drain cover he had found earlier in the day; on his way there, he stopped to climb the tree at the back of the house. He waited for the guards to pass, then tied the rope to the tree and lowered it down into the grounds. Hidden behind a tree within the walls, it was one hope of escaping if all went well; even if it was discovered, Ty didn't think it wouldn't give much away.

Ty froze as he saw a guard walk round and stop below him, lean against the tree, and light his pipe. The rope dangled just behind the guard, slightly too close for Ty's comfort. Then he noticed the guard's money-pouch attached to his belt by thin leather straps, and his thieving instincts took over. Without thinking he leaned out and grabbed the rope; wrapping his legs around it.

Suddenly realizing what he was doing, he froze in position, knowing it would be nigh on impossible to make it to the ground being so close to the guard. He tried half-heartedly to talk himself out of the temptation, then gave in to it fully and looked around. *How could I distract him?*

But he didn't need to create a distraction; just at that moment two patrolling guards came around the side of the house, each man holding two dogs on leather leads. The dogs began barking wildly and Ty readied himself to go, thinking they'd caught his scent. Then he realized the handlers were encouraging the dogs to play-fight against each other. This was the cover he needed. He slid down as quietly as possible.

After landing gently behind the guard, Ty remained motionless, making sure he hadn't been detected. When he was certain, he edged forward until he was directly behind the guard. Pulling out his tiny double-bladed dagger, he held one hand under the pouch and snipped the purse strings. Holding the purse, he waited, but the guard never moved except to call encouragement to his two comrades and their dogs. Ty slipped the pouch carefully into his pocket and quietly stepped backwards to the rope. Grabbing it with both hands, he pulled himself up until he was safely back on the branch. The dogs had moved on, and the guard took a few more puffs of his pipe, emptied its contents on the ground, and resumed his patrol.

Ty smiled to himself and opened the pouch to reveal a handful of silver pieces and a small key. He slipped the coins into his pocket and placed the key on the branch. Not the best haul he'd ever had, but he was still happy. *It isn't the loot,* he thought to himself, *it's the looting.* He thought briefly about the patrolling dogs and wondered if they might hinder things later, but time was short. *Cross that bridge when we come to it,* he thought.

He waited in the shadows until no one was about, and pulled four pieces of rag from his pocket. Rolling them up, he stuffed one into each ear and filled both nostrils. He then covered his mouth with another, larger rag, and made his way over to the drain cover. Once there he quickly wedged it open with the tip of his dagger, slid it clear, and squeezed in and onto a ledge, pulling the lid closed behind him.

After lighting a torch he looked down into the sewer. Filthy black water and rubbish ran along the bottom, and rats scurried in every direction. The jump down from the ledge looked to be about six feet; if there had ever been a ladder it had long since rotted away, so he had no choice. He tried to work out the depth of the water that flowed through the sewer; two feet max, he guessed.

He sat on the edge of the ledge and placed the torch between his teeth. He dropped into the water as smoothly as he could, but still made enough of a splash to wet the torch.

Don't you dare go out, he thought as he blew on the damp embers, and slowly the flames returned to life. *Hmm, maybe my luck is changing.*

Even through his rags, the smell of the sewer was astonishing, bringing stinging tears to his eyes as all sorts of rubbish floated past him. He held his hand over his mouth and gagged at just the thought of what was down here. Then he shook himself mentally. *No time to lose,* he thought, so he made his way against the current through the sewer. Knowing the house was on his right side, about a hundred steps or so, he took the first right turn and headed down a slope, counting his steps as he went. The lack of rubbish here was a welcome break. At the bottom of the slope there was another sewer running right to left. He estimated that he must be under the house grounds, roughly halfway to his destination. *Fifty steps to go.*

He continued until he began to notice light filtering in from drains above his head. Looking up through one, he could tell it was the kitchen; the smell of food made a welcome change from the sewage smell. He extinguished his torch and waited for his eyes to adjust to the darkness. With the light creeping in from the kitchens, it was just about possible to see.

After another fifty paces or so, he came to a hole at his head height. He peered into it and saw lights from the rooms above, shining through from drains on the roof of the narrow tunnel. A slight trickle of water ran down the tunnel and dripped into the sewer. *This must be it,* he thought. The hole looked tight, but part of Ty's early training had involved fitting into spaces normal people couldn't. It had helped him escape on more than one occasion, and Ty was particularly good at it. He shoved the swords and torches into the tunnel, then pushed his arms through after them. His shoulders were wider than the hole, but after a pull, a squeeze, and a few joints clicking out of their sockets, he lay in the tunnel.

He wriggled like a snake, slowly edging his way along until he was under the first drain. He bent his arm in front of his chest with a click; his dagger sprang from its holster and Ty chipped away at the grout and countless moons' worth of dirt that held the metal drain in place. He could hear voices from above, but chipped away as quietly as he could just in case he wasn't quite where he should be. Within a few minutes the drain was loose, and he gently pushed it up and slid it along. Not being very heavy or of any great size, it slid with ease. Using all his neck muscles, Ty peered out from the drain. He had come up in one of the cells; this one was empty but he could make out a person in the cell across the corridor. He hoped it was Kern, because he didn't relish the fact of trying to squeeze back down into the sewers and try again.

He pulled his head back down and slowly lifted one arm up into the room, followed by his head. He gritted his teeth as he dragged his dislocated shoulder up through the drain. After a lot of effort he was finally in the cell. He wrenched his arm and with a wince he clicked it back into its socket, then reached back down and grabbed the swords. He pulled the cotton from his ears and nose; looking through the bars he saw Kern, Galandrik, and Pedlyn.

Aside from the strangeness of having just broken *into* a cell for the first time, he also felt elation at having found the party, and wondered what elaborate way he should announce his presence. He hesitated when he remembered the last time he'd wanted to show off – it had nearly killed him. But... *what the hell,* he thought, *I'm the Rat.*

He crawled over to the door of the cell and, with infinite patience, contorted himself to squeeze through the bars. Then he slid out on his belly into the corridor between cells. He crept on his stomach over to his companion's cell; when he was within touching distance he snaked an arm through the cell bars. He was about to tap Kern on the shoulder, when Kern spun round and grabbed Ty's forearm. With a yank he pulled the thief into the bars, his head cracking against them.

"Ouch!" Ty shouted.

Kern let go. "What the hell are you doing, you fool?" he shouted back.

Ty slumped back, rubbing his chin. "I… I thought you were dead. I couldn't see if it was you, I mean…" he spluttered, realizing that his attempt at a grand entrance had backfired monumentally.

"Hang on a minute, forget all that," Pedlyn said. "How did you suddenly appear in here?"

"Yeah, and what took you so long?" Galandrik asked, gripping his cell bars and looking through.

"What about *'Thank the gods you're not dead,' 'Thanks for coming,' 'Good to see you'*?" Ty said angrily.

"Just let us out, you fool," Kern replied.

"No." Ty folded his arms.

Galandrik grinned at the childish stance and said, "You broke into our jail house to *not* save us?" He started laughing. "That's brilliant, lad!"

"Well, it's obvious you don't need me – I'll just go out the way I came then," Ty said, turning round.

"Okay, everybody calm down," Kern said. "Thank the gods you're not dead, and thanks for coming. Now open the damn cells," he finished, with a hint of sarcasm.

"Unbelievable," Ty muttered, and he set to work at Pedlyn's cell door. In a matter of minutes, all three companions were freed.

"What's your plan then?" Pedlyn asked, taking a short sword from Ty.

"What's *my* plan? I don't do plans, and unless you can squeeze your fat head down that drain over there, we are leaving through the front door," Ty answered.

Kern walked to the main door of the room and listened. "Right – we know the way out. It's along the corridor and up a couple of flights of stairs to the back door. We'll definitely encounter some guards, so be on your game."

"What happened to your nose?" Ty asked, knowing that answering would hurt Kern more than the actual injury had.

"It was your mate, Bok," Kern answered.

Then Ty remembered. "Bok! That's it!" He rapidly explained the red-robed man's death and how he had fallen with the body, as his companions listened in fascination. He decided not to mention the dragon, and hoped he would survive this, lest the last dragon die in a cupboard.

Finally they were ready to make their escape. Kern slowly tried the door handle; it was locked, he shook his head at Ty. Within seconds the thief had unlocked it. *Such a basic lock,* he thought, *and so old.*

Kern edged through the open door and cautiously looked down the corridor. It was empty but he could hear voices coming from the end. The group tiptoed slowly down the corridor towards the T-junction at the end, the voices growing louder as they approached.

Leaning with his back to the wall, Kern looked back at the others and held up three fingers of one hand, his sword raised and ready in the other. One finger folded to begin the countdown, then a second; then his hand swept down and he spun around the corner, swinging his sword as he went. The guard was slightly further away than Kern had anticipated, but still near enough. The sword crashed against the guard's armour, and the second guard lunged forward, drawing his own weapon.

Galandrik stepped forward into the space under Kern's outstretched arm and sank his blade deep into the second guard's throat. The wounded man dropped his weapon and fell to his knees, grasping Galandrik's sword as if to tug it free – then fell onto his side and died.

The other guard, seemingly frozen in fear, reached hesitantly for his weapon but then quickly raised his hands above his head. "Please, please don't kill me," he begged, "I have a family!"

Galandrik recognised him as the guard who had pissed into his cell. "You hate dwarves, do you?"

"I was only joking, master dwarf!"

Galandrik let the guard continue to beg for a few moments before interrupting him. "Get it out now and let's see you piss," he said angrily.

"You... you... you want me to get it out now?"

"Or die," the dwarf snarled.

Slowly the guard undid his leather straps and dropped his trousers. Ty shifted as if he were about to say something, and Kern held up a hand to silence him.

"Hold it in your hand," the dwarf ordered.

The man's hand was shaking like a leaf, but he obeyed.

Galandrik raised his sword high and roared, "Now say goodbye to it!"

The guard fainted and sank to his knees, slumping over on top of his dead companion with his bare behind sticking up in the air. Galandrik looked at Kern and smiled cheerfully.

"You wouldn't have, right?" Kern asked uncertainly.

"You'll never know," Galandrik said, still smiling as he stepped over the unconscious guard.

"Should we cover him up?" Pedlyn asked, looking down as he followed Galandrik.

"No, let the rats wake him," Ty laughed.

At the end of the corridor were steps leading up. "Right – it's up here and along to the left about twenty paces," Kern explained, "and there is the door that leads out. The guards patrol that door on the outside."

"Surprising there are not more guards inside here," Pedlyn said.

"No one's ever broken out – or in – before, that's why," Ty answered boastfully.

"I have an idea," Kern announced. "I'll knock on the door and when it's opened, I'll drag the guard in."

"Still full of good ideas, I see," Ty sniggered. He got a shake of the head from the ranger in return.

Kern banged three times on the door with the hilt of his sword. The jangling of keys could be heard, and after a few seconds the door started to open inwards.

"You're too early, Jakob," the guard said as he opened the door. Kern grabbed the guard by the scruff of his tunic and dragged him inside. The guard's shock was evident on his face, but before he knew anything else Pedlyn's elbow had smashed him straight in the nose, and he sprawled on the floor unconscious. Kern looked outside. "All clear," he whispered.

Galandrik looked at Pedlyn with a shocked expression – he would never have expected such a devastating elbow from the mild-mannered elf.

"I don't know where that came from," Pedlyn said, rubbing his arm while Galandrik shook his head in amazement.

"You see that tree over there? There is another tree behind it; I tied a rope to it before I broke in," Ty announced proudly. "We can climb it and get over the wall quickly."

"Who's a clever boy then?" Galandrik whispered back.

Ty grinned, too pleased with himself to realize that the comment had been made in jest.

"Get back – two guards are coming," Kern said, closing the door. They heard voices from outside, getting louder and louder.

"Piko, Jakob, Tiran," they heard one of the guards call.

Kern put one finger up to his lips.

"Where the hell has Piko gone? I bet he's playing dice again with Jakob," the guard complained.

"Go down and find him. If he is, I'll have his guts out," a second guard said. The door was pushed open; the guard looked horror-stricken to see the party on the other side of it, but before he could scream Galandrik had cracked him with the hilt of his sword.

The second guard ran shouting, "Under attack!! We're being attacked!!"

Ty stepped out into the night air and pulled a knife from his belt. He flipped it and caught the blade by the tip, then launched it; it struck the guard behind the knee, and he fell to the ground, still screaming.

"Why didn't you kill him?" Kern shouted. "He's loud enough to wake the whole town!"

"You've knocked the last two out; I thought we were being subtle," Ty replied angrily. He ran towards the rope, followed closely by the others.

Ty and Pedlyn began climbing the rope as three guards ran around the corner of the building; Kern and Galandrik stood to face them at the bottom of the rope.

"Over there, behind the tree!" the guard on the ground shouted, holding his leg.

"Up you go, dwarf, no time to argue," Kern bellowed.

"You'll never take all three of them on your own," Galandrik replied, refusing to move.

"There will be another three after these. Go!" Kern insisted.

"Come on, let's move!" Ty shouted from above.

Galandrik didn't budge as the guards closed in on them. Kern parried one blow and struck armour with his riposte, but his short sword was no match for the guard's armour. Another guard launched an attack at Galandrik, and with a parry he shouldered the guard to the floor. Before the dwarf could step in for the kill the third guard jumped in and sliced at Galandrik; he dodged the attack but not quickly enough, and it slashed across the top of his arm. Stepping back Galandrik then countered another attack, his blade slicing the forearm of the guard.

Kern rallied again; he landed blow after blow on his attacker but to no avail. He was weary and underfed, and each swing drained him more.

The guard pressed his advantage and launched several blows at Kern. He parried and blocked, but a sudden rush of fatigue hit him and he fell backwards. From the ground he parried another blow, but his sword was knocked from his hand. The guard, seeing his opportunity, stepped in and raised his sword above his head. Kern knew he was looking at his own death, and he shut his eyes.

Looking down, Ty saw Kern fall; he moved to the edge of the branch, drawing two daggers as he went, then turned around and leapt. Landing behind the guard's back he struck, stabbing twice in between the guard's armour, sinking deep into flesh. As the guard fell forward, Kern rolled out of the way and grabbed the guard's sword.

Kern saw that Galandrik was struggling; with his free hand he picked up his abandoned rusty short sword and threw it with all his might. It stuck Galandrik's opponent full in the face, hilt first, spinning him round and giving Galandrik enough time to pick his spot. He stabbed the guard in the back of the neck, just below the helmet line. The last guard stood facing the party – and hesitated. Ty, Kern, and Galandrik all ran screaming at the guard, who dropped his sword, turned, and ran. They let him go and scrambled up and over the wall as quickly as they could manage.

Soon all four were on the outside, running through the small side alleyways with Ty leading the way. When they reached the Red Horse, after making sure no one was about Ty led them into the stables. A few of the horses whickered at the intrusion, but most ignored the party.

Finding an empty horse bay, they entered and sat down on the fresh hay.

"I thought that was it then. I couldn't do anything," Galandrik said, lying back in the hay.

"Me too," Kern agreed. "We haven't eaten in days, and swinging that sword felt like swinging a ton of rocks."

"Are we staying here tonight?" Pedlyn asked.

"I don't think that would be wise," Kern answered. "Every guard in the town will be looking for us."

"Yes, unfortunately we must move north as soon as possible," Ty added.

Pedlyn stood, a look of regret etched across his face as he looked around at the others.

"You're not coming, are you?" Ty questioned.

"No. I appreciate everything you've done, but I would be useless. I need books, herbs, magic – there's no point. I would only hinder you all, and I know you couldn't afford to buy what I need so I will take my leave. There are people I know here who can help me stay safe."

Kern stood and held out his hand. "My thanks," he said, "and may luck be with you."

Galandrik did the same. "I will always owe you, elf," he said.

"Be lucky!" Ty said, remaining seated.

"Thanks again," Pedlyn said, smiling. "I hope you get out of here safely and do… whatever it is you do." At the entrance of the stable, he looked left then right, and with a last swift wave he was gone into the night.

"We couldn't afford everything he needs? What a cheeky –"

"Leave it, Ty. He did just save Galandrik's life."

"And what did *I* just do, then? I don't expect paying for it!"

"Neither did he," Kern answered wearily.

"Whatever." Ty stood up. "I think we can go upstairs. There is a back entrance so we won't have to walk through the front; it'll be shut or nearly shut now, anyway." After making sure the coast was clear, they crept around the side and through a back door, up some stairs, and into Ty's room. While Ty locked the door, Kern slumped in a chair and Galandrik sprawled on the bed.

Ty paused in front of the cupboard; then sheepishly he said, "Right, I have something to show you."

Kern leaned forward and said. "I don't like the sound of this."

Galandrik covered his face.

Ty explained the story with the dogs and the corpse, how he had left the egg on the ground and turned his back on it for a few moments.

"Don't tell me somebody robbed it. Have you lost the egg?" Kern said, standing up in alarm.

"No, I haven't lost the egg – well, not exactly," Ty said. Turning round, he slowly pulled the cupboard door open. The dragon sat on the backpack looking up expectantly. Ty looked over his shoulder at Kern once more, then stepped to the side, revealing the dragon.

"Oh my god, it's hatched?!" Kern said.

Galandrik sat up and looked. "Where's the other one?"

"The other egg? Still in the chest. I didn't know what to do," Ty replied, bending down. He gently picked Sleeper up and walked to Kern, cradling the baby dragon. When Kern reached out to stroke the dragon, Sleeper snapped at him, squealing and trying to flap his wings.

Ty stepped back. "Whoa, I know he's an ugly brute but take it easy," Ty said, smiling at Kern. "Watch this," he continued. After placing Sleeper down on the floor, he pulled the box from the top of the cupboard. Reaching inside he pulled out a mouse and dropped it on the floor, Sleeper pounced, almost flying toward it; soon he had gulped it down.

"Nice," Kern said, sitting back down to watch as the second mouse met the same fate.

"Yeah, he's partial to the odd mouse."

"He doesn't mind rats either, by the look of it," Galandrik said, watching as Sleeper stood on Ty's foot, waiting to be picked up.

"Ty, can you go get some food? I'm starving," Kern asked.

"All right. I need to get a bath first, because I absolutely stink."

Kern saw Galandrik open his mouth as Ty placed Sleeper back in the cupboard, and he quickly shook his head at Galandrik, knowing that whatever comment he'd been about to make would probably have resulted in Ty not bringing back any food.

When Ty returned an hour later, he was cleaned up and carried a bag full of bread, cheese, fruit, vegetables, and a couple of water canteens. Standing in the bedroom he looked on for a moment at his snoring companions.

He woke them, and they ate heartily, seeming to revive a bit with the food. But it wasn't long after finishing the meal that Galandrik's head began to nod, and he soon started to snore again. Ty reached into the cupboard and pulled out a blanket, which he tossed to Kern. Kern curled up on the chair and thanked him wearily.

"I am popping out again to see what chaos you have caused."

Kern smiled. "And Ty… thanks for today."

Ty turned around, pride swelling his chest. "Oh, it was nothing. I simply found the sewer entrance, slid in when no one was look–" He stopped mid-sentence as he heard Kern start to snore. With a shake of the head he turned and left the room, locking the door behind him.

Chapter Twenty
The Last Stretch

Kern awoke early the next morning and sat up stretching his neck, which was aching from the uncomfortable night's sleep. Galandrik sat at the small table in the corner of the room, eating a big bowl of beef stew; the previous night's leftover bread and cheese covered the table.

"Good morning," the dwarf said around a mouthful of his breakfast.

"Good morning," Kern replied, standing up; he stretched and pulled out a chair next to the dwarf. "Where's Ty?" he asked, sitting down ripping off a big chunk of bread.

"I don't know. I woke and this was here – I didn't need to be asked," he replied, filling Kern's bowl with beef stew.

Apart from the selection of food Ty had managed to grab for them in the early hours of the morning, this was their first decent meal since Forkvain. Their three nights without food in the cells were still fresh in their memories, and the polished off the pot of stew in a very short time. As they were picking over the crumbs, the door opened and Ty walked in with an enormous sack slung over his shoulder. He swung it off and it landed on the bed. "I'm never doing *that* again," he said, struggling to catch his breath.

Kern stood up and walked over. "What've we got?" he asked.

Ty emptied the contents of the sack onto the bed: Rations, rope, torches, daggers, two complete sets of leather armour, three small backpacks, and small crossbows complete with bolts.

"Where're the big weapons?" Galandrik said, standing up with hands on his belly.

"In the stable with our horses," Ty said. "And this is it – there's no more gold." He helped himself to some bread and used it to sop up what was left of the stew.

"Are we skint?" Kern asked.

"No, *I* am skint! I had to sell gems and everything. This room plus the horses has done me in! I am officially broke," Ty said, wiping gravy from his chin.

"Not even a silver coin for a bath?" Galandrik asked.

"No, and you'd be spotted anyway," Ty said. "There are guards patrolling every street corner, and double on the gates," he added.

"How can we leave then?" Kern asked, picking dirt from his fingernails with a dagger.

"No idea. Jump the wall on your horse?" Ty replied with a smile.

"I think the dwarf may have trouble there, on his little pony," Kern laughed.

"Hey!" Galandrik objected.

"Catapult him over?" Ty suggested, dropping a mouse into the cupboard for Sleeper.

Just then there was a knock at the door. "Who is it?" Ty said in his grand trader's voice.

"It is I," came the response.

"And who is 'I'?" Ty said, exchanging a wary glance with Kern.

"It is I, Pedlyn," the voice revealed.

Ty quickly unbolted the door and pulled it open. "Hello…wait, you're not Pedlyn!" Ty said, looking at an old man leaning on a stick.

"Yes I am, now get out of my way before I fire another lightning bolt at you," the old man said, shuffling past him. "Hello Kern, Galandrik," he continued.

"Who are you?" Kern asked in alarm, brandishing his dagger.

"I told you, I'm Pedlyn," he replied, reaching into his cloak pocket.

"Careful what you pull out, old man!" Kern said, holding the dagger up higher and moving one step closer to the hunched figure.

The old man retrieved a leather bag from his pocket and handed it to Kern. "There you are."

Kern moved to toss the bag to Ty, still holding the dagger in his other hand.

"NO! Don't throw it!" Pedlyn shouted in alarm.

"More eggs?" Kern said.

"Not eggs, but just as fragile. It's glass."

Kern passed the pouch to Ty with a sharp nod. He kept a suspicious eye on their elderly visitor as Ty opened the bag. Inside were nestled three glass vials, cushioned in cotton. Ty held them out carefully for Kern's inspection. "And these are?" Kern asked.

"Disguise potions," Pedlyn said.

"So you have… taken one?" Galandrik said, leaning forward and looking closely at the old man.

"No, he aged forty years since last night," Ty quipped.

"I see some things don't change, then," Pedlyn replied. "Yes, Gal, I've taken one. They last for anywhere from one to three hours; there's no way to know exactly how long the disguise will last so make your escape and be quick about it," he explained. "Now I must leave you again, before mine runs out," he said, turning to Ty "Thank you very much, but we cannot pay you," Ty said, tapping his pockets to indicate his lack of coinage.

"You saved my life twice – consider it partial repayment."

"You are very kind. I do have one question," Ty began.

"Yes, friend?"

"What do we get disguised as?" Ty asked.

"It's random; some are better than others," Pedlyn said with a cheeky smile. After a last quick round of thanks from everyone, he was gone.

They took turns washing as best they could in the little corner sink. After Ty fed Sleeper the last mouse, he placed the dragon in the backpack, which was now well-padded with bedding Ty had bought in the market.

"Shall we do the potions now?" Kern asked when they were all ready.

"I think we can make it to the stables without being seen," Galandrik answered. "We'd better make every minute count, in case the potions wear off sooner rather than later."

"Point taken." Kern replied.

Then they gathered up their new equipment and crept down into the stables, dodging all passers-by and keeping their cloak hoods up. Once they were safely in the stable, Ty shifted some loose hay and uncovered Galandrik's axe and Kern's sword.

"Where did you find these?" Galandrik said, looking his axe up and down with a loving gaze.

"I had a little go last night back through the sewers; I knew all the guards would be out in the town. Where did you think I got the gold for the horses?" Ty explained.

"Thanks again," Kern said, slipping his sword into its sheath.

They quickly got acquainted with their new horses and saddled up inside the stable, not wanting to risk the exposure of the stableyard. Once mounted, they each uncapped one of Pedlyn's glass vials, then counted to three and drank. Ty swallowed his down and opened his eyes; in front of him were the two horses, but in their saddles were now a young elf and old human. He laughed and said, "Look at you two!"

Kern looked at Galandrik and said, "You're an elf."

"And you're an old man – why'd I have to be a bloody elf!" Galandrik exclaimed, feeling for his beard which wasn't there.

Ty was still chuckling, and Kern said, "Before you laugh at us, take a look at yourself." Kern smiled at Galandrik.

Ty looked down at his hands; they looked rather feminine, he thought. "No, please don't say…" He jumped from his horse and ran over to the horse trough. He leaned over to look at his reflection in the water, and staring back at him was a beautiful young human girl.

He turned to look at the others, stunned. "I don't believe this," he said, his voice getting higher-pitched with each word. He looked down at his slender form, dressed in light green leather amour. Then he noticed his breasts, and raised both hands.

"Don't even think about it!" Kern laughed.

"What?" Ty answered, dropping both hands quickly and jumping back up onto his mount. His face was beginning to turn red. "I was just going to… *adjust* myself."

Kern and Galandrik's belly-laughs echoed around the stables.

Soon all three were riding through the town; the gate was only five minutes away. Guards patrolled the streets and they could see carts being stopped, barrels ripped open and hay being pierced with swords and pikes in search of any hidden, living, cargo. "I think we are being sought," Kern whispered as they rode.

"I think you are right," Galandrik added.

Then, "I don't believe this!" Kern said angrily.

"What?" Galandrik asked.

"There, over there, sitting outside that inn. That's that bastard who broke my nose!" Kern spat.

"Bok," Ty said, grinning.

"Yes, bloody Bok," Kern replied.

"How long we got?" Ty asked.

"Enough time for him, I think," Galandrik said.

"Let me," Ty said, jumping down from his horse and awkwardly fluffing his new chestnut curls. He passed the reins to Kern, "Meet me over there in ten," he said, turning.

"But… I wanted…" Kern sputtered.

"Okay then, follow me when I move," Ty said over his shoulder.

Soon Ty was just a few feet away from where Bok sat. As he passed Bok's table, Ty deliberately nudged the table with one shapely hip as he passed. Bok looked up and smiled at the lovely young woman passing by. The "lovely young woman" – Ty – smiled back coyly, then winked and carried on into the Inn. Within seconds Bok was standing next to Ty.

"Well *hello* there," Bok said. "Can I get this round?"

"Oh! Most certainly," Ty said, acting tipsy. The barman put two jugs of ale on the bar and Bok picked them both up, throwing some coinage on the bar.

"Outside?" he suggested, and Ty nodded. "What's your name, my dear?"

Bok asked over his shoulder.

Ty felt a stab of panic; he hadn't thought this far ahead. He blurted the first name that came to his mind: "It's Ty..la! Tyla. How do you do?"

After the formal introductions they were soon chatting companionably at their outdoors table. Bok explained that he was a bounty hunter travelling the land, and Ty did his best to look appropriately impressed. Twenty minutes and two flagons of ale later, Ty asked, "So are you staying here?"

"Yes, for now. I'm searching for someone very dangerous at the moment, and will be moving on soon."

Ty chuckled to himself at the blatant lies, but carried on looking impressed. "What are the rooms like?" he asked.

"They are all right. Nothing special – I have had better," Bok replied, missing the point.

"You could show me?" Ty asked with a smile.

Bok looked up with bright eyes, and Ty knew the penny had dropped. "Yes, I… ok… let's…" he babbled.

"What room are you in?" Ty asked.

"Number forty-four."

"Well, why don't you go ahead and take some ale up, and I'll follow in two minutes."

"Great! See you soon," Bok said, and skipped past the innkeeper, tossing a silver piece onto the bar top as he went.

As Ty walked past Kern and Galandrik, who had taken a table at the edge of the outdoors seating area, he whispered "Room forty-four, five minutes."

Standing outside the door to room forty-four, Ty knocked twice.

"Yes?" Bok called from within.

"It's Tyla," he answered in what he hoped was a seductive tone.

"Come in." Ty opened the door to see all Bok's worldly goods lying on a chair, while Bok lay in the bed.

"Get up, honey," Ty commanded in a sultry voice, and Bok climbed out of the bed in all his naked glory. "Now shut your eyes. I have a surprise, something you're going to like," Ty said in a smooth whisper, licking his lips.

Bok smiled back and closed his eyes. Ty took a step back, and kicked Bok straight between the legs. Bok grunted and doubled up, falling to the floor. Ty opened the door for Kern and Galandrik.

While Galandrik stood at the door and kept watch, Kern strode over to Bok and hauled him up to sit, groaning, on the edge of the bed. "This is from Kern," he said, and smashed his fist square into Bok's nose. Bok fell backwards, holding his face and howling. Kern grabbed Bok by the hair and pulled him upright again. "This one's for Galandrik." He smashed him again, this time holding on to Bok's hair to stop him falling backwards. "And this one's from Ty!" Kern shouted. Bok's rapidly swelling eyes popped open at the name, then shut as Kern delivered a final punch, knocking him out cold. Kern let go of Bok's hair, and he slumped to the floor.

Blood covered Bok's face and Kern's fist. Kern wiped his hands on Bok's bedcovers while Ty finished ransacking Bok's goods and balling up his clothes. Opening the window, he launched all Bok's clothes, leather armour, and backpack into the street. The gear was gone in seconds, street urchins and beggars getting whatever they could.

"We'd better leave," Galandrik warned.

"Not just yet." Ty bent down over Bok with his dagger drawn.

"What're you doing?" Kern asked.

"It's just a little thieves' guild trick," Ty replied as he cut deep into Bok's thumb and forefinger on both hands. Blood trickled from the cuts onto the floor, but Bok did not move.

Kern looked perplexed. "What the hell?"

"Ever tried picking a lock or a pocket with cuts like that? It's nigh on impossible for weeks. He'll know where it came from," Ty said, re-sheathing his dagger.

At that moment Bok stirred, and Ty spun around and kicked him in the stomach. "And *that* one's from Tyla! She's not that easy!" Turning to Kern and Galandrik he said, "*Now* we can go." They left Bok curled on the floor, bleeding and coughing.

Soon all three were saddled up and riding towards the gate. They were stopped and given a cursory search at the gate, but "Tyla" distracted the guards, and they were ushered through without any problems. Then they were out and on the path north to Tonilla, the dragon's lair.

"This should be the final stretch," Ty said, to no one in particular.

Bok opened his eyes, and the pain hit him like a hammer to the face. He slowly sat up and gently felt his nose, then winced from the pain in his hands. He inspected them and saw the dry congealed blood on his fingers and thumbs. He tried to bend them, but the thick dried blood added to the pain and stopped him. *Ty*, he thought, *only Ty would have done this!* A punishment to all thieves caught stealing from another member in the guild. Then Bok remembered the beautiful girl,

"Tyla," he said out loud in the empty room. "I can't believe he done me with a disguise!" Bok was absolutely disgusted that he had been outwitted by a simple disguise spell.

He clambered to his feet and looked for his belongings, but found nothing. Anger welled up inside him as he walked to the cupboard; it too was bare, everything gone. He pulled the bed over – trying not to bend his injured finger and thumb – and stepped up on it. Looking on top of the cupboard, he grinned and reached for his money pouch. Hiding it this way was something he always did when inviting a woman back to his room; if she ending up wanting to be paid, he would only show what was in his tunic.

He wrapped the bed sheet round him and walked into the hall, his head still thumping. "Heckton!" he shouted. *"Heckton!"* Soon the fat innkeeper was thumping up the stairs,

"Yes, what would you…" He stopped short at the sight of Bok's face. "What the hell happened?" he asked.

"I fell. Now send a boy out to buy me a full set of clothes and boots, and be quick about it!" Bok tossed Heckton a couple of coins and stalked back into his room. He stepped into the bathroom and inspected his face in the mirror. What he saw was a mess. Both eyes black and swollen, his nose off-centre and split across the bridge in two places. He looked at his hands and winched; he knew how long cuts like these would take to heal; even wielding a sword would be agonising. He splashed his face and hands gingerly with water, cleaning himself up carefully as he went over the events in his head. He seemed to remember an old man punching him with the force of a kicking mule, with the words 'This one's for Kern.' It was all a bit hazy after that, but he thought he remembered one standing at the door. The girl, the old man, plus one at the door – it had to be them, he thought, the three who escaped, all disguised. He continued to wipe the blood from his face, but even after it was clean he still looked a mess.

Once the boy returned and Bok was dressed, he left the Inn and headed over to Conn's house. After a brief discussion with the guards at the gate he was led inside and into a downstairs room, where Svorn greeted him. "Hell, you get kicked by a horse?" he asked.

"Not quite; a Rat," Bok answered.

Svorn's eyes widened. "Please don't tell me…"

"I don't want to say I told you so, but…" Bok said, sitting down.

"I don't believe this. Why won't that little pig die?" Svorn said, slamming a hand down on the table.

"He will, trust me," Bok hissed.

"Forgive me for mentioning, but how long have you been chasing him now?" Bok didn't answer. Svorn continued, "We've sent a wyvern – make that *two* wyverns, the King's guards, and bounty hunters, and still he's walking!"

Bok said nothing, and after a few moments Svorn sighed and sat opposite Bok. "I will gather the men and inform Conn that this little shit is still about, and may still have his chests," he said.

"How did they escape?" Bok questioned.

"We don't really know. They must have had hidden lock picks. We had searched them before locking them up, and we didn't find anything," Svorn replied.

"It was Ty. The others are not thieves. He got in somehow and released them, trust me."

"Rubbish," Svorn answered angrily. "The guards didn't see anybody, and the back door was definitely locked all night."

"Who said he came through the door?" Bok said, shrugging his shoulders.

"Well, he didn't slide under it!"

"I never said he did. There are plenty of ways of slipping in unnoticed. Was anything delivered? He could have disguised himself as a delivery boy."

"No, they all go through the main entrance. We would have noticed."

"Upstairs window?"

"Maybe, but we have guards patrolling all night. Surely they would have spotted him."

"He is a trained burglar; he would easily hide in shadows and dodge your guards. His climbing skills are second to none. It would be easy."

"Not buying it, the windows are barred or guarded, and the rooms that aren't in use are locked from the outside."

"Ever heard of lock picks?"

"That would be a hell of a lot of work to go through. Our walls are sheer, no way he'd be able to climb them. Besides then he'd have to get through the whole house without alerting anyone."

"Maybe not... what about the chimney?" Bok shrugged.

"Now you are clutching at straws!"

"You'd be surprised how versatile some thieves are."

"More chance digging a tunnel than coming –"

"That's it! Tunnel!"

"Now you *really* are clutching at straws," Svorn scoffed. "You think he dug a tunnel and –"

"No, not dug a tunnel – the drains. Is there a drain in the cell he could have come through?"

Svorn stood up. "Tez!" he shouted, and the door opened.

"Yes, Svorn?"

"Go down to the cells and check the drain covers. *Now*," Svorn said, waving his hand.

Twenty minutes later, Tez knocked and entered. "In the cell opposite, the drain cover was loose, and it's been moved recently," Tez said, bowing his head. "But there's more," he added.

"Go on," Svorn said, folding his arms.

"The stores were robbed last night," Tez said, embarrassed.

"How? What's gone?" Svorn said, walking over to Tez.

"The three men who escaped, it's just their weapons – an axe and a sword," Tez answered.

"Give the store guard ten lashings and ready ten men; we leave at once," Svorn shouted.

"Yes, sir," Tez answered, backing out and closing the door behind him.

Svorn sat back down. "He steals from the king, kills the king's wyvern, breaks into Conn's house, kills his guards – he will pay for this," Svorn snarled.

"The sooner the better," Bok agreed.

"Be ready in one hour," Svorn said.

"I'm ready now," Bok replied.

Chapter Twenty-One
Up North They Go

The party continued northwards. Sleeper sat in front of Ty, his wings flapping every so often, much to the annoyance of the thief. "I think we should camp soon. It's getting dark and this little one keeps trying to bite my mount," he laughed as he looked over at Kern.

"Good idea. Let's head towards the Eastern Mountains; there is bound to be a shelter we can use, and we'll be off this track if they send out any search parties," Kern suggested.

"Do you think we should have killed Bok?" Galandrik asked, drawing a finger across his throat.

"We only kill when we *have* to, remember? Killing a defenceless man lying naked on the floor is hardly our thing," Kern replied, shaking his head.

"He'll follow us, you know, and probably tell others. Only bring us grief in the end."

"Maybe we should have stuck him in a barrel and sent him to Blame on a cargo wagon," Ty said, scratching Sleeper's head.

"He won't follow us now; he'll still be nursing those wounds," Kern laughed.

"Oh, he'll follow. He's that stupid he won't let it lie," Ty replied.

"Look over there," Galandrik interrupted, pointing at a path that snaked up into the mountains.

The party followed the path up the rocky terrain. The trail didn't take them in towards the deep heart of the mountains; they rode just along the eastern ridge. Down to the east at ground level they could see the pathway that ran adjacent to the one they were on. The fields and trees of eastern Bodisha spread eastward below them, covering the land as far as they could see.

Soon they came to a rocky outpost that had clearly been used many times before. A rock jutting out of the side of the mountain protected travellers from inclement weather. Their position was good for setting up camp, and looked down onto the path leading north. The northward path they were on led higher up along the Eastern Mountains.

"Good spot, but a fire's out of the question. Everybody for twenty leagues would see us," Galandrik said as he dismounted.

"Good point, friend. Dried rations and blankets it is for tonight, then," Kern nodded, swinging himself out of the saddle.

Ty brought his mount up alongside Kern's, and stretched out the hand that was holding Sleeper. "Just grab him for a second, Kern," he asked, but before Kern could reach him, Sleeper leapt from Ty's grasp.

Ty made a grab for the dragon, but missed – and Sleeper dropped like a stone. Kern and Galandrik were frozen in place, cringing, and Ty clapped his hands to his head. Sleeper, flapping frantically, fell halfway to the ground, but then seemed almost to hover in mid-air. Still flapping madly, he held his position for a moment, then dropped again. This time his descent was slower and more controlled, his flapping seeming to help him decelerate.

It wasn't the most graceful of landings, but as soon as the dragon touched ground, he ran over to a small rock and overturned it with a talon. A field mouse ran out from its hiding place under the stone, but Sleeper was too quick and the mouse was swallowed within seconds. Then he simply tucked his wings neatly behind him and began sniffing his new surroundings.

Ty swung his legs round and landed on the ground. "We may need to put him on a lead; he'll be flying off before we know it."

"I agree, but you have to admit, there's nothing wrong with his sense of smell," Kern laughed.

They made camp without a fire and bedded down for the night. Ty made a little lead from leather strips and tied it carefully around Sleeper's back leg – which, to everyone's surprise, didn't seem to bother him at all. Kern handed out some dried rations and they ate and talked, trying not to worry about the hardships that might lay ahead of them.

They passed an uneventful, night, with each of them taking turns at keeping watch, Kern had the third turn, and he watched over his friends as the halfling and dwarf slept, with Sleeper curled up close to Ty. Kern wondered if he would have believed anyone who, a few days ago, had told him he'd soon see his halfling friend snuggling with a dragon.

The morning sun was rising and Kern welcomed the warmth of her rays. Birds were chirping all around, which always pleased him; his father had always said that no birds in the sky meant bad things were about to happen, as the birds could sense upcoming danger. He sat on a boulder and started to wonder: He knew where they were going and he knew why, but *how*? How they'd manage to get a baby dragon back to its mother was a mystery. Would the mother even accept it back? Was the mother still alive? Where exactly did the mother live? He remembered Nuran mentioning the great orc wars just north of here – could they pass that way with a baby dragon in tow? Maybe they should head straight up through the Eastern Mountains, staying on this trail; could that be the answer? Maybe they could stay out of sight all the way to the dragon-mother's den.

Kern scratched his chin as Galandrik rolled over. He stood up and began to walk around the campsite, stretching his aching limbs and kicking the odd stone down towards the northern pathway to Tonilla. He wondered if the mother dragon would eat them all, and shivered.

He decided to put it out of his mind, and started to tend to the mounts. It was the worst thing about having the early watch; you got the mounts ready for the day's travel while the others slept in. He stroked his horse's head and thought, *Oh how simple it would be to be a horse.*

Just then the horse reared, pawing the air with its front legs. As Kern toppled backwards, he saw that an arrow had struck his horse in the rump.

The horse bolted down the trail they had come up – along with Kern's supplies.

Kern quickly rolled over and looked down at the northern path, Bok, Svorn, and a dozen of the King's guards were all looking directly up at him. Ty appeared next to him as arrows flew past their heads.

"What the hell?" Ty said, squinting in the bright morning sun.

"It's bloody Bok!" Kern said, ducking an arrow.

Bok, Svorn, and five of the guards headed south towards the path that would lead them up into the mountains, directly to the campsite. The remaining guards continued to bombard them with arrows.

"Quick – let's get mounted up before they get round to us," Kern hissed and then ran towards the two remaining horses. He gave a Galandrik a kick as he passed. "Up dwarf, we must go!" he said as low a voice as he could manage. "I reckon we have ten minutes before they get down, around, and up to us," he added.

Galandrik sat up like a startled rabbit. "What, where – orcs? I'll kill them all!" he mumbled like a waking drunk.

Ty dashed past Galandrik and scooped up Sleeper, then carefully lowered the dragon into his backpack. Galandrik stood up, still dazed, as another arrow flew through the camp, just missing the top of his ginger braided hair.

"Another inch and it would have bounced off your thick head," Kern said, mounting up and offering an outstretched hand to the half-awake dwarf.

"Where's *your* horse?" Galandrik asked, picking up his axe and swinging his backpack over his shoulder.

"I'll explain along the way," Kern said, waving his hand in a hurry-up motion. Galandrik accepted and Kern pulled the dwarf up behind him.

"We can't go down towards them, it's so steep; and we can't go back, so it's straight up and into the mountains," Ty said, giving his mount a hard kick.

Soon both horses were moving up the rocky path. Down to their right side was the pathway north; on their left was a sheer rock face that was slowly getting higher as they travelled. As the path levelled out and curved downwards into the mountains, their view of the green trees and the pathway to Tonilla was replaced by rock and scree.

After twenty minutes the path split, one side leading deeper into the mountains, the path twisting downwards into the depths of its stone belly. The other offered a slow, steady climb along the west edge of the mountains. The landscape was getting harsher and they knew they had to choose a direction. Both pathways were obviously there for a reason and led somewhere, but where was anyone's guess.

"Well, what do you think, up or down?" Ty asked, looking behind him, half-expecting to hear the chasing horses.

"Up. Dragons don't normally live *under* mountains," Galandrik replied.

"No, but fat dwarves do!" Ty replied, feeling stung that he'd missed the obvious. Once more he kicked his mount and raced past the others.

Kern and Galandrik followed Ty up the rocky incline, slowly getting deeper and higher into the eastern mountains. The small clusters of vegetation that still lingered gradually disappeared as they gained elevation, until the last fading resemblance of their starting point was gone. It felt colder and damper up here, as if there was a light rainfall freezing to their faces.

They could now hear the pursuing pack. Galandrik and Kern were moving more slowly than their pursuers. Although the path had slowly widened, its incline was steeper, and the steam from the horses' hides was a clear indication that were feeling the strain. The path gradually turned in, westwards, into the heart of the mountains, and it seemed ages before it curved again, this time to the north. Ty was about a hundred paces ahead of the others, scouting for a hideout or anyplace that might offer an escape from the guards chasing them. Looking around desperately, he saw a gap in the rocks. It was too smooth to be natural; about ten feet high, it appeared to be a doorway.

Ty jumped from his horse and looked down through the gap in the rock. It was very narrow but seemed well made. He scanned the entrance quickly for traps but found nothing. Picking up a fist-sized stone from the ground, he threw in down the passageway, where it landed without commotion. He hesitated, then threw a second rock in, a little further. This time when the stone landed he heard another noise – then two slabs of solid stone, one from either side of the tunnel, slammed together, crushing the stone into dust. *Nice trap,* Ty thought to himself as dust from the pulverized stone wafted out of the tunnel.

Kern and Galandrik rode up alongside Ty, their mount's sides heaving with every breath. Kern looked at the gap as he dismounted. "What is it?"

"I have absolutely no idea, but they'll catch us up soon and I think this is our best option. You cannot fight in a two-foot tunnel," Ty said, shrugging his shoulders.

Galandrik peered into the opening. "Also," he said, "you cannot *fit* in a two foot tunnel."

"We've lost too much time already," Ty said, grabbing the packs from the two horses. "Go on, get out of here! Run!" he shouted as he slapped the beasts on their rumps. The horses galloped away up the path. Ty turned to the other two. "I'll go in first. There are foot pad traps; you stand on one and you're dead, simple as that. I'll let you know where each one is. If you touch it or even breathe heavy near it, two slabs will make you part of this mountain." Ty had slowly edged into the tunnel while he'd been talking. "Also, I suggest Galandrik come next. That way one of us can push and one can pull," he added with a grin.

One by one, they entered the stone corridor sideways on, Ty announcing traps every few minutes. After thirty slow steps, they heard the sound of horses galloping past. As Ty eased down the corridor it very slowly opened up a bit, and he could see daylight at what appeared to be the end of the tunnel. So far he had found six foot traps, and all his senses were on high alert. When they reached the end of the passageway, Ty stepped out into open air and onto a ledge that was no more than two feet wide.

Arms wind-milling, he lurched forward on his tiptoes, balancing precariously on the edge. His arms waved frantically as he tried to regain his balance, and he began to fall forward. Just before his centre of gravity toppled him over the ledge, he was stopped with a jerk.

"I got ya, lad," Galandrik said from behind. With a tug Ty was pulled back onto the safety of the ledge. His heart beating twice its normal rate, he turned to Galandrik.

"Give us a pull?" the dwarf – wedged in the opening of the tunnel, unable to squeeze his girth through – asked with obvious embarrassment.

With a careful pull from Ty and a push from Kern, Galandrik was soon out on the ledge, and he shuffled sideways enough for Kern to step out. Below them stretched an abyss, blackness, down and down it went. In front of him was a rope-and-plank bridge was spanning the abyss, and on the other side another corridor – the mirror image of this side, another tunnel leading ever deeper into the heart of the mountain. They could only press forward, or go back.

The rope bridge was anchored into the wall on either side of him, and appeared to be well-secured and sturdy. Ty rested his foot cautiously on the first wooden plank and pressed down carefully. It seemed firm enough; so did the second.

"That was too close for comfort," Kern said, looking around. They could see birds soaring in the sky high above them, and could feel the cool wind sweeping down the mountains. "Well, only one way now," Ty said. "I'll go first to test it, then I'll come back for your backpacks and weapons. It'll make you lighter." He began walking slowly forward.

Kern and Galandrik were watching Ty's advance when Kern heard a noise from behind. He peered down the corridor, and saw an arrow lying a few feet from the opening. He couldn't see to the far end of the corridor, but he could hear the commotion and knew that their pursuers had found the freed horses, and backtracked.

"They've found us. Quickly, we must move," he said urgently.

Ty was about halfway across the bridge, taking every step as carefully as he possibly could. He didn't seem to be alarmed in the least by Kern's announcement.

Suddenly the ground shook; Ty managed to swing with the motion of the bridge, while Kern and Galandrik grasped each other's arms and the bridge's wall-anchors to steady themselves.

"What in Hades?" Galandrik gasped, looking down to the abyss anxiously.

"Remember those traps?" Ty called, taking another anxious step forward. "I think someone just found one."

After a few more nerve-wracking minutes he was across, looking down the next corridor to be sure it was passable. "Looks okay! All right, same as the last corridor," he explained as he walked back across the bridge, more confidently than before. "Pass me a backpack." Moving more quickly now, Ty soon had all their weapons and gear on the far side, and Galandrik began slowly making his way across the bridge.

Another earth-shaking boom rippled the ground beneath their feet, this one much louder and more ferocious than the first. Kern wobbled and held onto the metal anchor-ring that secured the bridge.

Ty watched as the bridge swung from side to side, Galandrik struggling to keep his footing on it. *Please don't fall,* he thought as the dwarf lurched from left to right and back again. Somehow, the more Galandrik tried to stabilize himself, the worse the swing got. Ty bent down and opened one of the backpacks, and Sleeper's head poked out curiously.

Reaching inside the other pack, Ty pulled out a coil of hemp rope, and quickly he started fastening one end to the iron ring embedded into the wall. It looked rusty, but he had no other options. Ty turned back to Sleeper to make sure he was safe; visualising the dragon falling into the abyss, Ty tucked him back in and pulled the drawstring tight.

Ty looked round just as Galandrik fell, his arms waving helplessly.

Fortunately, the dwarf's fall was cut short when his foot got caught between two of the bridge's wooden slats – upside down he hung, dangling over the abyss.

"Help!" Terrified, Galandrik was still waving his arms around frantically.

"Keep still, you idiot" Kern shouted. As quickly as he dared, Ty walked out to where Galandrik hung, the bridge creaking ominously under the strain of two bodies. When he reached Galandrik Ty tied the rope around Galandrik's boot, then scrambled back to his spot on the far ledge.

"I've got him secured – what now?" Ty shouted.

"Hold on – I'm coming," Kern replied, and started to walk across the bridge. He could hear the voices in the corridor behind him getting closer.

At that moment one of the two wooden boards pinioning Galandrik's foot split, and his foot slid through. Ty overlapped the rope through the ring so the ring would take the strain, but just in case, he braced himself.

Galandrik screamed in terror as he fell. Then with a jolt that felt like it had popped his ankle out of the joint, he began to swing towards the wall below Ty.

The rope held strong and Ty needed minimal effort to hold him; the overlapped rope stayed firm. Galandrik hit the wall with a thud, and his world went dark.

Kern, finally reaching Ty's side, grabbed the rope and began to pull as Ty kept the rope anchored. With a grunt and a heave, he stopped.

"No good, we'll need to lift him together," he said to Ty. Together they both heaved on the rope but it was no good; Galandrik's weight combined with the weight of his armour was too much for them.

"This isn't working, we need some other way of lifting him," Ty said, looking round.

"I got it! Quick, grab the rope." Kern grabbed the rope from Ty and held it fast. Ty grabbed the other loose end and hopped and skipped as lightly as he could across the bridge. Once across, he threaded the coil through the iron ring on that side. Then he knelt down and started paying out the rope. Kern couldn't see exactly what he was doing, but it looked like he was creating a loop in the rope. Ty dashed back across the bridge and grabbed the rope with Kern.

"Slide into the tunnel," he instructed.

"What?" Kern said, taking a step backwards into the darkness. "What about traps?" he shouted.

"I checked, there aren't any," Ty replied, hoping Kern wouldn't spot the blatant lie. In a few moments they both squatted a short distance into the tunnel.

"Are you going to tell me what exactly is going on?" Kern demanded.

"You'll see," Ty replied, looking across the bridge. "Keep hold of the rope – when I tell you to, let go."

"But Galandrik will fall!"

"Just trust me," Ty answered.

A few minutes went by before they spotted the first of the guards, his helmeted head popping out of the passage on the other side.

"I hope they don't notice Galandrik," Kern whispered.

"No chance, unless the buffoon wakes up and screams," Ty whispered back. The guard looked down the corridor behind him, and soon another one stepped out. *Hold on…just a little further,* Ty thought as the first guard stepped cautiously onto the first wooden step, and the second guard soon followed.

"I'm going to count to three," Ty whispered to Kern. "On three, let go. I just hope I hit him sweet. All right – one, two… three!"

Ty stepped forward from the shadows and unleashed a dagger, sending it speeding through the air. Kern let go of the rope, and it screamed as it whizzed through the ring, pulled by the dead-weight of Galandrik. Ty's aim was true, and his dagger thudded into the guard's eye socket. Galandrik's falling weight made the rope around the guard's feet tighten and constrict around their legs. The dead guard toppled forward off the ledge, the rope snared tight around his legs, and his weight was enough to drag the second guard over. As they fell, the rope screamed again – in the other direction, this time.

Kern stepped out of the tunnel as Galandrik's feet appeared just below their ledge. Looking over the edge, Kern saw that the dwarf's axe was caught, keeping him from rising the rest of the way.

"Quick, grab him," Kern said. Together, they pulled the dwarf up and over the ledge, the weight of the two guards doing most of their work for them. Once Galandrik was safely up, Kern drew his dagger and cut the rope. The trailing end whipped through the two rings until it fell free, down into the abyss, the screams of the falling guard following.

Kern slapped Galandrik's face, trying to rouse the unconscious dwarf. A trickle of blood seeped out from under his helmet as Galandrik grunted and his eyes rolled in their sockets.

Another guard appeared on the other side. "I'll cut the bridge," Ty said, pulling a dagger from his belt.

"Don't; this may be a dead end," Kern said, helping Galandrik stand up.

"Good call," Ty replied. "Quick, then, follow me," and he stepped into the corridor. Sleeper hissed as Ty slipped an arm through the backpack strap and swung it roughly onto his shoulder.

"What happened?" Galandrik asked, rubbing his forehead.

"Explain later, friend. Follow Ty," Kern said, pushing Galandrik into the gap. An arrow pinged against the wall next to him as he followed Galandrik into the next tunnel.

This second tunnel was even darker than the first. It bored straight through the rock, and had no light coming in from above. Ty lit a torch and looked around carefully for hidden traps as he led the way. The corridor ran on for a good hundred paces on a slight incline. It opened onto a circular chamber, and Ty stepped forward and lit the wall torches on either side of the room. There was one door, which appeared to be the room's only other entrance or exit. Ty examined the door as Kern brought a still-dazed Galandrik up to date regarding his adventures on the rope bridge.

"No traps," Ty said, "and I think I can pick it." He knelt down and unravelled his lock picks, and soon the lock clicked open. Ty stepped back and gestured to Kern.

"Your hands broken?" Kern asked, but he stepped forward without hesitation. He placed an ear close to the door, then eased it open, tilting his head to one side to peep round the corner. "It's just another corridor," Kern said, opening the door fully. They filed into the new passageway, Galandrik limping slightly from the rope burns he'd sustained earlier.

Ty knelt down and re-locked the door behind them. "I can't see Bok opening this," he laughed.

"Why, because you're the best?" Kern said rather dismissively as he gazed around the room. He spotted another door and went to investigate it.

"No, because I messed his hands up, remember?" Ty sniggered.

"Oh yes – I'd forgotten about that," Galandrik said, placing his hand on Ty shoulder.

Kern placed his hand on the door handle and listened. "It seems all quiet," Kern announced.

Before Ty could reply, the door flew open, knocking Kern backwards into Galandrik, and eight lizard warriors ran into the room. Spears pointed at them from every direction.

The lizard people were an enormous race – the shortest among them stood seven feet tall, and their tails were the same again in length. Renowned for their organization in battle and stubborn refusal to die easily, they were fearsome warriors. Most wore only light leather armour; there was the odd shield, but always they fought with spears. Their reach with their chosen weapons made it nigh impossible to challenge them with daggers and short swords.

Sprawled on the floor, Kern looked up at Ty and shook his head. The three of them raised their arms.

"Put down your weaponsss," the lead lizard hissed.

"Okay, we will do as you ask. We mean you no trouble," Kern replied, kneeling and laying his sword on the ground in front of him.

"Ssshut it, human!" the lizard said, using his spear to push Kern off balance. Then he spied Galandrik. "Oh look, we have a dwarvesss. Oglar likesss the tassste of dwarvesss," he hissed.

"This 'Oglar' must have real bad taste then," Ty said with false cheer. The lizard turned to face the thief.

"What have we here, thensss, a little wormsss?" He levelled his spear against Ty's chest and slowly pushed him backwards until he was pinned against the wall.

"I have sometimes been called a Rat, but never a worm," Ty said, his voice sounding slightly less amused. The spear creaked and bent slightly against his light leather tunic; at any minute, Ty thought, it was penetrate straight through him.

"Oglar likess them alives, Ssied!" said another lizard from behind Ty's tormentor. The lizard Sied relented, but he continued to glare at Ty. His reptilian eyes reminded Ty of cat's eyes, bright green with jet-black pupils. It was like looking into the eyes of death itself, Ty thought with a shiver.

Sied slowly stepped back, releasing the pressure from Ty's chest. "I know thisss, Kaleem. Bring themss!"

Bok, his ear pressed to the door, looked up at Svorn and put one finger up to his lips. "Shhh," he said softly.

"What's going on?" Svorn whispered back.

"Lizards, lots of lizards," Bok replied. "We can't get through this way; we need to find the western exit and catch them there."

"What makes you think they will make it past the lizards?" Svorn asked, clearly sceptical.

"He is an elusive little bastard; it would be wise to remember that," Bok replied.

"All right, we'll wait for twenty-four hours, but I'm not giving him any longer than that. If he doesn't show up by then, we will presume him dead," Svorn said, turning to leave.

"He will escape. He *always* escapes," Bok hissed quietly as he followed Svorn.

Chapter Twenty-Two
Big Trouble Little Worm

The lizards rounded them up and led them along a new corridor. "You should probably thank Kaleem," Kern whispered.

"I thought I was a goner," Ty admitted.

"Keep your mouth shut then," Galandrik added.

"Sshut itsss mouth upss," Sied said, turning back. The metal spearhead knocked the top of Ty's head, making him squint.

The lizards led them down one corridor after another, all lit by lanterns hanging on rusty brackets. They passed spaces which looked like they'd been offices and living quarters, dating back to when these mountains had been used as barracks, many hundreds of years earlier. After a good walk they arrived at two massive doors rising twenty feet high. Sied banged on the door with his fist. They heard gears churning, chains rattling, clicks and bangs seeming to come from within the mountain itself.

Slowly the great doors started to open; wind rushed through the widening gap between the doors, and the smell of roasted meats filled their nostrils. Ty felt Sleeper stirring in his backpack and knew the dragon couldn't be kept hidden in there much longer. Sleeper needed food and, one way or another, he would get out; the tantalizing aroma of the food would only make the baby dragon more curious.

The doors finished opening and the party walked through, prodded none too gently by the spears behind them. This looked like a feasting hall;

lines of tables and chairs squared the room, and giant lizard tapestries lined the walls, depicting battles from many moons gone by. From the ceiling hung a giant wooden chandelier filled with candles. Behind the head table, two massive thrones studded with gems and covered in gold leaf overlooked the room. Bright red cushions adorned the seats of both. The worker lizard men and women scurried around the room, preparing for what looked to be an event of some size. Ty tried to assess the value of the wealth in this room, but it staggered him; so many gems and trinkets were embedded all around, he couldn't even begin to count them.

They were prodded along through the hall, until they finally exited into a corridor opening at the far end. A hundred feet down the corridor, the path forked; they were ushered to the left and down some stairs. The stairs spiralled down and down for what seemed like hours and then, when the steps eventually levelled out, after a few more paces the group was pushed into an empty room. The door slammed shut behind them. Ty immediately inspected the door, "No lock," he said, shaking his head. "Must be barred from the other side."

"Walls look like they won't be knocked down in a hurry," Galandrik added, rubbing his hands along the wall. "The craftsmanship is quality."

"Knocked down with what, anyway?" Kern asked irritably. "Got a siege engine in your backpack? We don't even have our weapons!" He sat down and rubbed his hands along his arms in an attempt to generate some body heat.

"I'm glad they did leave our backpacks alone," Ty replied, lifting Sleeper from his pack. "If they'd found him, it would have been all for nothing."

"And it still WILL be all for nothing, when they feed us to this Oglar," Kern laughed bitterly.

"Let's be optimistic here, we're not dead yet," Ty replied, stroking his pet. Sleeper was beginning to lift off the ground now. With only a few flaps of his wings he could easily rise to the level of Ty's head, and he was even starting to go forwards and backwards. His constant squawking appeared to be an attempt at breathing fire, but so far but only small puffs of smoke had ever emerged.

"They grow quick, don't they?" Galandrik said into the silence.

"Yes. I hope we find the mother soon," Ty replied.

"Find the mother? Have a look around you, for fuck's sake. We have a hundred lizard warriors and an 'Oglar' to worry about! If it wasn't for you and that the blasted dragon, we wouldn't even *be* here!" Kern shouted.

"Listen, no one made you come! I could have left you in the orc mines, or Conn's dungeon! Would that have been better?"

"Oh, here we go again. Ty *the saviour!*"

"Tell me I am wrong then," Ty said angrily.

"No, no – you are dead right. We were in those places, and we were there because of you!"

"How in Hades is it my fault?"

"It's always your fault!" Kern said, turning his back.

"That's right, turn away," Ty said sarcastically.

Kern spun round and walked towards Ty. Galandrik could see the fury in his eyes and stepped in front of him. "Calm down, lad, this isn't helping anyone." He held Kern by the arm for ten tense seconds, and finally Kern shook his head in disgust and, with a grunt, turned away again.

Galandrik pointed at Ty as the thief opened his mouth to say something else.

"Don't," Galandrik said softly but decisively.

Nothing else was said for a few hours until, in the ringing silence, they heard footsteps outside the door. Ty quickly offered the backpack to Sleeper, who slid inside obediently.

The door opened and six guards stood outside. "Get out," the lead lizard said; Kern recognised him from their earlier encounter: Kaleem. Hands in the air, they walked from the room in single file.

Once more they were led down corridors full of twists and turns, eventually coming to a great rounded door. Kaleem rapped twice on the door, and again they heard the clunks and clangs of some hidden mechanism. The door rolled open to reveal an enormous circular room. Three imposing pillars formed semi-circles along either side of the room, and lit torches were mounted on each pillar, casting a smoky, flickering light. On the other side of this room, across a sand-covered floor and directly opposite the doorway in which they stood, was a ten foot tall steel-barred gate.

All three were pushed into the room and the door slammed shut behind them.

"Like lambs to the slaughter," Kern said quietly out the corner of his mouth, as if not to awaken anything that might be lurking in the darkness.

"Indeed," Galandrik quietly replied.

Ty padded quietly in the direction of the nearest pillar, scouting out the room. As he drew nearer to the pillar, something on the ground behind it caught his eye. Bending down, he picked up a bastard sword. "Catch," he said, tossing it to Kern.

Kern caught the blade and examined it closely. "This is older than the mountains."

"Here's another," Galandrik said, picking up a scimitar.

Before long each member of the party had picked up a weapon, Kern had also found a wooden buckler, but he doubted it could withstand a blow from a child, let alone from an Oglar, whatever that was.

Ty shrugged off his backpack and laid it down behind one of the pillars. Unbuckling the leather straps, he whispered into the bag, "If this turns bad, go find your mother."

Suddenly they could see lights from above. The ceiling glowed resplendently; embedded with rubies and emeralds, it seemed to sparkle and dance. The reds and greens reflected down onto the arena floor, giving it a very colourful look; as the torchlights flickered, the reds and greens made the floor shimmer and move in a magical display of lights.

Lizard men and women appeared on the balcony encircling the top half of the room. Before long the balcony was full, and the noise and cheering was deafening. At the far end of the balcony, above the barred gate, were two empty thrones, flanked on either side by two guards in glistening white armour. They stood erect and immobile, holding their spears and their bright golden shields; each of their helmets was crested with a plume of white feathers and their breastplates featured the emblem of a snake twining around a hawk.

A few of the lizard people began throwing pieces of rotten fruit down into the arena, but the threesome easily dodged the slimy missiles. Ty bent down to pick a piece up, intending to throw it back into the crowd, only to find two rusty daggers in the sand. He tucked them into his belt and thought wistfully about the lost invisibility ring, wishing he still had it at his disposal.

The crowd went quiet just as a piece of rotten fruit landed at Ty's feet. Into the suddenly hushed arena walked two regally dressed lizards – well, as close to royalty as a lizard could get. Each wore a crown of gold smothered in gems that glistened in the torchlights lining the balcony. Their flowing robes were heavily embroidered with multi-coloured silks and silver thread, each with an elaborate belt closely cinching the waist. Silver daggers rode in gem-studded sheaths affixed to the belts, and even from where he stood on the arena floor, Ty could make out the diamonds embedded in the daggers' handles.

The lizard Queen sat whilst the lizard King stood staring down at the threesome. Slowly lifted his arm and pointed, then spoke in a clear, carrying voice. "Todayss, you threess will fight to sssurvive. You breakss into our homess and tryss to sssteal our gemssess," he said, the room deathly quiet apart from his echoing voice. "Now you payss!"

Ty stepped forward, whipping a dagger from his belt. He hurled it towards the lizard King, but it had barely left his hand before two loud cracks resounded in the stillness. Lizard guards on either side of the balcony stood, each holding a whip; the tongue of one whip flicked the dagger out of the air and it landed harmlessly in the sand in the middle of the arena. Ty felt the other whip lash across his face, and before he even realized what had happened, he was lying on the ground, one hand to his cheek. The pain seared through his head, at first dull, then blossoming into a bright flame of agony. He could feel the warm blood trickling through his fingers.

Kern quickly bent down. "What are you doing, you fool?" he whispered harshly, examining the cut across Ty's face.

"Help me up," Ty replied. Kern extended a hand and pulled, and Ty stood up, flicking the blood from his hand to the floor. He stared steadily at the King, as if the whip had been nothing but a graze, though his face throbbed and he could feel the blood running from the torn cheek. He resisted the urge to wipe his face, and held the lizard King's gaze in silence.

The two guards closest to the King had stepped forward at Ty's first movement, moving their shields together to form a protective wall in front of their King. Now they slowly pulled them away, revealing a grinning King. "Ssuch sspirit for ssuch a little worm," he said, laughing. "Releassse Oglar!" he shouted, and the crowd screamed with joy.

"Spread out," Kern ordered, hoisting the shield in front of him. He spun the rapier in his other hand a few times, finally resting it on top of his shield, pointing towards the portcullis. "Our best chance is a three-pronged attack!" he shouted, hoping his friends could hear him above the cheering of the crowd.

The giant barred door lifted slowly; two lizards worked tirelessly at a system of rotating wheels, ropes, and pulleys to raise its massive weight.

Ty dashed behind a pillar on the right side of the arena, and Galandrik took a similar position on the left. "I'll grab his attention, you two strike when you can," Ty said as he leaned against the pillar, gathering his courage. He glanced over his shoulder at the slowly rising gate; sweat streamed down his cheeks, mixing with blood and stinging his open wound fiercely. The sweat was running into his eyes, but he found his hands were trembling so he kept them at his sides, clenched into hard fists, and tried to blink the droplets away.

When a tomato squelched against his shoulder, Ty looked up and saw a young lizard laughing to another and pointing. Ty moved forward to the middle right pillar, away from the young lizards and the distraction of their missiles. Kern noticed Ty's movement, and gestured for Galandrik to do the same; if he could lead his foe past the middle pillars, maybe – just maybe – his friends would have the opportunity to attack from behind.

The gate had reached its zenith and the arena went quiet. Kern could feel his breath quickening, his heart nearly bursting from his chest. It wasn't the fight, he thought; it was the crowd, the spectacle of it all; the intimidation levels were immense. He wasn't a gladiator; he was a ranger – a hunter, a fair fighter, but no gladiator.

Into the sudden hush sounded slow, thudding footsteps, the ground trembling beneath the unwilling combatants with each step. An immense, hulking shape began to resolve from the darkness, until finally it stepped into the torchlight of the arena: a mountain Troll, at least eight feet tall, his forearms and legs bulging with muscles, and nothing but a loin cloth covering his modesty. The troll carried a club in one hand, a length on chain in the other. His huge head and bulbous eyes were menacing and mean; hundreds of scars lined the troll's face and chest from years of arena fighting. Around his neck was a thick metal collar, with one large ring hanging under his chin. Leather straps bound his feet with a similar metal ring on either side; *they must keep him restrained,* Kern thought, *when he's not ripping people's heads off for a bloodthirsty crowd.*

The troll extended his arms and roared his battle cry into the hush; the crowd roared with him, and the cacophony of shouts, screams, cheers, and jeers returned threefold. He lowered his arms and looked directly at Kern, snorting like a horse, before moving forward. Kern held his stance.

As the troll passed the middle pillar, Galandrik looked at Ty and nodded, and they both ran to spring the ambush. Galandrik let out a war cry as he ran and the troll turned, swinging the chain in his right hand towards the dwarf. The chain wrapped around Galandrik's sword, snatching it from the dwarf's grasp; the blade went flying towards a wall, snapping in two on impact. The crowd howled.

Ty saw his chance and ran directly towards the troll's back. From the corner of his eye he saw Kern step forward to within attacking distance. Just before Ty was about to strike he heard the crack of the whip again and felt it, almost instantaneously, wrapping around his middle. He was lifted from the floor and fell backwards.

Oglar turned to Ty, who was staring up in shock at the lizard holding the whip. The troll raised his great club and sent it crashing down towards the thief, but Ty rolled at the last instant, just managing to evade the blow. The whip was now wrapped around his waist twice; he grabbed its coils as he jumped to his feet.

Kern launched a sweeping attack towards the troll's midsection; with the back of his hand Oglar swatted Kern's attack aside, bowling him over again.

Galandrik ran at Oglar's blind side and jumped up, landing on the troll's knee then wrapping his arms around the enormous head. With all his strength he tried to choke the great beast.

Ty looked up at the lizard holding the whip and pulled as hard as he could, using all his strength and body weight. The lizard guard, caught by surprise, came crashing down head-first next to the troll. Ty loosened the whip from around his waist.

Oglar dropped his chain and club and reached up behind his head; with one hand he plucked Galandrik loose and tossed him to the floor. As Galandrik lay winded by the force of the throw, the troll picked up his club and brought it down towards the dazed dwarf.

Just before impact, Kern struck the club with his shield, parrying the blow to the floor so that it just missed the dwarf's head.

Oglar screamed in frustration. Looking to his left he spied the lizard guard getting up; he raised one giant foot and squashed the lizard's head like a watermelon. A groan echoed around the arena, and the queen turned away, closing her eyes.

Ty darted in and grabbed the fallen lizard's spear, throwing it under the troll's legs to Kern. Pulling the rusty dagger from his belt, Ty leapt up and grabbed hold of Oglar's loincloth with one hand, stabbing repeatedly and ferociously at the troll's side with his other. Blood gushed from the new wounds and Oglar's roars seemed to shake the entire mountain.

Grabbing the spear, Kern knelt and readied himself for a strike. The troll twisted and finally managed to grab Ty by the back of his neck and lifted him away. With a quick flick of his wrist he sent Ty sailing – right into Kern.

All three companions were now lying, dazed and bloodied, in front of the Oglar. The troll raised his giant foot and brought it down onto Kern's and Ty's feet, trapping them both.

Ty let out a scream with the pressure of the troll's foot on his own.

Luckily the troll's weight was concentrated on his standing leg, and the sand underneath them offered some cushioning; otherwise their bones would surely have been crushed like the lizard's head.

Kern desperately tried to reach the spear, but it was a fingernail length out of reach. Galandrik eyes rolled as he struggled to focus.

The crowd screamed all the louder, as they could sense a bloody end nearing. The troll stretched out his arms again, club in one hand, and screamed to his adoring crowd; the only wound marking his body was the flow of blood running down his leg from Ty's stab wounds.

"Grab the damn spear!" Ty shouted, pushing against Kern.

"I'm trying," Kern replied, arching his body in an attempt to grab the weapon.

Ty sat forward, in agony as his foot was twisted under the troll's foot. He pushed against the troll's leg, trying to release his own. Galandrik gained some focus and started mumbling.

The troll looked down at his victims and brought both hands together on the handle of the club, raising it above his head.

Kern had managed to get close enough to touch the spear with his fingertips, but still was not close enough to grab it. Ty frantically lashed out at the troll's leg, but it was having no effect.

The troll raised the club to full height and let out one final roar. Ty grabbed the shield and laid back, covering his head. Kern still scrabbled desperately in the sand, trying to reach the spear.

Just before Oglar unleashed the club Kern saw something flicker above the troll's head; a black shadow hovered over, then covered, the troll's face.

"Sleeper!" Kern shouted, as the baby dragon latched onto the troll's face, biting and clawing at his eyes and nose.

The troll stumbled backwards, the club forgotten on the ground where it had fallen. He waved and grabbed out for the dragon, but Sleeper was too quick, darting in and out of reach as the troll lurched and swung, and always aiming for the troll's eyes.

Freed from the troll's pinioning foot, Kern rolled over and grabbed the spear in the same movement as he scrambled to his feet. Ty grabbed

Galandrik and together they struggled to stand. Kern waited for an opening as the troll lashed out at Sleeper, then attacked, thrusting the spear into Oglar's belly.

The troll grabbed the spear with one hand and spun around, still trying to swat the dragon with his other. Blood streamed down his face as he blindly turned and twisted.

Sleeper landed next to Ty and they all watched the Troll stagger around the arena. The crowd sat in stunned silence as the lizard King stood up in disbelief. Kern dashed over to the dead lizard and pulled the guard's sword from its scabbard. Moving behind the troll, he waited, dodging flailing arms and legs – then he struck, forcing the sword up deep into the troll's spine. Kern jumped back and stood next to the others, watching as the troll staggered for a few more seconds, then stopped. Slowly, like a massive oak tree falling in a forest, Oglar toppled to the ground. The whole arena shook when he hit the floor, smashing the spear into tiny pieces, and then all they heard was silence.

Finally the lizard King's enraged voice shouted from above, "Kill them!" Spears stuck the ground around them as Ty grabbed his backpack and all three ran towards the only exit, the troll's cave, Sleeper flying ahead of them. Arrows and spears were flying all around them and Ty struggled to dodge them. His ankle felt like it was broken and he winced through the pain. He looked up in time to see the whip-bearing lizard lift the lash up, ready to bring it cracking down. Ty threw his dagger desperately, but its flight was true, hitting the whip-bearer's arm. The lizard dropped the whip as he screamed in agony.

"Close the gate!" the lizard King screamed.

They put everything they had into a last burst of speed, dodging cracking whips and spears. Ty's ankle gave out and he rolled the last few feet, the iron gate crashing into the ground inches behind him.

Chapter Twenty-Three
Déjà Vu

Kern, Galandrik, and Ty hastened down the corridor from which the troll had entered the arena. Ty, dragging his injured foot, was being helped by Galandrik, who was now fully recovered from his disorientation. The corridor led down to a circular room, a stench emanating from it that stung their noses and made their eyes water. Bones of all sizes lay scattered around the troll's nest; bedding of filthy, mouldering straw was positioned in one corner and a campfire, still alight, sat directly in the middle of the room.

There was small door on the eastern wall and a pit in the northwest corner. A brief examination of the pit showed it to be a trash pit for the bones and troll rubbish.

"What sort of troll tidies up after himself?" Galandrik asked, holding his nose.

"No troll would, but lizard men who use a troll for sport might," Kern replied.

"They must come in through that little door over there," Ty said, pointing.

"No chance," Kern said, examining the door. "I would struggle to get through that, and those lizards are huge – they would never fit down there. Anyway it looks like this door hasn't been touched for ages," he added.

"It will be soon; they're opening the cage," Ty said, tugging at the door handle. From up the corridor, they could hear the grinding and creaking of the iron cage door being laboriously raised again.

Galandrik walked over to the small door. "So the lizards wouldn't be able to get down here, then?"

"Not a chance," Kern replied.

With that, the dwarf kicked the door; it creaked and cracked but stayed firm. Galandrik took a step back and kicked again, and this time a few shards of wood smashed inwards. Heartened, he stepped back and repeated his kicks until the door was completely broken through, revealing a little corridor heading downwards, Ty gathered up his backpack, along with Sleeper, and they all entered the corridor one after the other. Kern was nearly kneeling as they edged their way down; the corridor was only just wide enough to get down, and it got darker as they went. They could hear the lizard men shouting and arguing in the room behind them, their voices echoing down the tiny corridor.

Soon they were in absolute darkness, with Galandrik leading the way; Ty was next, his ankle still throbbing from the troll's abuse. Sleeper was perched on Ty's backpack.

"I can't see a thing," Galandrik moaned.

"Just keep sweeping your hand in front and tapping your foot as you go. I have hold of you," Kern answered from behind.

After a while Galandrik stopped. "Wait! I can't feel the floor. I think it's a pit." The dwarf felt blindly around the walls and floor of the corridor, reaching out in front of himself but feeling nothing. "It's a doorway," he explained, "and the floor just drops down, and I can't feel anything."

"Drop something down and listen for how deep it is," Kern suggested.

"Just push him," Ty added, sniggering.

Galandrik knelt down and found a small stone. "Be quiet and listen." He dropped the stone and almost immediately heard the noise it made as it hit the ground below. "It's not that deep, if I back into it and hang from the edge here, it should be ok," he suggested.

"We can help lower you down if it helps," Kern answered.

"Okay, let's do this," Galandrik said, and squeezed himself around in the corridor until he was facing Kern and Ty in the blackness. He knelt down and swung himself over the side, Kern and Ty holding his arms. Slowly they lowered him down as far as Ty's shorter arms would allow. "I still can't feel the floor," he said.

"On three we'll let go," Kern said. "One, two, three!"

"Argggh!" Galandrik fell only three or four feet, but landed on what seemed to be a slide of some sort. Off he slid; faster and faster he seemed to go, his voice getting quieter and further away.

"That didn't seem to go too well," Ty said. "I'm not sure we should follow him."

"I don't think we have much choice; listen!" Kern said, turning his head down the corridor.

The noise was unmistakable; the lizards had released tracking hounds; by the sounds of the barking, they weren't far behind.

Kern turned and lowered himself at his full arm's reach, but his feet still didn't touch the floor. "I can't reach either. Here goes – see you on the other side, Rat," he said. Letting himself drop, he was soon hurtling down the slide.

Ty turned to Sleeper, still sitting on his backpack; he knew he couldn't land on his bad ankle, so he bent his leg back behind him as he lowered himself down. He gently nudged Sleeper off the backpack and grabbed it. "Follow me; I can't risk landing on you," he said to the dragon as he shut his eyes and dropped.

Galandrik flew out into from end of the tunnel, his world whirling and turning. He could see lights but everything was spinning so fast he couldn't focus properly. He felt himself land in what felt like an elastic bed; he sank in deeply, then sprang back upwards, then back down again. He gradually came to a stop, and realized that whatever this was, he was firmly stuck on it.

Kern came flying out of the tunnel and landed above Galandrik, also bouncing a few times before stopping. Then Ty flew out of the tunnel and landed on Kern; once more they were all jostled forward and back, but this time Ty fell free and landed on the floor.

Kern focused his eyes and realized that they were in a spider's web, about ten feet off the floor. Ty lay below them, face down, groaning with pain from his re-injured ankle. The room was large, with two exits leading out; white eggsacs clustered around the room seemed to pulsate in the light. In the middle of the room was a pool filled with bright green water. There seemed to be a light source below the surface, lighting the room in a ghostly greenish luminescence. Ancient bones lay all around, alongside armour and swords, all covered in tangled, sticky webs.

"You ok?" Kern asked.

"Yes, but I am stuck firm," Galandrik replied.

"Ty!" Kern shouted down at the thief, but there was no reply. He thought he could see a slight movement in Ty's chest as he breathed in and out.

"Sod our luck, how many damn monsters live under these mountains?" Galandrik said, struggling to break free from the web.

"If I could just get one hand free, I could grab my sword," Kern said, fighting the web.

With a squeak and a squark, Sleeper flew out of the tunnel, flapping madly and veering away just before hitting the web. He made a careful sweep of the room, then landed next to Ty.

"Wake him!" Galandrik shouted down to Sleeper. "There's a good boy, go on, wake him up!" He added a few words in dwarvish.

"I don't know if dragons understand dwarf," Kern said wryly.

"I think they do," Galandrik said, looking down at the dragon.

Sleeper was nudging Ty's head, walking around him and pushing one side and then the other. Slowly Ty began to move his head, then lifted himself from the floor. He shook his head to rouse himself, then stopped and squinted in pain. It felt like his brain was bouncing from side to side in his skull. He rolled over onto his back, blinking his eyes. After a few moments his eyesight cleared and he saw Galandrik and Kern above him, stuck in the web.

Galandrik's head was pointing towards the floor, his face red and eyes bugging, shirt drooping down to reveal his rounded belly; Kern hung next to him, right-side-up but in no more dignified a pose. Slowly a smile appeared on Ty's face, and soon his laughter echoed around the room. Still laughing, he got to his feet and brushed the dirt from his clothes.

"What's so funny?" Kern growled.

"If you could only see yourselves!" Ty answered still chuckling.

"All right, now cut us down," the upside-down dwarf said.

Ty limped around the room until he found a short sword lying among the debris. Studying the web, he identified the main silky strands holding the structure up and began to hack at them. It took some time, but eventually his companions were free and pulling gooey webs from their clothes and hair.

When they made an examination of the room they found a large hole in the ceiling, evidently for the spider's use. The two exits didn't reveal much, but the pool was very strange. The liquid filling it was thicker than water, and gave off a radiant green glow. Kern picked up a leg bone and wrapped a rag around it. After dipping the rag-wrapped end into the pool he held it aloft; it easily gave off enough light to use as a torch.

Galandrik had been rooting through the weaponry, and had found himself a hand axe. "Better than nothing," he said, spinning the axe in the air.

"Right, now before the spider returns, which way do we go?" Kern asked, holding the improvised torch in the entryway of one of the corridors, trying to make out what was in the distance. Sleeper flew off down the other corridor, stopped, and shrieked.

"I think someone knows the way," Ty said, raising an eyebrow.

"He's never been here either," Kern replied.

Ty looked at the dwarf and shook his head.

They followed Sleeper down the corridor until it ended at a wooden door; the door had no lock and just one handle.

Kern carefully pushed the door open to reveal a square room, a table and four chairs arranged on the west side of the room. On the table were platters of bread, fruit, roasted chicken, and vegetables; bottles of red wine stood at one end. The delicious odours filled their nostrils and set their stomachs to grumbling.

"Smells mighty fine," announced Galandrik, but Kern put a restraining hand to his shoulder.

The food was tempting indeed, but Kern and Ty were looking around at the rest of the room. A massive bear skin rug lay in the middle of the room; on the east wall opposite the table and chairs was a tall metal cage, secured to the wall. The only exit was opposite the door through which they had entered; another door with no lock, only a handle. The walls were covered with framed pictures of Bodisha in every season, the Eastern Mountains and Lake Fortune given pride of place, and torches lit the room.

"Trapped to high heaven?" Kern whispered.

"Let me have a look around," Ty whispered back. Limping past his companions, he checked around the doorway in which they stood. Getting down on one knee, he examined the floor and rubbed his hand along the bottom of the door frame. "It looks all clear to me," Ty said finally, standing up.

Carefully he stepped into the room, rusty dagger in hand. When no traps were sprung after his first few footfalls, he walked straight over to the table laden with food. Using his dagger, he stabbed a cooked potato and held it up to his nose. "My favourite, cooked with fresh parsley and garlic herb butter," he said happily.

Kern and Galandrik entered the room behind him. Kern stooped and lifted the head of the bearskin rug using a rusty sword he had picked up from the spider's room. Galandrik examined the cage; above it was wooden plaque and written in elegant script it said 'Lock me up, it's time to move on.' Inside were wrist and ankle shackles, two at the bottom of the cage and two attached to iron rings at the top. They shimmered with a magical red light.

"This is new, never been used," Galandrik said. "The floor and the metal bars are clean."

"Not as fresh as these potatoes!" Ty replied, taking a bite.

"Freshly poisoned!" Kern said sharply, standing up.

"Who would prepare this delightful meal just to ruin it?" Ty scoffed, ripping off a leg of roast chicken and throwing it on the floor for Sleeper, who immediately gulped it down while Ty tore off another for himself.

Galandrik joined in, saying, "I'm that hungry I'd *eat* poison!"

Kern held out, but when he saw that his companions were coming to no harm, he gave in and sat down with them. Soon all three were relaxing, laughing around mouthfuls of food and washing it all down with rich red wine.

"Say – where's the door we came in through?" Kern said, looking at a solid, blank wall where the entrance had once been.

Galandrik rose to examine the wall. "No idea," he said, "but this must be magical."

"You think so, eh?" Ty scoffed as he wiped chicken grease from his chin.

"Listen, you little –" Galandrik started to say when the other door opened and in walked a human, dressed in leather armour and holding a long-sword. The door shut behind him, and he glared at Ty. "Who dares eat Redvine's food?" the newcomer asked in a deep, authoritative voice.

Ty stood up, dropping his dagger into his hand behind his back.

"Calm down, we have been traveling for a long time and needed to eat," Kern explained.

Redvine turned to face Kern. "Was I speaking to you?"

"I thought you were speaking to all of us," Kern answered.

"I wasn't, so unless you want to feel my cold steel in your throat, be quiet." He turned back to Ty. "Who dares eat Redvine's food?" he repeated.

Ty leaned against the wall and crossed his arms. "Well, it doesn't take a genius to work it out, now does it," he answered casually, tossing a half-eaten chicken leg onto the table.

Redvine stepped forward. "Pay me now for the food, or die," he hissed through gritted teeth, levelling his sword at Kern.

"Are you talking to me now, or still him?" Kern said, gesturing towards Ty, his other hand dropping to the hilt of his sword.

The man lunged forward with astonishing speed; Kern leaned back, barely dodging the tip of the blade and drawing his own sword in the same movement. Ty stepped forward to attack, but Redvine spun on his heel, knocking the dagger from Ty's hand. Kern lunged forward and Redvine parried, using a small wooden buckler strapped to his arm. Galandrik stepped up, to Kern's right, and brought his hand axe down. Redvine dropped his shoulder trying to evade the blow, but the axe blade caught his forearm just above the buckler. It sliced through his leather armour, but didn't seem to do much damage. He swung back around, making Kern duck from his attack, and in the same motion he thrust towards Galandrik, only to be parried by the dwarf's hand axe.

Ty picked up a nearby jug of wine and threw it, smashing it against the side of Redvine's head and knocking him sideways. In blind anger, he swung back towards Ty but the halfling was too quick; even with his injured ankle, Ty evaded the strike. Redvine shook his head, seemingly blinded by the wine. Kern saw his opportunity and stepped in with a slice low across Redvine's stomach. The slice cut through amour and skin, and blood oozed from the wound. Using the edge of his buckler Redvine knocked Kern sideways. Kern rolled to his side as Galandrik stepped over him and struck again, catching his foe on the shoulder. Redvine, still cringing from the stomach wound, dropped to one knee from the force of the attack and swung his sword at Galandrik's legs, but the swing went wild and the dwarf easily stepped out of the way.

Kern rolled back to his feet and lunged forward with a thrust towards Redvine's face, only to be parried away with his buckler. The distraction gave Galandrik his chance, and he struck sideways with his hand axe, striking Redvine clean in the forehead.

He dropped his sword; his eyes rolled as he fell backwards, and then Redvine lay dead on the floor.

Kern looked down at the man. "All for a piece of chicken?" he muttered as he sheathed his sword. Ty retrieved his rusty dagger as Galandrik placed one foot on the human's chest and pulled the hand axe from Redvine's forehead. With a sickening squelching noise it came free. Ty searched Redvine's body, but he carried nothing of interest. Kern examined Redvine's long-sword, but the hilt was broken.

After eating their fill and packing some food into their backpacks they made for the door; with no lock to pick, they soon left the strange room behind them. The door opened onto another corridor, which led, after a short while, to another door identical to the one that had led to the last room. Ty listened at the lockless door, then shrugged at Kern, opened the door, and peered in.

The room was identical in every respect to the room they had just left. Kern looked at Galandrik and Ty with a frown and stepped into the room. "What the hell?"

The others followed hesitantly behind, with Sleeper hovering calmly above. "How weird is this! It's even the same food," Ty said, pointing at the table where a spread of piping hot food awaited.

"I could eat again, too!" Galandrik announced rubbing his belly.

"You're always hungry," Ty said, "but saying that, I think I could eat a little myself."

"There is no way we should still be hungry after what we just ate," Kern said worriedly.

"No, something is strange here," Ty answered. "I *am* hungry, though – and look, even Sleeper is!" The dragon landed on the table next to the roast chicken and was sniffing, clearly preparing to eat.

Kern turned round. "Look, the door! It's gone again."

"The bearskin rug is still there – and the cage, as well. Too strange. Who would set these rooms out identically?" Galandrik wondered aloud.

"I don't know, but I'm having another potato," Ty said, stabbing one and taking a bite.

The door on the other side of the room flew open, and once more a human dressed in leather armour and bearing a long-sword walked into the room. He was almost identical to the last man, but looked slightly larger; as the door shut behind him, he looked at Ty and challenged, "Who dares eat Redvine's food?"

The potato fell half-chewed from Ty's mouth as he slowly turned to Kern.

"We just killed you!" Kern mumbled.

Redvine turned and faced Kern. "Was I speaking to you?"

Glancing from Galandrik to Ty in confusion, then back at Redvine, Kern held up a hand as he raised his sword in the other hand. "Listen, we killed you once. Don't make the same mistake twice."

Redvine moved forward to the table. "Pay me now for the food, or die."

Galandrik raised his hand axe. "Here we go again."

Redvine stepped forward, aiming a blow at the dwarf. Galandrik parried it, and Kern swung for Redvine's midsection. Knowing the human would try to parry with his buckler, Kern tilted his sword just before the parry was made, and felt his blade cut deep into Redvine's thigh. With a scream, Redvine directed his next attack at Kern.

As Kern closed with Redvine, Ty stepped onto a chair and leapt for Redvine's back. Holding his dagger in both hands, he plunged it deeply into the base of the neck, straight through Redvine's spine. The human twisted and fell soundlessly in a heap.

Kern helped Ty to his feet. "What the bloody hell is going on?" Ty asked, wiping the blood from his blade.

"I don't know, but I think I can guess what's down the next corridor," Kern said, shaking his head.

"Look at his sword – it's broken again," Galandrik added. "In the very same place."

"Do you think if we paid him, he would stop?" Ty asked. "I hate to part with the coins, but it might be less trouble."

"Maybe. It's worth a go," Kern agreed. They searched around the room and, as before, found nothing. They left the room and came once more to an identical door. After entering the room, Kern paused, holding the door open. "I wonder – if we went back now, would it be the same?"

Galandrik moved over and to hold the door. "Go check."

Kern walked up the short corridor and back. "Door's gone," he said. He stepped inside the third room and they watched the wall as the dwarf let the door close. The door shimmered and seemed to melt into the wall; after a few seconds it was gone. A brief inspection of the room showed that, again, it identical.

Ty fished a few silver coins out of his pocket and held them ready.

"Right, here we go." He picked up a carrot and began to eat. Sure enough, after a moment the door on the other side of the room flew open and an armoured human walked in holding a bastard sword. He looked even bigger than the last two but was otherwise almost identical; Kern noticed, however, that the wooden buckler was now metal and the armour was hybrid, made of leather and chain mail.

As the door shut behind him, he looked at Ty. "Who dares eat Redvine's food?"

Ty stepped forward next to the table. "It is I, Ty the Rat, and here is payment for your food." Ty dropped the two silver coins onto the table.

"Who said you could buy my food?" Redvine said, pointing his sword at Ty.

"You did," Ty sneered.

"Don't mock me halfling!" Redvine said, stepping forward.

"What do you want then?" Kern said, stepping forward.

"Was I speaking to you?" Redvine said, turning to Kern.

"*That* sounds familiar," Galandrik said, readying his weapon.

"You will pay – in *blood!*" Redvine said, moving forward and swiping a blow at Kern

Kern sidestepped the attack and took a swing of his own, which Redvine parried. Ty came in jabbing with his dagger, but Redvine stepped out of the way and returned the attack. Ty ducked and rolled away as Galandrik stepped forward and swung his hand axe up towards Redvine's chest, but the blow was parried by the buckler. Kern swung again, catching the top of Redvine's arm, but the chain armour took most of the blow.

Redvine swung his buckler, connecting hard with Kern's shoulder and knocking him back. Galandrik stuck again, this time catching Redvine's sword hand; instantly the sword clattered to the floor. Redvine stepped backwards, blood pouring form his injured hand, and Kern jumped forward, landing a crashing blow against the buckler. Ty advanced, swinging his dagger, and Redvine raised his forearm in an attempt to block, but the dagger sliced easily through the leather. Moving further back, Redvine tripped over the head of the bearskin rug, falling backwards. His head hit the stone floor with a sickening thud, and the human lay still.

"I can't go through this again," Kern said, panting.

"Or me," Ty agreed, flopping down on one of the chairs.

"What shall we do with him? And look, his sword isn't broken," Galandrik said.

"When we kill him, his sword breaks and everything repeats itself." Kern thought for a moment, then walked to the door. "Galandrik, hold the door open for me," he said, and walked down the short corridor and tried the next door. "It's shut tight. Won't budge; it feels like a solid oak door now," Kern said as he walked back into the room.

Ty stood up. "But when we *don't* kill him, we can't enter the next room," he said, puzzled.

"Well, we can't leave him here to wake up and attack us again. I have had enough of this bullshit," Galandrik said. "Why don't we tie him up?"

"Tie him with what?" Ty responded.

Kern looked around the room. "What about the cage? Put him in the cage – that way when he wakes up we can question him."

Ty nodded. "That sounds better than killing him again. I just wish he had a pocket full of gold each time, I'd stay here all day."

Kern grabbed Redvine's arms and the others took a leg each, and they moved him over to the cage. As Kern opened the cage door he looked up and spotted the wooden plaque with the inscription above it.

"That's it!" he exclaimed. "Look! 'Lock me up; it's time to move on.' That's the riddle; if we lock him in here, things will go back to normal!" he said excitedly.

They maneuvered Redvine into the cage and, using the magical-looking shackles, secured his hands and feet, then closed the door, slid the bolting bar along, and latched it shut.

As soon as they had shot the bolt home, the shackles on Redvine's hands and feet started vibrating. His body began to pulsate and his eyes opened wide. It got worse, and began to look like he was being electrocuted; his body and limbs thrashed about, blood pouring from the cuts inflicted by the arm shackles.

Ty took a step back and watched the human's frenzy, horrified. "I think we should have killed him!"

Then it all stopped and Redvine slumped in the shackles, hanging lifelessly. Blood dripped to the floor from Redvine's bowed head, as the exit door clicked and creaked open.

"That must have been it," Galandrik smiled.

"Trust me!" Kern said, as if congratulating himself.

Ty was first to the exit. "You are not going to like this," he said, shaking his head. Kern and Galandrik joined him to see what lay on the other side of the door.

The corridor had gone and now they were looking into another room exactly the same as the first three, apart from what was on the table. There was no food this time; instead there were playing cards and bone dice. The cage and bearskin rug were still there, but this time the inscription above the cage read, *'Thou who failst to know will know only me.'*

"What the hell is going on?" Galandrik yawned.

"I think we are in some mage's game rooms; they like to test and test some more," Kern answered.

"Well, I don't like it," Ty barked, walking into the room. "Why can't they just fight and be done with it?" The door melted into the wall behind him. "Oh great, here we go," he added.

The door on the far wall opened and in walked Redvine. This time he wore no armour, carried no sword or shield; he was dressed simply in a cloak and sandals. "Hello, my good friends," he boomed, holding his hands aloft before pulling a chair out. "Please be seated. I mean you no harm – this time."

"But… but you have died three times today! And now you stand in front of us, all full of the joys of spring?" Ty burst out.

"Oh, nonsense; does anybody really die? Please sit," he grumbled, taking a seat.

The three adventurers sat around the table, eyeing him warily. "Right, here is the game," Redvine began without preamble. "One of you stands in the cage, and I will ask a question of the remaining two. If you get if wrong, the one in the cage stays and we move to the next room; get it right and the next person stands in the cage. Get all three questions right and you are free to leave."

"What if we decide not to play and just leave?" Ty asked, placing his dagger on the table.

"That wouldn't be very wise, now would it?" Redvine chuckled.

Ty leaped from his chair with a yelp; his dagger had turned into a snake and was slithering across the table. "What the hell?!"

"Oh, sit down, it's only a grass snake," Kern said, and flicked the snake with his hand. It fell from the table, and landed with a clinking sound; Ty's dagger lay on the floor in its place. Looking at Kern. Ty shook his head before picking up his dagger to examine it. "This is getting strange."

Redvine walked to the cage, opened the door, and gestured for someone to go in. "Who is first?" he quizzed.

"I had better not go first and leave you two to answer for me. Let me get the two of you free first," Kern said, smiling.

"Sod this, it's just too weird for me," Ty said, sitting back down.

"We can't fight against illusionists; they mess with your head," Galandrik answered.

"He is right, you know," Kern said to Ty, then winked at Galandrik. "Go on, dwarf; in you go, you'll be fine."

The dwarf stood with a sigh; he walked reluctantly to the cage and stepped in. *Clink,* and the cage door locked. "Oh, splendid! I do love a game," Redvine said, clapping his hands.

He returned to the table and announced, "Right, listen very closely. You can discuss the questions, but when you say the words 'Answer is,' I will take the very next word as your final answer. Is that clear?"

"Yes. Give us his question," the ranger replied.

"Question one!" Redvine said with glee. *"Iron roof with glass walls, burns and burns but never falls."*

Kern looked at Ty. "Iron roof and glass sides?"

"Burns and burns?" Ty replied.

"Right, what burns?" Kern asked.

Redvine stood up and folded his hands behind his back. "Be quick now."

"Candle, torch, camp fire," Ty murmured, scratching his chin.

"No, 'iron roof' – cauldron or something," Kern replied.

"What about those candles people have, with the metal guard, so when they walk it doesn't blow out?"

"No, we need glass… That's it!" Kern burst out. "A lantern! It has glass sides and a metal roof; it has to be a lantern."

"Are you happy with that answer, Galandrik?" Ty asked. The dwarf simply shrugged, gesturing to his mouth.

"He can't speak," Redvine answered for Galandrik. "Once in the cage, your voice is mine."

"Right then. Answer is *lantern*," Kern said, smiling.

The cage door clicked and Galandrik stepped out, pausing to shake Kern's hand. "Thanks," he said, with a tremor of relief in his voice.

"No problem. Right, Ty, in you go," Kern ordered.

"Okay, but get it right, please," Ty said, as he walked into the cage and the cage door shut behind him with a *click*.

"Question two," Redvine began. *"I weaken all men for hours a day, and show you strange visions while you are away; I take you by night and by day give you back – none suffer to have me but do from my lack."*

Turning to Galandrik, Kern said, "It has to be sleep! 'Visons' are dreams, and 'suffer from lack' – of sleep!" Kern leaned back in his chair and looked very smug.

"Good answer," Galandrik agreed.

"Answer is *sleep*," Kern said, looking triumphantly at Redvine.

The cage door clicked open and Ty stepped out. "I knew that, easy," Ty said, looking at Kern.

"Oh, you need a harder one?" Redvine asked with a smile.

"Ty! Keep that big gob shut!" Kern said as he stepped into the cage. The door clicked once more. Redvine leaned back and lifted his feet up onto the table.

"Third and final question," he said, with glee in his voice. *"Two bodies have I, though joined as one; the stiller I stand, the quicker I run!"*

Ty looked at Kern, who looked just as puzzled as Ty felt, then at Galandrik. "Two bodies that stand still and run?" he said, puzzled.

"What about rivers?" Galandrik suggested. "They are bodies – of water – and they run."

"No, it doesn't make sense," Ty said, rising to pace the room. "The stiller I stand the quicker I run? What about those animals with….no, still doesn't make sense," he pondered.

"I am going to give you a countdown," Redvine said, pulling an hourglass from his pocket and placing it on the table. "In two minutes the game will end, and your ranger friend here will stay if your answer isn't correct," he finished with an evil grin.

"Two minutes?" Galandrik protested.

"It took your friend less than that to get the last two combined," Redvine smirked.

"Come on, Galandrik, think!" Ty said.

"I did think. River, remember?" he answered. "Okay, okay, give me a minute – stands still and runs…two bodies…" Galandrik placed his head in his hands. "Think, think," he muttered. Finally he looked at Ty and said, "I think we need to go with river."

Ty looked at the hourglass; only a few seconds remained and he knew 'river' was their only option.

Ty turned and looked through the bars of the cage. Kern gestured for Ty answer the question, concern etched upon his face. Twisting back around, he looked at the remaining sand dripping through, racking his brain for any other answer to the riddle.

Galandrik said anxiously, "Ty, the sand's about to run out."

Ty gave himself a shake and said, "Right, here goes. The an… No! Wait! That's it, *hourglass!* Two bodies have I, though joined as one, the stiller I stand the quicker I run – that *has* to be the answer." Galandrik nodded in approval.

Ty looked at Redvine. "The answer is *hourglass*."

The cage door clicked open and Kern stepped out, visibly relieved. "Thanks. I really didn't think you had me then."

"Well played." Redvine rose, a faintly disgruntled look on his face, and turned to exit the room. "Please help yourself to the contents of the chest, and you are free to go," he said over his shoulder as he left.

The group looked around the room and saw, where the entrance door had been, a large chest. Ty searched it for traps then opened the lid to reveal freshly minted weapons – a long-sword, a double-headed axe, and ornately made daggers – a purse with five gold coins, and some basic adventurers' equipment.

Galandrik hefted the axe. "Fine double axe, this; looks like it's an orc-seeking one by the colour."

Kern looked at the long-sword. "Yes, indeed; mine is the same make."

Ty spun the daggers in the air; catching one by the tip, he launched it at the door, where it thudded in. "These seem nice too. I think they're snake venom too, magically poisoned by the tiger snake. You never need to apply the poison yourself, because every strike does poison damage magically."

They shared out the five gold pieces, taking one coin apiece then rolling the dice for each of the other two pieces. Much to Ty's disbelief, Galandrik won them both. Lastly, they grabbed the equipment – torches, rope, flint and tinder, and rations – and divided as evenly as possible.

Kern pulled the door open to reveal another corridor. Ty led the way down the corridor, searching for traps as he went. After a long walk and a few twists and turns, they came to a large square room. At the far end of the room were two doors, and in front of those doors stood two giant paladins, complete with full plate armour and two-handed swords which they rested their gauntleted hands on. The three adventurers entered the room cautiously.

"Are they real?" Ty asked in a hushed voice.

"I don't know, but they look it," Kern replied.

"So did Redvine's death," the dwarf added.

"They *are* real, and they are bloodthirsty, and they will kill you if you attack," Redvine said from behind.

All three spun around. "Redvine! Got a few more questions?" Kern hissed.

"No, but you have," Redvine said, walking past the trio. "In front of you are two paladins and two doors. One of these doors will lead you safely out, and the other will lead you to your deaths. The trouble is, you have only *one* question to ask only *one* of the paladins," Redvine explained.

"Simple!" Ty said, walking forward.

"BUT," Redvine continued, "one paladin will always lie and the other will always tell the truth. Remember: One question and one question only, and may the God of Luck be with you." Redvine walked past them and out up the corridor.

"Easy, just ask if the door is good," Ty said.

"But what if he's lying?" Kern answered.

"Do the opposite then," Ty replied.

"Yes, but how do we know?" Galandrik added. "He might *not* be lying."

"Ask him if he's lying? No, we still won't know." Ty scratched his head and sat on the floor, watching Sleeper chase his tail next to him.

"If we ask one if the other is lying?" Kern said, thinking out loud.

"No, that still won't work because we still wouldn't know if he was telling the truth," Galandrik said. "Besides, we only have one question."

"This is too confusing. Let's just pick a door, it's an even chance," Ty said.

"He said death!" Kern argued.

"But, *does anybody really die?*" Ty joked, mimicking Redvine's voice.

"Very funny."

Galandrik looked at the paladins closely; his head came to just above their waists. "I thought paladins protected the good, not the evil," he said, eying the paladins' great two-handed swords. No one had an answer for that observation.

Three hours went by as the three companions sat against the wall and pondered every possible question they could ask find out which door led to safety. Their tempers had all flared more than once, and each of them had a splitting headache.

"Let's just pick a door!" Ty exclaimed, not for the first time. "It's an even chance and we have been lucky in the past." He stood up and stretched, then walked over to the paladins.

"Yes, but what if our luck has run out?" Galandrik replied.

"Then we fight death," Ty said, shrugging. "The way I see it's fifty-fifty. Galandrik has been lucky lately, let him choose," the thief added.

Kern got to his feet. "It's a massive gamble, though," he said, stretching.

"Are you a real paladin?" Ty said, looking at the one on the left.

The paladin slowly moved his head to look down at the halfling. "Is that your question?" he asked.

"No!" Kern quickly barked.

Galandrik stood up to join the other two. "What if we asked the paladin if *he* would go through the door?" he suggested.

"But he could be lying. What about if we ask the paladin what the other one would do?" Kern replied.

"But he may still be lying," Ty argued.

"Yes, but then if we did the opposite of the answer, it would be right," Kern said, his voice getting a little more enthusiastic.

"How could it, if he is lying?" Galandrik said, shaking his head.

Ty added, "And what if he's telling the truth?"

Kern bent down and drew two doors in the dirt floor, each with a stick-figure paladin in front of it. "Let's say left is a liar and right tells the truth, and the left door is good, right door is bad," Kern began. "If we asked the truth paladin, *'What door would the other paladin tell us,'* the truth paladin would tell us the bad door because he's telling the truth, so we do the opposite. If we ask the liar paladin, *'What door would the other paladin tell us,'* he would lie and *also* say the bad door, so again we do the opposite! It has to be right," Kern said, standing up.

"I still don't understand," Ty said, shaking his head.

"Trust me," Kern smiled and walked to the left paladin. "I have a question,"

"Better make it a good one," the paladin replied.

"What door would the other paladin tell us leads to safety?"

With a tiny hint of a smile the paladin answered, "He would say the door behind him."

"Then we would like to leave through the door behind you," Kern said assuredly.

"You choose wisely, ranger," the paladin said, grabbing hold of the handle and pulling it open. Kern turned to Ty and winked as they hurried from the paladin room.

Chapter Twenty-Four
Shalamia

The corridor went for only a few hundred yards, twisting and turning, before it began gradually turning into a tunnel, the walls getting rougher and the floor increasingly damper and uneven. Ty walked with care, making sure he never rolled his ankle. Sleeper was in his backpack, and Ty could hear the dragon's snores.

"He's getting heavy," Ty announced into the silence.

"Who is?" Galandrik asked.

"Sleeper. They grow quickly! I'll need a bigger backpack soon," Ty said, rearranging the straps of his pack. They came to a fork in the tunnel, and they chose to go left; after the paladin doors, it seemed a lucky omen. The tunnel slowly inclined as they walked for ages, stopping once to eat. They finally came to a circular room, empty apart from a few barrels, crates, and boxes. On the east side of the room was a doorway.

Ty peeked through the doorway; it was an old store cupboard. More boxes and crates were piled up inside and the stench was terrible. Ty held his nose. "Nothing in here," he said to his companions. As he turned to leave, he noticed an old piece of paper flapping next to his knee. He leaned over and held his hand out, and felt a slight breeze.

After Ty started moving the boxes out of the way, he noticed that a section of wall had been patched up with wooden slats, and concealed by the boxes and crates. "Come quick, I think I've found something," Ty shouted.

Kern and Galandrik stopped their search of the other room and came to stand in the doorway.

"What is it?" Kern asked.

"I think there's a way out here; there's a draft coming through and some light." Ty removed the last box and passed it to Kern. He used his dagger to pry loose a few of the wooden slats, and looked behind them. "Yes, it's an escape route," he said. "I have seen loads of these; it's a rope going down to another level."

Ty examined the rope and the wooden beam above that anchored it. "Looks all safe. I'll go first." Ty grabbed the rope and stepped out, wrapping his legs around it. The wooden beam creaked a little under his weight, but held firm. He slowly lowered himself out of sight.

After sliding down some twenty feet he landed in a round alcove. Peering out, he saw a massive round room, with pillars spanning upwards and out of sight. On one side of the room, fallen rock formed a ramp which led up to an opening, through which he could see daylight beyond. Looking up, he saw another opening far, far above. The room seemed to be shaped like a cone or an inverted funnel, and he was standing in the wide base.

It wasn't long before Galandrik and Kern joined Ty, and they all stood peering around the room. "What sort of place *is* this?" Ty wondered.

"It looks almost like an old volcano; it gets narrower as it goes up," Kern replied.

"The base here must be five hundred steps wide! It's truly massive," Galandrik said, stepping out into the room.

"Something lives here, by the look of things," Ty said, pointing out a pile of carcasses as the three of them walked around the edge of the massive room towards the slope leading up. "Maybe it's the dragon's den," he laughed.

"I thought dragons slept on a pile of gold, not bones," Galandrik replied.

"Typical if the one we found liked bones instead of gold!" Ty chuckled.

They made their way carefully up the slope to a circular exit; looking down, they could see Tonilla in the distance. The many street lanterns made the town sparkle against the moonlit sky. To the south of Tonilla they could see a massive camp with thousands of tents and camp fires. The view was remarkable, Kern thought to himself. The wind was cold and damp, and he knew they were high up in the mountains.

"Is that Nuran's war?" Ty asked.

"Yes, I should imagine so," Kern replied, squinting to see, "protecting Tonilla from the advancing orc hordes."

"It sure is a delightful sight," Ty said. "Not the war, I mean, just the scenery."

"I'm hungry," Galandrik said, rubbing his belly.

"I see some things never change," Kern said with a laugh, putting his arm around his dwarf friend.

They went back down into the big room and found a nice spot to rest for the night. Galandrik started setting out Redvine's gifted rations and Kern laid a fire. Ty gently placed his backpack on the floor, saying, "We'll wake him soon enough. Let him eat, then get a good night's sleep; maybe in the morning he can lead us to the mother dragon."

Galandrik shared out some bread and fruit and they all began to eat, feeling content that their mission was almost accomplished. They had barely finished their first few mouthfuls when Ty felt a cold blade at his throat. Out from the darkness behind the pillars stepped Svorn and six guards, each with a crossbow pointed directly at one of the party.

Kern grabbed his hilt of his sword. "Don't even think about it!" Svorn said, lifting one hand; all the crossbows were raised with intent. Ty felt the pressure of the blade under his chin, and slowly stood up with his hands held above his head.

Bok stepped from behind the pillar still holding the blade to Ty's throat. "Didn't think you'd see me again, hey little worm?" he said, grinning through black rotted teeth.

"Oh, hello," Ty said brightly. "Last I saw you, you were slightly less dressed – and if I remember rightly, it was *you* who had the 'little worm'."

Bok jerked the blade away, then smashed the hilt against Ty's temple, knocking him over into a slump. Bok slowly walked towards Kern. "Oh, I have been waiting to speak to you," he began, but Svorn cut him off.

"Leave it, let us get the chests and then you can kick and punch them until your black heart is content."

Looking over at the unconscious Ty, Kern saw that his friend's body was covering the backpack. "We don't have the chests," Kern said.

"I think Bok may have had the right idea after all," Svorn smiled.

"The lizard men stole them," Galandrik added.

"Search them!"

As the guards stepped forward, a roar was heard from above and the room seemed to grow darker. Everyone looked up. "What was that?" Bok asked.

"Fuck knows," Svorn answered, just as the roar sounded again.

Swooping from above, an enormous dragon came into sight, swirling down through the small opening, twisting in flight. Massive wings flapped to control the landing, and the dragon thundered down onto the stone floor in front of the ramp. Her wings folded back and her head arched forward; with her mouth wide open and razor sharp teeth on display, she gave another deafening roar.

The guards stepped forward, along with Svorn. "Spread out," he shouted, "three left and three right, on my command," he commanded, raising his shield. Bok disappeared behind them, vanishing into the shadows; Kern and Galandrik picked up Ty and the backpack, then stepped back to the comparative safety of the next pillar.

The dragon took a step forward. "Who enters Shalamia's home?" she boomed, a trickle of smoke wafting from her nostrils.

"We wish you no harm, Shalamia," Svorn replied.

"No harm, but you all raise weapons against me?" the beast replied, her voice echoing around the cavernous room.

"We will drop them if you let us pass," Svorn stuttered.

"But you haven't answered my question. Why are you in my home?" she asked again, as she slowly looked around the room.

"We were searching for someone, and his track led us here."

"Did you find him?" the dragon said menacingly, stepping forward, and the guards all took a hasty step back.

"No, we were just leaving, then, sorry if we intruded." Svorn was practically babbling in his effort to placate the dragon.

Shalamia looked steadily at Svorn, then turned her head towards one of the guards. Svorn could see the man's crossbow shaking. "Solider, be at ease; steady there, Jardon," he said in what he hoped was a calming voice.

The dragon moved her head forward in Jardon's direction, smelling the air around him, and gave a snort. With that Jardon stepped back and tripped over the leg bone of some long-devoured cow. His crossbow fired and struck Shalamia below the eye.

The dragon drew herself up on her back legs and roared. The noise was like thunder in the room and the floor shook. Then she brought her head forward and roared again. This time flames flowed from her mouth to engulf the guard, and he screamed in agony as he lay thrashing and burning.

"Attack!" Svorn ordered.

The rest of the guards fired their crossbows then dropped them to run at the dragon with swords raised. A few of the blades struck home and the dragon spun, her tail smashing into a pillar behind her and sending shards of rock flying. Once again flames erupted from her mouth, and three guards were engulfed, screaming as they burnt to death in a matter of seconds.

Svorn ran forward to join the last two guards. He struck at Shalamia and his blow cut into her scales. She arched her back in pain; stretching her giant neck she brought her head forward, grabbing Svorn in her mouth. Her razor-sharp teeth pierced and ripped his torso, and Svorn screamed and brought his sword up to strike at the dragon's long muzzle. With a quick twist of her head she spat Svorn out of her mouth. He flew across the room, hitting a pillar and falling to the floor already dead.

The last two remaining guards dropped their weapons and ran towards the slope and freedom. With a quick swish of Shalamia's tail and they were sent flying into the wall. The guards' bones were instantly smashed and their bodies broken by the force of the blow, and their bodies slumped down to the floor, then laid still.

Silence settled as Shalamia looked into the shadows at the edges of the room. "Come out, come out, little friends. I won't hurt you," she said.

Kern stepped out first, arms upraised. "We wish you no harm, Shalamia. We have brought you a gift." Galandrik and a dazed Ty came out behind him, no weapons showing on either of them. The dragon shifted, and Kern could see a couple of crossbow arrows protruding from her side. "We'll help you," he said. "We can remove the arrows."

The dragon followed his gaze down to her side; it was as if she had never known the arrows were there. Sitting back, she seized the arrows between two of her talons and flicked them onto the floor. "I don't need you to remove anything; I have lived here for a hundred and ten years without needing humans. I can take care of myself," she grumbled, her head arching forward.

"I apologise," Kern replied meekly, bowing his head.

"Are you the people the others were chasing?" Shalamia asked, smoke trickling from her nose.

"Yes, they have been chasing us for weeks – and *we* have been looking for *you* for weeks," Ty explained.

"Looking for me? You thought I slept on a bed of gold?" she asked, her voice a little harsher. "Had riches beyond your wildest dreams?"

"No! We have brought you a gift, as my friend said," Ty said, picking up his backpack.

"Be careful what you pull out, halfling." Flames twisted between her teeth.

Ty loosened the backpack fastening and set it on the floor. A few tense moments passed before Sleeper's head appeared, blinking away his tiredness and the moonlight shining through the cave entrance. Shalamia stepped back, her head tilted to one side. "This your kin," Ty said.

Shalamia sat back on her haunches as Sleeper rose from the backpack. Flying straight to his mother, he circled her excitedly, the joy in his actions as clear as a dog's wagging tail. Shalamia and Sleeper embraced as dragons do, neither of them seemingly aware of the three friends watching their reunion.

Ty reached into his backpack and pulled out the second chest. He pushed the gems and the lid popped up. Taking a few paces back he laid his backpack down, and set the egg gently on top. He stepped back to stand next to Kern.

"I hope she doesn't think we took them," he whispered.

"I hope the other egg isn't damaged," Kern whispered back.

"*I* hope she isn't hungry after all this excitement," Galandrik added, and both Kern and Ty glared at the dwarf.

"And what about dragflu?" Kern whispered out of the corner of his mouth,

"You don't believe that old rubbish, do you?" Ty said, raising an eyebrow and smiling at Kern. Galandrik shook his head.

Sleeper was sitting perched on his mother's shoulder, as if he had been sitting there every day since he'd hatched. Shalamia turned to the party and spotted the egg; the look in her eye was nearly human. She leaned forward, gently taking the egg between her huge front teeth, and with a couple of flaps of her enormous wings she lifted from the ground. The gusts of air from her liftoff nearly knocked the three adventurers over, and they shielded their eyes from the dirt the wind had disrupted. When the dust settled a bit, they looked up to see her flying away through the opening above them, Sleeper following just behind.

"Let's go, before she returns," Ty offered, picking up the empty chest and stuffing it in his backpack.

"No, wait, they'll come back," Kern argued.

"No, let's go, dragons eat people," Ty said, walking towards the slope. He stopped to search the crushed bodies of the guards, and relieved them of their no-longer-needed gold coins.

"He may be right," Galandrik added.

"No, you're just gutted that Sleeper has left you!" Kern said, stepping forward.

"Don't be stupid. It's a dragon, not fifty gold pieces," Ty said, standing motionless, looking up at the full moon in the black blanket of sky.

"Yes you are. I have seen that face before," Kern insisted. "You took a shine to Sleeper and now you're sad that he's back with his mother." Ty didn't bother to reply; he didn't even move, just stood there looking up.

The noise of Shalamia's flapping wings sounded once more, and they turned to watch from the bottom of the slope. She swooped down majestically, spinning and spiralling, seeming to glide through the air like a fish swimming through reeds. As she neared the ground, a rush of wind smothered them and she hovered and landed, folding her giant wings behind her. Even though her landing was perfect, even delicate, the ground still moved under the impressive mass of her weight.

"I hope she's not hungry," Ty whispered.

"She'll eat the dwarf first," Kern whispered back.

"We dragons have very good hearing, you know. And we don't eat human, dwarf *or* halfling. You taste revolting."

"That's a relief," Ty said with a smile.

"Unless we are *really* hungry – then the odd halfling might do," Shalamia continued with the slightest hint of humour. Ty's face was a picture, and Kern fought back laughter.

"Thank you for bringing my children back," she said, her voice much less intimidating now. "Who found after my first kin?"

Ty raised his head. "I did," he replied.

"What did you call him?"

"I named him Sleeper," Ty said sheepishly.

"Then that will be his name; my second, I will name." There was a long pause, and it felt uncomfortable. Then she continued. "I have nothing to give you. Dragons do not keep wealth as so many humans believe. Many have learned that by coming here. Unfortunately, those who *did* come here never left to share their knowledge. Still, I am grateful, and one day hope to be of service to you, to repay you," she said, as Sleeper appeared, hovering above her head.

"You saved us from the King's guard – that is payment enough," Kern replied.

"I did that for my own reasons. They threatened me, and they paid the price. A day may come when I can be of assistance to you and replay my debt. But for now, if you please," she said, "I have much to do, and I am sure you do as well, so let us not linger over our goodbyes." Then flapping her giant wings she launched into the air and out of sight.

Kern heaved a sigh, then straightened and said, "Right, then, let's get packed up and go."

"I thought we were camping here for the night?" Galandrik asked.

"That was before we knew a dragon lived here," Kern answered.

"Kern's right – I think we may have outstayed our welcome, giving back her kin or not."

The dwarf sighed. "I guess we walk *again*, then."

They gathered their belongings, Ty headed up the slope ahead of the others but paused, turning to look up one last time. He was still hoping Sleeper would fly to him for a final goodbye – but he didn't.

Kern stood beside him. "He's there... watching." Ty forced a smile, then with a sigh turned and resumed his walk up the slope. After a few steps he felt a sharp, sudden pain in his chest.

He realized almost instantly, though, that it was not grief clutching his heart; the pain had a more immediate cause. He looked down at the arrow sticking out of his tunic and watched as a circle of blood appeared around it. He grabbed the protruding arrow with both hands. His mouth opened and he tried to shout, but no sound emerged; his eyes rolled in his head and he fell over backwards.

Kern and Galandrik watched in shocked horror as Ty hit the ground in front of them, an arrow sticking up from his chest. A movement caught Kern's eye; at the top of the slope he saw a form silhouetted against the opening, a horse and rider. A mocking voice rang out into the stillness: "See you in hell, little worm!"

Bok.

He gave a contemptuous salute; then he was gone, down the path towards Tonilla. Galandrik gave chase, and Kern knelt, holding Ty's head. "Hold on, friend, we will get you to Tonilla, a healer –"

"I don't think so, this time," Ty said, his voice just a whisper.

"You can make it!" Kern shouted.

Ty looked up, eyes wide. "It's been good, but this time I beat you. I go first."

Kern looked down in shock as Ty's eyes seemed to lose their focus. Frantically he slapped Ty's face, but to no avail.

The thief was dead.

Chapter Twenty-Five
The King's Gold

Sleeper flew down and landed next to Ty, sniffing his head and his wound; then, letting out a small screech, he was gone. Kern sat on the ground holding Ty's head, numb with shock and grief.

Galandrik came back, panting and sweaty. "The coward has gone," he said to the back of Kern's lowered head, and waited for a response. Kern didn't seem to have heard him; he sat motionless looking down at Ty's still form. After a few moments of silence the dwarf put a hand on Kern's shoulder and bent closer. "Is he… is he okay?"

Kern looked up and shook his head dazedly. Galandrik turned and walked away up the slope, his hands clenched into fists at his sides. "*Damn* you bloody thieves! Revenge and back-stabbing, that's all you know."

"Bring him here," Kern heard Shalamia say from the middle of the room. So deep was his shock, Kern hadn't even heard her return. But he didn't hesitate; he carefully lifted Ty from the ground and carried him in to the dragon. "Lay him in front of me," she ordered. Kern laid Ty's lifeless body gently where she indicated; Sleeper flew over and sat next to his head, making small mournful noises.

Shalamia leaned over Ty's body and used her talons to remove the arrow from his chest. Her gentleness and precision took both Kern and Galandrik by surprise; with her wings folded back, she seemed less daunting, and was nothing as immense as in the stories they'd heard growing up.

She turned to face them. "I can help, but I have never done this on a halfling," she said. "There may be... strange effects."

"Please," Kern begged, "do what you can."

Shalamia turned her attention to Ty's form. Raising a foreleg, she folded back all the talons but one, its razor-sharp point clear to see. Carefully she placed the tip of the talon into the wound left by the arrow. Slowly at first, fantastical lights and sparks began to swirl around Ty's body; his lifeless form began to twitch and jump uncontrollably as the lights whirled faster, until his arms and legs flapped wildly as the blue and red sparks danced all around him.

Kern and Galandrik leaned away from the strange, wild lights, raising their arms to shield their faces, but Sleeper sat still and calm by Ty's head. Transfixed by their grief and the spectacle in front of them, neither of them was really aware of the precise moment the dragon began chanting.

'Dreams dance on the fading shadows of the night, taking the wisdom of their secrets deep within... The brief memories left in your waking mind... run fleeing from the morning sun... leaving scars to remind you of something unknown... The unconscious mind is a fearsome thing, filled with power... delve into your worst nightmares, Ty the Rat, and return to us... return to us... return to us...'

Ty opened his eyes calmly, as if waking in a comfortable bed after a long night's rest. He blinked, then saw Kern and Galandrik kneeling next to him, looking worried. Slowly he sat up, as Kern and Galandrik scrambled to their feet. "What happened?"

"Bok tried to spoil your plans. Welcome back, old friend," Kern said, offering Ty his hand. Ty took it and stood up.

"Welcome back? I haven't gone anywhere." Rolling his shoulders and neck, Ty looked down at his tunic, fingering the little hole in the bloodstained fabric. Then, distractedly, he skipped from side to side. "Huh. My limp has gone; in fact, *all* my aches have gone."

Kern looked at Galandrik and shook his head.

"It's good to see you feeling well again," Galandrik said, offering Ty the dwarf handshake, which Ty accepted.

"So where did Sleeper go?" Ty asked, rubbing one eye and looking upwards.

"He's right here," Kern said as he turned, but both dragons were gone. He looked up to the opening above them. "No, he's up there with Shalamia," he corrected himself. "His mother."

"I guess they will be getting to know each other," Ty replied.

"Does this mean no one is looking for us now?" Galandrik wondered aloud.

"I guess it does," Kern smiled back.

"This is cause for a celebration! To Tonilla, and the first round is on me!" Galandrik said, picking up his axe.

"Sounds like a good idea, friend," Kern said, clapping Galandrik on the shoulder as they made their way up the slope and out of the dragon's lair.

Ty turned and looked up at the darkness in the mountain. *'Later, Sleeper,'* he thought to himself. A moment later, he seemed to hear a whisper in his mind.

'Later, Ty.'

Ty smiled and, after a moment, ran to join the others. "So what actually happened back there, and why have I got blood on my tunic?" he asked when he caught up with them.

Kern laughed as Galandrik draped an arm over Ty's shoulder. "We'll explain everything over a nice pint of mead." They walked on in contented silence for a time, down the southern slope that led away from the mountains and into western Bodisha.

"I think our luck is changing!" Galandrik said.

"How do you figure that?" Kern asked, confused.

Galandrik pointed down the path, where three of the King's guards' mounts stood at the side of the path, eating what little foliage grew in the harsh mountain environment.

"Maybe it is," Ty agreed. "It's still a shame that Conn was so full of shit, though. That reward would have sorted us out."

"What would you have done with your share?" Kern asked of no one in particular, approaching one of the horses and scratching it between the ears.

"Me," Ty replied, "I would have bought a set of black leather shadow armour, two heart seeker daggers, and a set of fine lockpicks."

"I see you have it all planned then," Kern chuckled.

"Oh yes. Then once I had the equipment, I would head over the Aeneanin Sea to a dungeon called Magnoross. Apparently there is a black market there, where you can find the finest thieves' items. Items that cannot be bought over the counter."

"Magnoross, eh?" Kern smiled at Ty's outrageous ambitions. "What about you, Galandrik?"

"Me? I would buy the biggest and sharpest double-axe in Bodisha, then head back to Sanorgk Tower and take the head of that orc who whipped me in those damn mines," Galandrik said with a chilling smile.

Ty laughed at Galandrik's answer as he mounted one of the horses. "What about you, Kern?"

"I don't know. It has never really crossed my mind."

"Oh, come on – you must want something," Ty pressed.

There was a slight pause before Kern answered, "Sometimes, just… to be normal. You know? A farm somewhere, wife and children."

Ty and Galandrik looked at each other in silence, then burst into laughter. "You, a farmer?" Ty mocked.

"What? I might… one day," Kern said defensively, refusing to look at the laughing pair.

"I can just see you milking a cow!" Galandrik said through his laughter.

"Kern Ocarn, Farmer from the North." Ty added, and their amusement redoubled.

"Laugh away. I wish I'd never said anything now," Kern said, kicking his horse into a canter. Galandrik and Ty followed, still chuckling at the thought of Kern the Farmer.

They arrived at Tonilla in the early morning, and the hustle and bustle of day-to-day life surrounded them as the town began its day.

"I need a bed," Kern said with an exhausted yawn.

"I agree totally, I am knackered," Galandrik added.

"Nonsense!" Ty said. "The day is early; let's have a drink, it's been many moons," he coaxed enthusiastically.

"All right, one – then we get a room and sleep for a week," Kern laughed.

"Sounds like a plan," the dwarf said, pointing across the street at a sign for the Factory Inn. Soon they were all inside, sitting at a table amongst a crowd of elves, dwarves and humans all enjoying an early morning flagon of mead. Judging by their coal-stained faces, most were miners coming off the night shift at the Eastern Mountains Refinery.

"Right – I will get these," Ty said, standing up. "Then I will find a buyer for these chests. The gems must be worth one hundred gold each."

"I'll take a bucket of ale," Galandrik laughed.

"I'll have the same," Kern said with a smile.

As Ty headed off to the bar, Kern turned to Galandrik and asked, "What are you going to do now, friend?"

"I don't know. Have you any suggestions?"

"Well, we do need to go back to Finn the ferryman and pick up those horses…" They both laughed.

Kern looked at Ty and back at the dwarf. "I'm sure something will turn up," he said wryly. "It always does."

"It's strange, isn't it? Just look at him," the dwarf said, indicating Ty with a tilt of his head. "He's had many wounds since we left Raith, and now he looks as fresh as a daisy."

"I agree. I don't know what that dragon has done, but it's certainly put the life back into that old dog." Kern yawned contentedly.

Ty stood at the bar and knocked for the innkeeper's attention. The barman turned to him with a smile, and Ty returned it. "Three flagons of your finest ale, sir."

"Of course," the barman said. "Shall I bring them over to your table?"

"No need," Ty replied, thinking of the tip the man might expect. "I'll take them." The innkeeper nodded and turned to his task, taking three wooden flagons from the top shelf.

Ty pulled a gold coin, freshly stolen from one of the King's guards, from his pocket and flipped it. He looked idly around the inn, sizing up the customers. Perhaps a game of dice or cards against some unwary fellow would fill his pocket with ready money.

A burst of girlish laughter next to him caught Ty's attention, and he turned to see a young farmer chatting to three human young ladies, obviously trying to impress them. The lad preened as the girls giggled at his story and batted their eyelashes at him. The young man shifted, and coins jingled in the leather purse hanging from his belt.

Ty rubbed his thumb and forefinger together and glanced around the room.

No one was watching.

The End

AUTHOR'S ACKNOWLEDGEMENTS

Back in the early 80s, my friends and I let our imaginations run free during many sessions of the popular role-playing game *Dungeons & Dragons*. *The King's Gold* is a retelling of the adventures we had back then.

Thanks to the role players and still good friends, Tryston Wilson (Kern), Jason Connell (Nuran), Shane Butterfield (Galandrik), Gav Wilson (Jarrow) – and of course the dreaded Dungeon Master (and best friend), Shaun Saunders, who held the fates of our beloved characters behind his screen, encapsulated inside weird-shaped dice.

I'd also like to say thank you to…
My parents, Billy and Hazel – I really don't know how they managed to put up with five noisy teenagers in the house playing Dungeons & Dragons three or four nights a week, but I thank them dearly for doing it. My mum always had dad's tea ready when he'd come home after a hard day's work, but he'd have to eat it on his lap while we role-played up the table. Now and then my mum would escape us by going to bingo, but when she came back, there we were – the five of us still immersed in our world of magic and monsters, and dad trying to hear the television over our chatter. Mum would fix us all cheese-and-onion sandwiches, and keep us supplied with coffee into the night until my dad uttered those inevitable words, "Pack that lot up now." Every time, it was just at the point in the game where we were

about to kill the final monster in a dungeon or open the last chest and discover what the loot was. All we'd be able to think about the next day at school was how it ended, and when and where we could continue the adventure.

It wasn't until I had my own kids that I realised why my dad would go out for a swift pint when my mum wasn't at bingo, but now I completely understand why… five teenagers and Dungeon & Dragons.

My wonderful partner, Cheryl – who has supported me along the whole journey, from setting down the first scribbles to finally getting this published.

Rob Stebbings who gave me the idea to write a book in the first place, and Jenny Jackson, my poetic friend.

Marina and Jason at http://www.polgarusstudio.com and Ashley at http://www.redbird-designs.net for their invaluable assistance, advice, and patience during the nuts-and-bolts phases of publishing.

Olie Boldador at https://www.facebook.com/OlieBoldadorArt/ for bringing the cover art to life. (Accepting commissions at rboldador@gmail.com)

Elayne Morgan for editing assistance.

Printed in Great Britain
by Amazon